Raven of Dispersion

Steve Dewey

An original publication of watwo

Raven of Dispersion

Edition 2
Copyright © 2020
Steve Dewey

ISBN-13: 978-0993222269
ISBN-10: 0993222269

http://cometodereham.co.uk
http://www.watwo.me.uk

Cover design: Paul Vought

watwo, longhedge, wiltshire, uk

Steve again thanks Lizzie for her eyes and ears

For John,
and the rest of the Streetwalkers

August 1975

Prologue

A handful of torch bulbs was all he needed, just six of them, which he would screw into the sockets on the wooden frame tied beneath the four helium-filled balloons. The bulbs would be powered by batteries, also fixed to the frame. When Peter Richards switched the lights on and released the balloons, they would drift into the night sky, high over the heads of the crowds assembled on the road at Copsehill. There would be excitement, awe and wonder. When people later left the hill, they would be dazzled still, they would carry with them a glow. They would believe they had seen a flying saucer. Because Peter was a hoaxer.

The night was perfect. The wind was light, and the sky was clear. Peter and his friend Phil stood just below the ridge of Red Post Hill, about a mile from Copsehill. Here, Peter had decided, was the best place from which to launch their device. Peter's other two friends, Martin and Rob, had already walked over to Copsehill. At just after eleven o'clock, they would direct the attention of the waiting skywatchers to the lights in the sky.

Screwing in the bulbs was always the last thing Peter did. The bulbs were the most delicate part of the device. Without them there would be no hoax. Phil held the strings that tied the balloons to the wooden frame, while Peter screwed in one of the bulbs to test the connection between the battery packs and bulb holders. Peter flipped a switch and the bulb lit up. He tried a couple more bulbs in different sockets. They all worked.

"Careful!" Phil whispered. "We don't want the skywatchers to see us."

"It'll be fine," Peter said, calmly. "Relax. We're below the ridge." He screwed in the remaining bulbs, and then took hold of the frame. "Okay," he said to Phil.

Phil released the strings, and Peter felt the balloons pull at the frame in his hands. They wanted to fly. They soon would. He looked at the fluorescent hands on his watch. It was just before eleven. "Right," he said to Phil. "It's nearly time." He flicked the switch quickly on and off one more time. He just wanted to be sure. The six bulbs dazzled him.

"Don't do that," Phil said. "We know the bulbs could blow any time."

"Stay cool, Phil." Peter licked his finger and stuck it into the air above his head. The wind was light and blew in the direction they needed it to. "It seems we picked a good night."

"It's time," Phil said.

Peter flicked the switch for the last time.

"Let it go, let it go," Phil urged.

Peter did let it go then, and the balloons slowly lifted the frame into the sky. The balloons rose vertically at first, but then, as they climbed higher, they began to drift towards Copsehill. Blinking away after-images, Peter could see that all the bulbs still shone brightly.

"Brilliant!" whispered Phil.

"Indeed it is." Peter replied.

By now, the light from each bulb had merged into one dazzling point. The balloons were rising faster than they were moving forward. With luck, they would lift the lights two hundred, perhaps three hundred, feet above the heads of the skywatchers.

Peter and Phil crawled up the slope of the ridge, until they had a view over Copsehill.

"I hope the balloons don't burst," Peter said. The fun they had perpetrating hoaxes would soon be over if batteries and bulbs fell on the upturned faces of awe-struck skywatchers. The balloons began to accelerate and within two minutes were passing over Copsehill. A gust or eddy caught the balloons and the lights beneath them swirled. "That looks great," Peter whispered. "Pity we can't make that happens any time we want." He paused, and then said, "Look what they're doing." He pointed towards Copsehill. Some of the skywatchers shone torches into the sky.

Peter wondered what was going on. "Are they trying to see what it is?"

"I don't know," Phil replied. "Hey! What are they doing now?"

The skywatchers were flashing their torches on and off.

"Are they trying to communicate with the balloons?" Peter wondered.

"Oh! There goes a bulb," Phil said.

Peter looked back towards the lights in the sky, which now drifted slowly into the darkness over Salisbury Plain. He couldn't tell if a bulb had blown or not; the light being generated was still impressive. He saw the next bulb blow, however, and the next, until there could only be two or three bulbs left.

The balloons had now been floating across the Plain for five minutes. "How far away do you think they are?" Peter asked.

"Who knows?" Phil said. "If the wind at that altitude is 10 or 15 mph, they must be... a mile or two away," he finished, uncertainly.

"I'm amazed we can still see them."

A few minutes later, the last bulbs blew. Phil sighed. "Ah well, it was impressive while it lasted."

Peter and Phil crawled to the top of the ridge. Phil lit a cigarette. They quietly sat and looked out over Copsehill. Peter idly speculated on the effects of brighter lights, coloured lights, and wondered how many balloons would be required to lift a lava lamp or oil wheel and a car battery. After fifteen minutes or so, Peter heard footsteps and heavy breathing. "Did you see the lights?" he said.

It was Martin who replied. "Yes, but they were not as bright as the face of the Lord."

Phil snorted. "One day we'll find a couple of Jehovahs up here passing out *The Watchtower*, then we will be confused."

"I think they'll be as confused as you," Martin said. He and Rob settled onto the grass.

"How did it go?" Peter asked them.

"Fantastic!" Martin replied. "The skywatchers became very excited when they spotted the lights. We didn't really need to do anything."

"How did the lights look from down there?" Peter said.

"Great," Rob said. "I know we've done a lot of tests, but they looked really good."

"Did anybody try guessing the size or height?"

"Some did," Martin replied. "But nobody was anywhere near right."

"We thought they were about two or three hundred feet above you," Peter said.

Martin nodded. "Yes. That's what we guessed, too. But they were talking thousands of feet high. They thought it might be the size of a car, or thirty feet across. They were making wildly inaccurate guesses. And they all thought the lights were travelling much faster than they really were. I'm sure I heard somebody say a thousand miles per hour."

"Why did they start flashing their torches?" Phil asked.

"Aha!" Rob replied. "We need to get a few more UFO magazines posted out to us. There's been a development. It appears that skywatchers can now communicate with our friendly visitors by flashing Morse code messages at them with their torches."

Peter was surprised. "That was Morse code?"

"Well, probably not, because, after all, how many people know Morse? But the intention was there. Two of the bulbs blew out just afterwards, so the dimming of the light was taken as a meaningful reply."

"Really? How fascinating," Peter said quietly. He was thinking.

Martin looked at Phil. "Oh, and by the way, the next time you spark up a cigarette, do it below the ridge, not right on top of it."

"Why?" Phil asked. Realisation quickly dawned. "Oh," he said. "You could see me."

"Yes, we could see you," Martin said. "Luckily everybody was still excited about our japery, so the skywatchers assumed that the sudden appearance of a dancing amber light was somehow related to our balloons. In fact, that's why we got here so quickly. We said we'd investigate before somebody else had the same idea."

"If we don't go back," Rob said, "they'll think we've been abducted."

"Well, hurry along," Peter said. "We'll come and join you in half-an-hour or so."

Rob and Martin left. Peter and Phil picked up the bottle of helium they had used to fill their balloons, and the bags in which they'd carried everything else. They began to walk along the footpath that led to Phil's car, parked on the road to Copsehill. An idea was forming in Peter's mind. The people on the hill had tried to communicate with balloons! The idea tickled him. What would happen, he thought, if his lights could talk back?

He had no idea now where his lights would lead, what darkness they would illuminate.

Spring
1976

1

Oh, Imo, Imo, Imo. Charlie wondered if he would ever stop thinking about Imogen. He sat with Stuart on a bench beside Brixham harbour. They both licked ice creams. He looked at Paul on the opposite side of the harbour, wrapped in the arms of Fiona.

"Doesn't it bother you," Stuart said, "that your ice-cream tastes faintly of fish?"

Charlie hadn't noticed. "What do you mean?

"The harbour stinks of fish," Stuart said. "It affects the taste, doesn't it?"

Charlie frowned and licked his ice cream. "You might be right." He licked again. "I don't care, though. It kind of reminds me of fish-fingers and I like fish-fingers. Fish-finger ice cream with fishy chocolate sauce and a fishy flake. What could be better?"

"You're a weirdo, man," Stuart said. He had one last lick of his ice cream, stood up and walked to a bin where he dumped the remains of his cone.

Charlie watched the inquisitive, voracious seagulls advance cautiously towards the bin, then he looked back across the harbour, between the bobbing boats and idling tourists, where Paul and Fiona walked hand in hand. They stopped and wrapped into each other as only young lovers can. Charlie was jealous. He could feel it bubbling in him. He was older than Paul by a few months and still hadn't had a girlfriend, hadn't even had a serious kiss. Stuart had. James had. Paul had. Charlie would be the last of them to do so. He remained unloved, un-kissed, a virgin.

"Do you want a knife and fork with that?" Charlie shouted across the rippling water towards the happily engrossed couple.

Paul and Fiona didn't, or couldn't, hear him over the babble of tourists and the Easter Bank Holiday traffic burbling around the narrow streets. They continued sucking on each other, oblivious to everything. Charlie carried on staring at them. There was more than jealousy inside him. Envy, perhaps. Frustration.

Paul and Fiona finally broke away from each other, then Fiona skipped along the harbourside. Charlie could see the small smile on Paul's face as he watched his love dance between the crab pots and black iron bollards. She disappeared behind a row of wooden huts selling fishing trips and boat tours to Dartmouth and Torquay. Paul ambled between the pedestrians, in no hurry, despite Fiona's flight along the pavement. Charlie caught brief glimpses of her in the gaps between the huts. He looked back to Paul, who was now laughing. Fiona appeared at the end of the row of huts, laughing too. What darling thing had she done while out of his sight, Charlie wondered, that made her beam so? She sat on a bench to wait for Paul.

Charlie leaned back against the hard, wooden slats of the bench. The feelings he had – the jealousy, the envy, the anxiety – bothered him. He would be nineteen in a few months. He hadn't had much time for jealousy in his life, but he had nonetheless learned over the last few months its forms, its shades, its edges, its subtleties, and knew intimately now the sharp thrust of it. What he felt now wasn't quite the same. It *was* envy, he thought, a close relation that he was slowly learning to differentiate from other feelings. He felt envious because Paul had something he didn't.

Stuart interrupted his thoughts. "Wonder what they were laughing about?" Charlie looked up at Stuart. He was smiling, still standing near the bin. Stuart too had watched Paul and Fiona, had been captivated by their smiles, their movements, and the happiness on their faces. Stuart was not bitter, was not envious, was not... well, whatever it was that Charlie felt. Stuart could appreciate Fiona and Paul and their love for what it was. Stuart probably fancied Fiona, anyway. He would see in Fiona what Paul saw in her, he would revel in her smile and talk and movement as Paul did. The difference was that Stuart didn't want her as Paul did. He simply appreciated her.

There had been one or two romances for Stuart in the last couple of years. He had the type of personality that encouraged the girls they knew – and particularly Imogen – to hug him, and touch him, and bestow friendly, playful kisses on him. And now, remembering how Stuart and Imogen touched, and hugged, and kissed, the pain in Charlie's ribs became more acute, somewhere on the left-hand side, just below his heart. Something always hurt, or became tense, or wheeled like butterflies in a breeze when he imagined Imogen and Stuart together. The feeling was never the same, but always the same. Nothing made him more jealous than thinking of Stuart and Imogen as a couple. Which was odd, because they had never been a couple. In fact, Imogen was going out with James. They'd all fancied Imogen – Charlie, Stuart and their friend James in Dereham. In the end, she'd gone out with James. But for a long time, she'd been closest to Stuart. Yet when Imogen did choose James, Stuart didn't care, even though he knew now that he couldn't have her, he could never have what James was having. He carried on flirting with her, hugging her, touching her arm, her back, her cheek. And yet – for some reason Charlie couldn't understand – Stuart's behaviour never bothered James, who had been Stuart's friend for so long now they were almost like brothers. And, of course, Stuart's behaviour never bothered Imogen, who had always been so close to him. Now, James and Imogen had split up – again. They were always splitting up and getting back together. James was drinking too much, taking too many drugs, Imogen said. She didn't like it. She wanted James to get his shit together. All of which meant Imogen was potentially available to Charlie. But whenever she split with James, she inevitably drifted towards Stuart. And when James and Imogen got back together Stuart would still be there, Imogen's favoured confidante, her rock, her shoulder to cry on.

James and Imogen were still friends despite the split, and Imogen was still one of the gang. So Charlie was fretting, as always, about what Imogen and Stuart might have done without him noticing, or what they might yet do while he wasn't looking. And, as usual during these interludes the images, memories, and reminders of Stuart and Imogen touching, hugging and kissing – however innocently – became more fervid, stoked by reminders of their behaviour around each other. Like at Kate's party last week, to which James hadn't come. He was giving Imogen some space, he said, and he also wanted to keep away from drink. Imogen had instead gone with Stuart. She had leaned in close to him, smiling, laughing, stroking his arm. When she stood to get herself another drink, or to talk to another friend, she'd give Stuart a kiss on the cheek, or place her hand gently on the top of his head as she walked away. *She never does that to me.* Charlie was beginning to resent Stuart - which was, he knew, ridiculous. Stuart was one of Charlie's best and oldest friends. And why did he not resent James? It was all very puzzling to him.

Charlie caught sight of Fiona again. She walked around the far end of the harbour, past the amusement arcade, towards him and Stuart. She looked good in her jeans and desert wellies. A wide leather belt, with a big, shiny steel buckle nipped in her collarless shirt at the waist. Some kind of military blouson, about two sizes too big for her, kept out the wind. She was a sloppy paramilitary hippie. Paul had increased his pace and was catching up with her, but she would reach them before he caught her. Stuart watched Fiona approach, and she smiled at him. The same warmth existed between Stuart and Fiona as existed between Stuart and Imogen. Charlie found himself confused, as he often did. What did it all mean? Who *did* Stuart like? Imogen? Fiona? All of them? If Stuart's affections could be so profligate, so promiscuous, Charlie wondered why he was so jealous of the obvious affection between Stuart and Imogen. In a rare moment of insight, he realised he wasn't jealous because Stuart was so close to Imogen. He was jealous because Imogen had feelings for Stuart, feelings she'd never had for Charlie.

Fiona reached up to Stuart and brushed his long, fair hair back from his face. Bloody typical, Charlie thought. She looked at Charlie. "What were you thinking about?" she asked.

"When?" Charlie said.

"Well, for the last five minutes or so."

"Nothing much."

"I was sitting over there." She pointed to the bench she had occupied. "You were staring blankly at me. I waved at you, but you didn't notice. When I started walking over here, you carried on staring at exactly the same spot. Then I knew you weren't staring at me."

"Were you disappointed?" Charlie said.

"Hardly, you looked like a bloody weirdo."

Stuart snorted. "Doesn't he always?"

Paul walked up behind Fiona and slipped his arms around her narrow waist. He nuzzled away her hair and kissed her neck.

"What did you do that was so funny?" Stuart asked.

"When?" Fiona said.

"You did something behind the huts over there. Paul was laughing and when you came out from behind them, you were laughing too."

"Oh! I held a crab pot on my head and did what I thought was a passable imitation of Carmen Miranda."

Stuart smiled. "Good one."

"Guess you had to be there," Charlie said, flatly. He looked over the harbour again, his gaze following a bright seagull as it glided down towards the water.

"What next?" Stuart asked.

"Berry Head, naturally," Paul replied.

"Why don't we just walk out along the breakwater?" Charlie said. He could, in fact, happily have gone back to Paul's parents' house, grabbed a book, and sat in the garden reading.

Paul frowned and shook his head. "There's too many grockles out on the breakwater. It has to be Berry Head."

Charlie sighed theatrically. "If we must," he said, and reluctantly stood.

Paul and Fiona walked slowly, hand in hand. Every time it looked as though Stuart might stride on ahead, Fiona reached up and pulled at the back of his long hair. "Woah there boy," she'd say.

Charlie found it amusing that this small girl could rein in Stuart's energy. Stuart was about six feet tall and broad across the shoulders. Fiona was small, only five feet three, but with a confident personality that made her look about three inches taller. Like Stuart, she enjoyed sports, and particularly shared his enthusiasm for badminton. Charlie didn't like sports, but he liked to walk. They all did. When Charlie, Stuart and Paul had all lived in Dereham, they had taken to walking around the downs. When Paul's family moved to Devon, Paul had found himself again living among hills, which he had soon explored. He was also within walking distance of the sea. Soon, Charlie and Stuart were old enough to hitch-hike down to Devon, and they had explored the hills and beaches with Paul. They soon began to think of Torbay as their second home. The route from Brixham harbour to Berry Head was as familiar to them as the walk from Dereham to Copsehill.

Charlie's mood had changed. He had relaxed and was now rather enjoying the walk to Berry Head with his friends. They were talking about music and books. Stuart had finally read Colin Wilson's *The Occult*, which Paul and Charlie had already read. Paul had been the first to read it. He had become intoxicated with it at the tender age of fifteen. He had become enamoured of Aleister Crowley, obsessed with Faculty X and fascinated by occult rituals and practices. Charlie and Stuart were also interested in the occult but had no desire to become practitioners. That was, Paul said, because they didn't have the discipline. He thought discipline was the essence of occult practice. The occult – and everything that, for him, related to it, such as meditation, Buddhism, Zen, and flirtations with yoga – was Paul's avocation. His bookshelves already included fat tomes by Crowley, Eliphaz Levi and members of The Golden Dawn.

"What did you think of the book," Paul said.

"Well, it was interesting," Stuart said. "But it was also a bit vague sometimes, don't you think?"

"He does gives lots of examples of the strange things that happened to people like Daniel Dunglas Hume. And what about Madame Blavatsky?"

Charlie agreed with Stuart. "A lot of the stories in it were very... anecdotal," he said.

"It was an enjoyable read though," Stuart continued. "I like his style. It's not often you can race through what is, essentially, a fat history book."

"Shame they didn't set that for O-level History," Charlie mused. "We'd have all got top grades."

"Yes," Paul said. "Colin Wilson could make a telephone directory sound interesting."

"Hah!" Fiona exclaimed. "That sounds like a quote. Who said that? Not you, I bet."

"Somebody on the back of *The God of the Labyrinth*," Paul admitted.

"Ah yes. *That* book," Fiona said. "A passable thriller with an unreconstructed vision of the female, if you ask me."

By now, they had reached the Berry Head Hotel, and they turned onto the track that led up to the Head. The path was, at this point, surrounded by trees and at its steepest. They walked in silence for a while, although Fiona still had energy enough to jog a few steps, or to dance off into the understorey. They passed under a dark and damp smelling arch of branches.

"It's a bogle kind of place," Paul remarked.

"Yes, I can imagine the bogles often a-bogling about these parts," Stuart added.

"It's probably an old bogle path," Paul mused.

"To where?" asked Fiona, who had just reappeared from among the trees.

"To the University of Bogle," Charlie said, "to learn their bogle-y ways."

"I love to go a-bogling," Fiona sang, stepping into a stiff march, "along the bogle way..."

There was silence for a moment.

"If any of us could remember the next lines, I'm sure we could come up with something amusing," Stuart said.

Fiona's voice floated back from up ahead. "La da dee daaa, la da dee daaa, a-Goblin on my back."

"Yes, please," said Paul.

Charlie snorted.

"Fol de ree!" hollered Stuart.

"Fol de rah!" replied Fiona.

"Fol de reee!"

And all four, with much snorting and giggling, broke into "Fol de rah hah."

The tree cover thinned, and the slope became easier. Then the way opened out to cropped grass and gorse. The sunny spring weather had encouraged the dazzling orange-yellow flowers to open.

"Have you done anything lately? You know, rituals or... whatever?" Stuart asked Paul.

"Nothing *meaningful*," Paul replied. "Not that I feel I could do anything important. I am only a lowly neophyte, after all."

"True, true... certainly lowly," Charlie muttered.

"I've been practicing visualisation, and concentration. I've been learning how to meditate. I'm slowly developing my abilities. You need a solid bedrock in the fundamentals."

"So we don't need to bring any goats down for you yet?" Stuart asked.

"No. Nor any nubile virgins."

"Just as well," Fiona replied, with an exaggerated wink at Paul.

Charlie caught the wink and wondered if they were having sex, and how often. Paul and Fiona hadn't been together for long, a few months, and Charlie hadn't been down to see Paul for a while. In the exchange of letters that had happened in that time, it had seemed indelicate to ask Paul if he and Fiona were doing it. Charlie knew that Paul and his previous girlfriend, Monica, had done it. Paul was experienced now, and Fiona was bubbly and fun. How could they not be doing it?

They walked over the stone bridge that crossed a deep ditch and led to the gateway in the grey walls of Berry Head Fort. The fort had been built to protect this stretch of coast during the Napoleonic wars. Inside the walls were a lighthouse and a café, housed in what once had been a guard house. Rough stone and shale pathways were cut into the grass that was still, despite a dry spring, a bright green when the sun came out from behind the clouds and lit up the day. The breeze that whipped across the Head was refreshing after the long walk up from the harbour. Stuart and Charlie wandered over to one of the low perimeter walls of the fort. Charlie climbed on top of it. There was about six feet of grass and rock between the wall and a fall to the floor of the quarry two-hundred feet below.

"Come on up," Charlie said. "The view's lovely!"

"The view from here is fine," Stuart said.

Charlie laughed, then jumped down from the wall. Sitting in its shelter, he rolled himself a cigarette. He shouted to Fiona. "Want a fag, Fi?" She turned and nodded, then gave Paul a kiss on the cheek. As Charlie rolled the cigarette, he watched her walk towards him. His hair blew around his face.

"You're going to get knots in your hair," Fiona said. She sat down beside him and took the proffered rollie. Charlie's lighter caught after several attempts at lighting it and, shielding it from the wind, he lit his and Fiona's cigarettes. Stuart had continued walking towards Paul, who was a few yards away, looking out to sea over the wall. They both turned and wandered off across the grass towards the farthest point of the Head. They were walking close together, talking.

"I wonder what they're talking about?" Charlie said.

"Probably magic," Fiona replied.

"Probably," Charlie said. "That's what we're like. Books, music, UFOs and magic. What a ridiculous bunch of freaks we are."

"Yes, you are." Fiona frowned. "But Paul is a *little* more obsessed with the occult than the rest of you."

Charlie imagined Paul in his bedroom, intent on some text by Israel Regardie, barely acknowledging Fiona as she brought him a cup of tea. "He'd say he was disciplined, though, wouldn't he."

"I suppose so. Studious, he might also say."

Charlie smiled. "Anyway. It could be worse."

"How?"

"He might instead have a potting shed, in which he meticulously polishes his hoes and trowels every night."

"But I like flowers," Fiona said.

"Too bad. He'd grow championship marrows. Only marrows. He'd have a garden full of marrows. He'd feed them bonemeal and water them every night."

"I could love a man with a big marrow," Fiona replied impishly.

Charlie guffawed, accidentally spitting his half-smoked rollie onto his lap.

"Bugger, I've burnt my own marrow now," he said, making a grab for the cigarette and brushing away the embers from his jeans.

He looked up to find Fiona's brown eyes looking at him. She pushed away the strands of the long blonde hair that had blown across her pale round face, then reached out and brushed Charlie's long brown hair behind an ear. She regarded him quizzically for a moment.

"What are you looking at?" he said.

"When are you going to get your bloody beard cut?"

"Beard cutting is a bourgeois indulgence," Charlie said.

"You're just a lazy sod."

"There is that. And what about Stuart's?"

"Oh, his is fine," Fiona said.

"Only because he's not yet a man and can't grow a proper one," Charlie said.

"That's very true," Fiona replied.

Stuart and Paul had wandered past the lighthouse, towards the cliff edge. "Shall we follow them?" Fiona asked.

"We'll stay here, cosy behind the wall."

"Yes, let's." Fiona threaded an arm into Charlie's. They dragged on their fags. For a while, they talked about music.

Paul looked back at Charlie and Fiona crouched beneath the wall. He pulled his coat tighter around him to keep out the wind. "I wonder what they're talking about?" Paul said.

"You, I should think," Stuart replied.

They reached the cliff's edge and looked out over the slate grey water of Torbay. A large ship was at anchor a mile or so away. Grey clouds scudded beneath high, white cirrus through which the sun sometimes broke. For a moment, a sunburst caught the ship and the dull white and rusty red of its bridge and hull glowed against the grey backcloth of the sea. Stuart approached the cliff edge gingerly and looked down what appeared to be a sheer face. It wasn't sheer, though – it angled out slightly, and all the way down were lumps and bumps on which gulls nested. Paul joined him but stood closer to the edge. Two hundred feet below, waves exploded against the rocks and gave up their energy in a cloud of white foam. He heard the cries and cackles of the kittiwakes and fulmars that drifted into the air below him, leaving and then returning to their ledges, gliding in white and blue-grey streaks.

"Nice view," Stuart said.

"Never did like heights, did you?" Paul said, moving a little closer to the edge.

"My fear is not only for me, so please step back."

"It's perfectly safe." Paul grinned, and began to jump up and down on the gnarly grass.

"If these weathered rocks should choose this moment to give way, I'm not going with you." Stuart moved back further.

"Bloody neurotic. Live a little!"

"No, I intend to live a lot, which is why I'm not jumping up and down on slimy grass two feet away from a terrible precipice."

"It's not two feet, it's more like four. And the grass is perfectly dry."

"Well, you carry on enjoying yourself, in your reckless, foolhardy way."

Paul did. He threw in some star jumps and squat thrusts for effect.

"I'm not watching," Stuart said. He turned and waved at Charlie and Fiona. Fiona blew a kiss. Charlie stuck up two fingers. Fiona leaned over and said something to Charlie, at which they both laughed. Then Fiona stood, brushed away grass and dust and walked quickly, with a light, bouncing step, towards Stuart and Paul. Charlie lazily levered his long frame from against the wall and walked over at a more leisurely pace. Paul was still doing squat thrusts.

"Watch out, the girls are on their way," Stuart said.

Paul stopped performing his calisthenics and stood to face the oncoming Fiona and Charlie. He opened his arms to the ever-accelerating Fiona, who leapt into them and wrapped her legs around his waist, and her arms around his neck. Paul noticed Stuart's wince. "You thought Fi was going to knock me off the cliff, didn't you," he said to Stuart. "You thought we were going to plunge to our doom."

Stuart pulled a face and nodded.

"Darling!" Fiona said with mock theatrical exaggeration, before planting a wet kiss on Paul's lips.

Stuart looked towards Charlie and smiled. Stuart opened his arms and Charlie began an exaggerated slow-motion run. He leapt into Stuart's arms, imitating Fiona's cry of "Darling!"

"Well," Fiona said. "We make a lovely couple and so do you."

"I was worried," Paul said to Charlie, "that when you finally met, your beards would rub together and set you both on fire."

"They only need the burning fire of their love for each other," Fiona said.

Charlie unwrapped himself from Stuart's embrace. "Can't you just toss her over the edge?" Charlie said.

"Oh, he has done many times." Fiona twinkled. "Haven't you my little darling?" She pinched Paul's cheek and shook his head from side-to-side with playful affection.

"You are a very rude girl," Stuart said.

They turned away from the edge of the cliff and began to walk back, past the lighthouse and guardhouse. Paul looked at his watch. "We'd better get back into Brixham," he said. "Mum is making a stew for five thirty. It'll take half an hour to get back into town, then an hour or so on the bus."

Although Mrs Maas was the type of mother who thought it lovely when they all sat down to dinner together, Paul also knew she would keep the stew warm in the oven until they arrived if Mr Maas decided he could wait for his dinner no longer. Paul was, however, disappointed that they had to leave. Walls and earthworks stretched further around the headland, and he had hoped to visit them. He was enjoying being on the headland, in the cool breeze, with his friends around him. Still, a stew sounded good. The fresh air had given him an appetite.

They made their way back through the gateway and followed the path back into town, talking about music, books and films all the way. They reached the grey concrete bus station just in time to catch their bus to Paignton, where, at another grey concrete bus station, they waited for the bus that would take them to Charlton.

Waiting for tardy teenagers had made Paul's father testy. Mr Maas complained that they treated the house like a bloody hotel. Charlie was distracted by Paul's younger sister Jane, who blundered into the dining room and clomped across the parquet floor in her red plat-form boots. She was sixteen years old. Her blonde hair was feathered and streaked. She was what he and Stuart called a *smooth* – she was not one of them, not a hippie, not a freak. But Charlie adored her, almost as much as he adored Imogen.

The dining room was small and the seven of them were crowded around the table. The meal was hot and good. Paul's father asked how they had spent the day. Paul described their walk around Brixham and Berry Head. At least, Mr Maas said approvingly, they hadn't sat around in Paignton all day long, drinking beer from tins and plugging money into one-armed bandits.

Charlie was pressed up close to Jane, which he rather liked. He could smell her perfume, so different to the patchouli, sandalwood and musk he usually associated with his friends. Sometimes Charlie couldn't tell the boys from the girls by smell alone. No wonder his parents always seemed confused. But this scent, this smooth's perfume, was very feminine. It would immediately identify the wearer as a girl. He couldn't imagine Imogen wearing it. Which was a shame really, it would smell good on her, so different to the patchouli she was so fond of.

"What's the perfume?" Charlie asked.

"*Havoc*, by Mary Quant," Jane replied.

"Sounds expensive."

Jane giggled. "If it was expensive, I wouldn't be wearing it."

Charlie felt daring. "It smells good on you. What are you doing tonight?"

"I did think about going into Paignton with some of my girl-friends. But, if it's okay, I'd quite like to hang around with you."

"Of course," Paul said. "But I warn you, we'll just be talking and playing Scrabble."

"That's fab," Jane said. "I only get to play games with you." She turned to Charlie. "My girlfriends don't like playing games. They think it's boring. But I like it sometimes."

"We should go for a walk on Blue Tor first though," Stuart said. "It's traditional."

"Not another bloody walk," Charlie moaned. But a final ramble on the hill had become a tradition on the last evening of their visits. Tomorrow he and Stuart would hitch-hike back to Dereham. Yet, at this moment, he'd rather stay here and flirt with Jane. He was about to make an excuse to stay behind, when, as if unconsciously prompted by his thoughts, Jane said she'd like to join them on the walk. Paul would say that was an example of telepathy, or synchronicity, or something. Fiona was right: Paul was obsessed with the paranormal.

But Charlie knew he had his own obsessions.

2

Jane made her way with the others through the deep Devon lanes. They found, between tall hedgerows, the farm track that climbed up to Blue Tor. It was mid-April. Although the nights were drawing out, it was already twilight. Here, between the hedgerows and beneath the trees, the darkness was even deeper. Stuart and Fiona, still full of energy, had accelerated ahead. Jane could only just see their dark shapes; they pushed and jostled each other playfully. She could hear their giggles and odd fragments of their conversation.

She looked up at the sky. "Do you think we'll see a UFO?"

"We always wonder that, and yet we never do," Charlie said.

"And you still haven't seen one?"

"No. Not at all. Not yet anyway. I'm beginning to think we never will."

"That's mad," Jane said. "Dereham's a hotspot!"

Charlie shrugged. "Perhaps there's nothing there. Perhaps it's all just stories."

"I hope not," Jane said, feeling a little disappointed. She was intrigued by flying saucers and longed to see one. She'd heard all about Dereham and Copsehill from Charlie and Stuart. She hoped she would soon be allowed to visit Dereham with Paul, to stay with Stuart or Charlie and go to Copsehill with them. She'd mentioned this to Paul, and he hadn't said no, he had only said that she should wait until she was a little older. Well, she'd be seventeen next January, and felt sure her parents would let her hitch to Dereham with him then. Just let them try to stop her. She was determined to get to Dereham. "Charlie," she said. "Would you mind if I came and stayed with you next year?"

"As long as you leave your brother behind, you'd be most welcome at my humble abode."

"Are you crazy?" Paul laughed. "I wouldn't leave her alone with you, you half-crazed zombie woof. I wouldn't want you putting your disgusting hands on her and infecting her with whatever gutter-derived infections you might be carrying. No. You can rub your calloused hands over *me* instead. Jane can stay with Stuart."

"Stuart?" Charlie said. Jane noted the tone of incredulity in his voice. "He's a flirt! A Don Juan!"

Paul laughed gently. "Don Juan? Hardly!"

"But look at him. How can you trust him with your own girlfriend?"

Paul looked down the track towards Stuart and Fiona. "I trust him. All he ever does is flirt. He's harmless."

Jane listened with interest. She thought – indeed, she had hoped for a while now – that Charlie fancied *her*. She'd overheard conversations between Stuart and Charlie that had piqued her interest. And some of the things Charlie said to her sounded meaningful – like when he'd asked about her perfume. But then, she'd also heard him talking about Imogen. Charlie fancied Imogen, she knew that. Absolutely *everybody* knew that. But Imogen was with James now, so Charlie wouldn't be going out with her any time soon. Perhaps he'd forget about her.

"Do you think we'll ever see James down here?" Jane said.

"Who knows?" Charlie said. "Every time we come down, we say to James he should come with us, but he never does. He likes being at home, I think. He feels safe in town."

James was a mystery to Jane. He was the only one of Paul's old Dereham friends who had never visited. Yet he still wrote letters to Paul, in which he passed on Dereham gossip, moaned about Stuart and Charlie, and told Paul about interesting bands and books. He even phoned occasionally. Jane found both Charlie and Stuart slightly exotic – crazy, beardy hippie boys who turned up every few months, had intriguing conversations about art, culture, the occult and UFOs, and then disappeared again. She'd grown attached to both of them and looked forward to their visits as much as Paul did. If she did go to Dereham, she would much rather stay with Charlie, while Paul stayed with Stuart – even if that also meant listening to Charlie's weird prog-rock music. She preferred Charlie. He was tall, skinny, pale – a bit gothic, perhaps. He had something about him though. He was, perhaps, a wan Romantic. She would like to sit with him while he told her stories about flying saucers and Copsehill and ghosts. But she knew this would remain a fantasy, for now at least. And if she ever did go to Dereham with Paul, she wouldn't be able to stay with Charlie. Paul was far too sensible. She'd probably end up sharing a tent with him at the campsite in Dereham.

Ahead of them, Fiona, silhouetted against a tree on the right of the track, had lit up one of her Benson and Hedges. The amber tip of it brightened in the darkness as she sucked on her cigarette. Stuart leaned against a tree on the left. Charlie began to roll a cigarette.

"Do you want a fag, Jane?" Charlie asked. They all knew she smoked once out of sight of her parents.

She did want a cigarette. But she wanted one of Fiona's smooth Bensons. The thought of Fiona holding out the crisp, golden packet towards her increased her desire. "No thanks," she said. Charlie, Jane and Paul caught up with Fiona and Stuart, who peeled away from their trees and followed behind as they walked out into an open, ploughed field, beneath a sky now clear but for scattered, scudding clouds.

The wind still had a keen edge. Jane pulled her grey duffle coat tightly around her. They walked and occasionally stumbled across the furrows turned by the plough, until they reached the summit of Blue Tor. From here, they could see orange streetlights and the amber glow of Torbay, red warning lights atop a pair of tall communication masts, and the flashes of light from the lighthouse on Berry Head. Paul and Fiona had walked on a little way and were kissing.

Jane looked up at the sky. She could see a faint light, gliding slowly, changing colour from red to a dull yellow and back. "What's that!" she said.

"Where?" Stuart said.

"Near the Plough. Just to the right. See it?"

"Yes."

"I see it too," Charlie said.

"It's probably a plane," Stuart said.

"It can't be!" Jane exclaimed. "I mean, it's not going straight across the sky. It's zig-zagging."

"Zig-zagging?" Charlie said.

"Okay, perhaps not zig-zagging. Moving from side to side."

"A low-frequency sinusoidal motion?" Stuart said. Jane could hear the smile in his voice.

Jane also smiled. "Well, maybe, if I knew what that meant. But I do know it's zig-zagging."

"That's caused by your own head," Stuart said.

"What do you mean, my own head? My imagination?"

"No, no." Stuart said. "One theory is that your eyes move backwards and forwards very slightly as you track the light, and against the black background of the sky it appears as though the light is moving from side to side."

"Saccades," Fiona said. She'd stopped kissing Paul and also looked up at the sky. Jane turned to her. "Your eyes move rapidly to establish fixation points," Fiona continued. "You can see it when people are reading." She paused and looked at Jane. "So, it seems that A-level psychology is useful for something."

"But it could be a UFO," Paul said.

Jane was grateful for her brother's support. She'd been excited by the thought that she'd seen a flying saucer; she hadn't expected the cold water of Stuart's scepticism.

"Well, it is, by definition, a UFO," Stuart said. "After all, we don't know what it is. It remains unidentified. And an object."

"And flying," Charlie added.

"To really identify it as a plane," Stuart continued, "we'd have to phone up airports and find out flight-plans and routes, and everything. And I can't be bothered with that amount of hassle."

"Even then it could be a military aircraft," Charlie added. "And then we'd never find out anything."

Stuart put an arm around Jane's shoulders. "And anyway," he said, "what Paul really means, and what you want it to mean, is that it could be an alien spaceship carrying little green men."

"Well, why not," Paul said. "If we can't identify it, then it could be."

"Why jump to that conclusion," Charlie said. "Just because something is, at this moment, unidentifiable, that doesn't mean it must be an alien spaceship."

Jane was disappointed. Whenever she went out on these walks with Charlie and Stuart, she so wanted to see a UFO with them. Tonight, she thought she'd seen one, and would be allowed entry into their world. But her sighting had been almost instantly dismissed. "You two sound like sceptics sometimes," she said. "Why do you even go up Copsehill? You must believe people are seeing things there, or you wouldn't go."

"Oh yes," Charlie said. "We think people see things. Mainly misinterpretations of the... mundane'

"Very eloquent," Paul said.

"But there are some stories from the hill that make me think there might be something to it," Charlie said. "The close sightings that people sometimes report, bright and low. Who knows, perhaps aliens really are coming for a quick peek at berks freezing on a hilltop."

"So, I might see one just like that when I come up," Jane said.

"Depends. If you're a berk, you might." Stuart said. "Are you a berk?"

"Sometimes," Jane said.

"Alternatively, you might see nothing, like we do," Charlie said.

"Which means you're not berks," Jane said.

"Exactly," Charlie said.

The wind was cold now, and Fiona suggested they start back. Jane asked Charlie and Stuart about Dereham, about what they'd seen, about what happened on the hills, and about the folktales associated with those hills. She'd asked these questions and had wanted to hear these stories many times before, and knew she would ask again and again, until she finally visited Dereham and experienced Copsehill for herself.

They walked along the path at the side of Paul's house, and entered quietly through the back door. Had it been earlier in the day, they might have crashed through it full of adolescent energy. However, they had all, except for Jane, walked more than ten miles today. They instead passed quietly into the flickering white brightness of the fluorescent-lit kitchen, and then into the dining room. Fiona went to Paul's bedroom and returned with night-lights, which she set into saucers, lit, and then placed on the dining-room table. She switched off the light. Jane and the others sat around the table.

"Who's for a game of something?" Paul asked.

Stuart, Jane and Fiona agreed. Charlie shook his head. "I'm going to read my book."

"What is it?" Jane asked.

"Herman Hesse. *Gertrude*. There's only a few pages left, and I want to finish it before we leave." He fetched the book from Paul's room, then took one of the nightlights and set it in a saucer on the dresser just behind him. He opened the book and began to read.

Paul asked if the others would prefer to play canasta or Scrabble. Canasta was the favoured option. Paul went to his bedroom to find two packs of cards, while Fiona made coffee for everybody. She returned a few minutes later balancing steaming mugs on a silver tray and carrying a packet of Bourbon biscuits under her arm. Paul also returned. He shuffled and dealt the cards. Charlie rolled a cigarette. Fiona offered one of her Bensons to Stuart, who sometimes smoked. He always said he could take it or leave it. Jane looked on enviously as Stuart did take a cigarette, which Fiona lit for him. She would like to be able to do that, just have a cigarette, without anybody caring. She wished she'd bummed one from Fiona when they'd been on the hill. She couldn't have one now. If either of her parents came into the room a7nd found her with a cigarette, she wouldn't hear the last of it. Nonetheless, she felt a little stab of desire for the burning cylinder of dried leaves between Stuart's lips. She instead took a Bourbon biscuit and dunked it in her coffee. The others were all pleasantly fatigued after the two walks they had taken that day; they relaxed and concentrated on their canasta hands. Conversation became hushed and intermittent. There was an occasional rustle as Charlie turned the pages in his book. From the lounge where her parents sat came the muffled sound of the television.

"I love these evenings," Jane said. She looked at Charlie and Stuart happily. "They only happen when you're here."

"What do you do the rest of the time?" Charlie said.

"Oh, I go out with my friends. Although I have to get back early because of the buses. Well, unless dad is feeling very generous and is willing to pick me up."

"Which isn't often," Paul said. He melded some cards and disposed of a three of clubs.

"Sometimes I spend an evening with Paul, talking and playing cards."

Paul was only a year and a half older than Jane, yet, until recently, she'd thought him very adult, very grown-up. She thought he lived in a different world. His interests – in the occult, in art and literature, and in obscure music she'd never heard until it drifted from his bedroom – seemed so unusual. When only a little younger than she was now, she'd thought Paul's interests – especially in the occult – were a bit silly. She'd rather be down the park, listening to the Bay City Rollers on a transistor radio, and talking about boys with her friends. Fiona was lovely, and sometimes took her for a drink or went shopping with her. It had been Fiona who first noticed a change in her and had lent her *1984* and *The Female Eunuch*. She had dipped into the latter but found it hard work. Soon afterwards, perhaps prompted by Fiona, Paul had talked to her about the poetry he was studying for A-level and had suggested she look at his copy of the *Selected Poems of T S Eliot*. One evening she did. Although her only exposure to poetry had been at school, bored by a droning teacher reciting something from a book she seemed to remember was called *The Golden Treasury*, she soon found herself intrigued by *The Love Song of J. Alfred Prufrock*, and baffled by *The Wasteland*.

This, she knew, was the world she wanted. Coffee and candle-light, Canasta and Scrabble, Charlie reading in the corner, Paul and Fiona discussing books and music – Orwell and Ravel, Freud and Soft Machine – Stuart sucking on a Benson and Hedges, pushing his long hair away from his face as he studied his cards. When Charlie and Stuart visited, she joined their world for a while, became a part of it. She felt a door was opening, and Paul and Fiona were inviting her to a party where Charlie and Stuart sat and read in a room full of books.

*

It was an excellent night to be on Copsehill, Peter Richardson noted. The air was crisp. The sky was clear and studded with stars. A silver sliver of moon touched the horizon. A good crowd had gathered on Copsehill, as it always did on Bank Holiday weekends. Peter and his friends had returned to Dereham, and stood atop Derebury Hill, a mile or so east of Copsehill. The hoax they'd perpetrated the previous August had been a resounding success. Many of the mimeographed UFO magazines had reported the dazzling UFO sighting at Copsehill. One report had described the lights – the ordinary torch bulbs powered by ordinary batteries dangling beneath ordinary balloons – as the most extraordinary thing the witness had ever seen, and the most spectacular UFO sighting of the year. Peter had an even more spectacular idea for the coming summer, but he felt the need to first repeat his experiment of last summer, if only because it amused him. The skywatchers would be watching, waiting for the elusive sighting – a flying saucer, a spaceship, an alien craft. In short: a UFO. And he would provide one.

Peter knew his audience well. He and his friends had also once believed in the imminent arrival of the spaceships. They had ranged across the North Downs at night, waiting for UFOs. Late in the summer of 1974, they'd at last seen a bright light dancing low across the sky, blinking on and off, changing colour from red to yellow to white. It had defied all rational explanation. It could only be, they whispered to each other, awestruck, a UFO – by which they meant, although they were reluctant to say it, an alien spaceship. Yet when Peter and his friends had revisited the scene of their excitement the following day, they saw what they hadn't seen when they'd arrived, in the dark, the night before. In the distance was another hill; a hedge-bound road zigzagged across it. Peter peered through the binoculars he'd brought with him. A car travelled along the road. It passed behind a farmhouse; further on, it disappeared into a dip before reappearing, and then sped through a small colonnade of trees. What their UFO had been was now obvious to them.

Disappointed, the group had climbed into Martin's car and headed back to Peter's house. There, they consulted an Ordnance Survey map that clearly showed the road twisting and turning, hugging the contour lines. They felt foolish – foolish for investing so much in the light, foolish for never thinking to consult the map before leaving the previous night. That evening, they talked over coffee about how elated they had been the night before, full of awe and excitement, and how they felt now. They felt cheated in some way – as if some great present had been given to them and then taken away before they could unwrap it and find the cosmic secret hidden within. They continued talking into the night about misperceptions, about their desire to believe, their need to see something. As they talked, a suspicion began to form. Perhaps all the spectacular sightings they'd read about were based on misperceptions.

Peter and his friends – Martin, Phil and Rob – were science students at university. Performing experiments had become second nature to them, and they thought it would be interesting to perform an experiment to stimulate misperceptions. They'd discussed how they could do this, and finally settled on the balloons and lightbulbs they still used. They wondered whether anybody would see through their hoax, see it for what it was. It was worth trying, surely, Peter had said. As they talked, they also realised something else; if they were willing to create a hoax – a fake flying saucer –the others had also been ready to do the same. By the end of the night they had a plan. They all agreed there was only one place at which their hoax should be perpetrated. Dereham.

In 1972, the small West Country town of Dereham had become the centre of a quite extraordinary wave of UFO sightings. It was the breathless newspaper reports about lights in the skies there that had encouraged Peter and his friends to skywatch on their local hills. They had made their first journey to Dereham a year ago now, during the cold Easter of 1975. They'd taken with them their balloons and helium, their batteries and torch bulbs, their tape and string. On the night, everything had gone wrong. Strings had snagged, torch bulbs had broken, and batteries had been lost in the dark. The one attempt to send aloft an underpowered two-bulb hoax in the gusty north-westerly wind had foundered in a tree.

They had tried again during the summer, which, after a strangely cold June, had been a season of warmth and sunshine. Their next attempt was successful. So buoyed were they by this success they had returned to Dereham several times, sending up balloons and also flying kites. They knew some of the UFO reports they had later read about had been a consequence of their visits. Nothing had been quite as effective, though, as the hoax they had perpetrated during the August bank holiday. Another Easter had arrived. There would be no failure now. They knew what they were doing, they were experienced. They expected their hoax to be as successful as that of last summer – more successful, in fact. Everything was bigger – bigger batteries, brighter bulbs, and bigger balloons.

Phil was counting down. When he reached one, he said, "Let them go!" Peter released the balloons, and the lights lifted away from Derebury Hill and into another clear sky. The lights were, as he had expected, spectacular. But not as spectacular as the device he had planned for the summer. It was more elaborate, more intricate, less likely to work. If it did work, however, Peter knew it would be a sensation. *A sensation!*

Charlie woke with a start. He'd been dreaming about something, but the content of the dream faded in an instant as he tried to remember where he was. He'd fallen asleep in the chair, his book on his lap. Only he and Jane remained in the dining room. Stuart had gone to his sleeping bag on the floor of Paul's bedroom. Jane was asleep, her head on her arms on the table. Charlie stood and stretched, then sat by Jane and stroked her hair. He could hear indistinct noises from the lounge, which at this time of night could only be Paul and Fiona.

Fiona puzzled him. Why was she so close to Stuart? Stuart had something about him, an air, a quality, Charlie knew that. Perhaps it all came down to Stuart. All his anxieties, his fears, everything. Although he wasn't quite sure what everything was. But if pressed to find the reason for everything, it had to be Stuart, who was so relaxed around women, so funny and charming, that they in turn relaxed around him. Charlie envied him that. And yet, Stuart didn't have a girlfriend. Why not? There had been a couple of girlfriends in the last year, short-lived flings, nothing long-term. Perhaps then,

Charlie thought, Stuart was also obsessed with Imogen, just as he was. In fact, perhaps they were all obsessed with here. He and Stuart and James and, oh, all the others they knew in town, Simon and Mark and Nick and Gaz. Even Julie and Chrissie and Sarah. Perhaps everybody in Dereham. And even in Wiltshire. Charlie smiled ruefully to himself. He knew that wasn't true. Because only he was that obsessed.

Jane's head moved beneath his fingers and she mumbled something in her sleep. He looked down at her face. She was pretty. He liked her a lot. And yet, even with this pretty young girl so close to him, his mind continued to circle around the twin conundrums of Imogen and Stuart. He wondered if these thoughts would ever end. The idea that they might continue, day after day after day, caused panic to rise in him. He forced the feeling back down.

After a few minutes Jane woke, looked up at Charlie through half-closed eyes and gave him a sleepy smile. "Hello, Charlie," she said. "What're you up to?"

"Just waking you up in the gentlest way I could."

"What time is it?"

Charlie looked at his watch. "Nearly three."

"Why didn't Paul wake me?"

Charlie nodded at the lounge door, which remained closed. "I think he has other things on his mind." He paused. "Or just on him. It doesn't bear thinking about, really, that ugly little homunculus slobbering over the lovely Fiona."

"Ugh. Stop it, Charlie. I don't want that image in my head before I go to bed. And I really must go to bed."

She took hold of Charlie's hand as she stood, gave it a gentle squeeze and then kissed it. "Thanks for waking me up so nicely."

"My pleasure."

"Night, Charlie. I'll see you in the morning."

"Night," Charlie said. He gave her a little wave with his un-kissed hand and watched her retreating figure pass through the door into the hallway. He heard the soft tread of her feet on the stairs as she tried to avoid the creaky steps.

Charlie rolled a cigarette. He'd known Jane since she'd first moved with Paul and his parents to Dereham. She'd been eleven or twelve years old then. Paul, Charlie, Stuart and James had become friends at the comprehensive school they had all attended. Back then, Jane had merely been Paul's little sister, somebody to joke and play games with. After two years, Paul's parents, always restless, had moved to Devon. Before leaving, Paul had told his friends he'd write to them. At first, Charlie hadn't taken much notice of this – he had never known people who wrote letters. But, after a few months, a fat letter, addressed to all the friends, had arrived at Charlie's house. Charlie, Stuart and James jointly wrote a letter back. Some weeks later another letter from Paul arrived, this time at Stuart's house. So it had continued – Paul writing a letter to each friend in turn, his friends jointly writing a letter back. In that way, Paul had remained friends with them all, despite the hundred miles between Devon and Wiltshire. Charlie had seen little of Jane after the family had moved. Then he and Stuart had begun to hitch-hike down to Devon during school and then college holidays. Charlie would see Jane two or three times a year, and she seemed to grow up in fits and starts, one moment thirteen, the next fourteen and then sixteen. And the last had been the most radical of these transformations. The sixteen-year old Jane seemed to bear no relation to the gawky kid he'd once known. Now she was a teenage girl and would soon be a young woman.

There was a part of Charlie that still saw Jane as Paul's little sister, and that part of him felt a little odd about fancying her. But was liking her so outlandish? After all, he was only eighteen. If you considered the dates on which their birthdays fell, there was, really, only eighteen months or so between them. He slowly smoked his cigarette, thinking about her. He unfolded the zed bed and threw some sheets and blankets across it. Jane's presence had disturbed him, and the kiss still lingered warmly on his hand. He found it difficult to sleep. He was awake when Paul quietly passed through the dining room on his way to bed. When he did finally drift off, he dreamed of Jane.

3

Charlie returned slowly to consciousness. It was morning and, judging by the bright daylight that lit the room even through the closed curtains, a morning that appeared almost over. He was hitch-hiking back to Dereham with Stuart today. He sat up and looked at the table. Jane wasn't there. He remembered, now, that she'd gone to bed, after kissing his hand, early this morning. He had dreamed of Jane, he remembered. But then he had dreamed of Imogen. There had also been a demon, he thought. Or a bird. His dreams had been confused, as dreams so often are. He stood, pulled on jeans and a tee-shirt, and then went upstairs to the bathroom. Before making his way back downstairs, he tapped softly on the door to Paul's bedroom, and then opened it. Stuart's sleeping bag was empty. He would be in the kitchen, Charlie supposed. Paul was still asleep. There was no sign of Fiona. She would have slept on the front-room sofa. Charlie glanced at the clock on the chest beside Paul's bed. It was quarter to ten, not as late in the morning as he'd thought.

Charlie left the room and walked down the stairs carefully, avoiding the squeaky riser, and then went down the hall to the dining room. Mr and Mrs Maas would have been up and about a couple of hours ago, and were now out of the house, at their jobs. Charlie turned down the hall towards the kitchen. The door was closed, but he could hear music from the radio. He opened the door and found Stuart dancing to *Heaven Must be Missing an Angel* and making toast for everybody. A plate of it sat on the work surface. "I see you're dancing to funky music again," Charlie said. He found a side plate and took a slice of toast.

"I love to boogie," Stuart said. "Jitterbug boogie."

"That's true," Charlie said, as he buttered his toast. "You do love to boogie." Charlie didn't like dancing. He couldn't dance. He was a music snob, too, and thought this song and songs like it were smooth's music. Fine for Jane. Fine for smooth girls who went to discos at the football club on a Saturday night. But not for him. He leaned against a worktop as Stuart took more toast from beneath the grill and piled it on the plate.

"Good day for a hitch," Stuart said.

"I haven't really noticed," Charlie said.

"Sunny," Stuart said, still dancing. "No rain."

Fiona came into the kitchen, her wavy blonde hair even more dishevelled than usual. She wore an old blue dressing gown of Paul's, which hung open to reveal a tee-shirt long enough to pass as a night shirt. She walked bleary-eyed over to Stuart and gave him a hug. She turned to Charlie and gently smiled. "Sorry, but you've got butter fingers," she said.

"Oh, don't you worry, I understand," Charlie said. "Stuart is a fine figure of a man and he almost distracts me." He knew Fiona would never have hugged him, anyway. Not like that.

Stuart rested his chin on Fiona's head and closed his eyes. He looked relaxed as she curved into him. He was enjoying the sleepy, morning warmth of her. "You smell of cigarette smoke and patchouli," he said, softly.

Of course she would, Charlie sarcastically thought. The toast was dry in Charlie's mouth, despite the butter. He poured himself a cup of tea from a brown teapot. Fiona opened her eyes then and looked at Charlie while addressing Stuart. "Don't you think Charlie and Jane would make a nice couple?"

"I was thinking the same," Stuart said. "They would make an interesting collision of smooth and freak."

It was more likely, Charlie thought, that Stuart had been considering how soft Fiona felt beneath the cotton of that tee-shirt. "She's a nice girl," Charlie said. "But why would a smooth young thing like her be interested in a freak like me?"

Fiona moved away from Stuart, picked up a piece of toast and spread butter and jam on it. "Clothes aren't everything. The music she likes doesn't define her," she said. "And she's become more interested in the same things as us."

"Has anyone yet convinced her *Larks' Tongues in Aspic Part II* is a towering achievement of art-rock?" Charlie said.

"Nobody has yet convinced me!"

"Yes, but beneath your gaudy apparel, I know you're really a smooth," Stuart said. "Once you leave us you go home and listen to your secret stash of Slade and Sweet records."

"Hey, *Ballroom Blitz* is a classic, alright?"

"Alright!" Stuart said.

Fiona said no more about Jane. Each of them buttered more toast and poured more tea. A few singles passed by unnoticed on the radio. Then the distinctive voice of Noosha Fox came from the small speaker, singing *S-S-S-Single Bed*.

"I love this song!" Fiona said.

"So do I!" Stuart replied.

"Oh god," Charlie said. "You're going to dance again, aren't you."

Fiona nodded emphatically, and then began moving to the rhythm. She and Stuart moved towards each other, attempting a jerky kind of dance.

"Oh, no," Charlie moaned. "This is like being at the worst social club disco ever. But with toast."

Fiona put her arms around Stuart. She started moving slowly from side to side, singing along softly. "This is a better kind of dance, don't you think?" Fiona murmured.

"Keep doing what you're doing, and you'll get no complaints from me," Stuart said, sliding into her rhythm.

"Hey, Stuart?"

Stuart looked down at her. Charlie could see the mischief in her cocoa brown eyes.

"Do I appear to have a low-frequency sinusoidal motion?"

Stuart laughed. "You could call it that," he said.

"What else could you call it?"

"Kinda snaky."

"Are you feeling kinda snaky?"

"Yeah. I just hope you can't feel old snaky."

Fiona and Charlie laughed then. These people were his friends, Charlie thought. They amused him, no matter how odd and on edge they sometimes made him feel. Fiona stood on tiptoe and kissed Stuart quickly on the lips. That was yet another thing that Charlie knew he would never receive from her.

Stuart continued to dance slowly with Fiona. "Would you be a darling," Fiona said to Charlie, "and take the toast out from under the grill before it burns."

Charlie clattered the grill pan out onto the hob.

The music stopped and Fiona rested her head on Stuart's shoulder for a few moments. She would feel nice there, Charlie supposed. Any further thoughts about how Fiona might feel in his arms were interrupted by the kitchen door opening.

Jane entered. Unlike Fiona, she had already dressed and brushed her hair. "Morning everyone," she said, cheerily and grabbed a piece of toast. "Isn't Paul up yet?"

Fiona stopped dancing with Stuart and poured Jane a cup of tea. "I made sure he'd have sweet dreams."

Jane winced. "Please don't, Fiona! You'll put me off my toast!"

Jane took the mug from Fiona. "What are you doing today? Are you staying here with Paul?"

Fiona shook her head. "No. Paul said he wanted to practice his visualisation. Boring. So, I thought I'd go into Paignton and buy some paints and boards. I need to paint more before the exams."

"Can I come with you?" Jane asked. "I don't want to hang around here while Paul conjures up demons and stinks the place out with joss-sticks."

"Of course you can, my lovely," Fiona said. "I warn you, though, I might be a bit a bit of bore. I'm feeling *très fatigue*."

"Please don't tell me why," Jane said. "If I see any of my friends, I might hook up with them, if you don't mind."

"Why would I mind? If you can find something better to do than watch me stock up on Daler board, that's fine. We can nip into a caff and have a coffee." Fiona winked. "And a fag, if you like."

Fiona filled the kettle again. She looked at Charlie and Stuart. "I'm going to miss you two. I like the change in Paul when you come down. You're still his best and oldest friends. You bring news, gossip and nostalgia with you. He laughs more."

Jane turned to Charlie. "So, when are you two leaving?"

"Soon, soon," Charlie said. "We just have to get our shit together."

Charlie regretted now that he was leaving today. He'd rather spend the day in Paignton with Jane than hitch back to Dereham with Stuart. And what awaited him there anyway? Either Imogen would be back together with James, again, or she would be seeking Stuart's shoulder to cry on, again. He left the kitchen to pack his bag, his mood just a little lower than it had been.

Jane spoke quietly, knowing Charlie was in the dining room next to them. "Do you think Charlie fancies me?"

Fiona smiled. "Yes, I do. Do you fancy him?"

"I think so. But there is the problem of... well, Imo."

"Don't worry," Stuart said. "I'm sure he's over her."

"Are you *really* sure?"

Stuart's only reply was a shrug and a smile.

"I only see him when you come down," Jane said to Stuart. "And I can't go up to Dereham until next year, Paul won't take me until then."

Fiona put an arm around Jane. "Why not write to him? That's how Paul stayed in contact with the boys."

"Do you think Charlie would mind?"

"I think he'd love it," Fiona said.

Jane frowned and looked at Stuart. "If I write to Charlie, shouldn't I also write to you? Otherwise it'll be obvious, won't it?"

"Just write to Charlie," Stuart said.

"I don't want things to be obvious, to go too fast," Jane sighed. "Perhaps I shouldn't have said anything." She wasn't sure why she had said anything; the need to say something had suddenly come upon her when she realised that Charlie would soon be gone, and that she probably wouldn't see him again for a few months. And she needed to know if the others thought that Charlie fancied her, or whether what she felt was a silly fantasy. She would feel foolish if he didn't. He was older, more mature. She didn't want to look stupid in his eyes. Fiona had said Charlie liked her. Nothing was certain, though. And always, looming over anything related to Charlie, was the tall shadow of Imogen.

"Why be coy?" Stuart said. "You've known us all for years. Why don't you just tell him how you feel?"

Jane looked from Fiona to Stuart, biting her lip. "I'm not just worried about how Charlie feels," she said. "It's me, too. I don't know how much I like Charlie in that way, you know? We don't get a chance to go out together like we would if we lived close to each other. So what do I know about how we feel?" She looked at Stuart. "I mean, do I feel this way just because I've known you both for so long? Do I just like the fact you're so different to my friends? You both breeze in here, turn the world upside down for a few days and then you're gone. While you're here, it's exciting. But then you go back to Dereham and I go back to school and hang around with my friends and..." Jane lost the thread.

"You wonder if Charlie represents the excitement you feel when we're here, yeah?" Stuart said.

"I think that's what I'm trying to say, yeah." Jane paused. "I don't know. Perhaps I really do fancy him." Jane looked at Stuart gravely. "I don't want you two talking about me like boys when you've gone."

"You needn't worry about *that*. Charlie and I are big girls."

"Don't joke about this."

Stuart rested a hand Jane's arm. He looked into her eyes. "Sorry. You know you can trust me."

Jane could see the sincerity. "I know. You're like my other brother."

Stuart sighed. "It'll be on my gravestone. *Here lies Stuart Garland. He was like a brother to me.* Signed, *all the girls he's ever known.*"

Jane smiled. "Well, you are. And there's nothing wrong with it." She kissed him on the cheek.

Charlie returned at that exact moment. Jane hoped he wouldn't take that kiss the wrong way. "Right then," he said to Stuart. "We'd better get going."

Paul met them at the bottom of the stairs. He was in his dressing gown, yawning and rubbing his eyes. The hallway was small, and there was barely room for the five of them. Charlie and Stuart reached into their pockets. Each took out a five-pound note and passed it over Fiona's head to Paul.

"For your mum," Stuart said. "For our keep."

Paul thanked them. "I'll see you in a couple of days' time."

"I'll have the pit ready for you," Stuart said.

"I wish I could go with you," Jane said.

"Your time will come," Stuart replied.

Fiona hugged Charlie and kissed him on the cheek. Then she hugged Stuart, kissed him on the lips and winked. "See you soon, snaky," she said. Stuart smiled.

Jane hugged Charlie. "It's been really, really good to see you," she said. She kissed his cheek. She turned to Stuart, who swallowed her in his arms.

"Your secret is safe with me," Stuart whispered in her ear.

"I know," Jane whispered back.

Stuart opened the front door. "Goodbye, darling," he said to Paul and blew him a kiss.

Paul grinned. "I'll be counting the days until I can feel you in my arms again. Now go, all of you, hence, before I embarrass myself and cry." He put a hand to his forehead.

Charlie and Stuart walked up the garden path to the lane leading to the ring road. Jane had followed them a little way, looking at Charlie. She wished she could be sure of his feelings for Imo. She wondered if Charlie's obsession was as bad as Paul and Stuart had sometimes insinuated.

How could that be? He might be older than she was, but he was too young for such madness. *Surely?*

Paul was alone in the house. Jane and Fiona had left for Torquay. Fiona was returning to her parents in Totnes tonight. Paul wouldn't see her now until he came back from Stuart's. He would miss Fiona. She had looked so lovely when she'd left. He wondered if she fancied Stuart. He knew Stuart fancied her because Stuart fancied everybody. But he trusted Stuart – although, considering they were all horny young men, he didn't know why. Yet he did. It was because he knew Stuart was loyal to his friends, he supposed.

He looked at his watch. It was only eleven thirty. Jane wouldn't be back for a few hours yet. There would be time for him to perform some kind of ritual. He sipped his tea and decided what he could do in the time he had. He looked around the room. Pictures adorned the walls – posters from Athena, postcards, and rock gods from music magazines. He could see Seurat's *A Sunday Afternoon on the Island of La Grande Jatte*, Waterhouse's *The Lady of Shalott* and Ernst's *Europe After the Rain*. There was a large poster of Robert Plant and Jimmy Page in full flight, while in a smaller poster stood the wind-blown members of Yes. There were postcards from friends: of Cornwall, the Yorkshire Moors, and Wiltshire downs; there were cards from museums: of Egyptian gods, Viking gods, Celtic gods, and Celtic bronzes; there were art postcards, Klee and Ernst, Millais and Burne-Jones.

The Banishing Ritual would be apt, he thought. It was the first ritual he had learned, and he knew it by heart. He lit a jasmine joss stick. He pulled down the flap of his bureau and placed a yellow cloth over it. This was his altar. He had no need for an altar for this ritual, but he liked to open the bureau. For him, that action alone marked the beginning of his practice, the entrance to another world. He slid open a drawer in the bureau and found his ritual knife. He finished his tea and lit another jasmine joss stick. He opened his bedroom window and allowed the cool breeze into the room.

Paul sat on his bed cross-legged and shut his eyes, breathing slowly. In for a count of four, out for a count of four. In and out, concentrating only on his breathing. He followed the flow of his thoughts, which had focused on the smell of jasmine and the petalled flowers in his mother's garden, the pansies and tulips. Images of flowers flooded his mind.

He stood slowly and picked up his ritual knife. He faced east and said, in a low growl, "Ateh." He imagined a bright light descending from above. It stopped just above his head, where it formed into a shining white ball. He touched his stomach and growled the word, "Malkuth." From the ball of light above him he drew out a ray, which snaked towards his feet. At the bottom of the ray he formed another shimmering ball of light. Using his knife, he dragged a stream of light from this ball, up to his right shoulder, which he touched and said, "Ve Geburah." He created another ball of light and again dragged a sparkling ray across his body, this time to his left shoulder, where he intoned, "Ve Gedulah." Another ball formed. He said, "Le Olahm," then brought his hands together. The knife was between his palms, its blade pointing towards the ceiling. The light now formed a cross on his body. Finally, he said, "Amen." He paused for a moment, breathing slowly. Light danced around him and passed through him. He revelled in its brilliance.

Paul used his knife to drag slivers of silver from the spheres and drew a pentagram in front of him. He pushed the knife into the centre of the pentagram, saying, "Yod Hey Vow Hey." He pointed his knife towards the floor and turned towards the South, drawing a semicircle of light as he did so. When he reached the South, he stopped and drew another pentagram, saying this time, as he thrust his knife into the pentagram, "Adonai." He did the same for the West, saying, "Ehyeh," and the North, saying, "Ahgalah." He finished the circle by returning to the East. He extended his arms, forming his body into a cross.

"Before me," he said, "Raphael."

The Archangel appeared in front of him, dressed in white. The sword in Raphael's hand pointed upwards. The scent of jasmine blew past Paul on the fresh breeze. Raphael was illuminated by a light similar in colour to the cloth over his altar.

"Behind me, Gabriel."

He could sense the form of the Archangel behind him, looking at him, holding a silver chalice. Around and about Gabriel was the sea, the sea Paul knew well, flowing as quiet waves over the sands at Paignton, or crashing on rocks at Brixham. Paul took a deep breath, catching a salt breeze that had drifted across the fields from Torquay and slipped through his open window.

"At my right hand," he then said, vibrating the name with his peculiar growl, "Michael."

Michael was to his right, as dazzling as Raphael and Gabriel, holding a red wand that was encrusted with diamonds. Flames surrounded the archangel. Salamanders writhed in the fire.

"At my left hand, Ariel."

Paul turned his head to look at Ariel, who held a disk at the centre of which was inscribed a pentacle. The pentacle burned with the same white light Paul had used to create his pentagram. Trees surrounded Ariel. The scent of flowers wafted through the bedroom window.

Paul regarded each Archangel, studying the symbolism that inhered in them and their associations with the Tarot. There was Raphael the sword-bearer, representing the Swords of the minor arcana, thought and intellect; Gabriel, the cup-bearer, representing the Cups – emotions and feelings, the cup of love, the shared drinking vessel; Michael, to his right, represented the Wands – drive, energy, the source of fire; and finally Ariel, holding the plate, represented the Pentacles – practicality, the home, family, the good earth. When he'd finished studying the bright Archangels, he said, "About me flame the pentagrams and in the column shines the six-rayed star!"

He reimagined the complete circle, the shining, mercurial light with the dazzling pentagrams at each quadrant and finally, the Kabbalistic Cross running through him. He remained still, visualising this light for a few moments, then deconstructed his Kabbalistic Cross by reversing the steps he had used to create it. When he finished, he waited a moment, then stamped his foot hard on the floor. He liked to stamp, he liked the physicality of it, the way it grounded him back in the world after being inside himself for so long.

Paul slowly opened his eyes and breathed deeply. He'd earlier thought he would follow the Banishing with the Invoking Ritual of the Pentagram. But he was tired. Fiona had kept him awake for a long time last night. Instead, he folded the yellow cloth on his altar and closed the bureau, which became again just another piece of furniture in his bedroom. He sat on his bed, feeling calm, then fell onto his back, closed his eyes and relaxed. After a few minutes, he sat up again and recorded in his occult journal everything he'd done and everything he'd seen and felt. He really believed he was at last learning to control the world around him.

4

Charlie sat on the floor in James's attic rooms, looking through the extensive record collection. Jane drifted through his mind – her face, the way she moved, her smile – but still he was impatient for Imogen's arrival. He took the Sobranie James offered and lit it. "What the hell are you wearing," he said.

James's waistcoat was particularly loud this evening, a crazy purple paisley affair with a yellow back panel. He smiled at Charlie. "Do you think Imo will like it?"

Charlie looked James up and down. "What do I know?" He selected Roy Harper's *Flashes from the Archives of Oblivion* and put it on the record deck. Both he and James drank cups of coffee that had been brought to them by James's mother. She had told James, before she returned downstairs, not to play the music too loudly. James had turned the volume down while she went down the stairs, then slowly turned it back up.

"They're both as deaf as posts," James said. "I don't know why they bother."

It certainly wasn't for the neighbours' sake, Charlie thought. James's parents owned a large, stone-built, detached house in Church Street, a quiet, well-to-do, tree-lined road in Dereham. The house was probably fifty feet from its nearest neighbour. James had the attic rooms to himself. One room housed his stereo, the sofa on which he sat, shelves of books and records, a desk and a pine chest; the other room contained a bed, a chest of drawers and a wardrobe. His parents were well off; thus, James was too. Of the four boys, he had the most books, the most records, the most art-prints on his walls, and the most dope secretly stashed away. He could also afford bottles of Martell and Mateus Rosé. Even though he could certainly get by on his extravagant pocket money, he also had a Saturday job. James liked money.

"How was Devon? How was Paul?" James asked.

"Devon was beautiful, as always. Paul talked too much, as always."

"He should be here by now, shouldn't he?"

"Yes, he arrived a couple of hours ago. He went straight to Stuart's." Charlie looked at his watch. "They'll be here soon. Then Paul can bend *your* ear for a change."

"And how was the delightful Fi?" James asked.

"Lovely. Spikey and funny, as always. Although she spent far too much time with her arms wrapped around Stuart."

"Jealous, Charlie?" James asked.

Charlie envied Stuart, he had no doubt about that. He could not bring himself to say it, though, in front of his friend. "Me, jealous? No way," Charlie said. But jealousy and envy gnawed at him constantly these days. Fiona and Stuart had looked so comfortable dancing together the other morning. They'd been so close, smiling at each other, moving slowly around the kitchen. "It'd be a shame if Paul got upset because of Stuart's thoughtlessness."

"Fi's thoughtlessness, surely? If Stuart spent the weekend with Fi's arms around him, then surely if anyone is to blame, it's Fi?" James was protecting Stuart. Just as Paul was still Charlie's closest friend, James was closest to Stuart.

Would Charlie have danced with Fiona if the opportunity had arisen? He doubted it. He knew he was a musical snob. The song they had been dancing to held no interest for him. What's more, he didn't really dance. Whenever he had the chance to dance with a girl, he stood at arm's length from her, trying too hard, trying to find the rhythm he couldn't really feel. He was all arms and legs, shouting jokes and small talk over the music, filling the space with anything to hide his bony awkwardness. Perhaps that's why he liked prog-rock music so much, he thought. *It's head music. Nobody can dance in seven-four time. We can just sit around, smoke a joint and enjoy the players' expertise.* Stuart always claimed he too couldn't dance. But he played guitar, he had rhythm. And Charlie particularly noticed that sense of rhythm when he danced with a girl – like when he had danced with Fiona in the kitchen.

James sipped at his coffee. "Did you see much of Jane?

"Yes. She hung out with us some evenings. She played Scrabble and joined us on our rambles."

"She must be growing up now."

Charlie sucked on his Sobranie. "She is. She's cute. She's a smooth, though. A cute smooth."

"Don't be a snob. There's nothing wrong with a smooth."

"Yeah, but it would be weird going out with somebody who listened to Gary Glitter and Terry Jacks. *We had joy, we had fun, we had seasons in the sun.*" Charlie shook his head. "Weird."

"Open your mind to new experiences!"

Charlie turned to look at James's record collection. "I don't see any Terry Jacks on your shelves. Or even Fleetwood Mac."

"Your bigotry has blinded you. Look somewhere between Emerson, Lake and Palmer and Focus."

Charlie scanned the shelf. James was right, of course. Between *Welcome Back My Friends to the Show that Never Ends* and *Moving Waves*, Charlie found Fleetwood Mac's *Fleetwood Mac*. "Bloody hell," he muttered.

"I really like *Rhiannon*. I'll have you know," James said.

"What about the rest of it?"

"Dross."

That was one advantage of having money, Charlie thought. You could afford to buy an album for just one track you might not even like very much anyway, and only listen to it once a year.

The age-worn brass handle on the plank door rattled. Stuart and Paul entered.

"Hi, kiddies!" James said.

Paul jumped on James and kissed his head. "Hello, my love. How I've missed you."

James pushed him away, laughing. "Get off, you bloody homo!"

Stuart sat on the floor, next to Charlie. Paul was about to sit next to James but found a wad of writing paper on the cushion. He picked it up to move it out of his way, glancing at it as he did so. "Are you still writing lyrics for Honeyhouse?" He put the writing paper on a small table beside the sofa.

"Yes. They seem to like them, and I enjoy writing them," James said.

Paul beamed affectionately at James, then punched him on the arm. "I haven't seen you for ages!"

"Not since the last time you were here," James replied.

"Obviously. But when are you coming down to Devon? You'd enjoy it."

"I keep meaning to, man, but, well..."

"Well, what?"

"I did think about coming down this time," James said. "But then Imo told me there was an Inshaw exhibition in Bath. Unfortunately, the only time she could go was at the weekend, so..."

"Where is the lovely Imo?" Paul asked.

"She'll be here soon. Do you guys want a coffee?"

Stuart and Paul said they did. James went downstairs to the kitchen.

Charlie looked at Paul. "What did you do after we left?"

"A Banishing Ritual. To remove the noisome spirits you left behind."

"Sometimes I think I'd like to learn the rituals," Charlie said. "But I just get side-tracked by the historical stuff. The Golden Dawn, the reinvention of Wicca, the witch burnings, whatever." He slid Fleetwood Mac from the shelf and looked at the cover.

"Jane's got that," Paul said. "I'm surprised James has it. Seems a bit lightweight for him."

"James is eclectic, man – like me," Stuart ventured. He returned to the subject of rituals. "What is the Banishing Ritual? I mean, I've heard you mention it before."

"You do it before you do another ritual," Paul said. "It creates a psychically clean and safe space."

"If you do the banishing, do you have to do another ritual?"

"Not necessarily. As I say, I banished the other morning to remove the foul stench and psychic disruption brought about by having you two energy vampires sucking on my Faculty X."

"Hey, I never sucked anything of yours," Charlie said.

"What is the Banishing Ritual anyway?" Stuart asked.

Paul described the cross, pentagrams and circles of light. James came through the door, a freshly lit black Sobranie in his mouth, two mugs clinking against each other in one hand, spilling drops of coffee down his jeans and onto the carpet, as Paul described the silver spheres of light he'd visualised at his shoulders.

"Are you talking about the Banishing Ritual?" James said.

"Yes, I'm explaining it to Stuart."

James put the mugs down on a small coffee table. He went to his bookshelves and pulled out Conway's *Magic*. He threw it to Stuart. "It's all in there," James said. He ran his finger along the spines of the books, found what he was looking for. He pulled out a fat tome by Eliphaz Levi and tossed it over. "That also has something about it."

"Thanks," Stuart said and began flicking through the books.

James sat down beside Paul again. "Have you tried any other rituals?"

"Israel Regardie's healing ritual," Paul said. "The Middle Pillar Exercise. Do you know it?"

"Yes, I know it."

"I've done some pathworking on the Tree of Life. I'm also exploring the symbolism of Tarot cards through inner imagery and meditation. Oh, and I'm learning all the magic tables in Conway."

"Wow! You'll be invoking demons next," Charlie said, sarcastically.

"Well, in pathworking, you can invoke a false Guide," James pointed out. "Which is something like a demon."

Stuart looked up from the Eliphaz Levi. "What would happen if you did?"

"The books are vague, perhaps intentionally. But it can't be good, to have the wrong Guide, can it?" James said.

The door rattled again, and Imogen came into the room. "Hey, guys!"

"Imo!" James squealed.

Imogen smiled and dropped her striped canvas bag on the floor. She went around Charlie, Stuart and Paul, giving them a kiss on the cheek. As she moved, a collection of cheap bangles tinkled on her left wrist. When she returned to James, she ran her fingers through his long dark hair, and then planted a full kiss on his lips. Her own long red hair fell across their faces. When she broke away from James, she tossed the curls away from her face and removed her blue and white striped blazer. She sat on the arm of the sofa with her left arm around James.

"Nice to see you," Paul said to Imogen. "I hear you went to see an Inshaw exhibition."

"Yes, it was good. He was showing some new pieces as well the old favourites."

"*She Did Not Turn?*" Paul asked.

"Yes. And *The Raven. The Badminton Game*, obviously. The usual."

Charlie wasn't as interested in David Inshaw as the others were. While they talked about the exhibition, Charlie admired Imogen instead. She was one of the most striking young women in Dereham, there was no doubt about that. Tall and slim, she was a perfect example of middle-class nutrition and education, a dream girl, almost unreal, as if James had fashioned her from the many Pre-Raphaelite women in the prints on his walls. Her long hair, full of curls and ringlets, was naturally auburn but she hennaed it a brighter red. She wore flared jeans, red baseball boots and a baggy old granddad shirt of blue and white stripes. The shirt was mostly unbuttoned to reveal a red tee shirt. Her big brown eyes suddenly turned on him. "How are you, Charles?"

"I'm fine, thanks." He looked at Paul with a smile. "Despite him lecturing us most of the time."

"I have to teach you yokels something," Paul said.

"Do you want a drink?" James asked Imogen.

She nodded towards one of the Mateus Rosé bottles on the shelves. "I wouldn't mind a glass of wine."

James usually had a corkscrew and glasses to hand. He opened a bottle, then picked up a glass, and inspected it. "I think I need to get you a clean glass," he said. He asked if anybody else wanted a drink. Paul asked for more coffee. "But you still have half a cup," James said. He poured himself a glass of Rosé.

"I will need another one. I'm very thirsty. It'll save you walking downstairs again."

James nodded. "Very true." He took a sip of his wine before heading for the stairs.

"How was Devon?" Imogen asked.

"It was good." Charlie said. "Lovely weather. The landscape was lovely."

"I'd like to come down," Imogen said.

"Well, James has never visited in nearly three years, so you might have a long wait," Paul noted.

Imogen frowned. "Very true. I can get him to exhibitions, gigs, plays, down the pub, but I can never convince him to leave town for a more than a night. He talks about coming down to see you, but he never even begins to make a plan. There's always something else to do instead."

"You can come down with me one day," Charlie said.

Imogen reached for the faience bead on her necklace and rolled it between her fingers. "Yeah, sure. I'll come down with you and Stuart one day."

Charlie had intended his comment to sound off-hand and frivolous. Yet, the manner of Imogen's reply told him that he had instead been clumsy. He was also suddenly filled with apprehension. Why did Imogen need Stuart there? Why did she seem always to drift towards him? He was just an empty-headed, silly flirt. There was nothing serious about him. *Why should she prefer him to me?* Stuart just wanted to play games, walk the hills and laugh. Fiona was more Stuart's sort. *If Stuart lived in Devon, would Fiona fancy him instead of Paul?* Stuart could be a child sometimes. Surely a girl like Imogen would prefer somebody more serious, more level-headed than Stuart. And then he thought: *woman.* Imogen was becoming a woman. She was no longer a *girl*, she was maturing – unlike Stuart and James.

James entered then, with another mug of coffee for Paul and a glass for Imogen. His return brought Charlie out of his reverie. Paul was speaking, "...so occultism allows you to develop Faculty X."

"James has told me about it," Imogen said. "It's this psychic faculty we're all supposed to have, right?"

Paul nodded. "Yes. Wilson thinks we all possess it but aren't conscious of it, except, perhaps, through occasional flashes of psychic experience, like telepathy."

"So, if we could develop Faculty X, we'd become telepathic?"

"Yes, telepathy and telekinesis are a natural by-product of it. The more you develop your Faculty X, the more naturally psychic you become."

"Which would elevate us above the rest of the proles," James said.

Charlie wondered how many times he'd listened to Paul rambling on about Faculty X over the last three years. "When do the demons come into it?" he asked. "I mean, I've seen a lot of horror films and it's the demons I want to know about. Somebody has to conjure up a demon at some point, so it can chase us for eternity, yea, even unto the fiery pits of hell. Or Southleigh. Whichever comes first."

Paul chuckled. "I had an idea. Just before I die, I'd like to invoke Pan. What a way to go!"

Imogen sipped her wine. "Would it be impressive?"

"It would be monumental! Indescribable!" Paul said. "After I'd gone – and they'd probably find no trace of me – they'd put up a plaque, or a monolith, or something, in the place where I performed the ritual. It would become sacred, hallowed ground, the place where Pan had appeared in all his glory. It would be called Panfield, or Pangate. Perhaps they'd build a temple there."

Charlie was still intent on a little mischief. "Very impressive I'm sure, but does Pan count as a demon? I mean, will we have to get Peter Cushing to come and rescue Fiona from your dribbling, insane figure?"

"We should phone him now, in that case," Stuart said.

Paul ignored them both. "When I invoke Pan, it'll be too late to phone Peter Cushing. I'll be gone. In my place will be ... will be... lights and fire, like the most fantastic firework show you've ever seen."

"Even better than Dereham Town Council's annual Bonfire Night extravaganza?" Stuart asked

"I believe so," Paul said thoughtfully. "Invoking Pan would be *huge*. Spectacular."

James looked at Charlie, and then Stuart. "Talking of spectacular, have you heard about the UFO sightings at Copsehill over the weekend?" Both Stuart and Charlie shook their heads. "Imo and I went down The White Lion on Sunday evening," James said. "We had a drink with Danny and Mark. You know them," James said to Paul. "The guys from the Honeyhouse."

"Yes, I know them," Paul said. "I've met them a couple of times."

"They'd heard reports about a UFO sighting at Copsehill on Saturday night. Three huge lights flew over, or something."

"Bloody typical, isn't it?" Charlie said. "One of the few weekends we're not on Copsehill, bloody great UFOs fly over."

"That's what Danny and Mark said," James said. "We had a good old moan about how we can walk around Copsehill for years and see nothing, then a bunch of kiddies arrive at Copsehill and spot something on their first skywatch."

"Where were they from?"

"Oh, the Midlands. Worcester, Stourport. Some infernal industrial hell-hole."

"Hah. Bloody Black Country oafs," Charlie said. "And their fine porcelains."

Stuart laughed. "How did Danny and Mark find out?"

"They were passing the UFO Centre and thought they'd pop in and catch up on the latest ufological gossip. These kids from the Midlands were there. About the same age as us. They chatted about music for a while, then they told Danny and Mark about the UFOs they'd seen."

"Bastards," Charlie said. He sucked on a roll-up. Stuart had taken another Sobranie from James. Paul told Stuart he would become addicted.

"I'm fine," Stuart said. "I can take it or leave it."

"You won't be able to play badminton," Imogen warned. "You'll stop being chunky." She winked. "I might have to stop hugging you."

Chance, Charlie thought, would be a fine thing. He felt a stab of jealousy again. He wanted these feelings to stop. Jane offered the possibility of escape from these obsessions. He liked Jane a lot. And Imogen was with James. He should stop this madness. He attempted to conjure the thrill he'd felt earlier in the evening at the mention of Jane's name. He found it hard to recapture.

Stuart had finished skipping through a poetry book and had picked up the Conway. He riffled through the pages, stopping to read now and again. He looked up at Paul. "It's very complicated... All these words you have to remember..."

"It's like learning lines for play," Paul said. "Just like Imo does. It's no more or less difficult."

Imogen looked rueful. "I usually only get a couple of lines a play. Everybody knows that if they give me more I'll get stage fright, freak out and forget what to say. I should leave the drama group, really."

Charlie sipped at his cognac. "No matter how many lines you need to learn, it seems you still can't conjure a demon."

Paul leaned back, put his hands behind his head. "I think you've got the wrong idea about magic, Charlie. You've watched far too many horror films."

"The horror films are, at least, exciting."

"But the magic I do is exciting to me. I feel my life is more intense because of occultism."

"Better living through magic!" James said sarcastically.

Paul ignored James. "Which isn't to say life gets any easier," he mused. "Or that studying the occult has helped me through my young adult angst. But I'm doing something vital–"

Charlie snorted. "Oh yeah, like the world really cares."

"I mean *vital*, with *intensity*. Magic takes me to places deep within myself."

"Not very far then," Charlie said.

Stuart sniggered. "Good one."

Paul sighed. "It clarifies my personal vision. You might think that learning magic is about controlling the world, the exterior world. But it's not. It's about controlling *your* world. No other world is real except the world you construct. So, when you control magic, you control the world."

"And yet you still haven't conjured a demon."

"You must get over this obsession with the dark side you see portrayed in films." Paul paused. "When I meditate, I draw together all the strands of what I'm learning. I think I'm doing really well."

"Such modesty," Simon said.

Paul smiled. "If I carry on at my current rate, I'll be the new Aleister Crowley, I tell you. Or the next Robert Graves! Tying together mythologies, making links, making sense of it all."

"Steady on old bean," James said.

"Sorry. I don't mean to sound pompous."

"Yet you manage it anyway," Stuart said.

"We should perform a ritual on Copsehill," James suggested. "There seems to be something there. Some elemental force, or something. Everybody comments on its atmosphere. And the place is buzzing with UFOs–"

"So crazy people say," Charlie said.

"Yes, perhaps," James said. "But it just feels like a place of power. Doesn't it?"

Paul sat forward excitedly. "Yes! That's a great idea. Let's do it. Let's have a skywatch this weekend and do it!"

Imogen looked at Charlie. "No demons, though."

Charlie held up his hands. "I wasn't going to say anything."

"And no summoning Pan," Imogen said to Paul. "I don't want any fireworks exploding and blowing my little lambikins to smithereens."

"Little lambikins indeed," said Charlie. "He's more like a shaggy goat, the hairy bastard." He laughed. "More like a satyr."

James ran his fingers through his full, dark beard. "It *is* an intriguing idea, though, isn't it? We don't have to do anything spectacular, do we? "

"No, we don't," Paul said. "But we can't really do it this weekend. We need to decide what we're going to do. We need to prepare for it."

James pouted. "Spoilsport."

"A skywatch sounds cool, though," Stuart said. "Who's up for it?"

They all were, and they began to make arrangements for the following evening. Charlie was pleased Imogen had agreed to come; she didn't always join them at skywatches. Stuart and James, his two rivals, would be there, but he could live with that. He liked to spend time with Imogen, even though he knew he would undoubtedly end up worrying about what how Imogen and Stuart were behaving with each other, what they were secretly planning to do the next time she and James split up.

Imogen stood up, saying she needed a pee. Charlie watched her walk to the door, admiring her legs. When she'd left the room, James threw a balled-up piece of paper at Charlie's head. "You can put your tongue back in now."

Charlie was embarrassed, although his beard hid his blush. "Well, she is gorgeous," he said. "What do you expect?"

"I expect you to behave like Stuart. A perfect gentleman."

Stuart, who had become absorbed in another book he'd found on James's floor, looked up and around, said, "Hmmm?" and then went back to the book.

Charlie wondered why both James and Paul showed so little concern about the way Stuart behaved with their girlfriends. He would have to ask one of them. It intrigued him. For the moment, he let it go as well as he could.

Imogen came back through the door, singing. Charlie recognised the song as one she'd written with Stuart and James. Stuart lifted his head from his book and sang with Imogen. Charlie loved Imogen's voice. Because she suffered from stage fright, she couldn't face singing in front of an audience. Stuart was the same. He'd played guitar twice on stage with Honeyhouse and had hated every minute of it. Imogen had tried singing with them once at a local gig and freaked out. Instead, Stuart and Imogen now played and sang together. Sometimes Mark from the band joined them. They wrote songs together using James's lyrics. She would sing them beautifully. Stuart would harmonize with her and, when it worked, Charlie loved hearing it. Yet at the same time it made him jealous. Singing was another thing that Stuart shared with Imogen that he couldn't. Their voices locked together almost intimately. They would look at each other as they sang, smiling, their eyes bright. James – who was, apart from Charlie, their only audience – would become enthusiastic, and insist that they get a band together, or work as a folk duo, or something, *anything*, and get back on stage again. Stuart and Imogen would dismiss his ambitions. They knew the stage wasn't for them.

Stuart and Imogen stopped singing and smiled at each other. Charlie could see how close they were at that moment and hated it. Suddenly, he felt alone. James and Imogen. Paul and Fiona. Stuart and Imogen. He felt the familiar twinges inside him. Given how they were behaving, Charlie supposed that James and Imogen had got back together while he had been in Devon. He didn't want to see them kissing each other. And yet, because he wasn't certain of their status – nothing had been announced, after all – it was still possible to imagine that Imogen and Stuart would finally get together. He looked at his watch. Eleven o'clock. He could go home now without it appearing out of character. Charlie faked a yawn, although he *was* exhausted, tired of these endlessly circling thoughts, of all this imagining, of all this *wondering*. He needed to go home and get some sleep. He needed to find some space. Tomorrow, he would avoid them all – until the skywatch, at least. Paul and Stuart would find something to do together, and James and Imogen could go to the pub. He needn't be with any of them.

Charlie stood up. "Right. I'm off."

Paul also stood. As he did so, James and Imogen collapsed into each other on the sofa.

"Good night, sweet friends," James said.

Imogen giggled as James snuggled into her. "Take care, darlings."

They looked to be very much together, Charlie decided. He needed to redirect his thoughts. He needed to think about somebody else. He needed a reminder of Jane. "Can I borrow the *Fleetwood Mac?*" Charlie asked.

"By all means, Charles," James said, already nuzzling Imogen's neck.

Stuart smiled down at James and Imogen and stroked her head as he passed. Imogen gripped Stuart's hand briefly as it trailed away. Charlie picked up the album and followed Stuart and Paul down the stairs. They all stood together briefly outside James's house.

"We don't have any plans for tomorrow," Stuart said to Charlie. "I expect we'll just wander about. If you want to meet up, phone me."

"I might well do that," Charlie said, while having no intention of doing so. He would stay in, read a book and listen to music. He would avoid everything, everybody and empty his mind. He would read something light and easy, some science fiction, perhaps. He would certainly avoid novels about people and feelings, about thoughts and relationships. He'd see everybody, anyway, tomorrow night at the skywatch.

Charlie nodded down the road, in the opposite direction to the one he knew Stuart and Paul would take. "I'm going to walk home across the fields." It was a slightly longer, circuitous route, but he needed some air. Stuart and Paul said goodnight and turned right. Charlie turned left. He heard Stuart and Paul talking as they walked away into the night up Church Street back towards the town centre. Charlie strolled down the road. At the bottom of it, he crossed a stile to a footpath that cut across a field.

Out in this empty space at the edge of town, he breathed deeply. He looked up at the sky, across which raced ragged scraps of cloud. Between the clouds, the stars shone brightly. For a moment he wandered only among the stars, naming the few constellations he knew. He scanned the sky for the bright planets. Now he was alone he felt light and free. He bounced across the field with a jaunty step. He wondered what Jane was doing. Was she in her back garden, looking for the elusive flying saucer she so wanted to see? Was she looking at these same stars? Most likely she was asleep, tucked up in her bed in the small room at the back of the cottage. Now he had removed himself from the overwhelming presence of Imogen he could think about Jane again. He wished he could talk to her, right now. Was there any reason he shouldn't just phone her and make small talk about Imo and James and Stuart? About these stars? He wished he could still smell the *Havoc* on her neck

5

Imogen opened her eyes and realised, sleepily, that she was looking at the ceiling of James's bedroom. It wasn't unusual for her to stay at James's house; she lived in one of the villages outside Dereham. There were no buses at night, and she didn't always want to leave as early as her parents would demand should she ask one of them to pick her up. She rarely risked, however, waking, at eleven in the morning, semi-naked on James's bed. *Oh well, it seems I'm back with James again.* She quickly stood up, rubbed sleep from her eyes and went to the bathroom. She met James's mother half an hour later, when she went to the kitchen to make a cup of tea. Mrs Sands asked how she'd slept, believing Imogen had made her way, as usual, to one of the three spare bedrooms. Because James's friends had been around the night before, Mrs Sands had left Imogen and James to sleep in. Imogen was relieved. She would be so embarrassed if Mrs Sands walked in with a nice cup of tea for James and found her asleep wearing only a vaguely buttoned striped shirt and a pair of white cotton socks. James came downstairs and into the kitchen, where his mother asked if he'd had a good sleep. James said he'd had a very relaxing night, thank you. He winked at Imogen as he walked over to the teapot. She wished he wouldn't do that. She got enough of that from lecherous gits as she walked around town.

Mr Sands was already out and about, working, as James had once explained, to continue the Sands' comfortable lifestyle. The work involved stocks and shares, long bonds, antiques and paintings. He was always buying, always selling and somehow always taking a sizeable cut along the way. His father's facility with money had led to a reaction in James, who now read Karl Marx and Herbert Marcuse and accused his parents of being bourgeois reactionaries. His reading had yet to dissuade him, however, from accepting considerable pocket money and working on Saturdays in the record section of Benton's, Dereham's only department store.

Imogen needed to call her parents and tell them she was going on a skywatch at Copsehill tonight. Imogen asked Mrs Sands if she could stay over for another night and if she could use the telephone. Mrs Sands said of course she could, there was no need to ask. Imogen couldn't imagine not asking; it would be impolite. When she returned from making the call, she found James had put on his Afghan coat and was holding her striped blazer ready for her. During a sleepy conversation the night before they had decided they would spend the afternoon in town.

Imogen slipped into the blazer. She loved the blazer. It was a prized find in a charity shop in Salisbury. Rarely was she seen without it, sometimes perhaps in winter when something warmer was required, or at the height of summer when she sometimes wore a red denim jacket. When it rained, she would wear a knee-length brown leather coat that James had bought her. Most of the time, though, she wore her blazer. She knew the vertical stripes accentuated her height, made her look even taller than she was. Just before she walked out of the door, she checked herself in the hallway mirror. What little make-up she wore – the blue mascara and eyeliner to define her large brown eyes – she'd applied before coming downstairs. She ran her fingers through her hair. It was a bit of a tangle, but she could live with that.

Imogen and James left the house and walked up Church Street, passing other imposing houses. At the top of the street stood St. Peter's, the grey stone parish church of Dereham. Imogen looked up at the tower. The church had a functional simplicity she admired. Both she and James were atheists, but they appreciated architecture. They had been to see the cathedrals at Salisbury and Wells, Bath Abbey, and other local churches. James took Imogen's hand and led her into the High Street. They turned right and crossed the road into the Market Place. They headed for Dereham's only bookshop, located in the crescent of shops around the north side of the Market Place. The Market Place no longer held markets; it was now a car park for the White Lion, which sat at the centre of the crescent. She thought the pub would be their most likely destination after the shop.

The shop was small and had a limited selection, but James could rarely resist browsing its shelves. Imogen loved the smell of it. The odour of paper and ink mingled with those of the polish and wood from the planked floor. Imogen went to the look at books on the art shelves, while James went to the small science fiction selection. She picked out an illustrated book about Max Ernst and flicked through it.

James had by now quickly scanned the other shelves and found nothing of interest. He looked at the book she held. "I'll buy that for you," he said.

James was kind by nature, Imogen knew that. He would pay for everything if she let him. She didn't want that. They'd only got back together again last night. It would feel wrong if James paid for the book. "Thank you, James, but I have enough money to pay for it." She took the book to the till, and they then left the shop. As expected, James steered Imogen towards the pub. They went up the steps, through the front door and then turned right into the saloon bar, which was popular with the freaks, students and weekend hippies of Dereham. There were only a few people in the bar at this hour, among them Chrissie and Jake, and Julie and Sarah. Imogen knew them all. She gave Julie a wave. Julie and Sarah had seemed deep in conversation, and Jake and Chrissie were kissing, so Imogen and James took their glasses of wine to a window seat. James smoked a Sobranie, while she admired reproductions of Ernst paintings and sipped her wine.

Imogen heard the door to the bar open; then a voice called out. "Imo! James!" Imogen recognised Kate's voice. She looked up from her book. Kate waved at her from the bar. Kate carried her drink over, kissed Imogen's cheek, ruffled James's long hair and said hello to them both. She waved at Julie, and then at Chrissie, before sinking onto a chair with a sigh. She put her half pint of IPA on the table and pushed her black hair away from her face. She put her shoulder bag on the floor beside her, and then smiled at Imogen. "I've been trying to find a decent pair of shoes for the last hour. And considering Dereham only has two shoe shops, that's quite an achievement." She looked at Imogen's book. "What are you reading?"

Imogen flipped the book closed, to show off the cover. Kate glanced at it. "Ah, an *artiste*," she said with disdain. "I've never been interested in *artistes*, as you know. What have you two been up to?"

"We woke up late, went to the bookshop and then came here," Imogen said.

"We'll be walking around town after we've finished," James added.

Kate grabbed Imogen's hand. "Can I join you? Please? Please?"

"That would be great." Imogen was so pleased to see Kate, who was her oldest friend. They'd known each other since secondary school. After entering sixth form they'd seen less of each other; the only class they shared was A-level psychology, and then Imogen had started seeing James, and now spent more time in Dereham. It had become more difficult for them to get together, but when Imogen needed somebody to talk to, she always went to Kate.

"Do you have you any plans for this evening?" Kate said.

"We're going up Copsehill for a skywatch. James's friend Paul is up from Devon," Imogen said.

"I remember Paul. I've met him a couple of times. Will Stuart be there too?"

"Yes," Imogen said. "And Charlie."

"Can I come with you to the skywatch?"

Imogen couldn't pass over the opportunity to have Kate around for the night. "Yes, yes, you surely can. You've never been on a skywatch, have you?"

"No. But you've told me about them. They sound fun."

"Sitting around listening to Charlie and Stuart talk bollocks isn't necessarily fun," James pointed out.

"Well, it makes a change from listening to you talk bollocks," Imogen said.

James snorted. "Point taken. I suppose we all talk bollocks, don't we."

"Oh, I'm all excited now," Kate said. "What do you do? Do you just sit around all night looking for UFOs?"

"That's about the sum of it," James said.

"And talk bollocks, naturally," Imogen added. "It's like a pyjama party. But in the open. With a bonfire. And no pyjamas."

"I think Charlie would like it if you wore pyjamas," Kate said.

"Or no pyjamas," James said.

"And how is Charlie's obsession?" Kate asked.

"Still festering nicely," Imogen said. "Although, it seems to have calmed down a bit lately. Of course, this might only mean he's hiding it better than he used to and brooding even more. But I think he's slowly beginning to understand that I love my little lambikins."

Kate looked at James. "Aww, who's Imo's little lambikins then?"

"If I'm going to be reduced to a small, cuddly farm animal I, uh, need a drink," James said. He asked if Kate wanted another drink, even though her glass wasn't yet half empty. She shook her head. He went to the bar to get two more glasses of wine.

"So you two are back on?" Kate said.

"I think we are," Imogen said uncertainly.

"Does Charlie know?"

"Well, we were all around James's last night, and there was kissing."

"With everybody?"

"You are a very silly girl. Only with James." Imogen frowned. "Mind you, I believe we've confused everybody, including ourselves, with all the splits and the reconciliations. Anyway, I think Charlie has a soft spot for Jane, so he might finally move on."

"Jane? Who's Jane?" Kate said.

"Oh, Paul's younger sister."

"Paul?"

"Paul. Paul, the guy who moved to Devon."

"Ah yes, Paul. I've heard you mention him."

"Anyway, Charlie and Stuart went down there last week. And we all know Charlie has a soft spot for Jane."

"But does Charlie know? And would it really make a difference."

"There's the rub. I tried to suss it out last night, but he didn't say anything."

James returned with the drinks. He asked Kate how her piano lessons were going. While the two of them chatted, Imogen wondered whether could catch Stuart alone tonight. She needed to ask him about Jane and Charlie. As much as she liked Charlie, she had found his continued obsession with her over the last year or so disquieting. She felt comfortable with Stuart. He flirted with her, but it was open, honest. And, anyway, she liked Stuart a lot. But Charlie's infatuation was always there, always lurking in the background. When she and James had got together, she had seen a change in Charlie. Stuart had been fine, had accepted her decision and carried on flirting with her in his own sweet way. Charlie, however, seemed to withdraw into himself. While he had believed there was a chance to be with her, he had seemed so open and warm, playful even. Now he'd become dark and sarcastic, he had shut off a part of himself. Surely James and Stuart knew how deeply Charlie brooded? She thought Stuart did. James and Charlie tended to think that Stuart was a bit silly, but he had intuition and empathy, features James and Charlie often lacked. Stuart had said something to her a few weeks ago about Charlie and Jane, about how he'd noticed a spark between them the last time they'd gone down to Devon. It would be such a relief to Imogen if Charlie could get over his obsession with her. She knew Charlie had eyes for nobody else in Dereham.

James excused himself and made his way to the toilets. Kate watched him walk towards the door and then leaned in towards Imogen. Her voice was low. "And how's it going with the *lambikins*?"

"Time will tell. He's a little love, really." She looked into her drink reflectively. "You know, I always felt a bit intimidated by him. He's incredibly bright. Charlie did his best to put me off. He told me that James was stoned all the time, that he drank too much, that he was obsessed with the occult and only ever talked about music and books."

"I know. It was true about the drink and dope, though, wasn't it?"

"It's all true. And yes, he does drink too much," Imogen said. "And he probably smokes too much pot." She mainly worried about James's drinking, though. He was only eighteen – well, nearly nineteen – and she knew her concern about how much he drank seemed odd to their friends. She had watched a much-loved cousin drink herself to death. Her cousin had only been in her mid-twenties when she died.

Imogen didn't want the same to happen to James. She didn't want to see that happen to any of her friends. So, Imogen would split up with James, hoping he'd see sense, and every time, James said that he would change, that he would stop drinking. And, for a while he would manage to do so, and Imogen would begin seeing him again. And then James, happy now he and Imogen were back together, would start drinking. Charlie and Stuart knew what was happening, were aware that she and James kept breaking up. Unable to meet and talk to Kate as often as she'd like, Imogen would turn to Stuart for advice and consolation. She knew this only added to Charlie's confusion.

"He said he'll change," Imogen continued. "He'll change for me, because I asked him, which is sweet. And we share so many interests, like books and art and music. I don't really want to be without him. And I do love him."

"I know, I know," said Kate. She squeezed Imogen's hand.

James came back. He carried more drinks. When he'd put down the wine glasses, Imogen took his hand and kissed it, and looked into his eyes with a smile. "Thank you, lambikins."

"Bah!" James said. "Can't I at least be *goatikins*? Or *tigerkins*? Give me some respect."

"A lambikins you are and a lambikins you shall stay," Kate said. "Once a girl has named you, so you shall remain." James laughed. "So, what else happens at a skywatch?" she asked.

"Oh, it just makes itself up as it goes along," James said. "Idle chit-chat punctuated by boredom. Deep and meaningful conversations that end up nowhere. Half-hearted attempts to look at the sky for longer than five minutes. Then, perhaps, a few moments of intense excitement which is inevitably punctured by the realisation we've been looking at a satellite."

"Charlie builds a bonfire," Imogen added. "He lovingly tends it until daylight – if we make it that far. We walk to the copse. Or to hedgerows behind which we pee. And then, if we're *really* lucky, Charlie nags Paul into conjuring a demon and we're never seen again."

"Sounds like fun," Kate said. "It's a bit like a Girl Guides' camp, isn't it? Apart from the demons. Can we sing songs?"

"You can sing as much as you want. It's a mile and half away from town, so nobody will hear you. Well, as long as nobody else is up there."

"You'll need to wrap up warm," James pointed out. "It can get chilly, especially at this time of year."

Imogen looked Kate up and down. She wore a denim jacket over a white tee shirt, red denim jeans and desert wellies.

"Yes, you can't wear what you're wearing. You'll freeze."

"Oh well. I'll catch the bus home later and get my mum to bring me back in. What should I wear?"

"Lots of layers," Imogen said. "Tee-shirts, shirts, jumpers, whatever. Wear tights under your jeans, to keep your legs warm. I've tried to convince James to wear my tights, but he's not having it."

"Far too pervy," James said. "I'm a man's lamb."

Kate finished her drink. James asked if she wanted another. She shook her head. "You're very kind, but no thanks. I'll turn into a ninny if I have two halves at lunch-time."

James and Imogen swigged down their wine, even though Kate told them there was no need to hurry. They left the bar and walked down the steps back into the Market Place, then into the High Street. Imogen felt a little tipsy. James suggested they go to the Oxfam shop. Imogen knew he wanted to look through the second-hand books. She and Kate agreed – there were, after all, also clothes in there. Imogen found a pair of leather, calf-length, stacked-sole, conker-coloured boots. She called out to Kate. "Hey, Katie! Come here! I think I've solved your shoe problem. What were you looking for?"

"Something to keep my feet warm and dry until summer arrives."

Imogen held up the boots. "How about these? They're your size and they're nearly new."

Kate tried them on. The soles were about an inch thick and the heels two inches high. She was almost as tall as Imogen.

"I suddenly feel very powerful," Kate said, excitedly. "Should I tuck my jeans into the boot, do you think?" she asked Imogen.

"Outside," Imogen said. "You'll look taller without being obvious." She looked Kate up and down. "You look great!" Imogen said.

"I feel great! Such a simple thing. You buy new boots and suddenly the whole world smiles with you."

James came over to them.

"Find anything?" Imogen asked.

James shook his head. He looked at Kate. "Have you grown?"

"Of course not. It's the boots Imo found for me." Kate looked down at them. "Aren't the great?" She went to pay for them. The lady behind the till chuckled when Kate lifted her leg onto the counter to show the price tag. She crammed the desert wellies she'd been wearing into her shoulder bag. Imo, Kate and James left the shop and almost collided with Stuart and Paul. James reintroduced Paul to Kate.

Stuart touched Kate on the arm. "Nice boots. You look good."

Kate blushed. "Thank you," she said. "Imo found them for me."

"I should've guessed," Stuart said. "Where are you going now?"

"Just around the shops," James said. "You guys?"

"We're going to dive into Oxfam," Stuart said.

"We'll wait for you," James said.

"Oh, and Kate is coming to Copsehill with us," Imogen said.

Stuart looked at Kate. "Cool. Brilliant."

Stuart and Paul went into the shop. James lit a Sobranie. Imogen knew Stuart well enough to see he was interested in Kate. Had he always been interested in Kate? Stuart buzzed around all his female friends – it was sometimes difficult to know who he had his eye on. "I see your new boots have already had a devastating effect," she said.

Kate looked at her boots, and then at Imogen. "What do you mean?"

"Don't pretend you don't know. Stuart seemed very interested in you."

"Surely not."

"And by your blush, ma'am, I'd say you fancied him too."

"No, ah... Well, I... we've only met a few times."

"Enough to make an impression, it seems. On both of you." Imogen turned to James. "Has Stu ever said anything to you about Kate?"

"Umm. Ah. Yes, I believe he did, after the party at Burnt Norton, at Jake's place. He asked me about Kate. He was trying to be casual about it, but I thought I detected a flutter of interest."

"A *flutter*," Kate said with mock peevishness. "I should hope there was more than a flutter."

James considered for a moment. "Being able to pick out a flutter in his habitual discourse about the fairer sex indicates a heightened level of interest. One could say his, uh, interest in you was a discernible signal amid the usual noise."

"What's he talking about, Imo?"

"Oh, Katie, I told you he talked the biggest bollocks." Imogen said. "He's just saying Stu *is* interested in you." She turned to James. "Why didn't you tell me?"

James thought for a moment. "What can I say? I'm a bloke. I probably made you a cup of tea and then bored you to death talking about an obscure paperback I'd found in Bath."

"You could never be boring, my little lambikins," Imogen said. She shoved him sideways with her shoulder.

Paul and Stuart came out of the shop. Stuart carried a waistcoat, which he showed it off. They began to walk through town. Kate and Imogen went in and out of clothes shops and charity shops while Paul, Stuart and James stood outside, chatting and smoking.

Finally, Kate looked at her watch. "If I'm going to get home and then come back into town for this skywatch, I'd better catch the next bus."

They headed to the bus stop in the Market Place. Kate walked beside Imogen, tall in her new boots. Paul and James chatted about their favourite films. Stuart talked to Kate. They smiled and joked with each other. They were flirting. Imogen was pleased to see it. It would be cool if James's best friend and her best friend got together.

Imogen had a sudden feeling of tenderness for them all, happy to have these people as friends, happy to be here with them, sharing their worlds, their obsessions and desires. The bus came and they waved Kate off. Stuart and Paul left them then and walked away along Town Road, back towards Stuart's house. As Imogen and James strolled into Church Street, she wrapped an arm around him and pulled him towards her. She kissed his cheek.

"I love you, lambikins," she said.

"I love you too," James whispered into her ear. Then he blew into it.

Imogen giggled. *I want it to stay like this forever. I don't want it to change.*

6

Paul rang the doorbell at James's house. James opened the door and led Paul and Stuart into the hallway. He then went to phone Charlie, to tell him they were on their way. They arranged to meet near White Street on the way to Copesehill. Imogen came down the stairs in a baggy jumper and a pair of faded jeans. "Hello, my darlings. Are we all ready for the evening's entertainment?" She carried her striped canvas bag. It bulged.

"Are you sure you have enough stuff?" Paul said.

Imogen patted the bag. "This is mine *and* Kate's. James has his own bag. Are you well prepared?"

Stuart held up a bulging rucksack. "I have the most important things. Sandwiches, bourbon biscuits and a flask of tea. Is Kate here?"

Paul looked at Stuart and raised an eyebrow. It was unusual for Stuart to care who was somewhere and who was not. As long as there was somebody to flirt with, he was happy. He did, after all, seem to fancy every woman they knew, Imogen and Fiona included. To specifically ask after Kate implied interest. He'd said nothing on the way back to the house earlier. He was playing his cards close to his chest.

Kate came down the stairs, smiling at Stuart and Paul. Paul glanced at Stuart, who watched Kate. Mr Sands came out from the lounge, regarded them all and looked at their bags with a twinkle in his eye. "I hope this means you're all leaving home and we'll never see you again. That'll save me a pretty penny."

"Unfortunately for you, pater," James said, "we'll be back."

"Don't come the *pater* thing with me, young man, or I'll stop your allowance. Anyway, if I'm lucky, you'll be abducted by aliens."

James's mother came into the hallway and fussed around James and Imogen, checking they had enough clothes and food for the night. Paul pushed Stuart playfully through the front door. Kate, James and Imogen followed, with Mrs Sands still fussing around them.

"Don't worry, Mrs Sands," Imogen said. "You know I'll look after James. I'll make sure he isn't abducted."

She would worry, though, Paul knew that. James was an only child and had suffered a life-threatening virus as a toddler. Mrs Sands had spent the ensuing sixteen years worrying about his health. The door finally closed. Imogen squeezed between Paul and James and put an arm around the waist of each of them.

Paul noticed something missing. "Where's your blazer? You look naked without it."

"I didn't want to get it dirty. I have my leather coat in the bag."

They caught up with Kate and Stuart. Kate wore a thick, long, brown wool cardigan over a striped jumper. The cardigan was belted at the waist. Her new boots peeped out from the bottom of her jeans.

"What did you do this afternoon?" James asked Paul.

"We played chess," Paul said.

"And I soundly thrashed him, three times," Stuart added.

James smiled. "Before or after the chess?"

Stuart and Paul laughed. "We don't need to ask what you were doing," Paul said.

"Hah!" James exclaimed. "Hold your depraved imaginings! Imo helped mother with the tea while I drank Martell upstairs. Imo then came upstairs, and we talked about the next essay deadlines. And then we ate, and then Imo helped with the washing up –"

Imogen interrupted. "While he sat upstairs drinking Martell. Again."

As they walked down Westfield Road, Paul could see the gangling shape of Charlie waiting at the junction of Bell Street, standing beneath a streetlight, wearing his greatcoat, smoking one of his roll-ups.

"You look like a bunch of degenerate freaks," Charlie said when they reached him.

"Exactly the effect I'm aiming for," James said.

They passed the terraced houses in Trowbridge Road, heading for White Street, chatting inconsequentially. White Street was a steep road that passed between Red Post Hill on their left and Derebury Hill and The Tump on their right. On either side of the road were semi-detached cottages and expensive detached houses. Paul could see, in bright front-rooms through undrawn curtains, people sitting in front of televisions or reading newspapers. They would be warm tonight, while he and his friends would be sitting on a cold hill. But we, Paul thought, will experience the world. We won't be cooped up in our petit bourgeois cells. We'll be outside the conditioned world occupied by those automata who are being fed televisual pap by the forces of global capitalism. And who knew, perhaps tonight he and his friends would glimpse something from outside this world, something that would make politics and economics irrelevant, something that would obviate the need for capitalism, socialism or anarchism.

They reached the top of White Street and then for a short while walked downhill on Lavington Road towards Red Post Farm. The Tump was now directly to their right, crowned with trees that were silhouetted against a sky burned amber by the streetlights of Dereham. Imogen and Kate had moved ahead of them, walking and talking together. Stuart and Charlie walked together, talking about UFOs.

"The whole thing has been exaggerated," Charlie said. "If there hadn't been so much written about it in the papers, Dereham would still be an unknown little town in Wiltshire."

Paul wanted to believe - like they all did, really - that flying saucers were real, but found it hard to disagree with Charlie.

The friends walked under the canopies of tall beech, ash and field maple that lined both sides of the road and formed an arch over them. Within this arch the road was very dark and would have been intimidating but for the lights of Red Post Farm a hundred yards away. Later, when they returned from the hill, the lights at the farm would be off and the walk along this stretch of road would be far more unnerving. Paul looked up at the thick branches curving above him. They reminded him of the gothic arches in churches.

The final half-mile was a long slog, a gentle enough slope, but uphill all the way. James complained, as he always did. He was a heavy smoker and not as fit as the others. No cars had so far passed them, Paul noted. That was good. It was possible there would be no other skywatchers on Copsehill tonight. When the hill was busy with skywatchers, cars would come and go, their occupants moving from hill to hill, endlessly searching for the elusive sighting, the unexpected phenomenon – anything that would bring awe and wonder into their lives. Into their drab, work-a-day lives, Paul couldn't help thinking.

Charlie broke away from Stuart and sidled up to James. He spoke quietly, but Paul could still hear him. "Have you got any dope with you, man?"

James nodded. "Yes. Not much, but it'll last the night."

Paul might take a few hits later, but he preferred hash on toast. Stuart and Imogen didn't smoke grass, so he was sure James's grass would last. He didn't know whether Kate smoked or not. Stuart now walked with Paul. They discussed Eliot and Pinter, Golding and Hughes, all of whom Paul was studying at college. James and Charlie slowed and joined them. Paul wondered where Imogen and Kate were. He looked up the road. They were ahead of him, dark shapes in the night. He wondered what they were talking about. Whatever it was, it almost certainly had something to do with relationships and nothing to do with authors.

At last, the road levelled out. Even in the darkness Paul could just about see the white gates that barred the old Lavington road. Dereham nestled in the folds at the edge of Salisbury Plain, and there were old roads that led from it crossed the Plain. But the Plain was now a vast military training area, and many of those roads were now gated. On the other side of the gates the roads had become lost through disuse. This was as far as they needed to go, anyway. To Paul's left a track led up to the copse of trees that gave the hill its name.

"Well, here we are," Imogen said to Kate. "Skywatch central! Copsehill."

Kate put an arm around Imogen. "Look at me, Ma! Top of the world!"

They would make their one-night camp here, where the road was wide enough to park a car and provided enough space for Charlie to build his fire. Grassy banks, topped with barbed wire fences, bounded the road. As Paul had hoped, there were no cars here tonight. Most skywatchers would have come the hill the previous Bank Holiday weekend. And today was a Friday, so any visitors would most likely arrive tomorrow evening.

Charlie took a torch out of his bag, switched it on and began to search for the stones he'd previously used to contain his fire. The others began to unpack their bags, pulling out flasks of tea or coffee, sandwiches and crisps, torches and jumpers, coats and cigarettes. James found his cognac.

"I'm glad we're here," Kate said. "My new boots were pinching. I don't know why they say you're breaking boots in. Surely the boots are breaking you in."

They sat on a grassy bank and chatted, and idly watched as Charlie search for his stones.

"Aha! Here they are!" Charlie said. "Stuart, come and help me with these."

Stuart walked over and shone his torch onto Charlie's find. Paul couldn't quite make out what all the excitement was about. Charlie and Stuart returned carrying a kerbstone between them. They placed it by the dark patch at the edge of the road where Charlie had built his previous campfires. "There's more," Charlie said.

"I think we'd better help." Paul said to James. They followed Charlie and Stuart. They found a pile of kerbstones, five or six of them.

As Stuart and Charlie lifted another, Stuart said, "I don't think this is a good idea."

"Why not?" Charlie asked.

"Because the heat will make them crack."

"It doesn't matter if they crack, as long as they contain the fire," Charlie said.

"Yeah, but they're damp. The water will turn to steam and then they'll... um... explode."

"*Explode?* What *are* you on about, man? Of course they won't *explode*. You worry too much. The fire will dry them out, anyway."

"Yes, by first turning the water to steam," Stuart muttered. "Which is what I'm worried about."

Between them, they soon had the kerbstones arranged in a rough circle. Charlie asked who wanted to help him find wood. James and Imogen said they would, and they climbed over the stile to the track leading to the copse.

Stuart, Kate and Paul looked around the road, banks and hedges for anything that could be used for kindling and threw what they found into the kerbstone ring.

"It's fun already," Kate said.

"It'll be even more fun when the kerbstones explode," Stuart mumbled.

"Charlie's right." Paul said. "You worry too much. It'll be fine."

Having scavenged all the paper, food wrappings and dried twigs they could find, they sat on the bank again. Kate poured coffee from a thermos into its plastic cup, took a sip and then passed it to Stuart. Paul looked at the sky. The weather had hardly changed all week. Small, wind-torn clouds, illuminated by the streetlights of Dereham, slid over the sky, driven on by the cool breeze. Stars were visible between the clouds, cold and bright in the clear sky.

"You guys have never seen anything up here, have you," Kate said.

"Nothing. Not in four years," Stuart said. He passed the plastic cup to Paul.

"How often do you come up here?"

"About once a week. We probably skywatch as much as anybody, but we never see anything. One wonders how that can be. But that's the way it is, apparently."

"You're a bit sceptical then?"

"A bit, I suppose. I think that ten per cent of the sightings are genuine. But the rest are something else."

"Like what?"

"Who knows? Hoaxes. Misidentifications. Optical illusions. I do think something's happening. What it is, I'm not sure. If we haven't seen anything, well, perhaps we're just been unlucky. We might see something, eventually. Tonight might be the night. You might be our lucky charm."

"What about you, Paul? Do you see it differently now you've moved away?"

"I still think there's something to these stories," Paul said. "But I put the number of genuine cases even lower than Stu. Five per cent, say. I think there's a lot of hype about Dereham. But I do feel this place, this hill, has power. I can understand why people are drawn to it."

"Particularly the copse," added Stuart.

"Yeah, the copse is really something," Paul said. "It's an elemental kind of place." Paul felt there were powers at work here; that was why he liked Copsehill so much. Perhaps the UFOs were manifestations of psychic and geological forces rather than alien visitors.

"So what about you, Katie?" Stuart asked. "What do *you* think of Dereham's great mystery?"

"Oh, I don't know. I've read some of Patterson's stories in the *Gazette*. I haven't read his book, though. I don't really know what I think. It would be nice if there was some kind of space brotherhood coming to Dereham to spread peace and light. God knows, we could do with some, with overpopulation and atomic bombs and wars everywhere. But I don't know much about it, how it all started. What did happen?"

"Richard Patterson, happened, I suppose," Stuart said. "Without him, there would be no mystery. He brought the events here to the world's attention."

Around the beginning of 1972, Stuart explained, Patterson – a journalist on the local paper, the *Dereham Gazette* – had heard rumours of strange sounds and lights in the sky. He wrote up some of these stories for the *Gazette*. After the stories had been published, other people came forward with similar tales. Patterson wrote these up, too. Witnesses sent letters to the editor of the paper. For a few months, the *Gazette* became the focus for information on an array of strange phenomena.

"Yes, I remember," Kate said. "I was young, only eleven or twelve, but I heard people talking about it. It all seemed so peculiar."

Stuart nodded. "Yes, it was. Then it all got weirder. Once UFO groups heard what was happening in Dereham, the letters page of the *Gazette* began to fill with theories and suggestions from all over the place."

"Oh yes! I remember," Kate said. "I read some of them. They seemed a bit wacky. It was hard to get my young mind around them."

Paul smiled. "Wacky is my kind of thing."

"Anyway, it was all bollocks," Stuart said. "Aliens from space, giant space arks, refugees from dying planets... Typical flying saucer stories. There were some letters about how the government knew what was going on and was hiding the truth from us. There were sceptics too, who pointed out that the town is on the edge of the Plain and that the military might be testing things near here. Anyway, Patterson began to write short articles about the UFOs for the national press. Then, in August 1972 I think it was, the *News of the World* sent a reporter down to Copsehill. And after that article was printed, the number of letters to the *Gazette* and reports to Patterson increased. People started arriving in town asking about UFOs and looking for the best hills to watch the skies from."

"So why this hill?" Kate said. "Why not Derebury or Red Post?"

"Simple. This hill is the easiest to reach by car. And the interest has never ended. Even now there's a steady trickle of eager people ready to watch the skies."

"*Skywatchers*," Kate said.

"Yes, the skywatchers," Stuart said. "See, you know everything already."

Kate nodded. "You can't live around Dereham and not know about skywatchers."

"You know Patterson, don't you?" Paul asked Stuart.

"Yes, I do," Stuart replied. "Haven't you met him?"

"No. You've never taken me to the UFO Centre."

"UFO Centre?" Kate said. "Now that sounds *very* important."

"Don't you know about the UFO Centre?" Stuart said. Kate shook her head. "It *is* very important. It is, after all, a *Centre*. I'm surprised you haven't seen the advert at the back of the *Gazette*," Stuart said.

"Oh, yes," Kate said. "Of course I've seen it. I'd forgotten. It wasn't important to me, so it had just drifted out of my mind."

Stuart smiled. "Indeed. I remember somebody once saying to me on this hill that everybody in Dereham must be thinking about

UFOs all the time, what a great place to live, et cetera, et cetera. But I pointed out to him that there's only a small number of people in town who have any interest in UFOs. For many people it was just a bit of temporary excitement, it wasn't something people took seriously."

"I know," Kate said. "I didn't. And I don't think I've ever heard mum or dad mention it."

"That's right. I don't think my mum and dad did either."

"Charlie's parents did," Paul said. "I remember. Charlie's dad was really into it for a while."

"Right," Kate said. "Now, what about this UFO centre?"

"Ah, right," Stuart said. "So, Patterson's reports got people fired up. They were turning up on his doorstep, looking for information, or a place to stay. Then he realised he could make himself a bit of money by creating a bed and breakfast and information centre for sky-watchers. So, a few years back he took out a mortgage and bought a dilapidated old house near the town centre. He did it up as cheaply as possible. He called it the *UFO Centre*."

"Very imaginative," Kate said.

"Yes, it was," Stuart said. "And the rooms soon began to fill up at the weekends."

"He must be well-off," Kate said.

"I don't know about *well-off*. There's no way any of this has made Patterson rich. So, yes, he did find a publisher for his book about the mystery, but it was only small company. The book sold okay, so he gets a little money from that, but Patterson has always said the royalty was small. He sold his own house to help finance the UFO Centre, and the Centre is a big house. His mortgage must be huge. And I know he doesn't charge skywatchers very much to stay in his B and B, although I hear the breakfasts are pretty basic, which saves him some money. And then there's the *UFO Centre Journal*, his newsletter, which makes him no money at all. He does it all for the love of the subject."

Oh yes, the newsletter," Paul said. He had read some of them when he visited Stuart or Charlie. "It's mainly filled with his own strange ideas and theories as I recall."

"Yes, that's right. The *Gazette* no longer carries stories about the Dereham mystery. The editor thought Patterson was making the paper a laughing stock."

"Do you think he was always interested in these things?" Kate said. "And the paper gave him a... uh... vehicle for his interests?"

"Most perspicacious, young lady. It turns out Patterson *had* been interested in the paranormal and UFOs before the flying saucers ever started visiting. So, when he heard that people were seeing things, he could hardly believe his luck." Stuart paused. "Since then, he's been hearing wild stories and receiving long letters about the paranormal and the occult. And now he's in contact with strange people all the time. He's the first port of call for skywatchers and journalists. That's why he thought it would be sensible to provide a meeting place for these people, and somewhere for them to stay. And, perhaps, make a few bob out of it all."

"And that," Paul said, "is when Stu got the job as his tour guide."

"Hah!" Stuart said. "So, Patterson is now absolutely convinced UFOs are alien spacecraft. He takes issue with anybody who thinks they might be optical illusions, or delusions, or misidentified military hardware. Oh, and he hates hoaxers with a passion."

"I can understand why," Paul said. "There are so many sightings around here. If you believed that hoaxers were an important element of the mystery would divert attention from the real thing. Whatever that is."

"Patterson says that hoaxers piss on the dreams of earnest seekers after truth. He was fooled a couple of times in the past by locals sending up balloons. He took a particular dislike to one local lad, Terry Dyson. Terry was a friend of my brother's, actually. Nice enough kid, but a bit of a show-off."

Paul heard voices on the path and an unexpected rustling. He stood and squinted into the darkness, and shone his torch up the track, illuminating first James and Imogen, and then Charlie. James and Imogen carried armfuls of broken twigs and fallen branches. Charlie had a bundle of twigs under one arm, but also balanced a large piece of timber on his shoulder, which he restrained with his free hand. Stuart and Paul went to the stile and took the bundles from them so they could climb over the gate.

"Where did you get this timber from?" Paul asked Charlie.

"It was just lying around beside the barn."

"Perhaps the farmer needs it for something," Stuart said.

"Well, he won't know we burned it when we've reduced it to ash."

Stuart frowned. "It's kind of irresponsible, though."

"What did I say? You worry too much."

Stuart was always the sensible one, Paul thought. Perhaps it had something to do with his anxieties. He hated heights, was afraid of dogs and was scared to be up here alone. He liked to be in control, to understand the consequences of his or other people's actions. He would probably hate to get in trouble with the police, too.

Charlie placed the twigs and smaller branches on top of the rubbish collected earlier. The timber – a piece of seven by two about ten feet long – would need breaking into smaller pieces. Stuart placed one end of the timber on the bottom step of the stile and one end on the road, then started jumping up and down on it.

"I thought you said it was wrong to use that wood," Paul said.

Stuart continued bouncing. "Well, it's here now, isn't it?"

Despite Stuart's best efforts, nothing happened. James joined him, but still the timber refused to break. Charlie began jumping on it as well. When the timber finally snapped, Stuart fell in a heap, much to the amusement of Paul and Charlie.

Stuart stood up quickly and dusted himself down. "We're never going to break that into smaller pieces.

"For a clown, you're very astute," Charlie said. He added the two pieces to the pile, then lit the fire. At first it sputtered, but then quickly caught the thinner twigs.

They all moved into a circle around its welcome warmth. Paul wondered if they would see a UFO tonight. He thought it unlikely. They never did. Jane would so enjoy being here, though. She loved Charlie and Stuart, and this whole UFO scene. It would be an adventure for her. And, according to Fiona, she especially loved Charlie. He had thought it would be Stuart. But, no, it was Charlie. James handed Paul a cup of Martell, and a joint.

Charlie looked at the faces tinted by the orange flame of the fire, *his* fire. Kate had Paul to her left, and Stuart to her right. To Stuart's right was Imo, and James sat next to her. Charlie was, therefore, between James and Paul. Stuart had somehow ended up between two girls. Charlie wondered how that had happened. Had Stuart arranged it, or was it luck? Or was this configuration perhaps the result of some subtle, unconscious agreement between the others? Whatever it was, it had worked to separate him from her. And if it was some unconscious agreement, then that meant, surely, that the others thought he *should* be separated from her. Charlie didn't like the implications.

Stuart talked to Kate - well, flirted with her, really. And why not, Charlie thought. She seemed a nice girl. Charlie had met her a few times. She resembled Imogen. They didn't look the same - Kate had long, straight, black hair that fell past her shoulders, blue eyes and was shorter than Imogen. And, obviously, Imogen was far more attractive. Kate's lips were thinner, her nose a little bigger. Yet there was something similar about them. What was it? It was something in the way the dressed, Charlie decided. Perhaps that's why Stuart liked her.

Charlie had thought a lot about Jane since returning from Devon. He wasn't certain how he felt. She was a smooth. Perhaps James was right; perhaps he was an inverse snob. A girlfriend could only be good enough for him if she was as hippie, as freaky, as he was. He thought Jane was perhaps a little young, and perhaps a bit silly. But then, Stuart, who was the youngest of the boys, also seemed young - Stuart was happy to admit that he had been a late developer - and was certainly a little silly. He could ramble about inconsequential trivia like a girl, but Charlie didn't hold that against him. Charlie and Stuart had been friends since they'd met in their first term at comprehensive school. They'd had the same interests in books and records, watched cricket and walked the hills together, and were amused by the same things. If Jane also liked the same things, would Charlie find her acceptable - even if she remained a smooth? She was acceptable, he thought; to think otherwise *would* be snobbish.

Charlie looked across the flames at Imogen. She was closer in age to him. Her birthday was in November, making her, like Charlie, already eighteen, more than halfway to nineteen. The tiny increments in all their ages resulted in subtle differences in their maturity and behaviour, he'd noticed. Charlie's birthday was in October; he was the oldest of the boys. Stuart's birthday fell in August and he was the youngest, nearly a school year younger than Charlie. Their beards marked out the difference in their ages. Stuart's was still fluffy, while Charlie's was thick. Neither of them, however, could match James's resplendent growth.

Charlie considered himself the most adult of them all. And Imogen seemed the most mature of the girls. She was a woman, Charlie reminded himself. Imogen was the first of the girls he knew who had developed into a woman. Was that why he found her so attractive? Her pale face reflected the light of his fire, giving her a warm and sultry look. She'd been listening to Stuart and Kate, but she suddenly looked at him. The fire caught in her brown eyes. He looked away, found a stick and gave the fire a poke. Butterflies of orange and red ash fluttered into the darkness above them. Charlie looked at Imogen again; she was now leaning over Stuart, hand on his knee, talking to Kate, while James rolled another joint. Paul listened to whatever Imogen was saying. Charlie felt alone here, in his own dark universe, poking his bonfire.

James lit the joint, toked on it a couple of times and passed it to Charlie, who hoped a few puffs would help lighten his mood. He knew he tended towards introspection; and lately had begun to think he might be a little obsessive. The last few days had seen him following the same thoughts over and over. Jane was young and a smooth, Imogen a woman and a hippie. He'd been obsessed with Imogen for so long now, he'd forgotten what it was like not to watch her, not to think about her, not to envy James and fret about Stuart. If he could think about Jane in the same way he thought about Imogen, it would be a relief. Even if Jane didn't feel the same as he did, perhaps just dreaming about her would provide a healthy distraction. He was aware his obsession with Imogen was damaging his relationship with Stuart. He could accept Imogen being with James – even if he had been jealous at first, even if he couldn't stop watching them together with a kind of horror – because he knew they wouldn't last. And given how often they had broken up, he felt he was right. Imogen's closeness to Stuart frightened him more, for reasons he found hard to define. Yet how could he blame Stuart? *Poor Stuart, I wonder if he's noticed?*

The faint remembered scent of Havoc teased Charlie. Jane was pretty. A pretty little smooth. All blonde wispy hair. He took another hit from the joint and passed it to Paul. He had spent the afternoon reading *Love Among the Haystacks* and had listened to Fleetwood Mac a couple of times. As James had said, *Rhiannon* was really good and a few of the other tracks weren't so bad. At least he'd have something to talk about with Jane the next time he saw her. He looked at the fire. The flames appeared more intense, but that, he suspected, was the effect of the dope. He poked the fire with his stick again, and then used it to rearrange the burning pieces of timber.

Paul offered the joint to Kate. She giggled. "Okay, but I don't do this often. I might get silly." She took a couple of drags, then offered it to Stuart. Stuart didn't smoke dope and neither did Imogen, so he took the joint and passed it directly back to James. Charlie felt light-headed and thought it was time for a walk to the copse.

"I'm off to collect more wood," Charlie said. "Anybody want to join me?"

Paul and James said they'd help him. Stuart asked James if he could bum a cigarette before they left, so James passed him a Sobranie. James took the joint with him, knowing the other three weren't really interested in it. They went over the stile and up the track.

Imogen was relieved to see Charlie go. She had felt his eyes resting on her heavily, darkly.

"I feel a bit dizzy," Kate said.

Stuart took a burning twig from the fire and lit his cigarette. "You'll be alright. It'll pass." He slipped an arm around her shoulder. "Here, I'll help keep you steady."

"Thank you, kind sir," Kate said. She snuggled closer into him. "Warm, too."

"Hey," Imogen said, smiling. "He's mine. Hands off."

"Don't be greedy," Kate said. "You've got James."

"I have enough love for both of you," Stuart said. He put his other arm around Imogen and pulled her to him. She rested her head on Stuart's shoulder.

Now that Charlie had gone to the copse; Imogen finally had a chance to ask Stuart what she had been wanting to ask since Stuart had returned from Devon. "What's happening with Charlie?"

"What do you mean?" Stuart said.

"Are there any girls on the horizon?"

Stuart paused before answering. "Not that I know of."

There was caution in his voice, Imogen noted. "I know he has a soft spot for Jane," she said. "I had hoped it might grow into something."

"I think he's beginning to recognise that he has feelings for her." Stuart paused. "The trouble is, they only see each other every few months." Again, Stuart seemed cautious.

"Why Jane?" Kate said. "She's bloody miles away. He'd never get to see her."

"There's nobody around here he likes." Imogen grimaced. "Only me. And Jane's the only other girl he's ever really talked about. It'd be good if he fell for her."

"Good for you, you mean," Kate said.

Imogen nodded. "Yes, for me." She lifted her head then and looked at Stuart. "And for you, too."

"Yeah, I know," Stuart said.

"Why?" Kate looked at Imogen, then at Stuart.

Imogen rolled the cool, glass bead of her necklace between her fingers. "You know why. Stu and I have always been very close. Charlie doesn't like it."

Kate's nodded. "Ah, yes. That."

They were all silent for a moment. The fire spat and crackled in front of them. Stuart found a stick and poked the fire, causing it to spark and flame brightly.

"Has anybody looked at the sky yet?" Kate said. "I mean, you all call it a skywatch, but aren't we just... fire-watching?"

"I do look at the sky sometimes," Stuart said. "Although having a bloody great bonfire in the way doesn't help." He tossed his cigarette stub into the flames. "If you want to do a bit of proper skywatching, you could lie back and look at the sky."

"I will, if you will."

"Okay, hang on." He reached into his rucksack and found his greatcoat. "We'll use this as a pillow."

Stuart put the greatcoat on the road and then laid his head on it. Stuart put his arm around Kate, who put her head on his shoulder. They looked directly at the zenith of the night sky.

"Such a lot of stars," Kate said.

"If it wasn't for the bonfire, you'd see a lot more." Stuart said.

"It's nice up here, isn't it? Do you know the names of the stars?"

"Not really," Stuart said. "I know some of the constellations, though. The Plough is... there." He pointed.

Kate giggled. "Even I can recognise that one."

"Yes, well, I said I didn't know much."

"I even know where the North Star is," Kate said.

"There's not much I can teach you, young disciple."

"Shall we go up to the copse later?"

"Yes, we shall."

Imogen thought Stuart and Kate needed some time alone. "I need a pee," she said and wandered away towards the hedges beyond the gate. Afterwards, as she stood on the other side of the gate zipping up her trousers, she could just make out in the light from the fire that Kate's head remained on Stuart's shoulder. Stuart had his arm around her still. Imogen smiled. *Good for them.* She so wanted Kate and Stuart to get together.

She began to feel the cold. She needed the leather coat in her bag, or to be beside the fire, but she was loath to disturb Stuart and Kate. She decided to walk to the copse and catch up with the other boys; it would warm her up. The copse was a few hundred yards to the northeast of the gates and at least a hundred feet higher. She walked up the sloping track at a brisk pace.

She hoped Charlie was falling for Jane. It wasn't as if Charlie's obsession was a physical threat to her. At least, she didn't think it was. But it had just gone on for so long, and it was always there, wrapped darkly around him like one of his huge black greatcoats.

And she didn't like the way he always seemed to blame Stuart for... something. She wasn't quite sure what. *After all, what could he know?* She folded her arms as she walked, to close her baggy jumper more tightly against her, to keep in the warmth and to shut Charlie out. She was in danger of becoming obsessed with Charlie, but not in the way he hoped. *Me, obsessed with Charlie! How tickled he'd be.*

As she neared the copse she heard Charlie's laugh, then footsteps and chatter coming towards her. James switched on his torch and shone it at her. She shielded her eyes against the sudden glare.

"Imo!" James said.

"Lambikins!" Imogen squealed and ran up to him.

"What are you doing up here?"

"I was cold. I needed a walk to warm myself up."

"Why didn't you go back to the fire?" Charlie asked.

"I wanted to leave Stu and Katie alone for a while," Imogen said.

"Oh god, I hope they're not kissing," Charlie said. "I want a sandwich when I get back. I don't want my stomach turned."

"Oh, don't worry. They weren't kissing when I left. They were just lying down, looking at the stars. He had his arm around her, and she had her head on his shoulder. It was sweet."

"Romantic twaddle," Charlie said.

"We found plenty of wood," Paul said. "It should keep the fire roaring a little longer and warm your frozen bones."

As they walked back down the track, Paul and James discussed occult rituals, and talked again about how *cool* it would be to perform one on Copsehill. Imogen shivered and whispered to James that she was cold. James moved his twigs under one arm and put his other arm around her. She snuggled in close to him and kissed his neck. James and Paul were discussing which ritual they should do. Something simple, Paul said, something they already knew, something that would increase their knowledge of the liminal world. James instead suggested they invoke Choronzon.

"Choronzon? *Qu'est-ce que c'est?*" Imogen said.

"The Dweller in the Abyss," James said dramatically.

"A Dweller in the Abyss sounds like a proper demon," Charlie said. "At last!"

"Choronzon is the gateway to enlightenment," James said.

"Yes," Paul agreed. "But Choronzon is powerful and should *not* be dabbled with. We're not yet adepts. Really, we should be much further along in our studies before we do something like that."

"Why?" asked Imogen.

"You need to prepare properly. If you *are* suitably prepared, then Choronzon can tear apart the ego, enabling bliss, enlightenment. But if you're *unprepared*, then..." Paul allowed the sentence to tail off dramatically.

"Then... what?" Imogen said.

"You're fucked, basically," James said.

"Oh, lambikins. I don't want you fucked! Not by anything but me!" James kissed Imogen's cheek. "And I don't want to be fucked by anything but you."

Paul suggested they try something simpler, more in keeping with their status as neophytes. "Do you remember when I last visited?" he said. "We came up here and discussed elementals. And we tried meditating. I said Copsehill feels like a hazy sort of Netzach."

"Yes. I agreed with you. Although I wasn't sure what you were talking about."

"Neither was I." They both laughed. "Anyway," Paul continued. "Why don't we try pathworking on Netzach? Perhaps then we'll find out what I was talking about."

"That's a splendid idea. That's what we'll do."

They arrived back at the stile. Imogen jumped over. Kate and Stuart were lying together just as they had been when she'd left them. She ran over to the fire and held her palms out towards it. It felt good to be warm again. Stuart waved his free hand at her. Kate had her eyes closed.

"The Prophets return!" Charlie announced. He threw his bundle of twigs onto the fire.

Paul and James dropped their wood into a pile by Charlie. Kate opened her eyes and sat up, looked around sleepily at everybody. "What Prophets?"

"*We* are the Prophets," Charlie said. "James, Stuart and me."

Kate frowned. "What *are* you on about, Charlie?"

"You don't know? Hasn't Imo told you about our Prophet... ness? Prophet... ability?"

"Prophethood," James said. "You ignoramus."

"No," Kate said. "What is this nonsense?"

"Ah, it's my fault," Paul said. "I was in the Lion one night, buying drinks for these reprobates, and I overheard some old guy at the bar speaking to Josh and he was looking–"

"Hold on," Kate said. "Who's Josh?"

"The guy behind the bar at the White Lion, you know him, the landlord."

"Oh, yes, him. Do carry on with your amusing anecdote."

Paul narrowed his eyes at Kate before continuing. "So, this old guy was talking to Josh behind the bar–"

"Why would Josh let the old guy behind the bar?" Kate said.

"What?"

"Why was the old guy talking to Josh behind the bar."

"The old guy wasn't behind the bar, Josh was."

"Oh, right. That makes sense."

Kate looked at Imogen then, smiling mischievously.

"So, this old guy in front of the bar was talking to Josh, who was behind the bar–"

"Right, I think I get it now," Kate said.

Imogen laughed.

"So, the old guy was looking at Stuart, James and Charlie and I distinctly remember him saying as if it were yesterday–"

"Perhaps it was yesterday," Kate said.

"No, I was at James's last night, this was last year," Paul said.

"Oh, right. So – what do you distinctly remember?

"I remember him saying, young lady, *Those daft sods look like a bunch of Old Testament prophets*. So I started calling them the Prophets that weekend."

"And the name kind of stuck," James said. "We rather liked it. It sounded suitably... stupid."

"Well, I'm about to be prophetic," Kate said. "If I don't go for a wee soon, I'll wet myself. What do I do?"

"There are some hedges beyond the gate," Imogen said. "Nip behind one of those. And make sure Charlie doesn't follow you."

"Very droll," Charlie said.

As Kate stood and dusted herself down, Stuart looked up at Charlie. "See anything?"

"Don't be ridiculous," Charlie said. He sat down and poked the fire. Flames leapt up. He began rolling another cigarette. Stuart asked what the atmosphere was like in the copse. Paul said it was fine, it wasn't heavy.

Stuart looked towards the gate, where Kate had gone.

"Go on, Stu," Imogen said. "Take her up the copse."

Charlie sniggered. "I've never heard of that sexual position before."

James's head was in Imogen's lap. Charlie watched as she idly played with his long dark hair. His eyes were closed. Charlie felt only a little jealous – James's grass and brandy had mellowed him. They had smoked another joint after Stuart had left them to find Kate. They talked about horror films. Charlie and James had recently been to the Regal cinema in town to see *Madhouse*.

"I've seen it," Paul said. "It wasn't very good."

"It had Vincent Price," Charlie said. "That makes it a classic."

"It had Natasha Pyne in it," James slurred. "That added some charm."

They talked about some of the other films they'd seen, *The Exorcist* and *Race With the Devil* and how they looked forward to *The Omen*, even though James and Charlie would have to go to Salisbury to see it. What they liked best though was a low budget British horror: *The Abominable Dr Phibes*, *The Beast Must Die*, *The Wicker Man*.

Charlie smiled and poked his fire. "Horror films led us astray."

Paul shook his head. "Hah! They made us into the fine fellows we are."

That was true, in a way, Charlie supposed. First, it had been the films – wangling their way into X-rated movies when they were fourteen and fifteen – then it had been cheap horror novels. Those had led to an interest in the paranormal and the occult and books by Alex Sanders and Richard Cavendish. Because Dereham was at the centre of a wave of flying saucer sightings, they'd started reading books about UFOs and aliens. The more speculative of these had introduced them to other topics. Paul had been the first to discover

Colin Wilson's *The Occult*, which had given the paranormal an almost academic lustre. He had subsequently written a long rambling letter to James about it. Charlie had read that letter, of course, and he remembered even now how excited Paul had been about his discovery. James had then bought David Conway's *Magic*. He and Paul soon began reading the occult masters of the Golden Dawn, Israel Regardie, Aleister Crowley, Eliphaz Levi, W. B. Yeats and Dion Fortune.

"I need a piss," Paul said. He stood, unsteadily and headed towards the bushes.

Charlie had noticed the blossoming intimacy between Kate and Stuart. He wondered what they were doing up in the copse. His thoughts invariably turned in on themselves. He began to wonder if he was to be the last spinster in this parish. Was it possible that he would be the first to eighteen and last to find a girlfriend? At least if Stuart and Kate got together, he and Imogen might leave each other alone. This constant fretting about Imogen was useless, pointless, tiring. Stuart, who Charlie had seen and continued to see as his great rival, his antagonist, was quite contentedly flirting with Kate, quite possibly wanted to be with Kate, was quite happily taking her up the copse right now. And Imogen, with whom he seemed constantly obsessed, stroked James's dark hair, smiling as she and James talked about films, the fire dancing in her eyes. Not one of them worried in the same way he did, not one of them was concerned with what the other was doing. They all did their own thing, enjoyed each other's company, laughed and loved. Only he ploughed the same furrows, followed the same groove.

There was a shriek from the bushes and Paul came jogging back, pointing into the sky. "Look! What's that, up there! The light!"

Charlie turned to look. "Is that what you're screaming about?"

"Yes!" Paul said. "What is it?"

"Take your time," Charlie said.

Paul stared at the light. A few moments passed. "It's a flare, isn't it," he said.

"It is," Charlie said.

"Even I knew that," Imogen said.

"But you're all veterans of the Plain," Paul said. "I don't see many flares over Torbay." Paul lay down on his back and looked up at the stars. "Shame, though. It would be really cool to see something."

Paul's excitement had failed to move James, whose head was still in Imogen's lap. She stroked back his hair and looked up at the stars. Charlie wondered what Jane would think of all this. She'd love to be here. What was she doing now? Probably tucked up in bed, fast asleep. Warm under her blankets. Wearing the pyjamas he'd often seen her in. Dreaming, possibly. Dreaming of what? When he thought about Jane – something he realised he was doing more often – he felt relaxed; there was none of the horrid urgency and lack of agency he felt when thinking about Imogen. And when he thought of Jane, Imogen was displaced for a while. This afternoon, half-reading the Lawrence but also thinking about Jane, Imogen had hardly crossed his mind. Yet he'd so loved – or had been so obsessed with – Imogen, she'd been so much a part of his very being for the past year, it was difficult to imagine how she could quickly fade from his immediate awareness. Her lips and eyes, her way of moving, they were all limned into his nerve endings and could not be easily erased. And the conflicts – all imaginary – with James, and then with Stuart, had played so much on his mind, they had scored ruts he constantly followed. How could these ruts be filled? By falling for Jane? Could it be so simple?

Kate and Stuart climbed over the gate. Charlie noticed Kate was now wearing Stuart's blue RAF blouson. Stuart put his arm around her waist. She pressed into his side.

"See anything?" James said.

"Well, yes. Did you?" Stuart said.

Charlie laughed. "I'm surprised you didn't hear Paul's scream from where you were. He went for a piss behind the hedge. While he was there, the flare went up. Then we heard a shout. *What the bloody hell is that?* So we wondered what the hell he'd seen. He came running over here and pointed at the big orange light. *Is that what you're screaming about?* I asked. *Yes*, he said, *yes*. Then James and I fell about laughing."

"But then, you have had another joint," Imogen pointed out.

Charlie started laughing again and pushed Paul's shoulder. "You big stupid screaming girlie."

"You all seem much more... jovial," Stuart said. "Everybody seems... happy."

Everybody did indeed seem happy, Charlie thought. He was certainly happy. Quite, quite merry. Stoned.

Imogen shrugged. "There's brandy everywhere. Even in the coffee." She sounded slightly less merry than everyone else.

"Does either of you want one?" James spoke slowly, his speech slurring.

"No thanks," Stuart replied. "Have you got any coffee left, Kate?"

Kate and Stuart sat down by the fire, close to each other, the right arm of one just lightly pressing the left arm of the other. Kate poured Stuart a coffee from her flask, then asked if she could have a drop of Martell.

"Certainly you can," Imogen said. She poured some into a cup and passed it to Kate.

"How civilized," Kate said. "Drinking cognac by a bonfire, under the stars."

Stuart's greatcoat was still lying on the road. He picked it up, dusted it down, and said to Kate that he'd swap it for his blouson.

"Right on," Kate said. "Imogen said I'd get cold. She was right." She removed the blouson and handed to Stuart and then pulled the greatcoat over her shoulders.

Before Stuart put on the blouson, he found another jumper in his bag and pulled it over his head.

Charlie sniggered. "You're beginning to look like the bloody Michelin man."

"Better than looking like a gothic ghoul," Stuart said.

James giggled. "I'm just a fucking freak, man."

"I'm devastatingly handsome," Paul added.

"That's all very well," Kate said, "but as you all know, there is nothin' like a dame. Nothing in the world!"

"How was it?" Imogen said. "The copse?"

"It's very quiet, isn't it," Kate said. "You feel kind of *alone* there.

The world seems... *emptier*, somehow. It has an atmosphere about it."

"That atmosphere changes every day, every night," Stuart said. "Sometimes it's unremarkable. But sometimes it can feel very heavy, like something is about to happen."

"And does it? Does something happen?" Kate asked.

"Hah! Good question," Stuart said. "Actually, no, nothing has ever happened. Well, except for me turning into a big scaredy-cat and whining and wanting to run back to the gates."

"How did it seem to you tonight?" Paul asked.

"A bit heavy. Not as bad as it can be."

"I protected him, anyway," Kate said. "And then we saw the flare."

"How did you feel when you first saw it?" James said.

"A bit awed, really," Kate said. "Like, yes, this is it! On my first visit!"

"Things do tend to feel different up here," James said. "Ordinary things become... spectacular. If you'd been down in Dereham, you wouldn't have given that light a second thought. You'd have known what it was instantly. But here, you expect things to happen. You expect them to have..." James struggled through his inebriated haze for a word. "Meaning."

Kate nodded. "Yes. That's how it was," she said. "I immediately thought *UFO!* It took me a few seconds to work out it was a flare. And then Stuart showed me a satellite. I hadn't seen one before."

"That's one of the reasons I like to come here," Stuart said. "I see flares, satellites, high-flying aircraft, distant helicopters, meteors, and, if I'm lucky, rockets over the Plain. Although not all at once, unfortunately."

"The sky is always randomly alive," Kate said.

"That's a good way of putting it."

James experimented with throwing Martell into the fire. The fire roared briefly. Then, one of the kerbstones exploded. Hot chunks of concrete flew out of it. One landed on Charlie's knee and burnt his jeans. "Bugger, piss, shit," Charlie said, brushing away hot concrete.

Another landed on James's chest. James rolled over. "It's burnt a hole in my bloody greatcoat!"

"I didn't expect that," Paul said.

"Well, I did," Stuart said with a theatrical sigh. "But nobody ever listens to me."

At which point, another kerbstone popped. A small shard of hot concrete hit Charlie's hand. He squealed and dropped his rollie into the cup of Martell on the road next to him. The cup burst into flames. Paul shrieked and jumped sideways. James watched the cup melting.

"I certainly didn't expect that," James said, confused.

Imogen was laughing. "How are you enjoying your first skywatch, Kate?"

"Early results of my participant observation indicate the skywatch to be a deeply serious investigation of paranormal activity," Kate replied, with mock gravity. Stuart playfully pushed her over. Kate sat up straight again and pushed Stuart over.

Charlie stood. "I fancy a walk up the copse. Anybody else up for it?"

Nobody seemed keen. "All right," Stuart said. "I'll go with you."

Charlie spoke to the others. "I can safely leave the rest of you alone for a while, can't I? You can survive without the light of my rationality? "

"We'll be fine," James mumbled. "Just get on with you."

Kate grabbed Imo's hand and pulled her up. "We're going for a walk, anyway." James rolled off Imogen's lap and onto the road.

"We are?" Imogen said.

"Yes, we are. We're going to talk about girly things."

Kate and Imogen ambled off along the road, arm in arm, giggling. James and Paul were flat on their backs, looking quietly at the sky.

Charlie and Stuart climbed over the stile. They walked towards the copse in silence for a while.

Stuart finally spoke. "Are you looking forward to seeing Jane again?"

"I think she's great." Charlie said.

"She *is* great."

"So you'd better leave her alone." Charlie wasn't sure where that had come from. He was brandy-soaked, certainly. The grass was no longer making him mellow.

"What would I do with Jane?" Stuart said. "I'm more interested in Kate. Even you should be able to see that."

"It's difficult to know who you're interested in. You flirt with girls all the time. When we were in Devon, you and Fiona were all over each other. You flirt too much." Where *was* all this coming from, Charlie wondered. He felt a little out of control. A little possessed.

"I talk to girls, and they like it," Stuart said. "I'm not going to apologise for getting on with them." They were silent for a few paces. "Look, if you fancy Jane, I'm happy for you." Charlie said nothing. "So... Are you over your obsession with Imo?"

"I am not obsessed, okay?"

"Okay, okay. You're not obsessed."

"You all think you know me, don't you?" Charlie muttered. "Anyway, why do you care? Worried Imo will want me, not you? "

Stuart's laugh was derisive. "You? You freak her out, man!"

"I do not!"

"You do!" Stuart spat the words out. He too was beginning to sound a little out of control.

"She's never said anything to me."

Stuart took a deep breath. He was calming himself before he continued. "She wouldn't. She doesn't want to upset our friendships. We've all known each other for years. She feels like an interloper."

"She used to confide in me all the time."

"I know," Stuart said. "It's just... Well..."

"What?"

"Well, you *did* freak her out, man. You were always going over to her house for coffee, you were always somehow in the pub when she was there, you were always buying drinks for her. And then you got all bitter and twisted when she started seeing James."

"I was just... *keen*," Charlie said, choosing a word that felt slightly odd in his mouth.

"You were probably too keen, too much in her face all the time."

Charlie was silent again for a few moments. When he spoke, he was surprised how hurt his own voice sounded. "Well, just don't flirt with Jane the next time you see her."

"I'll do what I like, Charlie. Why shouldn't I? "

Charlie's voice had begun to swing between drunk mumbling and aggression. He knew he sounded a little manic. "If you do flirt with her it'll really piss me off."

"Are you all right?" Stuart asked.

"I get pissed off with the whole lot of you sometimes."

"We've been friends for years, Charlie. What's happening, tell me."

"Wouldn't you like to know. Just so you and Imo can talk about me behind my back." Charlie grabbed Stuart's shoulder and pulled him around so Charlie could look into his face. "I'd probably be a lot more relaxed about going out with Jane if I didn't feel you lot were watching me all the time, waiting for me to admit Jane isn't good enough, that I only want Imo."

Stuart shook his head. "You go on about me messing with Jane, but you know you're the problem, don't you. So, are *you* going to mess Jane about?"

Charlie pushed both his hands against Stuart's chest, shoving him backwards. Stuart staggered. He struggled to keep himself from slipping on the broken chalk surface of the track.

"No, I'm not going to mess her about," Charlie said. "What do you know about me? What do any of you know? Do you think I can't move beyond Imogen? Huh?" He shoved Stuart again. He wondered what he was doing. He might be three inches taller than Stuart, but Stuart was stocky, fit and strong. "Is that what you think?" Charlie's voice was brittle. "You think you're so fucking good because girls talk to you. But you're not." Charlie shouted into Stuart's face.

When Stuart spoke, his voice was very controlled. Aggressively controlled. "Charlie, you're one of my best friends. But I wouldn't keep pushing me if I were you."

Charlie shoved him again. "Why, what are you going to do about it?"

"Christ, Charlie. Are you looking for a fight?"

Charlie jabbed a stiff forefinger into Stuart's chest. "What if I am?"

"I don't like fighting, Charlie, so I'll do very little."

Charlie pushed Stuart again. "You're a wimp. A little wimp. I wonder if Kate knows what a girl you are. Perhaps Imo's telling her now."

Stuart continued to keep himself under control. "Last warning, Charlie."

"Hah. You don't like fighting, so how are you going to stop me, Mr Wimpy? This is the way a friendship ends," Charlie said caustically. "Not with a bang but a wimp." He was pleased with that line. He shoved Stuart once more.

Stuart delivered a stinging slap to Charlie's cheek.

"What the hell?" Charlie spluttered.

"You're acting like a big bloody kid, Charlie! Grow up. Get over it, whatever it is!"

Charlie slowly sank down onto his haunches. To his embarrassment, he began to cry. Stuart stood apart from him for a while, also embarrassed. After a few moments, though, he squatted down next to Charlie. "Come on, man. Talk it out. Don't make me slap you again."

Charlie laughed between the sobs. "I don't know what's wrong with me. I really don't." He looked down at the ground between his knees, the sobs subsiding.

Stuart stayed silent but remained close. Time passed slowly. Stuart spoke again. "You're one of my best friends, Charles. You can talk to me any time. About anything." Charlie could hardly find the energy to speak. So much had been held back over the last year. "I can't make you talk to me, Charlie," Stuart said. "But I hope you'll tell me what's going on in that fat head of yours."

Charlie sat down on the stony track. Stuart stood up and looked over the orange glow of Dereham.

"I think I've smoked too much dope today," Charlie said. "Made myself a little paranoid."

"And you've certainly drunk too much brandy. That aggression didn't come from the grass. It came from the booze."

Charlie looked up at Stuart. "Sorry about that shit, man."

Stuart reached out his hand to pull Charlie up. Charlie grabbed it. "Sorry I slapped you. Let's get back to others."

"At least we can tell them there was a bad atmosphere up here now," Charlie said, grimly.

"I won't tell if you don't," Stuart said.

"Done," Charlie replied.

*

Imogen heard voices coming down the track, and then the gate clattered as Charlie and Stuart climbed over it.

"See anything?" James said.

"You're joking, right?" Charlie said.

Paul was still lying on his back. "Dark clouds have arrived," he said.

"That's no way to talk about us." Stuart said.

Imogen looked up. The stars had been shut away. She checked her watch. It was four-thirty. The piles of twigs and branches Charlie and the others had so recently carried down from the copse had rapidly dwindled. If they stayed longer, somebody would have to fetch more wood.

Charlie looked around him. "Well, the fire's nearly out, the sky is shit," he said sullenly. "We might as well call it a night."

James sleepily agreed and slowly stood, his arms held out slightly from his sides as he tried to maintain his balance. Stuart reached out a hand to Kate. She took it and Stuart pulled her up. Imogen was happy to see them together. Kate and Stuart had kissed in the copse, their first kiss. Kate had told her earlier. Paul began breaking up the fire with toe of his shoe. Charlie picked up the remaining wood and stacked it against the hedge, just past the gates. Imogen wriggled between Stuart and Kate, putting an arm around each of them.

"Did you enjoy your first skywatch?" she asked Kate.

"I did! I look forward to doing it again one day soon."

Charlie helped Paul break up the fire, using the stick that had been his poker for most of the night. Kate broke away from Imogen, bent down to put the plastic cup back on top of the flask, then put the flask away in Imogen's bag.

Imogen looked at Charlie. He'd been quiet since he'd returned from the copse. Something had happened up there. Had somebody said something? Should she ask him? He saw her looking at him and turned away quickly.

James searched the ground. "Where's the cup. Where's the fuckin' cup?"

"What cup?" Charlie said.

"The cup which is supposed to screw on to the top of this... this... this fuckin'... flask... thing."

Charlie pointed to the deformed plastic by the fire. "There it is. Try screwing that on your flask."

James started laughing. Charlie kicked the useless cup away down the road. The fire had been spread and reduced to glowing red and grey ash. They all picked up their bags and walked away from the hill, back down Lavington Road.

The lights were off at Red Post Farm. Paul and Charlie were lost in the darkness under the archway of trees. Imogen could just see Stuart and Kate ahead of her. James held her hand and leaned into her. He started singing one of the songs she and Stuart had written based on his lyrics. Stuart had his arm around Kate again. They slowed a little and Kate turned and kissed Stuart's cheek. Stuart then kissed Kate on the lips. It was a brief kiss, but Imogen could see the meaning in it, the promise of it. They began walking again as she and James caught up with them. Charlie and Paul had slowed, and when Stuart and Kate reached them, Stuart put his other arm around Charlie's shoulder and drew him closer. As they came out from the greater darkness beneath the arch of trees, James began singing *America* by Simon and Garfunkel. Imogen joined in with him and then Stuart also joined in, finding harmonies with Imogen. Stuart left Charlie and Kate then, and skipped over to James and Imogen. He put his arms around both of them as they continued singing. James stopped singing for a moment and then started with *Jerusalem* instead. This was a song to which they all knew some words, and they all joined in. Like James, Charlie couldn't sing. Paul's voice was passable. Kate began singing and surprised Imogen. She had forgotten Kate could sing. Imogen had heard her sing along to songs on the radio, and they had drunkenly sung together at parties, but now Kate was singing seriously, clearly, tunefully to impress Stuart perhaps. Her voice was strong and sweet, and she knew how to add a third harmony to the melody.

They walked down White Street, trying out various songs, many of which ended in garbled la-la-las, and retraced their steps into Trowbridge Road and then Westfield Road, where Charlie lived in one of the terraced houses. Charlie was hugged first by Imogen, then by Kate, then by a giggling James. Charlie said goodnight, opened the front door and was gone. James put his arm around Paul and the two of them walked down Westfield Road talking about T. S. Eliot again and Wallace Stevens and Ezra Pound, while Imogen, Stuart and Kate walked behind, comfortable in their silence. They cut down Bell Street, across the car park and along a path that exited into the Market Place, where they crossed the quiet main road. At the top of Church Street, they stopped under a streetlight.

Imogen walked over to James, took his arm from Paul's shoulders and said, "Come on, lambikins, time for bed."

James smirked drunkenly. "Yes please."

Imogen smiled, shook her head at Paul, and then mouthed, "No way."

Kate turned to Stuart and looked up at him. "It's been an education."

Stuart kissed her. "We'll see each other again, yeah?"

The streetlights sparkled in Kate's eyes. "Yeah. Phone me soon." She squeezed Stuart's hand, and then skipped over to Imogen.

Stuart and Paul were just turning to walk up the High Street, back towards Stuart's house, when James suddenly became more awake.

"The ritual! Don't forget about the ritual! We'll do it soon, yeah?"

7

Charlie walked into the house on a warm day in early May. His greatcoat had been relegated to the wardrobe and replaced by an old blue pin-striped suit jacket he'd bought from a charity shop. He carried books and folders under his arm. His mother came into the kitchen, waving an envelope. "It's not Paul's handwriting," Mrs Woolmer said. "It looks a bit like a girl's to me." She sniffed the envelope. "In fact, I'm sure I smell perfume."

"It could be Paul then," Charlie said with a smirk.

Mrs Woolmer stopped waving the envelope for a moment. "What do you mean?" She paused. "Oh, I get it. I see. You're saying your friend Paul is a big girl. Yes, very funny."

Charlie placed the books and folders on the kitchen table. He took off his jacket, hung it on the back of one of the chairs arranged around the small table, and rolled up the sleeves of his collarless shirt. He looked at his mother. "Well, give it here then."

Mrs Woolmer offered the envelope to him, then snatched it away. "Not until you tell me who it's from." Again she offered the envelope, and again she snatched it away, giggling.

"Come on, mum," Charlie said, petulantly. "Until I open it, I honestly don't know who it's from."

His mother considered, and then handed the envelope to him. He looked at the postmark. It was from Devon. He thought he recognised the handwriting that had addressed it. He opened the envelope and pulled out the single sheet of paper, at the top of which *Dear Charlie* had been written. He was sure now; the letter was written in Jane's large, looping handwriting. Still, he turned the page over to check, and saw *Love Jane*. Excitement thrilled through him. Why was she writing to him?

Mrs Woolmer poured a mug of tea for Charlie. "Well, who is it then?"

"Jane," he said.

Mrs Woolmer handed him the mug. "Who's Jane?"

"Thanks." Charlie paused for a moment. "Paul's sister." He found his tobacco and cigarette papers in his waistcoat pocket and began making a roll-up.

"She's but a slip of a girl," Mrs Woolmer said.

"She's not anymore, mum." Charlie popped the rollie into his mouth and started patted his pockets, looking for his lighter. He remembered it was in his jacket. He found, it, lit the cigarette, then slipped the lighter back into the jacket pocket.

His mother eyed him knowingly. "I see. It's like that, is it?"

"It's not like anything."

Charlie's mother winked. "Yet."

Charlie thought it best to take the letter to his bedroom before reading it, away from his mother's questions and prying eyes. He placed the letter on his pile of books, which he carried with his mug of tea carefully up the stairs. He didn't want to spill tea on his letter. He put the books and letter on his small desk, and his mug on his bedside cabinet. He went over to the record player and without much thought, put on *Fleetwood Mac*. He then took the letter from the top of the pile and sat on his bed, his back against the cool wall, the letter in one hand, the mug of tea in the other, the rollie still in his mouth. Before he started reading the letter, he quickly sniffed the paper. His mother was right; there was a hint of *Havoc*. Jane had probably dabbed a little on her wrist before writing the letter.

His rollie had gone out. He put his mug down on his bedside cabinet and tried to find his lighter, patting his waistcoat and trouser pockets. He then then remembered that he'd absent-mindedly put it back in the pocket of the jacket, which was still downstairs, hung over the chair. He put the letter next to the mug and slid open the drawer in the top of the cabinet. He rummaged through paper, pens and pencils and a diary he'd never used. A glint from beneath the diary caught his eye. It was his ritual knife. He picked it up and looked at it. He, James and Paul had each bought one at an occult shop in Glastonbury. He'd bought his on a whim, buoyed by the enthusiasm of James and Paul. Unlike them, he would never use it in a ritual. He put it back, closed the drawer and looked in the cupboard beneath. He found a half-full box of matches. He lit his cigarette again, replaced the matches – in the drawer this time – picked up his mug of tea and took a sip. He retrieved Jane's letter and began to read it.

Dear Charlie,

You scraggy hairy monster. What are you up to? Are you well? I am. Despite the monstrous hangover I had yesterday. I went to a disco in Torquay on Friday night and had a good boogie around. I drank too much though (groan). The bar staff shouldn't let under-age drinkers drink so much. Mind you, I saw a girl from school there who must be a year younger than me sinking rum and cokes like there was no tomorrow. Actually, there probably wasn't for her (haha). Anyway, we (me and Maggie and Marci) walked back (staggered more like) through Cockington, over the fields to Charlton, which helped clear my head a bit. Still woke up with a headache though. A real banger. A thumper. Oh, yes. Dad gave me surly looks. I think he knew what I'd been up to.

Before we went to Torquay, we caught a bus over to Totnes. I bought some new clothes while I was there. I really like them. I hope you like them too, Charles. I think I look fab.

Charlie paused for a moment. He took another sip of tea. She hoped he liked them too, he thought. *Interesting.* He continued reading Jane's letter.

I'm revising like mad for my O-levels (when I'm not drunk, haha). I still find maths really hard, Charlie. Do you? I don't care really, "cos I want to do English, Art and Psychology A-levels next year. I'm hoping I can go to KEVICs in Totnes. You know the one, it's where Fiona and Paul go. You've been there, haven't you? Totnes is so cool. I'm sure everybody must smoke dope, drink absinthe (I had to look that one up (embarrassed)) and have really weird conversations late into the night. They're all beardy weirdies, Charlie, like you.

How are you getting on with your A-levels? Are you a good boy? Do you do your homework every night?

Again, Charlie paused. *She wrote me a letter.* He wondered if she would also write to Stuart and James. Not James, he thought. James never goes to Devon with us; she can barely remember him. Would she write to Stuart, though? Was she going to start writing letters for fun, like he, Stuart, James and Paul had been doing? *Or is she writing only to me?* It excited him to think she might be.

> When are you coming to see us again? In the summer? I always look forward to seeing you guys. I hope I'll see you soon.

She hopes to see me soon! Just me! Not Stuart!

> I hope you don't mind me writing to you Charlie. I'd love it if you wrote back. You always make me smile. Write to me if you have time.

There were three kisses beneath her name. Sometimes, in the letters Paul wrote to his friends, Jane would add little asides or marginalia. When she did this, she also signed the letter and put two kisses. He thought back to the Christmas cards and postcards he and Stuart sometimes received from her. They would also have two kisses under her name. He revelled in that extra *x*. He crushed his rollie in the ashtray. He would write back. He lifted his mug of tea and sipped it. She wanted to know when he would next visit Devon. He would have to go alone. That should be easier now Stuart and Kate were together. Stuart would surely prefer to go there with Kate. But when could he to? When was the next college break? It was close, wasn't it? Half term for Whitsun and the spring Bank Holiday. He found a diary on his desk. The last Monday of May. He could go down any weekend, really, he could even go down this weekend. He didn't want to rush things, though. Perhaps, after all, he'd misunderstood the intent of Jane's letter. He would first reply to her. There were, though, only three weeks until the Bank Holiday. He needed to write soon. He would do it tonight, after he'd eaten, and phoned Paul.

Charlie held the phone to his ear, listening to the ringing at the other end, wondering what he should do if Jane answered. It was, though, Mrs Maas who answered, and then fetched Paul.

"Good lord, it's you," Paul said.

"Just a quick call. Can I come down at Whitsun?"

"That should be acceptable. Hang on."

Charlie heard a muffled conversation, which he guessed was between Paul and his mother.

"That's fine. Is Stuart coming?"

"Oh, he's spending a lot of time with Kate now," Charlie said. "He's got better things to do." *No way is Stuart coming down.* "I'll probably come down by myself."

After the phone call, Charlie went to his room again. Fleetwood Mac was still on his record player. He decided to play it again. He sat on his bed, with an A4 writing pad on his lap, a pen in his right hand and a rollie in his left. He tapped the pen on the pad and wondered how to begin. He found it difficult. The letters the boys wrote to each other were long, rambling epics, sometimes composed over months. Apart from gossip, they also contained ramblings about the masses, social control, politics, drugs, music and books. There would be silly plays, stories and odd poems. There would be long sections about being bored and having nothing to do except write, and apologising for writing about nothing; they would, therefore, attempt to write interestingly about nothing.

Charlie couldn't write a letter like that to Jane. He knew Jane sometimes read the letters they sent to Paul, but she could put those down if they bored her, she could walk away from them – they weren't written to her. He knew he should write something pithy, trifling and amusing, but which also said something essential. He thought for a while, and began to write a couple of times. Each time, however, he was always unhappy with his efforts. He sat back and leaned against the wall, wondering if he would ever succeed in this simple task. He'd never written to a girl before. He knew he had to write this letter differently. He was eager to finish it tonight though, if he could, and post it tomorrow. *If I can't manage this now, I'll never do it.* He picked up Jane's letter and smiled as he reread it. When he finished it, however, he still had no idea what to write. He wished, in a way, he could write like her. Then an idea came to him. Why not model his letter on hers?

Dear Jane,

What an unpleasant surprise it was to receive your missive. Haha, as you would say. Just kidding. Sorry to hear about your hangover. But that is the punishment for enjoyment we must all learn to endure as we grow up. Six aspirin and a glass of Andrews work for me. How are you now?

I can't say I've been drunk lately. But James did overindulge in — how can I put this delicately — certain substances the other day and instead of catching a train from Salisbury to Dereham, ended up on a train to Exeter, where he promptly fell asleep. No ticket collector dared wake the ugly hippie freak on the way down. However, on the way back, when he was conscious, a ticket inspector caught him and made him cough up for a ticket back to Dereham. The berk. Always said he smoked too much. He didn't get back until eleven... to find all his friends waiting in his dank attic rooms, mocking him.

So, notwithstanding hangovers, how are you? What are you up to? Have you spotted one of your elusive UFOs yet? Nothing much is happening up here. Oh, apart from Stuart getting together with Kate. She's a friend of Imo's. She's a nice girl. I don't see quite so much of him as I used to. Kate lives out Burnt Norton way, near Imo.

I was surprised to find James had that Fleetwood Mac album you've got. Fleetwood Mac by Fleetwood Mac. Macwood Fleet by Macfleet Wood. Flatpack Meat by Meatback Floop. Feedback Loop by Backloop Feed. You know the one I mean, doncha? Course ya do. Anyway, I borrowed it from James and I've been listening to it. Now I had it pegged as one of your smooth records, somewhere between Terry Jacks and Al Stewart. So imagine my surprise when I discovered that... it's not at all bad. Or, at least, not all bad. I've been listening to it quite a lot. I really dig Rhiannon. I'm listening to it now.

Your A-levels sound cool and I'm sure you'll be fair incredible at the O-levels (no hangovers the night before) even maths. Although A-levels are a struggle, man. I hate homework. I'm nearly nineteen years old and I'm still doing bloody homework!

Hey look, I'm coming down over the Whitsun weekend. I've already phoned Paul, to check it was okay with your mum and dad, so he's probably told you anyway. I'm looking forward to seeing you and especially your now legendary new clothes (it's all we talk about around here (haha (as you'd say))). I'm sure you'll look really cool in them. See you soon!

He signed it and then, daringly, wrote two kisses beneath his name. Not three, as Jane had done, because he was, after all, a young man. He read over the letter again. It struck, he thought, just the right note. He put it into a manila envelope and addressed it. He would post it on the way to James's house later this evening.

Imogen studied the lyrics inside the gatefold sleeve of a Van Der Graaf Generator album while James read a book that appeared to be, on first glance, somebody's Selected Works. The door rattled and Kate and Stuart came in. Kate went over to Imo, hugged her, then sat on the floor beside her. James looked up from his book and waved at Stuart and Kate. He leaned over and turned down the volume on the amplifier. He asked if Stuart and Kate wanted coffee, and then disappeared through the door and downstairs. Imogen turned the volume down a little more and asked how they were getting on. Kate pulled Stuart down onto the floor beside her and leaned her cheek against his shoulder. "I'd say we're getting on fine," she said.

Stuart ran his fingers through Kate's long black hair. "Yes, we are," Stuart agreed. He kissed Kate.

"I'm so glad," Imogen said. "I thought you might be when we hadn't seen you for a while. I always knew you two would be good together. That's why I left you to get on with it."

"Well, we *have* been getting on with it," Kate said.

Stuart looked at Kate. "We met up again a day after the skywatch."

"And we kissed again," Kate added.

"Yes, we did some hugging and kissing," Stuart said. He looked at Imogen, smiling. "Shall I carry on? This *is* the kind of thing girls like to hear isn't it?"

Imogen laughed. "Yes, indeed it is. Although hearing it from a boy is kind of weird."

"So, then we met up again the day after that," Stuart continued. "This time I rode my bike over to Burnt Norton. We went for a walk and then sat and made daisy chains in a green field speckled with daisies and dandelions."

"There were sheep and lambs in the field," Kate said "We were surrounded by the warm smell of grass and lanolin."

"Love the detail," Imogen said.

"Our kisses became longer," Stuart continued. "The time spent lying in the grass with our arms around each became longer. I made a necklace for Kate. A daisy chain necklace." He smiled at Imogen mischievously. "It was a warm day, and her cheesecloth shirt had been unbuttoned low at the neck, where the necklace of daisies hung to her breasts."

"Woah, there!" Imogen said. "Now this is turning into a cheap blue movie."

The door opened and Charlie came in. He frivolously rubbed all their heads as he passed them, and then sat on the sofa. He looked around at them all. "And how are you this fine evening?"

"I think we're fine," Imogen said. "These two certainly sound fine."

"I know I am," Kate agreed.

"And I was, the last time I looked," Stuart said.

"Ask me how I am," Charlie said.

"How are you?" Stuart asked.

"I'm good. I'm pretty damned good. Where's James?"

"Making coffee."

"Imo, do you think he'd mind if I pinched some of his Martell?"

"Of course he wouldn't. Go ahead."

Charlie inspected a glass, decided it was fit for use, and poured himself a large measure. He took off his jacket and folded it over the arm of the sofa.

"I'd like to tell you why I'm good–" Charlie began.

"In fact, why you're pretty damned good," Stuart interjected.

"Yes. Pretty damned good. But it would sound inordinately like boasting."

"But we like a boast," Stuart said. "It's traditional!"

"What are you on about?" Kate asked.

"For many years," Stuart explained, "boasting was *all* we could do. Mind you, I *am* a late developer, so I have an excuse. The other guys, however... Well, they couldn't get girlfriends either, even if James did start growing pubic hair at eight."

"But it's only ten to nine now, so that's only fifty minutes ago," Kate said.

Charlie spat a mouthful of Martell back into his glass and snorted. "Good one," he said.

Stuart snorted and punched Kate playfully.

"He hasn't stopped growing hair since," Imogen said. "He'll be a bloody yeti soon."

"Anyway, the point is," Stuart continued, "we're a bunch of pseudo-intellectual hippies growing up in this rural backwater. What's more, we get into UFOs, and science and science fiction when we're fourteen, and then into the occult at fifteen. As you can imagine, no girl will look at us, despite our rugged good looks and affable natures."

"Some of the girls at school even thought we were performing questionable rites on Copsehill," Charlie added.

"So, while our peers were off kissing every girl they could, we were lucky if a girl talked to us *at all*. If a girl did talk to us, it was a *big deal*, man. I can't remember which of us started it, but in the letters to Paul, if we had *any* interaction with a girl, however trivial, we would write BOAST in capitals–"

Charlie interrupted. "And in red pen, and underlined."

"Yes, all of that," Stuart said. "And give full details of what had happened."

"So what *was* a big deal?" Kate said.

"Well, something as innocent as walking arm in arm with a girl was a big deal. *Huge!*" Stuart emphasised. "Anyway, we'd start saying it in conversation. *Boast!* we'd say, and then relate some sorry tale of some trivial happening with a girl."

"Obviously, if you could spice it up without going into the realms of fiction, so much the better," Charlie said.

"You poor boys!" Kate said.

"Well, it got better as we got older. A few of the girls in Dereham started turning into freaks. Then, when we went to college, there were more freaks around. Freak heaven!"

Imogen held her hand up. "Yes, I'm one! I'm one! And I've got the biggest freak in Dereham!"

James returned with the coffee. "And here is the hairy yeti monster!" Kate squealed.

"Are you talking about me?" James said.

Kate nodded.

"I have it in my power to withhold the coffee, you know." He moved the tray temporarily out of her reach.

"You doity rat," Kate said.

James laughed and moved the tray back towards her.

Stuart looked at Charlie, who stared absently into his Martell. "Come on, then," Stuart said. "Out with it. What is the nature of your boast?".

"A boast!" James said, excitedly. "A boast! Why, we haven't had a fully-fledged boast for some months."

James reached for the Martell bottle, poured more into Charlie's glass and poured some into a glass for himself. Imogen watched as he poured. James sat on the sofa, next to Charlie and patted his knee encouragingly. "Go on with your boast, dear boy!"

"Oh, I don't know," Charlie said. "It might be something of nothing. Might hardly be boast-worthy at all, come to think of it." He swirled the brandy around in his glass, took a sip. He fiddled with his jacket, then moved it over so he could rest his glass on the arm of the sofa. He looked around them all with a smile and began to roll himself a cigarette.

"I might know little about the time-honoured boast," Kate said. "But it's not going well so far."

James offered Stuart a cigarette, which he took. Kate looked at him, turned up her nose and called him a stinky boy. Stuart lit the cigarette anyway, blew smoke into the air, removed the cigarette from his lips and poked his tongue out at her. Kate quickly leaned towards him, sliding her lips over his tongue. They kissed for a few moments, before Stuart pulled away from Kate and said, "Hey! Big boast! I kissed a girl today!"

Imogen gently kicked Charlie's calf with one of her black espadrilles. "C'mon, you tease, what's the boast?" She needed to hear it. She hoped it involved Jane.

"Oh, well. Okay. Here goes. *Boast!* When I got home tonight there was a letter waiting for me. From Devon."

"It wasn't from Paul then," James said. "That's not something to boast about. Well, not unless you've finally embraced that hidden side of yourself."

Imogen knew now who the letter was from. She felt an unexpected relief. She was surprised at how much tension suddenly fell way inside her. She hadn't fully understood until that moment how Charlie had made her feel.

"It was from Jane," Charlie said.

James frowned, then said, "Jane? Paul's sister Jane?"

"Of course! Do we know any other Janes?"

"You might have bumped into one in Devon."

"Had that been the case," Stuart pointed out, "we'd have been subjected to an earlier and mightier boast."

"True, true," James agreed. "So, uh, what did she say?"

"Nothing much," Charlie admitted. "It was a lot of gossipy stuff. I just got the feeling she was interested in me."

Kate leaned towards Charlie, eagerly. "Tell us more, tell us more."

"She said she looked forward to seeing me. She's bought some new clothes. She thinks they look good on her. She said she hopes I like them too–"

"You're in, big man," Kate said.

"Then she asked if I was coming down soon."

"Are you?" Stuart asked.

"Well, yeah. Bank Holiday weekend, I hope."

"That was a bit sudden," Stuart said.

"Well, you know I like her," Charlie said.

"Yeah, I do," Stuart said. "I hope something works out for you, man."

"You *are* going to reply to her, I hope?" Imogen asked.

"I already have. And posted it."

"Cool!" Imogen said. She played with the bead on her necklace. Would she finally be released from Charlie's obsession? She turned away and sipped at her coffee. She tucked her long hair behind one ear. Still, she knew, Charlie watched her.

Imogen hoped, for all their sakes, that Charlie would soon enter a new and very different world.

8

A week had passed since Charlie had sent his letter to Jane. He was again in the kitchen at home, and his mother again waved a letter under his nose.

"It's from young Jane, isn't it?" Mrs Woolmer said, knowingly.

"Well spotted, mother," Charlie replied. "Now give me the letter."

"Not until you say *please* and treat your old mother with respect."

"Oh. Okay. Dear mother, please would you pass the missive to me forthwith? I should be eternally grateful for your kindness."

"I only wanted some respect, not for you to turn into a bloody ponce," Mrs Woolmer said. She handed him the letter. "I'm not sure about this college education," she continued. "It's turning you into... into..." She waved her hands ineffectually.

"A pretentious git?"

"Is that a college way of saying ponce?"

"Close enough."

While they'd been talking, the tea Mrs Woolmer habitually made just before Charlie arrived home had been brewing. She poured him a mug. "Are you going to see her, or are you just going to write these... what did you call them?" She looked at Charlie cheekily. "Missiles? Mischiefs?"

"Missives."

"Yes, write these missives to each other, declaring your undying love?"

"Declaring our undying love would be a bit premature, mum."

"Oh, I don't know. Sixteen-year old girls can be very intense, you know. Why do you think I ended up marrying your father when I was still a bright young thing?"

"Because you were pregnant?"

Mrs Woolmer gently tapped Charlie's head. "Cheeky."

Charlie sipped up at his tea. "I'm thinking of going down over the Whitsun weekend."

"Don't take Stuart, he'll be a gooseberry."

"I think Stu has other, far more pleasant things to do than hitch with me."

"Oh yes, he's hooked up with that Kate girl, hasn't he?"

Charlie's younger brother, William, came into the room. "I've seen him with Kate. She's a looker."

Mrs Woolmer looked stern. "Will, Stuart is a lot bigger than you, so be careful what you say when he's around."

"Hah! I could take that big hippie," Will said. He shadow-boxed for a moment, before taking a biscuit from a tin. He then turned to Charlie. "Is that a letter from Jane?"

"Yeah, it is."

"What does it say? Does she *want* you? Is she *pining* for you?"

"How would I know?" Charlie said. "I haven't had a chance to open the bloody thing yet."

William winked. "I stopped mum from steaming it open."

Mrs Woolmer now gently tapped William's head. "What she says might not be fit for your young ears."

Charlie knew there was probably nothing in the letter unfit for William's young ears. At fifteen, he already had a girlfriend. Mrs Woolmer had often remarked on this state of affairs to Charlie, saying wasn't it about time *he* had a girlfriend, after all look at young William, off sowing his wild oats already. Charlie had pointed out that he looked a little different to the other young lads in the town and that his interests were at odds with the amusements girls usually demanded of a young man. He'd also tried to explain something of his obsession with Imogen, but his mother had said *that* was no way to carry on at his young age and his father had said there were plenty more fish in the sea, at which point Charlie had retreated to the sanctuary of his bedroom and listened to Genesis.

He went to his bedroom now, carrying with him his mug and the letter. He sat on the bed, rolling a cigarette, delaying the moment he would open the letter, increasing his anticipation. He picked up his mug, swallowed some tea, then put the roll-up between his lips and lit it. Finally, he ran his finger beneath the flap of the envelope, removed the letter and read it.

Dear Charlie,

Thanks for your letter. It did make me laugh. Well, at least once (haha (haha)). I was so thrilled when I saw your scrawl on the otherwise rather boring envelope mum handed me. I hope you're well. No hangovers down here at the moment.

I've had my hair done since you last saw me, I've been letting it grow. I no longer look like Farrah Fawcett. I hope you like the new style.

I've been out on Blue Tor a couple of times since you were last down, with Paul and Fiona. I keep hoping I'll see a UFO. We did see something, but Paul said it was only a satellite. I've been over to Paignton too, to the beach, just for a walk. It's nice, at this time of year, before the grockles arrive. There are only locals walking their dogs, and those weird joggers, and the oldies who come down on coach trips.

Charlie had been to Paignton at many different times of year and May was, indeed, a good time. The streets were uncrowded, the beach was almost empty, the air was warm and the wind light. Charlie liked it there in the early evenings – a stroll along the sand and then into town for a pint or two before the walk back to Charlton. He'd like to do that with Jane. He continued reading the letter.

I've been reading some more of Paul's books. I really enjoyed "1984" but it was a bit bleak (haha) and now I'm reading "Down and Out in Paris and London." After I finish it, I'm going to try "Brave New World", perhaps even "The Occult"!! And would you believe it!! While you're trying out FlickFlack Back, I've been listening to some of Paul's prog-rock. Yes and Genesis are pretty cool. It takes a while to get into, doesn't it... It's not as instant as T. Rex, is it? ('No' is the word you're groping for haha).

Some of my friends have noticed I'm changing. I think it's good I'm changing, isn't it? ('Yes' is the word you're groping for). I'm not sure my friends like it though.

Charlie was pleased that she was now listening to the kind of music he liked, and that her reading matter had extended beyond *Jackie* and school textbooks.

> I do look forward to seeing you at Whitsun, despite your
> ridiculous beard and odd dress sense. We can go for walks over
> the hills, or over to Paignton or Brixham or Torquay, or something.
> See you soon.

Charlie put the letter down and then lit his rollie. He picked up his mug and sipped thoughtfully at the lukewarm tea. She was changing. He wondered how much she'd already changed. He knew he should like her, smooth or not. And he did. She didn't really have to change for him. Yet, she had decided to make these changes. Charlie had said nothing to her, put no pressure on her. He knew, though, that she was only making these changes because she liked him. She was changing and alienating her friends out of a desire to impress him. He felt flattered, but also slightly guilty that he approved of this.

He would have to write back immediately. He picked up his writing pad, found a pen and rolled another ciggie. Again, he didn't know where to start. Nothing much had happened since the last letter. There wasn't even an amusing anecdote about James. Charlie decided to just wade in and see where that took him.

> Dear Jane
>
> It was an unalloyed pleasure to receive your latest epistle and to
> see you're learning the proper form and function of these
> missives. I'm really looking forward to seeing you at Whitsun. And
> now I also have your new haircut to look forward to. Oops, sorry, I
> should say hairstyle. What an oaf. Boys get haircuts. I'm happy
> you're changing.

Charlie paused for a moment, tapped the nib of the pen against his teeth. He ripped the sheet from the pad, screwed it up and threw it on the floor. He began writing again, opening in the same way, but after saying he looked forward to seeing her at Whitsun, he wrote

> I hope you're still enjoying the Yes and Genesis. I can bring some
> albums down to Charlton with me that Paul hasn't got. I'm still
> listening to Gabardine Mac and enjoying it more each time I listen.
> I sometimes imagine there's other music you like that I might like
> too.

Charlie grimaced. As long as it wasn't Abba or the Bay City Rollers.

> But then I think that's hardly likely (haha!).
> My anticipation at seeing the 'legendary new clothes' (still a hot topic of conversation in James's dusty attic rooms) is enormous. I am hugely intrigued by the nature of your new hairstyle. I'm sure when I mention it to the others, it will become as legendary as the clothes.

I have to say something about the changes. He wondered to phrase it. He wrote slowly, thinking as he went along, searching for the right words, still trying for a light touch.

> I hope you're not changing too quickly. And I hope you'll enjoy what you're changing into. I hope you'll enjoy the butterfly emerging from the chrysalis. I hope you don't upset too many of your friends by changing. Friends are important. Personally, I thought you were cute and funny when you were a smooth and you'd probably be cute and funny even if you turned into a greaser.

Charlie nodded. *That'll do.* His letter would show Jane that he liked her for her personality, not for the way she looked. Although if she didn't look as good as she did would he, he wondered, be interested in her at all? He fancied her and had always thought her very pretty. Not beautiful like Imo. But very, very pretty. So outward appearances did make a difference. But not her clothes and style.

He finished by again saying he looked forward to seeing her at Whitsun. He reread the letter. The final paragraph wasn't too heavy, he thought. He made some minor edits, then folded the letter and put it into one of his manila envelopes. He addressed it, found a book of stamps in the bedside drawer beneath his ritual knife and stuck one of the stamps to the envelope. He would post the letter later, on the way to James's house.

Not beautiful like Imo? What a horrible thing to think. But, with a feeling of excitement at the recognition of a peculiar emptiness that hadn't existed before, he realized this was the first time he'd thought about Imogen for a day or two, perhaps even three. He'd hardly thought of Imogen at all, even when he'd seen her at James's house. She'd simply been adorable, lovely Imo. There had been no ache of frustrated desire, no peevishness when Imogen gave Stuart a hug, no dark thoughts running constantly along the grooves he'd previously thought permanently etched into his mind. Jane was changing; and now it seemed that things were also changing for him.

9

Peter Richards and his friends had now designed and prototyped their new device. This time, the balloons carried beneath them a small, square, wooden frame. Each face of the frame held a set of bulbs. An electronic switch controlled each set of bulbs. Each switch could be turned on and off by Peter, using an old radio controller that had once belonged to a model aeroplane. If he moved the joystick one way, one set of lights would turn on. If he moved the joystick back to its central position, the lights would turn off. By moving the joystick in different directions, he could turn different sets of lights on and off.

The latest design had been inspired by the skywatchers at Copsehill. When Peter had seen them using their torches to send signals to recent hoax UFO, he knew what he had to do. If a skywatcher attempted to communicate with his hoax, Peter could signal back. He'd even learnt Morse code; if a skywatcher attempted to communicate using Morse, he could reply in kind. Because the switching mechanism was expensive, the balloon would be tethered and allowed to drift slowly into the air on two or three hundred feet of strong twine wrapped onto a spool. As a rule, skywatchers did not run excitedly towards UFOs, but instead watched in awe. If skywatchers did rush towards them, however, they could rewind the twine and retrieve their device.

Peter and the rest of the team had gone to the local hills to test the device, spooling the line out and rewinding it, allowing the balloons to float as high as possible and then bringing them back down as quickly as they could, before disassembling the device and packing it into rucksacks. They would carry with them, however, one item of emergency equipment – a pair of scissors. If they felt they couldn't get the device back to ground before hordes of overexcited skywatchers descended upon them, they would cut the tether and let it go. It would be a small price to pay to continue their experiments.

During the tests they were surprised, as always, at how striking a small number of torch bulbs could be, how bright and incongruous they appeared in the dark of the night, even when floating two hundred feet above them. Martin had played the skywatcher, flashing his torch at the UFO. Peter had flashed a message back, as fast as he could, in Morse code, disappointed only by his lack of wit in signalling *Bugger off*. Martin had, nonetheless, been amused to discover the meaning of Peter's coded message. Martin suggested this should be the message they always returned to excitable skywatchers. Although this would certainly be amusing, Peter said, there was always the small chance that a skywatcher would know Morse, and the earthiness of such a message from a supposedly extra-terrestrial source might lead to suspicion. The team somewhat reluctantly concurred.

They were ready to fly their device. They all agreed it would be best to wait until the colleges and universities had broken up for the summer. All-night skywatches on Copsehill were, after all, even more attractive during the long holidays. The summer months at Copsehill were always busy – the fine, warm weather attracted students looking to do something 'different'. Most students would be on holiday by the end of June. All the team had to do now was practice and wait – for the long summer nights, and for the unwitting and unwary.

Summer
1976

10

Charlie alighted from the bus at Charlton and walked along the lanes. He was nervous. He looked forward to seeing Jane, yet had no idea how she'd react, nor how he should react. At least it was sunny. The world was made a soft blue by the shining sky and the white cow parsley and hawthorn blossom in the hedgerows. Wild-flowers scented the air, sweet and sour and dusty. As he walked through the gate and into the garden of Paul's house, he found Mrs Maas bending over a flowerbed, planting violas. She looked up at the sound of the gate.

"Hello, Charlie," she said warmly. "How was your journey?"

"It was fine, thanks. It was slow though. The train stopped everywhere. But it's a lovely day. I didn't mind."

"Would you like a cup of tea?"

"Yes, please. Is Paul here?" Charlie asked, although he really wanted to know if Jane was home.

"No, Fiona and Paul went into Torquay with Jane. They said they'd be back by now. But then, to get back by now, they'd have been on your bus. And they weren't, were they?" Mrs Maas chuckled gently at her own wit.

She shook her hands in an attempt to remove the red soil that adhered to them, and then walked down the path to the back door, holding her hands out in front of her. Charlie followed. In the kitchen, he rolled a cigarette while Mrs Maas washed her hands, then set about making tea. She asked about his parents and his brother. Charlie took his cigarette from his mouth and blew smoke into the kitchen. He held the cigarette, as he always did, between his fingers, just a few inches away from his face. He noticed that his fingers trembled, very slightly, like leaves in a light breeze. He could feel the excitement in his stomach. He now wished he could hide his hand away from Mrs Maas, who would surely notice the trembling, although she was putting the few plates and cups from lunchtime into the washing-up bowl and turning the taps on, and was unaware of Charlie's pleasant state of agitated anticipation.

He wondered what he should say to Jane. He still wasn't entirely sure why she'd written the letters – perhaps she had only been bored and in search of something to do, or wanted to have a pen-friend because she was changing and becoming more like him and his friends. Yet he felt the references to her new clothes, and how he would like them, implied something, though he was unsure what that *something* might be. He knew what he hoped it might be; that Jane fancied him. And he remembered what Kate had said three weeks ago: *You're in, big man.* It had been nearly two months since he'd last seen Jane, but he could still recall the scent of *Havoc* on her neck.

Mrs Maas handed Charlie a cup of tea. "How are James and the lovely hippie girl?"

"James is fine," Charlie said. "And Imo is good too. They're starting to worry about the exams, but I suppose we all are. Apart from Stuart."

"And how is Stuart?"

"He's happy, too." *And he has a mighty slap.* "He's found himself a girlfriend."

"Really? How lovely. Who is it? Is she nice? Pretty?"

"She's Kate, a friend of Imo. She's a nice girl. And she's very pretty, I suppose." *But not as pretty as Imo.* Then he remembered what he'd just thought. *Or as Jane.*

Charlie knew very little about Kate. He'd spent so long thinking about Imogen, and now Jane, that hardly anything new had penetrated the fog of constantly-firing neurons that filled his head and through which he could discern very little except faint and distorted images. He thought about Kate. What else could he say about her? "She's funny too. She's a bit like Fiona, in a way."

"Is she another of those hippie girls?"

"Yes, she is," Charlie said. Although, he thought, less hippie than James and Imogen. Yet, somehow, very similar to Imogen. It was as if Stuart had taken bits from two of his favourite girls and melded them into one. Stuart had created a Bride of Frankenstein. Charlie smiled to himself.

"What are you smiling about?" Mrs Maas asked.

"Oh, nothing much. Just thinking how Kate really seems to be a cross between Fiona and Imo. It seems as though Stu has the best of both worlds."

Charlie heard voices coming down the path at the side of the house. The back door opened. Charlie had been caught unaware. He'd forgotten to prepare himself for Jane. He had been, he remembered, attempting to summon images of her and the smell of her neck before he'd been diverted by Mrs Maas's chatter. He felt butterflies; he felt stupidly scared. However, it was Paul and Fiona who came through the door first. Charlie stood up.

Fiona squealed and threw herself at him, wrapping him in her arms. "Charlieeee! How are you?" She planted a kiss on his lips.

"I'm fine, " Charlie told her.

Paul looked at him. "You're still an ugly bastard."

Mrs Maas giggled. "Oh, Paul,"

Although Charlie remained wrapped in Fiona's arms, he looked over her shoulder, towards the back door.

"She'll be here in a minute," Fiona said quietly. "She stopped to talk to one of her school friends." She pulled away and went to pour herself a cup of tea.

And then, in the doorway, stood Jane. She *had* changed. Gone was the big hair, the midi skirts, the frilly blouses. She had parted her blonde hair in the middle, and it tumbled down her back. She wore green bell-bottoms, Doc Martens, a checked shirt. She wore little make-up. She was gorgeous. She hugged him. And there, now, was the scent of *Havoc* at her neck.

"You smell good," he found himself whispering in her ear. And he realised he was smiling absurdly.

Morning sunlight streamed through the kitchen window. Charlie and Jane had gone out with Paul and Fiona the night before, first to the village pub for a couple of drinks and then up to Blue Tor. The night had been mild and clear. Charlie had bought some bottles of light ale, which he had taken to the hill and shared with Jane as they lay in a field, staring up at the stars. They'd all talked about music and books and then Paul and Fiona had disappeared for a while.

Jane and Charlie had slowly swigged from their bottles, trying to make the drinks last while Charlie smoked his rollups and Jane smoked some cigarettes Fiona had given her. They'd talked about the stars and UFOs and time and space and music. Charlie had found her adorable. When Paul and Fiona finally returned, they had all walked slowly back to the village, Jane's arm through Charlie's. They'd stayed up late, playing games and drinking coffee, laughing and smoking. Eventually, they'd all gone to bed, Charlie dossing down, as usual, on the zed bed. He fell asleep with thoughts of Jane swimming foggily in his head.

Jane had woken Charlie with a mug of tea and now they were alone in the kitchen. Mr and Mrs Maas had gone to work and Paul and Fiona had gone into the village to buy milk, biscuits and bread. The sun shone on Jane's hair, illuminated one side of her oval face. She was making toast for them both and moved between the sink, the fridge and the grill. Charlie noticed how tall she'd grown in the last year, how graceful she was. Her red jeans accentuated her long legs; her lumberjack shirt was open over a white tee-shirt that clung to her breasts. Desire stabbed at him with an intensity he hadn't felt since he'd first fallen for Imogen. He wanted to take Jane in his arms and kiss her. But at that moment she handed him a plate full of buttered toast and asked if he wanted more tea. He still wasn't sure what Jane felt, and he was even less sure this was the right time to say anything to her about how he felt.

After breakfast, when Paul and Fiona had returned, Charlie and Jane suggested they could walk over to Torquay for the day. Paul and Fiona said they would stay behind; they needed to revise before the start of the new term, they said. A likely story, Charlie thought. Not that he minded – he would be alone with Jane. They walked out over the green fields that were speckled with orange, yellow and white, along footpaths, and between low hedges. Charlie was always aware of Jane beside him. They talked about nothing as they walked. Sometimes Jane would hang on Charlie's arm and laugh. They crossed a stile into a lane and headed down towards Cockington village. Jane put her arm through his and walked close to him, her body warm against his. They moved into the shade of trees and were dappled by sunlight.

Charlie could feel his pulse racing. He had to say something. He had to say something *now*. He stopped and turned to Jane. "I really, really, like you. I know we live a hundred miles apart. But can we go out together, in some way? We could... Oh, I don't know. I'll try to get down here as often as I can. The long summer holiday is nearly here. Surely we can..." He looked over her head, gazed blankly down the lane towards the thatched roofs of the village. It suddenly seemed absurd and he sounded, even to himself, vague. His heart still hammered inside. When he looked at Jane again, she smiled at him.

"Yes, of course, I'd love it," she said. "I wanted you to ask. I've been hoping you'd say something like this. I wanted you to say something last night, while we were on Blue Tor. And I thought you were going to say something this morning. But I stupidly asked if you had enough toast."

Charlie smiled. "Well, I was going to say something. You looked gorgeous in the sunlight."

"Making toast."

"Yes, even making toast."

Charlie kissed her. Their first kiss. It was delicious. "I know it's a bit crazy," he said. "But we can work something out, can't we?"

"Yes, we can work something out."

He took Jane in his arms and kissed her again.

And at that moment, and for that moment, he didn't think of Imogen at all.

11

For the next month, Charlie hardly thought about Imogen. He had revised for his exams and, when he wasn't revising, he had thought about Jane. Then the exams had finished, and he was free. The summer holiday stretched before him. He had headed down to Charlton to see Jane as soon as possible after term had ended and had been in Devon for a week now. He had even forgone a party at Mark's this weekend so he would have few more days with Jane. He wasn't even bothered that he'd missed an opportunity to be near Imogen.

The days were long and hot and the nights warm and clear. Charlie walked into the lounge at the Maas's house. The sunlight of a hot July day flooded the room. Jane was lying on the sofa, holding a book above her, reading. Charlie sat on the edge of the sofa and slid a hand under her loose white tee shirt. He ran it over the over the soft, warm skin of her belly. That he was allowed to do such a thing had made the summer even more splendid. He asked what she was reading.

"Still this," Jane said. She tilted the cover of the book towards him. She had started reading it a few days ago. It was _The Interrupted Journey_.

"You're becoming quite the ufologist," Charlie said. He leaned over and kissed her forehead.

"It's fascinating, Charlie! You really haven't read it?"

Charlie shook his head. "Not this one, no." He hadn't read many UFO books at all, despite spending so many nights on Copsehill. Even though he hoped there was some truth to the UFO stories, he thought most sightings were mundane – misidentifications, misperceptions, or hoaxes. He did know that Jane's book described the Betty and Barney Hill case, but he had never wanted to read it. He thought abduction stories were too fantastic. Why would aliens travel light-years to abduct and examine a couple of ordinary Americans?

Jane, though, had been excited to learn about abduction cases. She had asked Charlie what knew about them not long after he'd arrived. He had told her about the Antonio Villas Boas case, which had been described in one of the few UFO books he'd read. He remembered the case because the story amused him. The tale of the Brazilian farmer's sexual antics with a perfectly formed, blonde haired space beauty had fascinated Jane. And then, last night, Jane had talked about abductions again. She wondered if the aliens were trying to create an alien-human hybrid. Then she thought perhaps the aliens were trying to escape a dying world or were searching for some characteristic they lacked but which manifested itself in humans, such as love, free will, inventiveness, or soul.

Jane looked turned her attentions from the book she was reading and looked at Charlie seriously. "They inserted a needle into Betty's navel," she said. "Do you think they were harvesting eggs?"

"I don't know," Charlie replied, still lightly stroking Jane's stomach, relishing the feel of her skin against his fingertips.

"But what if they were? It's just like I was saying last night... They need something we have, something in our make-up. Some... some, oh, what's the word, some... genetic thing. I think we have something they need."

"You have something I need," Charlie said. He ran his hand around to the small of her back, leaned over and kissed her on the lips. Jane moved her arm around his shoulders; Charlie could feel the book pressing against his spine.

After a few moments, Jane pulled away. "When are you and Paul leaving?"

"Soon now. I came to say goodbye."

"Sorry, Charlie, I've been so absorbed in the book... I should have helped you pack."

"Don't worry, there wasn't much to pack. And that kiss was worth the wait."

Paul came into the room, saw Jane lying on the sofa and Charlie leaning over her. "I hope I'm interrupting something."

"Just saying goodbye," Charlie said.

"Is that what you call it?" Paul said. "We need to get on the road."

As Charlie stood, Jane grabbed his hand. "Come back soon."

Charlie pulled her up off the sofa and hugged her. "I undoubtedly will." They kissed again.

Paul wrinkled his nose. "That's quite enough of that."

Jane giggled. "Now you know how I feel when I see you and Fiona at it."

Charlie and Paul moved towards the kitchen to fetch their bags. Jane followed, her hand still in Charlie's. "When can I see you again, Charlie?"

"I'll hitch down in a couple of weeks' time."

She looked up into his eyes. "You'd better, or there'll be trouble." She gave him one final hug.

Charlie and Paul left the house and headed towards the main road. When they had put some distance between themselves and the house, Paul said, "So, are you over your obsession with Imo?"

"I think so. Yes," Charlie said.

"Fi tells me Jane is becoming very attached to you. I wouldn't want you to hurt her."

"I won't. I think she's a darling."

"As long as you're not doing this on the rebound."

"I never went out with Imo," Charlie pointed out.

"You thought a lot of her, though, didn't you? She's been with James for, what, a year or more now. And you were the first to fancy her.

"Stuart did."

"What?"

"Stu fancied her first."

"Well, give or take a few days. Anyway. It's a long time to be obsessed with somebody."

"Obsessed is a bit strong, isn't it?" Charlie said, knowing it to be true nonetheless.

"Oh, don't deny it, Charlie. Your letters used to be full of her. And you talked about her all the time."

"How would you know that?"

"Well, it was obvious when you visited. And when you phoned. And Stuart told me."

Bloody Stuart, Charlie thought. Always sticking his nose in. "Well, yes, but Stuart might be a little biased. He was vying for Imo's affections as well, remember," Charlie said.

"I know. But when she went out with James, Stu got over it."

Only because he continues to get Imo's affection. "Are you sure he's over it? Perhaps he's just trying to cause hassles. Stir up some shit."

"I trust him, " Paul said. Charlie raised an eyebrow. "Oh, I know he's a flirt," Paul continued. "But he's very open about it." Paul thought for a moment. "Look, here's the difference. When Imo went out with James instead of him, Stu wrote to me about it, whined about it, and when he visited, talked to Fiona and me about it. He got it all off his chest, you know? But you said very little at first. Then in your letters, you were very bitter about James, calling him a pot-head pixie and saying he drank too much."

"But... But..." Charlie stuttered, knowing he was about to deny Paul's assertions. "I didn't mind! Honestly!" he said. Although he knew he had minded, had said those things, had behaved in those ways. He was surprised – *disturbed* – to hear his obsessions reflected at him through Paul, who had been, so he thought, detached from events in Dereham.

"It was obvious to me," Paul said evenly, "that you'd been bent out of shape. I don't know... Perhaps it wasn't obvious to you. And then, suddenly, you stopped talking about James and Imo and how you'd lost out. You stopped wondering what it was that James had and you didn't. Instead, your letters were full of complaints about Stu, about how he and Imogen were still so close, how they hugged and were kissy-kissy all the time. On and on you went."

They'd reached the main road. Paul stuck out his thumb. Charlie could feel the heat of the sun bouncing back from the tarmac. "Yeah. Well, that's all over now," Charlie said, believing it at this moment to be true. "I like your little sis. Jane's fun. I like to be around her."

"Just be careful," Paul said. "I worry about her. She's young and you're her first serious boyfriend. Fiona thinks she could easily fall in love with you."

Charlie was suddenly angry. Everybody knew so much about him. Only he seemed ignorant of himself.

Paul looked Charlie up and down. "Though why my darling little sister should fall in love with an ugly freak like you is beyond my comprehension."

Charlie wondered if he *was* an ugly freak. Perhaps that's why Imogen had preferred James. But no – Jane liked him. He may be a freak, but not necessarily an ugly one. Perhaps Jane did love him. The enormity of it struck him. She was still only sixteen. What did love mean to a sixteen-year old? And did he love Jane?

A car stopped. Charlie and Paul took the offered lift to Ilminster.

12

When Paul opened the door to James's attic, he found Imogen walking to the bedroom dressed only in her underwear.

"Good evening," Paul said.

"Nice," Stuart said. "Haven't seen you like that in a while."

Imogen laughed. "Avert your eyes, you perv."

Paul and Stuart walked into the centre of the sitting room and put down the bags they'd been carrying. The bags contained the clothes, sandwiches and flasks of tea and coffee they'd brought with them for the skywatch tonight.

Charlie sat on the floor, toking on a joint. James's parents had gone to Salisbury for the day and weren't expected back until late. Paul was surprised Imogen dared walk around the room half-undressed in front of Charlie. But she knew Charlie and Jane were together now, so perhaps she felt more comfortable around him.

"What's with the naked ladies?" Stuart asked.

"Kate and Imo have been shopping all afternoon," James said. "We decided to, uh, roll a spliff or three while they were out."

Charlie handed the joint to Paul.

"You certainly seem relaxed," Stuart said.

"I hear I missed some excitement last weekend," Charlie said. "At Mark's party. There was a fight I hear."

"Oh, that," Stuart said. "Not much of a fight really. Jake and Mark squared up, but Simon soon sorted it out."

"Simon?" Paul said. "He does kung fu doesn't he?"

"He does. And he used it on Mark, so I hear." Stuart said.

"Did you see it?" Paul asked eagerly.

"Sadly not. Kate and I had gone for a walk and we missed it. Simon told me about it."

Imogen returned from the bedroom. "Julie fancies Simon even more now. He's even more manly than anybody ever knew."

"Julie fancies Simon?" Charlie said.

"And Simon fancies Julie," Imogen said.

"Well, well, well," Charlie said. "Love *is* in the air."

Imogen asked about Devon and Jane. Charlie told her what had happened there. Now Charlie was away from Jane, he seemed to like her even more, Paul thought. He could hear it in Charlie's voice. Perhaps he had been worrying about nothing.

"You don't have to be a Prophet to prophesy Charlie will soon get laid," James said.

"Oh, *James*," Imogen said reproachfully.

Paul's world tilted for a moment. He hadn't yet considered that possibility. "Oh, my word," he said. "Do you have to blurt it out just like that? My pure, darling, little sister and this hairy fiend?"

"Can't say I've really thought about it yet, either," Charlie said.

Paul considered that most unlikely. Charlie had said it only to mollify him.

"When it happens, it happens. If it does," Charlie added.

Now James had encouraged Paul to think about it, he knew that Charlie must undoubtedly have already thought about it. Charlie was still a virgin, and the possibility of sex was probably weighing heavily on his mind. Paul knew Jane remained a virgin. Perhaps he should have a word with her. Perhaps he should have a word with Charlie, come to that.

Imogen and Kate returned to the room. Kate twirled to show off the collarless shirt she'd bought. It was so long it looked like a dress.

"You look lovely, darling," Stuart said.

"Thank you," Kate said. She bent down and kissed him.

"What do you think about alien abductions?" Charlie asked James.

"The only way Brazilian farmers can get a shag is from aliens who bark like dogs."

Paul and Charlie giggled.

Imogen sighed. "Looks like we'll get little sense out of the boys tonight," she said to nobody in particular.

Stuart broke off from kissing Kate. "Hey, I'm straight."

"True enough. But you and Kate will probably sneak off into the fields and leave me with these stoners."

"What car are you getting?" Charlie asked James.

"An old Vauxhall Victor," James said.

"Car? What car?" Paul looked from James to Charlie and back to James again.

"Lambikins is taking his driving test soon," Imogen said. "He's buying a car on Monday."

"I've already got the money out," James said. "I hope I can get the price down if the guy selling it sees cash."

"How much?" Paul said.

"He's asking two hundred and fifty quid. I want to get him down to two hundred."

"Two hundred and fifty quid? I don't think I've seen that much money in my life."

James reached into his waistcoat and found his wallet, from which he removed a wad of notes. He waved it under Paul's nose. "Smell the wealth!"

"Money makes the world go around, the world go around," Kate sang. She looked at Imogen. "I think lambikins loves the money as much as he loves you."

James carefully put the notes back into his wallet. "It *is* a close-run thing, but I, uh, hesitate to create an invidious hierarchy."

Imogen thumped James's arm. James pretended to look hurt enough to warrant a kiss. While in the middle of his kiss, James blindly offered the joint to Charlie.

Charlie passed the joint to Stuart, who passed it immediately to Paul. The music stopped.

Stuart smiled at Paul. "It's like pass the parcel," he said." You have to smoke it now." He put another record on the deck.

Paul dragged on the joint. Charlie at him looked quizzically. "Do you think you'll remember the ritual?" Charlie asked.

"Why," Paul said. "Why wouldn't I?"

"You're getting stoned."

Paul passed the joint back to Charlie. "I'm not *that* stoned. I've only had a few puffs. I'm just trying to nudge open the doors of perception."

"What about you, James?" Charlie said. "What's your current state?"

James waved a dismissive hand. "Sober as a judge. I don't need to do much anyway," he said. "Just write down what's happening and prompt Paul if he forgets something."

"If he keeps puffing on that thing, he's bound to forget something," Charlie said.

Paul handed the joint to James. "You'll probably find yourself getting sucked into it anyway," he said to James. "You know a lot of the ritual."

"I hope so. I want to travel the path of Netzach, too."

"This ritual isn't going to be very exciting for us, is it?" Charlie said. "We won't see anything."

"I suppose not. But we'll return with a record of our visions that will *astound* you," Paul said.

"There'll be at least one disappointment," Stuart said, with a sly smile.

"And what might that be?" Charlie asked.

"There'll be no demons."

"Bah!" Charlie exclaimed. Then he grinned. "But we can always hope."

Paul looked at his watch. "We should get going."

Imogen, Kate and Charlie picked up their bags and went out through the door. Paul stood, but James grabbed his arm and held him back. "Fancy heightening the sense of ritual? I have some acid."

Paul shook his head. "No. No. It'd be too intense."

"Wimp, James said. "I'm going to drop a tab. I'm only the amanuensis, after all."

"Do you think this a good idea?" Stuart said. "You've been getting yourself into enough trouble with Imo as it is."

James looked at Stuart foggily. "Damn and blast. I forgot you were still here." He raised a finger to his lips. "Mum's the word, okay?" Stuart shrugged.

"I suppose it might be interesting to enter into an altered state of consciousness," Paul said. "Just a little. But I'd need something less mind-bending than acid. Do you have any hash?"

James rooted around in the back of a drawer. He pulled out a small block wrapped in tinfoil. Paul unwrapped it and broke off a piece. He popped it into his mouth and chewed. James looked at Paul, then dropped his tab. "I think we're ready," he said.

Now he was on the hill, Paul felt less than ready. He'd felt fine on the walk along the quiet, dark roads, only a little vague after toking on the joint. The hash he'd swallowed had worked its way into his bloodstream. The distant amber streetlights of the town had become jewel-like. He sat on the road, and breathed deeply, slowly relaxing. The day had been hot and the asphalt beneath him was still warm. A muggy breeze blew across the top of the hill. It was one of those rare nights when the coats they'd brought with them would be unnecessary. They'd be comfortable enough in their cheesecloth tops and tee-shirts. Charlie hadn't even bothered to make up a fire. Kate and Stuart had gone for a walk to the copse together, after Kate had made promises to protect him from aliens and elementals.

Paul looked at James. "How are you feeling?"

"Fine. Or as fine as anybody who's been smoking weed all day can feel," James replied. "And you?"

"The joint has had its effect. Now the hash is beginning to kick in, I think."

Paul looked around him. He'd been afraid, earlier in the day, that other skywatchers would be here tonight, but he and his friends were the only people on the hill. If they were alone now, then it was likely they would remain so for the rest of the night. Which was just as well, Paul thought. Kate and Stuart would most likely end up in a field somewhere making love, and he and James would soon start performing their ritual in another field. Charlie, meanwhile, was so stoned he would probably laugh at any attempt to involve him in a serious ufological conversation. It would be a weird situation for outsiders to suddenly find themselves in.

Kate and Stuart returned from the copse. "See anything?" Charlie asked. This, for no reason Paul could fathom, caused Charlie to start laughing. "See anything," Charlie said again, to himself. "Too funny, man."

"They weren't gone long enough to see anything," Paul said, which started Charlie laughing again. Paul also felt a desire to laugh. They really were stoned, he realised.

"It's too small to see in the dark anyway," Charlie added and laughed some more.

"Had to come back," said Stuart quietly. "There's a weird atmosphere up there tonight."

Charlie laughed again. "Weird atmosphere! Hah! Nonsense. There's nothing here. There are no elementals! There are no UFOs! It's all a figment of your imagination!"

"No way, man," Stuart insisted. "It's really weird up there. And I did see a small orange light."

Paul looked at Kate. "Did you see it?"

Kate shook her head. "It was gone when I looked."

"It was only there for a couple of seconds," Stuart said. "Hovering near the ground. Like a firefly."

"Perhaps it *was* a firefly," Charlie said.

"No," James said. "Not around here. Wrong environment."

"The atmosphere *was* weird," Kate said. "I've never really noticed that kind of thing before. Stu felt it first. And when he explained what he was feeling, I started to feel it too. And when he said he'd seen a hovering light, it freaked me out a bit."

"Bollocks." Charlie said. "You're just feeding off his imagination." He stood up. "I'm going up there by myself. I bet I don't feel a thing."

"Don't blame me if you get eaten by a gremlin," Stuart said.

Charlie strode off. "Huh. Atmospheres," he said, as he climbed over the gate. "Load of crap."

"He'll bump into a dryad one day," Paul said. "That'll freak him out."

Kate and Stuart came and sat with those that remained. Paul could hear Charlie whistling as he walked the path up to the copse. Paul turned to James. "I'm beginning to feel very stoned. If we're going to do this ritual, we'd better do it now."

James nodded. "Yeah, good idea. I'm feeling nice and... relaxed."

Imogen leaned over and kissed James. "Be careful out there."

"We're only going to the field over..." James paused and looked at Paul. "Where are we going?"

Paul pointed in the direction of the field they'd chosen when they'd arrived. If James had already forgotten where it was then he must be more stoned than either of them knew. Paul stood up. James also stood.

"Woh!" James said and put his arms out at his side to keep his balance.

Imogen looked at James with concern. "Are you okay, lambikins?"

James rubbed Imogen's head. "Indeed I am, my love. We'll be back soon. Having looked into the abyss, we'll return with secrets of a most abstruse, arcane and occult nature." He paused. *"Abstruse, arcane and occult nature."* He laughed. "What a great phrase."

The field was surrounded by a low hedge, into which a gate was set. When Paul reached the gate, he heard a rustling in the bushes. "Just was well Stu isn't here, he'd have pissed himself by now," he said.

Paul and James moved slowly along the hedge toward the sound and finally reached its source, although they still couldn't make out the cause of it. James found his lighter from his pocket and lit it. The rustling noises increased. In the flickering light, Paul could see a blackbird, hanging upside down in the hedge, its leg caught and snapped in twisted branches. Paul examined the bird more carefully and saw that it also had an injured wing, which hung down uselessly beside it.

"It's in a bad way," James whispered. "We should put it out of its misery."

"I've never killed a bird," Paul replied. "It's not something I have experience of." He reached into the hedge, feeling for the knot of branches that had caught the bird's leg. "Hold your lighter over here, James." The bird had stopped struggling, perhaps in response to their presence, perhaps because it was exhausted. Paul extricated it and held it delicately, cupped in his hands. "How do we kill it?"

"Break its neck, I suppose," James said.

"That's easy to say. What do I do?"

"I don't know. We never learned that in Rural Studies. We could leave it beside the hedge to die, I suppose. Who knows, it might recover."

Paul willing agreed. He had no desire to break the bird's neck. He bent down and gently put the bird in the thick grass at his feet.

"Mind you," James said. "You do have your ritual knife with you, right? You could cut its throat."

"I could, I suppose," Paul said, uncertainly. He doubted that he *actually* could.

They stood without speaking for a moment. Paul looked down at the small, dark, twisted shape, barely visible at the bottom of the hedge.

"I've had another thought." James said quietly. "We could use it in the ritual. The bird. We could use it. It would be kind to the bird *and* add power to the ritual."

"Sacrifice it, you mean," Paul said. James nodded. Paul said nothing for a moment, thinking over James's suggestion. Then he said, "It's a bit dark, isn't it? A bit black?"

"Oh, I don't know... After all, sex and blood have always, uh, been associated with magic. This bird seems to have, uh, appeared at the right time. It's not as if we chose it for this purpose. We wouldn't have thought of it if we hadn't found it. So, it's not as if we had a black magic ritual in mind, is it."

"I'm still not sure," Paul muttered.

"Perhaps it's a sign."

Paul considered this. "Perhaps it is." He sighed. "I do believe in signs and significant coincidences."

"I know you do."

Paul found himself warming to the idea. The bird's presence here might well be a sign. "And if we do use its blood, the bird dies quickly, rather than slowly and in pain. And we add power to the ritual."

Paul reached down and picked up the bird, cradled it in his hand and stroked its head, shushing it as he and James pushed their way through the unlocked gate. They sat cross-legged in the centre of the field, facing back towards the gate, looking over the copse and the ridge connecting Copsehill to Red Post Hill. Paul put the bird down on the grass in front of him.

Paul might have accepted using the bird in the ritual, but he was still loath to the kill it himself. "I feel a bit squeamish about this," he said.

"I'll do it," James said. "I don't mind. Give me the knife."

Paul took the knife from a pocket in his corduroy jacket and passed it to James, who raised the knife rather theatrically and stabbed the bird through the breast. He then cut the bird's throat – although, as the blade of the knife was blunt, he sawed at it rather than slit it. Paul began to wish James hadn't started this. James finally lifted the bird by the tail. Small drops of blood, shining and black, dropped onto the grass in front of them. The blood amounted to very little, and Paul wondered if all the stabbing and sawing had been worth it. He stood, took the knife back from James, and used it to draw an imaginary circle around the drops of blood that were now barely visible in the darkness. He then drew a protective circle around the two of them.

"What do we do first?" James asked.

"We need to concentrate and visualise the temple of Malkuth," Paul said.

"Didn't I read somewhere that you should only visit paths in the correct order? You should start at Malkuth and work your way through the paths individually?"

Paul sighed. "Yes, you probably read that in the letters I sent you. I've already worked the paths below Netzach. I've been preparing for today. Do keep up."

"Yeah, you did tell me. Sorry, man. Just want to make sure we do it properly."

Of course they would do it properly, Paul thought. *I'm not a neophyte.* "I've already worked my to Malkuth," he said. "Now we need to work the paths towards Netzach. We'll start at the temp of Malkuth. So, now we need to visualise a temple. I'll guide you with the symbolism up to Netzach. As I'm the one performing the ritual, nothing should happen to you, but you should be able to see things, visualise them, feel them."

"Yes," James said. "I remember now. Get on with it."

Paul closed his eyes. He felt dizzy and could still see, behind his eyelids, as some dim, unreal shadow, the shape of the bird, held by its tail, dripping gobbets of blood from its throat. He wondered if James could still feel the tail feathers in his hand, could also still see the blood falling. Paul thought he'd better sit down. He shook his head and concentrated on visualising the temple. Suddenly it appeared, large and shining, like the New Jerusalem he'd once seen in a photograph of a tapestry that showed it descending before John of Patmos. The shape was the same as his imagined temple, all turrets and towers and crenellation, but he invested it with colour and texture, pure gold, clear glass, and a shining brilliance. A large wooden door was already open to receive him. For a moment, the blackbird's yellow beak and yellow-ringed eye appeared at the doorway and then were gone.

"We need to walk towards the temple," Paul said quietly. "When we're in front of it, I'll vibrate the godname of Malkuth." He felt the ritual knife in his hand and wondered why he was still holding it. He put it on the grass in front of him, and then folded his hands in his lap.

Paul imagined himself walking towards the temple, which shone with a brilliant white light. Each step seemed to take a moment longer than the last. Then he looked up at the shining temple. He swayed in front of it, taking in its gold and glass walls for some time. Then he growled, in the strange way he'd learned for ritual work, "Adonai ha-Aretz."

Paul had now to ascend the temple steps. The steps appeared enormous to him. How wondered if he would ever climb them. *I'm too stoned for this.* But he did climb them, reaching the fourth step at last. He growled, "Sandalphon," the name of the archangel Malkuth. He could feel a power growing inside him, an expansive feeling of warmth, of connection. He felt dizzy again, however, and wondered if it was because of that power. He put his hands, which had been folded in his lap, down on the grass beside him. He could feel, it seemed, every blade beneath his palm, each imprinting its contour into his skin, each vein in each blade limned with precision across his flesh.

Another four steps appeared, the last steps to the door of the Temple. Again, Paul wondered how he would ever mount the steps that loomed over him. Again, somehow, he did, with an ease that belied the size of each step. Now, he needed to become aware of the door, to take notice of its form. He became lost in admiration of the carving and texture, and of each long grain, before he remembered he must now vibrate three times the name of the angel choir of Malkuth. "Ashim," he said. "Ashim, Ashim."

The door opened. He knew what he should see inside – the temple filling with fiery creatures, creatures of energy and light. He could see, this, yes, he could, but among those creatures he could also see a dark shape moving, a black, feathered form, a broken-winged bird, its head canted at an odd angle, a bright red slash across its neck. He shook his head gently, trying to shake away the image of the bird. He concentrated instead on the light-forms. He tried to shut the black bird from his mind.

He focused his attention on just one creature, all intense white light, and entered the temple. The creature poured its energy into him and for a moment he was filled with warmth, with healing power. He looked around and could no longer see the black bird. The room was bright. Around the walls were doors, above which were letters from the Hebrew alphabet. He needed to leave through one of these doors, the door corresponding to the next path, and then follow that path to another temple. In that temple, they would perform a similar ritual, exit through another door, and then follow the path to Netzach. In a whisper, Paul described for James the door he should head towards. In his imagination, Paul crossed the floor of the hall. The creatures of light were around him.

Yet he sensed darkness following him.

Charlie had returned. He'd felt nothing in the copse. There had only been trees, and the wind through the branches. "I told you it was all bollocks," he said. "There's no mysterious atmosphere. Nothing out of the ordinary."

"How long will James and Paul be?" Imogen said.

Stuart shrugged. "They'll be a while yet, I think. I don't know much about the actual detail of the ritual. I do know Paul will have to work the paths from Malkuth to the temple at Yesod and from there take the path to Netzach."

Charlie sat down beside Stuart. "That's not the way I'd go. I'd take the B-roads to Malkuth, then around the Yesod bypass and take the

A666 to Netzach. Anything else is madness and you get caught in holiday traffic.

Stuart laughed. "Once Paul reaches the path, he should meet a guide who'll take him to the temple at Netzach. He'll enter the temple there and meet the shining ones."

"The *shining* ones. Wow!" Kate enthused. "Sounds like fun."

"It probably is," Stuart conceded. "But it takes a lot of practice and preparation. I know Paul has been working the paths to Malkuth for a while. But to do this ritual with James, he has to work the path to Yesod, which he only did a couple of weeks ago."

Imogen removed her denim jacket – she had reluctantly foregone her striped blazer on this warm, dusty night – and laid it on the grass beside her. "James has also been learning the ritual and all the symbolism, so he could follow Paul and prompt him if he forgot what he was doing."

"It might take them an hour or two," Stuart said. "It'll depend on what they find in the temples and on the paths."

Charlie nodded as he rolled a cigarette. "And don't forget they'll have to do the banishing ritual before and after. That'll also take some time."

"I hope nothing happens," said Imogen.

"What could possibly happen?" Charlie said. "It's all in their heads. Just like Stuart's *atmospheres*."

"You're just insensitive to elemental forces," Stuart replied.

"I just don't get freaked out by spooky stories."

"You felt nothing?"

"Nothing."

"I need a pee," Imogen said. She stood and dusted herself down.

"I'll come with you," Kate said.

"You don't need our protection, do you girls?" Stuart said.

"Or perhaps assistance?" Charlie said. "I'll warm my hands up."

"No, we'll be fine," Kate said. "It'll give us a chance to talk behind your backs."

Imogen and Kate walked away, talking quietly and then climbed over the gate and disappeared behind the hedge.

"So, you and Jane are getting on great," Stuart said. "Excellent news."

"She's cool. I really, really like her," Charlie said.

"Glad you've got your shit together."

Charlie looked at the fire for a moment. "I was talking to Paul about you," he said.

"Yeah? What have I done now?"

"You've been bad-mouthing me."

"What? I haven't been *bad-mouthing* you. I might have talked to Paul about you. It's what friends are for. To talk about relationships and... shit."

Charlie sighed. "Ah, I just get pissed off with you all sometimes. You all think you know so much about me. About my problems. Paul had a go at me when we hitched up yesterday."

"Why?"

"He wanted to be sure I wasn't leading Jane on. That I wasn't..." Charlie looked across at Stuart. "That I wasn't on the rebound from Imo." He laughed mirthlessly. "I don't need you all reminding me what an idiot I've been."

"Well... He knows what you've been like over the last few months. We all do. We've all been concerned."

Charlie felt the need to restrain himself. He could feel anger rising again. Only a few weeks had passed since he and Stuart had argued about Imogen and Jane on this same hill. He didn't want a repeat performance. He also didn't fancy another slap. Not that Stuart would catch him out like *that* again. "Yeah, well you don't have to worry any more. I've got Jane now and I'm really happy."

"Then I'm really happy for you, man."

"So, are you going to shut up about all this Imo stuff now? I don't really care *that* much about her, you know." Charlie hoped he spoke the truth, that Jane would work some magic on him that could stop the river, dam the stream and dry the source. He did know he spent less time now thinking about Imogen, if only because he spent more time thinking about Jane. However, he also knew that, sometimes, Imogen still leaked through the dam.

"I really like Kate," Stuart said. "I wonder if I'm falling in love," he mused.

Good old Stuart, Charlie thought. *He wants to change the subject as much as I do.*

*

Half an hour later, Stuart had wrapped himself around Kate, who dozed on the grassy bank. Imogen fretted about James. Then she curled up behind Stuart for a while, with her arms around both him and Kate, which Charlie found vaguely disturbing. Nobody said anything for a while. Then Imogen stood and paced the road.

"I'm grumpy," Imogen said.

"Aww, no," Kate said. "What's wrong?"

"James. I'm worried, because I know he's pissed. He brought more brandy with him than even I knew. I thought he'd brought a quart to share around. But he didn't. He brought two."

"Well, that isn't so bad, is it?" Charlie said. "We've all been drinking, except Stu. It's been shared around."

"The sharing bottle isn't even finished yet. He's been drinking from his own bottle, while he offered the other bottle to you guys."

"It's no big deal, is it? Not tonight? We're all chilled out, having a laugh."

"Yes we are, but that's not the point. I asked him not to get smashed tonight. I wanted the evening to be pleasant and relaxed. I wanted to not worry."

"There's no need to worry-" Charlie began.

"Ah, shit," Imogen said. "You guys don't understand what it's like."

She walked off quickly, towards a gate, and climbed across it into a field.

Charlie didn't know what to say. Nor, it seemed, did Kate and Stuart. They leaned up against the grass bank and looked at the stars. Eventually, the three of them began chatting about music. Kate drifted into a light sleep.

When Imogen returned, she sat beside Stuart, and played with the glass bead on her necklace. She was still worrying about James. He and Paul had been gone for over an hour, nearly an hour and a half. "How much longer do you think they'll be?" she said.

Stuart spoke quietly. He was trying not to wake Kate and to reassure Imogen. "I don't know. It'll be all right. Don't worry."

"How can I not worry? James is such a... prick... sometimes," she said. Charlie was surprised at the suppressed anger in her voice. "And I'm sure he's tripping. Just before they went off to do their stupid ritual, he looked really spaced out."

Stuart said nothing. His very silence roused Imogen's suspicions. "Did he drop a tab?"

Stuart shrugged. As a reply, it was ambivalent. Charlie knew Stuart would remain loyal to James no matter how close he and Imogen had become over the years; James was, after all, his oldest friend.

Imogen sighed. "Sometimes I wonder if James cares about me at all." She walked away again, back into the fields.

Ten minutes or so passed. Stuart began to doze. Charlie decided to revisit the copse. He told Stuart where he was going. Stuart mumbled something in reply. There was no sign of Imogen. He climbed over the gate and walked slowly up the track.

Paul had reached, in his imagination, the path of Netzach. He'd felt, as he worked the paths, James's reassuring presence beside him. There was no doubt, however, that the hash was working strongly on him. The colours he imagined were more vibrant than usual, images had more clarity and the imaginary world seemed more real. He wondered if James was really here with him, whether they'd now crossed some threshold and were in some place where reality and imagination had merged. If he were to look over his right shoulder, would he find James there, walking with him? Yet to look over his shoulder, to look out into the real world to see if James was there, on the grass, rather than here, in his imagination, would take a determination he was unable to summon, and would also involve leaving this bright, clear world he'd created with such effort.

Charlie began to feel uneasy. The chalk track glowed faintly white ahead of him. The further he walked, the more freaked-out he felt. It was just dope paranoia, he thought. He walked a few more yards, and then realised he'd walked more yards than he'd imagined. He stopped walking. For a moment, everything went very dark and very quiet. He started walking, and again found himself further along the track than he imagined he should be. He knew what was happening. He was blacking out. He'd drunk nearly all the other quart of brandy – Kate had only taken a nip or two, and Paul a few slugs – and smoked at least three joints today. He stopped walking and tried to get his bearings. He thought he must be halfway up the track.

Paranoia scrabbled at Paul. He had an unsettling feeling something had gone wrong. At some point, somewhere between James sawing at the blackbird's throat and then beginning their journey along the paths of the Kabbalah, they – or rather, he – had forgotten something, had missed a path, or omitted some important element of the ritual. Yet recalling how they had arrived here, the steps they'd taken since leaving their friends at the gates, was difficult. Paul wanted to move on, to meet the guardian, to move this world, the world of his own creation, forward. The path had formed before him, and he began to craft the temple to which the path would lead him. His head dropped forward for a moment. The world whirled around him. Then he remembered that he was a magician, an occultist, no longer a neophyte but an initiate, and that success came from the application of *will*. Discipline, he remembered, was the key. He willed himself to lift his head and look along the path, tried to remember what he was waiting for.

The guardian. I'm waiting for the guardian to escort me to the temple.

There was movement in the distance. A form manifested from the fabric of the darkness in which he stood, an emerging shape on the glittering road to the temple. The form became solid and took on an unexpected shape – part man, part bird. Paul wondered if he confused memory and reality, but then recalled that this was not reality, this was controlled imagery. Images returned to him forcefully – the knife in James's hand, James stabbing at the black bird, James sawing at its throat, and the blood in the circle before him. Paul considered the nature of the creature he had created. It seemed to have been shaped in the form of the angel he'd expected, but also by his memory of the bird, its yellow-ringed eye staring at him as it died. The creature approached and was soon so close Paul could see the fully-formed beak, the downy head and the heavily-muscled arms protruding from an amber and orange tunic that fell from feathered shoulders – a creature that was more cruel raven than gentle blackbird.

*

Charlie slowly sagged down onto the chalk. He wondered what Imogen and Stuart might be doing. She'd looked so comfortable spooning Stuart and Kate. The image kept returning to him. Each time he reimagined that moment of intimacy between the three of them, he found himself disturbed. Kate always faded away, leaving only Imogen pressed up behind Stuart, shaping into him, her arms around him.

Paul knew he must challenge the guardian, ask its name. He finally summoned the energy to do so. The creature seemed reluctant to speak at first, and then, Paul thought, looked sly before saying his name. Orev Zarak. He would be Paul's guide now, he said. Paul knew the name and felt some relief at that. He knew the name was a part of the world of this path. Yet his confidence was failing him. He was tired and dizzy. Cold fingers of paranoia continued to scratch at him.

He remembered James had also learned the paths, the symbols and the names. "James? The guardian... Who is the guardian?"

There was no answer.

"James? James?"

There was still no answer. Paul dared open his eyes to find James. Even in the darkness, he could see James staring into the circle they'd imagined in front of them, transfixed by the small dead body that lay there still. "Is it Orev Zarak, James?"

"You see him too?" James whispered.

Paul could hardly concentrate now. He was very stoned. For a moment he blacked out, a brief, disquieting and disorienting span of nothingness that passed quickly and was suddenly replaced by clarity, the azure of the night sky and stars. He remembered James had asked if he could see someone, or something.

"What can you see?" Paul asked.

"Orev Zarak. I see Orev Zarak. In the circle."

Darkness came again for Paul, followed by a startling image of the path he could still see in his mind and the raven-headed angel standing over him, close now, tall, very tall, looking down at him with a darkly glittering bird's eye. He thought he was falling and gripped at the dry grass to steady himself, knowing he'd done something wrong.

"The circle!" James suddenly said. There was fear in his voice. "It's broken!"

Paul wondered why James's voice carried such alarm. He opened his eyes and found, oddly, that he was looking at the zenith of the sky. He understood then that he was on his back. He was vaguely aware of James at the periphery of his vision.

James moaned. "Oh no! No! The circle *is* broken! It's broken!"

Charlie shook his head. The world had become black and quiet for a moment. He looked towards the copse, the canopy of which was just visible over the brow of the hill. He blacked out again.

Paul managed to lever himself upright with one arm – one eye closed, one open – only by summoning his last reserves of will. He was surprised to see an enormous white light, larger and brighter than he'd ever seen, somewhere between him and the gate. The light was intense, and he shut his eyes against it, immediately falling onto his back again.

Charlie opened his eyes. There was a dazzling light above the trees.

Paul could hardly remember why he and James were here, what they'd been doing. Another moment of blackness, of dark nothingness, of no thought, and then after-images of the light, the path, Orev Zarak. He thought he remembered James saying the circle had been broken, but what circle?

"He's coming for me," James said, anxiously. "He's out! He's out of the circle!"

Blackness came again, washed over Paul, and submerged him.

When he finally struggled to the surface, he heard James whispering something, all confusion. "The light! The light! Orev Zarak. Coming for me. So bright! So big!"

Paul thought he heard soft footsteps in the grass. There was an image of a beaked head. Orev Zarak. Then he passed out.

*

Charlie was running. He was frightened, but he wasn't sure why. He vividly remembered Imogen and Stuart entangled somehow. He remembered a bright light. His vision filled with colliding images and after-images of something and everything. He blacked out again while running and returned to himself only when he crashed into the rusty white metal gate at the bottom of the track. He climbed over it and ran towards the glowing fire. Imogen was walking up the road, returning from wherever she had been. Stuart and Kate were still lying together on the grass bank.

Charlie almost shouted. His voice was loud, excited, breathless. "Are you okay? Is everything all right?"

"Charlie?" It was Imogen's voice. "What's up, Charlie, what's going on?"

Stuart sat up now. "Calm down, Charles. What's up? Is it James?"

"Didn't you see it?"

"See what?" Imogen said.

Charlie twisted his head from side to side, looked wildly around the sky. "The UFO!"

Imogen glanced up at the sky, puzzled. "What UFO?"

"The UFO, over there!" Charlie turned and pointed at the ridge between Copsehill and Red Post Hill behind them.

Stuart turned and looked toward the hill. "What are you on about, man?"

"A bloody UFO!" Charlie exclaimed. He pointed again. "Over there!"

Kate sat up then, rubbing her eyes. "I didn't see anything," she said. "I've been snoozing."

Charlie turned to Imogen. "Did you see it? Did you see the UFO?"

"No, Charlie. I didn't see it. Calm down!" Imogen said.

"But it was so big and bright, man! How could you not see it?"

"I was lying in a field, staring at the stars over Derebury."

"Ah, shit, you were looking in the wrong direction," Charlie said.

"When did you go to the field?" Stuart said.

"While you two were sweetly dozing," Imogen said.

Stuart looked into the sky again, and then at Charlie. "What did it look like?"

"It came up from behind the ridge and hovered in the sky. At first it was just a bright, white light. But after a few moments, the lights started making patterns, turning on and off. I tried to follow the patterns, to make sense of them, but they seemed random. The lights all came on again and they stayed like that for a minute or two, then suddenly, the UFO just vanished–" Charlie clicked his fingers. "Like that. As if it had suddenly been sucked into a different dimension, or something."

"You're not having us on, are you Charlie?" Stuart asked.

"No. No way. It was fantastic."

Charlie paced backwards and forwards excitedly on the road, gesticulating as he described the UFO. When he finished talking, he sat on the grassy bank next to Imogen. "I can't believe I've finally seen one."

"Are you sure it wasn't a plane, or something sent up by the army?" Stuart asked.

Charlie shook his head. "We've been coming up here for years. There are no lights that could fool us. Take it from me, this was weird."

"Hey, I believe you, Charlie. You're the biggest sceptic of us all. If it impressed you, it must have been something strange."

Charlie began to roll a cigarette. "It was. I'm a bit freaked out to be honest with you. You know me, Stu. I'm always wandering up to the copse, telling you how pathetic you are. But sometimes when I go up there, I'm not as confident as I make out. And when I saw that...thing."

There was silence for a moment.

"When you *came to?*" Imogen said. "You were unconscious?"

"Completely out of it."

Imogen grabbed Paul's arms. "So where is James?"

Paul shook his head, then ran across the road to the hedge at the top of the bank and began to retch again. Imogen looked at Stuart.

"He's probably gone for a walk to the copse," Stuart said.

Imogen peered into the dim dawn light around her, looking for James. Paul returned to them. "Did James eat some hash too?" Imogen asked.

"No, he didn't. He–" Paul paused. "Well, he dropped a tab."

"I thought he did," Imogen said. "The silly little shit."

Imogen would be mad, Charlie thought. She didn't mind him smoking a bit of weed, even eating some hash, but she'd always been wary of acid.

"We'd better look for him," Imogen said.

"I'll look after Paul," Kate said.

Charlie, Stuart and Imogen climbed over the gate onto the track and headed towards the copse. Where they could, they spread out into unfenced fields. The sun had risen above the Plain and suffused the fields in watery yellow light. Mist drifted across the floor of the combes. As they neared the copse, Charlie peered into the trees, but there was no movement, no sound. They circled the copse and explored adjacent fields, but there was still no sign of James. They walked back down the path to the gates in silence, and found Paul, still pale, leaning against the grass bank.

"Where's Kate?" Stuart asked.

"She also looking for James," Paul said.

"You try that field," Charlie said to Imogen. "I'll try over there."

"I'll stay here," Stuart said. He looked at Paul. "I'll see if I can get some sense out of this berk."

Half an hour later, they met up again by the dozing Paul. They wondered what they should do. Stuart suggested they wait. They sat near the gates for another half an hour. They said little. Charlie desperately wanted to talk about his UFO but sensed that now was not the time.

Paul stirred. "Is James back yet?"

Imogen rolled the faience bead between finger and thumb. "No, he's not."

Kate put an arm around Imogen. "If he's tripping, he could have gone anywhere. Don't worry. It's a warm night. Once he comes down, he'll find his way home."

Paul was dozing against the bank again.

"Why don't you take Paul home," Charlie said to Stuart. He looked at Imogen and Kate. "In fact, why don't you all go home." Imogen was, he knew, becoming very worried. "Look Imo, James might have gone back to the house. You go and check there. I'll take a look around the fields again and join you later."

"But it's really early," Imogen said. "James's parents might not be awake, and if James isn't there, what will I say when I wake them up?"

Stuart put an arm around Imogen. "Hey Imo, stay calm. You have a key. I know you do, James cut one for you in case he ever lost his when he was drunk."

"I can't just walk into somebody else's house."

"Yes, you can. Mr and Mrs Sands really like you. They'll understand if you tell them James went for a walk or something. They might not even be up yet. And James might be there anyway."

"Yes, yes, you're right." Imogen breathed deeply. "We'll go back to the house." Imogen looked at Paul. "You'd better take him straight back to your place and see if you can get any sense out him."

They packed their bags, and then wandered slowly away down the road back to Dereham. Stuart turned and looked back at Charlie. "Good luck," he called out. Charlie waved, then climbed over the stile and walked back towards the copse, hoping he wouldn't black out again, hoping and fearing he might see the light again.

13

Charlie rang the doorbell at the Sands' house. It was only eight in the morning, but James's parents normally woke early. Imogen opened the door.

"Oh, it's you, Charlie." Imogen said, disappointedly. "Come on in." Kate came out of the lounge and into the hallway. "Well?" Imogen asked

"No sign of him," Charlie said.

Imogen frowned and her body sagged. She turned and led Charlie and Kate to the kitchen, where she made coffee. Charlie slumped wearily onto one of the stripped pine dining chairs around the breakfast table.

"We tried to talk to Paul on the way home," Imogen said. "But he was still stoned and rambled a lot. He told us how real the temples had been in his mind, and that he'd met a guide. As if we cared." She tapped a spoon on the back of her hand, thinking. "Paul seemed confused about the guide. He babbled about it being the wrong guide, about how he couldn't remember the name that should have been spoken. He still can't remember. What does it all mean?"

"I don't know," Charlie said. "Does it matter? It's all happening in their heads anyway. None of it is real."

"Paul remembers having blackouts," Imogen said.

"Blackouts?" Charlie said.

"Yes," Kate said. "He said he kept having brief moments of unconsciousness."

"Which means he can't remember everything," Imogen added. "His memory is confused."

"How are the parents?"

"They weren't up when I arrived," Imogen said. "Thankfully. When they did get up, we fobbed them off with a story."

Charlie yawned. "I need to see Stuart, find out if Paul remembers anything else." He gave Imogen and Kate a hug and left the house. He set off towards Stuart's house. A thunderstorm had moved over the town. The morning light was murky. Fat raindrops splashed against him. He turned up the collar of his jacket as lightning briefly lit the fronts of the houses and thunder boomed around the hills.

When Charlie arrived at Stuart's house, he was greeted by Stuart's father, who was, even at this early hour, in the garage, working on his car. "Good morning, Charlie. Stu's in the kitchen. Go around the back."

Charlie went through the back door, which gave onto the dining room. Stuart sat at the table, drinking tea. The house seemed quiet.

"Where's your mum?" Charlie asked.

"Gone around to see Gran," Stuart said. He stood and made a cup of tea for Charlie.

"Brothers?"

"One still asleep, the other was out at a party last night. We're not expecting to see him until this afternoon."

"Good," Charlie said. He felt they should discuss James's disappearance discreetly.

Stuart handed a mug of tea to Charlie. "Did you find James?" he asked.

Charlie shook his head. "Thanks. No, not yet. How's Paul?"

"Asleep now. Mum made him a fried egg, which he ate, but then puked up about ten minutes later. He drank some tea, though, then said he was going to bed. He looked pretty shitty, to be honest."

"Did he say anything about last night?"

"He was still trying to remember what they did. He had blackouts."

"Yes, Kate told me."

"He was having these... momentary... blackouts before he finally crashed out completely. They seem to have muddled him."

"In what way?"

"He's just not clear about what they did. He knows he reached some of the temples. He met the guardians and beings of light and power."

"He knew that was going to happen. When I was in Devon he gave me a rough outline of the ritual."

"He's still slightly stoned, so he's not being particularly... um... lucid. I'll tell you what, though, he's very worried they did something wrong."

"What could he do wrong?"

"I've been thinking about it. If they both freaked out, they might have forgotten to do the banishing ritual at the end."

"Is that serious?"

"I guess it is, if you believe in all this nonsense."

"Did he say anything about the UFO?"

"Well, yes and no. He did see a bright light. From what I could make out from his babblings, it would have been in the same place as the light you saw."

"But?"

"Well, he was doing a ritual," Stuart said. "So he associated the light with a guardian or a shining one."

"Or he might have seen my UFO and got freaked out by it."

Stuart frowned at Charlie, his eyes narrow. "Yeah, maybe."

"What's up?"

"You weren't trying to wind us up last night? Nobody else saw your UFO. You're the biggest sceptic of us all. It's all a bit..." Stuart waved his hands around. "You aren't playing a trick on us that's got out of hand, are you?"

"What do you think?"

"I don't know Charlie, you tell me."

"I did see something. I'm certain. Don't forget Paul saw a light too. I think he saw my UFO."

"Oh, I don't know. You both say you saw lights. And, I must admit, I'm more inclined to believe you both saw a UFO than he saw a demon. Although..." Stuart paused, thinking.

"What?" Charlie asked.

"Perhaps you both saw Paul's *shining one*. Perhaps he objectified it. Made it real somehow. Perhaps it became a part of your reality."

Charlie shook his head. "No. The UFO seemed to rise up from behind the ridge. His guardian or whatever should have appeared in his circle of power, shouldn't it?"

"Yes, I think so. So, if you both saw a light, it must have been your UFO, I suppose."

There was a tired lull in the conversation. Charlie knew he needed to sleep. He looked at his watch. It was still only nine thirty. Charlie squeezed his palms into his eyes. "I'm knackered, Stu. How are you managing to keep going?"

"I got an hour's kip after I put Paul in bed."

Hailstones rattled against the window. The thunder still growled. Charlie looked out of the window. "I don't fancy walking back home in this."

"Go and sleep on the front room sofa," Stuart said. "Dad won't be going in there with his oily hands. Mum won't be back for a couple of hours. And I doubt Andy will be out of bed for some time."

"Good idea," Charlie said. "I'd better phone my mum. I haven't been home yet."

"Go ahead. Get some shuteye."

"I will... Thanks."

Charlie went to the hallway, where he phoned home. His mother answered. He didn't mention that James was missing. He then went to the front room and sat on the sofa. He heard the low voice of Stuart's father talking in the kitchen, the clinking of mugs, the click of the electric kettle as it was switched on.

Charlie nursed his own secret concerns. He couldn't remember whole passages of the previous night. He hadn't lost consciousness, he thought, not completely, but like Paul he had suffered short, sporadic blackouts. He'd lost time. He had shared two or more joints at James's house, and James had rolled him at least one more on Copsehill. He had drunk a great deal of the Martell. Now he thought about it, he was surprised he had managed to remain sensible and vaguely upright. But long passages of empty time had passed during the night. He did remember feeling paranoid. He'd been walking up the path to the copse just before he seen the UFO. He'd been suddenly frightened of Stuart. Why? He remembered collapsing onto the track. Stuart and Kate had been curled into each other, on the grass bank, dozing. Then Imogen had turned to them and hugged herself into Stuart. Charlie wondered whether, if Jane had been there, she would have left his side and joined the other girls, lying with Stuart, her arms around him.

He recalled odd feelings. There had been fluttering in his chest, tension, breathlessness. Between the blackouts, there had also been irrational anger, jealousy and fear; he could remember thinking that Stuart was some kind of a sexual daemon, a minor god, like Pan, or Priapus, which was ridiculous, of course. He remembered trying to stand then, his heart heavy, about to walk to the copse. And then... He remembered nothing except the light in the sky. Then he was back at the gates, talking to the others, about James being missing, with no memory of how he came to be there. And then... He couldn't remember anything again, not until later, when he'd thrown up in the copse, alone, after the others had gone home.

What had happened during that missing time? When Stuart had asked Charlie if he'd really seen a light, whether he was having them on, he'd felt the world fall from under him. Because what had he *really* been running from? He was no longer sure. He *thought* he'd been running away from a light. He was certain he *had* seen a light. He would hold onto that. *I was frightened by a light.* He wished, though, he could remember more.

He lay down then, on the sofa, his head on an orange cushion. Rain pattered against the window. Lightning flashed through his closed eyes. He found himself counting the seconds between flashes and rumbles. Somewhere between a flash and a rumble, he fell asleep.

14

James had still not returned. Imogen knew she had to say something to James's parents. First, though, she needed to get the story straight. However, when she talked through what had happened again with Kate, it all sounded so ridiculous. Occult rituals, acid, guardians, and temples of light. She couldn't explain all that to Mr and Mrs Sands.

Kate on the kitchen table, frowning. "Do James's parents know he uses drugs?"

"Well, they might suspect he smokes dope," Imogen said. "But they probably don't know about the acid."

"Did you know about it?"

"I knew he took it sometimes," Imogen said. "I didn't like it. I don't mind him smoking a bit of pot. But I don't like acid. I thought he'd stopped."

"Did you ask him to?"

"Yes. But I wasn't going to stop him if he really wanted to do it." She sipped her coffee. "Anyway, whenever I mentioned it, he would just ramble on about the doors of perception and Huxley and a separate reality and Castaneda."

Kate put an arm around Imogen's shoulders. "Lambikins will be back, don't worry. With his tail between his legs."

They talked some more, about what a silly young man James was, trying to make light of it all. Mr and Mrs Sands arrived in the kitchen half an hour later.

"Is James still not back?" Mr Sands asked.

The sun, which had shone brightly through the windows for a while after the earlier storm, had slipped behind dark clouds again. Thunder began to growl in the distance.

"He'd better come home soon," Mrs Sands said. "He'll get wet through otherwise."

The storms came closer. Rain lashed against the windows. Flickering lightning illuminated the room.

"Foolish boy is going to get wet," Mr Sands said.

"We've got to tell them, Imo," Kate said.

"Tell us what?" Mrs Sands said, a note of concern in her voice.

Imogen fingered the glass bead on her necklace. "We've lost James."

"Lost him?" Mrs Sands said, incredulously.

"I suppose he was at the Martell all night?" Mr Sands said. Imogen nodded. "Oh well, this rain will sober him up. Then he'll be back."

James's mother seemed more concerned and asked if she should call the police. Imogen didn't know what to say. It was Kate who spoke. "I wouldn't, if I were you. We think he took some LSD before he went to Copsehill. We think he might have been tripping."

Imogen knew why Kate had said it – to stop James getting busted. James's father became angry. "The silly little sod. Drink's one thing, but drugs..."

"But what does it mean?" Mrs Sands asked.

"If he's tripping, he could have wandered off anywhere," Kate said. "When he comes... recovers... from the trip, he'll probably make his way back home."

Mrs Sands fidgeted around the kitchen, putting things away, concern on her face. "How long does one of these *trip* things last?"

"Depends on the dose in the tab he took," Kate said. "And we don't know that. It was warm last night, so there's no need to worry. He's not going to suffer hypothermia or anything."

Kate was trying to be helpful, trying to reassure Mrs Sands, but Imogen knew she couldn't have said anything more likely to worry Mrs Sands. Kate didn't know about James's childhood illnesses, didn't know how much Mrs Sands still worried. After all, if James was out in the open *now* he *was* going to get wet. If James got wet today and then spent another night outside, possibly unconscious, he might then get hypothermia. What if the storms went on all night? Mrs Sands was probably imagining all this now.

For a moment, sunlight bathed the kitchen. Imogen could still hear thunder in the distance. She got up from the table, went to the window and looked into the sky. Between breaks in the clouds she could see towering anvils, Distant lightning flashed in the cloud tops.

"Looks like it's set for the day," Imogen said. Poor, stoned James might be wandering around the countryside, not knowing where he was, soaked to the skin, pelted by hailstones. She'd never dropped acid, couldn't imagine what James would be feeling. She asked Kate what she knew.

"Perceptions change," Kate said. "Time is distorted. Objects can seem larger or smaller than they really are."

Mrs Sands nodded thoughtfully. "Does that mean James might think he's only been away for an hour or so and not know that he's been away for much longer?"

"Yes, he might think he's lying in a field at Copsehill and will get back to the rest of us soon, not knowing he's been tripping for hours."

Mrs Sands pulled at her bottom lip. "I still think we should call the police."

"But if what Kate is saying is true," Mr Sands said, "James might well turn up in the next few hours. And he'll get into trouble with the police if he's been taking drugs. I'd leave it for a while. I'll give him a piece of my mind when he does get back, though."

Imogen imagined James feeling the hail as bricks pummelling him, the lightning as demons out to get him. She wanted her lambikins back. She would give him a piece of her mind too; but she would also hug him to her, warm him with her body, smooth his return to reality with her kisses.

Kate and Imogen had managed to quiet Mrs Sands' fears. James's parents spent most of the afternoon in the lounge, watching television. Imogen phoned her parents' house just in case, for some unknowable reason, James had wandered over there. She told her mother that James had gone missing, and the circumstances of his disappearance, which earned a rebuke from her normally liberal mother for hanging around with a druggie. Kate then phoned her mother, to check James hadn't ended up there. Kate didn't mention the events of the night.

Imogen and Kate still sat at the table in the large kitchen, where Charlie had left them earlier in the day. Mrs Sands occasionally came into the room and asked if they wanted more coffee. In the middle of the afternoon the crashing of the storms died away and Kate fell asleep. Her head rested on her arms and her black hair spilled over the table. Imogen stroked her head as she slept, wondering all the time where James could have gone. Imogen found stroking Kate's hair in the quiet of the kitchen relaxing, although it was she who needed her head stroked, she who needed to sleep; but Kate had been a good friend and had stayed with her and supported her. Imogen knew she wouldn't be able to sleep anyway. She heard the doorbell and hoped it was James. However, she could tell from Mr Sands' voice that he was talking to one of the boys. Stuart and Paul came into the kitchen. Poor Stuart was worn out, Imogen thought. Paul still looked ghastly, pale and tired.

Stuart went to Kate and bent down to gently kissed her head. "How long has she been asleep?" he asked quietly.

"About half an hour," Imogen said. She looked up at Stuart, hoping he had news. "Any idea what's happened to James?"

"I went back to Copsehill earlier, to the copse and I searched around the fields." He frowned. "But, like Charlie, I couldn't find him. Then it started to piss down again so I came home."

"I'm worried about him, Stu."

"I know. Come here." Stuart knelt in front of her and gathered her in his arms. "Don't worry, Imo, he'll be back. Like a bad sheep."

"Like a bad, bad, lambikins," Imogen mumbled.

She heard the doorbell ring again and her heart skipped a beat, even though she guessed it would only be Charlie. The thunder had returned, each low long rumble rolling over the last. Lightning briefly illuminated a kitchen that had become steadily gloomier. Imogen felt calm here in Stuart's arms, as she always did. Her head rested on his shoulder; she felt swallowed by his warmth, comfortable. For the first time today, she wanted to sleep. Her eyelids became heavy, she blinked rapidly as she tried to keep them open, and then she allowed them to close. She heard, rather than saw, Charlie enter the kitchen, his footsteps first, and then his voice saying quietly to Paul, "You look like shit, man."

"Thanks. I feel it," Paul said. "At least I don't feel like puking anymore. But man, my head hurts."

The next lightning flash was bright and close. The clap of thunder followed almost instantly, rattling the windows. Imogen started in Stuart's arms.

"Shit!" Charlie exclaimed. "That was close!"

Kate woke then and lifted her head from the table. "What happened?"

Imogen looked across Stuart's shoulder to Kate. "Just thunder, darling."

Kate reached out a hand and stroked Stuart's back. "Stu!" Her voice lingered on the vowel. "Good to see you."

Stuart gave Imogen a reassuring smile, kissed her cheek and released her from his arms. He turned to Kate. "How long have I been asleep?" she asked.

A little while," Imogen said quietly.

Kate looked up at Stuart, then leaned over and kissed him. When she drew away, she looked into Stuart's eyes for a moment. "I'm dying for a coffee. Does anybody else want one?"

"You stay there, Kate," Charlie said. "You're tired. I can make it."

"Thanks Charlie. I need to move, though. I've got pins and needles."

Kate stood slowly, and then walked over to the hob where she set the kettle to boil. "Any news on James?"

Stuart told her he'd been back to Copsehill but had found nothing.

"Kate and I phoned our parents," Imogen said. "Just in case James had wandered out to Burnt Norton." She sighed. "What else we can do? I hate this waiting around."

"We could phone Mark and Danny," Stuart suggested.

"Good idea," Imogen said. "Those are the people he'd go to if not us."

Stuart went to phone Mark. The others waited in tired silence. The kettle whistled, and rain hammered against the window. Kate busied herself with the coffee.

Stuart returned. "Well, there was a band practice this afternoon," he said. "Mark has only just got back. As far he knows, nobody in the band has seen James. Nobody mentioned him, at least. Mark said he'd ring round. He'll phone back if he hears anything. I also phoned Simon. He hadn't seen James either. He said he'd phone Nick, Gaz and Julie." Simon looked at Imogen encouragingly. "The message will soon get around to everybody we know."

Stuart sat on Kate's chair. Kate handed mugs to Stuart and Imogen and then sat on Stuart's lap, one hand holding her mug, the other stroking Stuart's neck. She studied his face. "You look tired, darling. Have you slept?"

"I snatched an hour before Charlie arrived this morning," he said. "But Dad kept me awake after Charlie had gone. He needs me to help him with the car. After that, I went back to the hill."

"You and Imogen should go upstairs and get in bed," Kate said.

Charlie snorted.

Kate looked at Charlie. "I don't mean together, idiot. Mind you, if they wanted to, I wouldn't stop them. I trust them both. As long as they kept their clothes on."

"We could widen the net," Paul said. "There must be other people he might have gone to. Acquaintances, college friends?"

"Unlikely," Imogen said. "James has a narrow circle of friends. He loves you lot and doesn't feel the need for many other friends."

There was some embarrassed shuffling around the table from the boys.

"Oh, don't be so silly," Imogen said, looking at each of them. "Nothing makes him happier than one of you guys coming around to see him. Even if Stu nicks all his fags, and Charlie drinks all his Martell."

"Talking of which," Stuart said. "Roll us a fag, Charlie."

The boys laughed away their embarrassment.

"It is true, though," Charlie said. "The only other people he gets on well with are the guys in the band and their friends – Simon, Nick and Gaz, Julie, a few others. At least they all now to keep an eye out for James."

"Does that mean he might go down to my house?" Paul wondered.

"He might," Imogen said. "If he felt he needed to get right away. If he felt his parents might hassle him."

"I think Jane would ring us if that happened," Charlie pointed out. "And I've already talked to her today." He passed a roll-up to Stuart and lit it, began constructing one for himself.

Stuart took a deep drag on the cigarette, and then coughed. "There aren't many trains on a Sunday," he sputtered. "It would take him a while to get to Paul's place."

"Don't forget he disappeared while Paul was unconscious," Imogen said. "Which was before dawn. He's been gone for... "Imogen glanced at her watch. "Over twelve hours now."

Charlie blew smoke into the kitchen. "If he's stoned, it could take him ages to get his shit together. He could easily be on a station somewhere, sleeping it off. At Taunton, say."

"Why don't we ring the stations?" Imogen asked.

"Because we don't know the route," Stuart said.

"What do you mean?"

Charlie tapped ash into an ashtray. "He could be anywhere. If he caught a train at Dereham, he could have gone to Westbury and caught another train there. If he went west, he might have jumped off the train at Castle Cary, Taunton, Exeter, Dawlish, Teignmouth... Anywhere. He's stoned, don't forget. And who knows what he was thinking last night. Then again, he might have walked to Westbury and then caught a train to Bristol. So he could be at Bath, Bradford on Avon, or Trowbridge."

"Or on his way to Birmingham New Street," Stuart said.

"If the first train that came through Dereham had been heading to Salisbury, he might have gone *there* and then caught a train to Exeter."

Paul interrupted Charlie. "He did that a few weeks ago, didn't he?"

"Yeah," Stuart said. "Got stoned, ended up going to Exeter'

Charlie nodded. "And a slow train from Salisbury to Exeter stops at all kinds of weird places. Tisbury, Pinhoe, Feniton."

"Don't forget Whimple," Paul said. "I always liked that name."

"Yeah, Whimple too. He could be anywhere."

"I see what you mean," Imogen said. She bit her bottom lip. "We just have to wait, then."

I think so."

While they'd been talking, the sun had come out again. Imogen looked through the kitchen window. The road outside steamed in the sunlight. Cumulus clouds towered into the blue sky.

"Looks like we'll be getting storms for a while yet," Charlie said.

"Switch the radio on, Charlie," Imogen said. "I need something to help me stay awake."

Charlie reached behind him to the transistor radio on the worktop and switched it on. Some middle of the road music came out of the speaker. He retuned the radio to Radio One. Imogen asked him to turn it down a bit, said she only wanted some noise to distract her. They sat without talking, while *You to Me Are Everything* quietly played in the background, accompanied by the fizz and crackle of interference caused by the storms.

Imogen finally spoke again. She had been visited by an image of James, alone, cold, wet on the side of a hill. "Twelve hours. If he's crashed out somewhere, he'll be soaked."

Stuart found her hand and squeezed it. "At least it's warm out."

Now the sun had returned the day had become stickier still. Imogen could feel sweat beading on her. The weight of the air tired her. Fatigue crept over her. She looked at Kate, who sat on Stuart's lap with her arm around him and her head on his shoulder. They must be hot, she thought. But together. That's something.

Stuart looked over at Paul. "What's up?"

Imogen also looked at Paul, who was frowning. He was concerned about something.

"'I'm still trying to remember exactly what we did last night."

"Would it help if you could?"

"It might. I keep thinking about the ritual. We did something wrong. In fact, the more I try and piece it together. I think we did a lot wrong." Paul shook his head. "Man, I was stoned."

"So, what did you do wrong?" Imogen asked.

"The banishing, for a start."

"What about it?" Stuart asked. "I assume you did it?"

"No, I don't think we did."

"Bloody hell. Why not? It's elementary, isn't it? It's what you spend most of your time practicing."

"I know, I know. But..."

"What?"

Paul shifted uncomfortably in his chair. "We found an injured bird. So... Well, we thought we'd put it out of its misery. Break its neck. But we couldn't do it. And then James had this idea to use its blood in the ritual. He thought we could... help it on its way... using the ritual knife. He thought the blood would add more power to the ritual."

"And you agreed?" Imogen asked.

"Not at first. I thought it was a bit... dark. A bit *black*. But then I began to think, hang on, it's not as if we'd tried to find a bird to kill. It seemed... propitious... And we did feel we would help the bird by killing it."

"So you did it?"

"Yeah. We did it. But now I think killing the bird was a big deal, a much bigger deal than we thought it would be. James actually did it, but it still... disturbed me. So much so, I just went straight into working the paths. James didn't notice we hadn't done the banishing. And he was supposed to prompt me if I forgot anything."

"But what does all this mean?" Kate asked

"You should perform a banishing before you begin another ritual," Paul said. "It creates a safe psychic space. It grounds you in what you're about to do."

"So if you believe in this shit," Imogen said, "you really do need this banishing?"

"Yes." Paul said.

Imogen felt angry. She wanted to blame somebody, and at this moment Paul was the obvious target. Paul looked at Imogen then, as if sensing what she was feeling. "But it was James's idea to use the blackbird in the ritual," he reminded her.

That was true. The anger that had been growing inside Imogen quickly faded. "Stupid lambikins," she whispered.

"But there are some other things I might have forgotten during the pathworking."

"Like what?" Imogen asked.

"Well, I'm pretty sure I forgot the name of the guardian."

Imogen gave Paul a puzzled look.

"When you work the paths of the Kabbalah," Paul explained, "you meet guardians. There are the proper guardians, the good ones. The Sephiroth. But there are false guardians who try to deceive you–"

"Demons?" Charlie said.

"I suppose so. In a manner of speaking. Anyway, when we got to the path to Netzach we were supposed to meet a guardian whose name I couldn't remember. When he said his name was Orev Zarak, it sounded right. I knew the name. I knew it was associated with the path. When I woke up this morning, I checked my book. Unfortunately, it appears that Orev Zarak is the Qliphoth for that path."

"Ah, a Qliphoth," Charlie said. "The demon."

"Yes, a false guardian," Paul said. "Orev Zarak. The Raven of Dispersion."

"Ominous," Charlie said.

"If you believe in all this," Kate said. "Which I don't."

"I'm not sure I do either," Paul said. "But even if it is something I've created, even if it is something psychological, it felt very real to me at the time, and probably felt real to James."

"Did anything else go wrong?" Imogen asked.

"Of course it did," Paul said. "We were both stoned. After the pathworking, we should have performed another banishing. But I flaked out, and it looks like James bolted for some reason. It seems we never finished the banishing."

"Or actually started it," Stuart said.

Paul sighed. "Nothing was completed. Perhaps I took the wrong paths, as well. It's hard to remember every little detail when you're stoned."

Stuart laughed, a little derisively. "And you were so confident."

"Bloody stoners," Imogen said, bitterly. "Is that it? Anything else?"

"Perhaps the freakiest thing. Although you don't believe in any of this, so make of it what you will. Before I passed out, I thought I heard James saying that the circle had been broken."

"What circle?" Kate asked.

"It's a circle of power we draw in front of us. If something... uh...

unexpected appears, it should be contained in the circle. If the circle is broken-"

"The demon escapes and chases my little lambikins all around Wiltshire?" Imogen said.

"Pretty much, yeah."

"But I don't believe in this," Imogen said.

"Doesn't matter. Either it's real, in which case he's being chased right now, or it's all imaginary. In which case he *believes* he's being chased. Same difference."

Imogen sighed. "Oh, sod it all. Sod it." She stood up and stretched. "I'm going for a pee. What a load of bollocks..." she muttered to herself as she left. She knew she was swearing more than she usually did. She was tired and anxious.

When Imogen returned to the kitchen, the sun shone through the window even though thunder still rumbled in the distance. Paul yawned, and stood up. He said he still felt like shit and needed to lie down, so was going back to Stuart's house before it rained again.

Imogen hugged him. "Don't worry, I don't really blame you for this. You were both irresponsible, arrogant idiots."

Paul thanked her. He said goodbye to the others, said he'd see Stuart later. Kate moved from Stuart's lap and sat in the chair vacated by Paul.

Imogen spoke to nobody in particular. "There's not a lot we can do except wait, is there?"

The others said nothing. They were all tired, Imogen thought. Kate had the puffy eyes of somebody who had slept inadequately. At least Kate had slept, if only, like Stuart, for an hour. *I still haven't slept yet.*

Stuart put his head down on his arms, resting on the tabletop as Kate had done earlier. Imogen reached over and stroked his head, remembering how calming it had been when she'd done this for Kate. She noticed Charlie watching, while Kate leaned back in her chair, her eyes closed, unconcerned. Imogen wondered what Charlie was thinking as he watched her. He had Jane now, didn't he? Yet it would be difficult, she supposed, to shake off so quickly an obsession that had lasted for a year or more. *If he fell in love with Jane, he could forget about me.*

She wondered if he and Jane had made love yet. That would probably blow his mind and certainly give him something else to occupy his waking moments. She remembered how it had been for and James after they had lost their virginities with each other. She had spent a lot of time then thinking about James, and about sex. But she and James had plenty of opportunity to be together. Jane was a hundred miles away. Would *that* affect how Charlie felt? Would he compartmentalise his experiences? A Jane life and a Dereham life? Would he forget about her when with Jane, but return to his old obsessions when back in Dereham?

The phone rang, bringing Imogen out of her reverie and back into the world in which James was missing and had been for nearly fifteen hours. She heard Mr Sands talking on the phone, though she could make out no words. The conversation continued. Imogen supposed he was talking to one of his acquaintances. Mrs Sands came into the kitchen, asked if any of them wanted coffee. Charlie, Kate and Imogen said yes, but Stuart said nothing. Imogen looked at him, noticed his breathing had slowed. She assumed he'd drifted off. *I really should sleep too*, she thought. Mrs Sands bustled around, refilling the kettle, setting it to boil on the hob, rinsing out their mugs. "Do you think James is all right?" she said.

"I'm sure he's fine," Charlie said. "Just crashed out in a barn somewhere."

"I still think we should call the police," Mrs Sands said.

"If you're really worried, you could check the hospitals."

Imogen shook her head. "Mr Sands has already done that. He phoned a few of the local ones earlier today, after Kate told him James had taken acid. But James didn't appear to be at any of them."

"I think he might phone them again later, just in case," Mrs Sands said. The kettle boiled and Mrs Sands made the coffee. She handed around the mugs, and then put a biscuit tin in the middle of the table.

"You all look done in," Mrs Sands said. "Perhaps you should go home and get some sleep." She looked at Imogen. "Do you want to stay the night, dear?"

"Yes, please, Mrs Sands."

"Would you like young Katie to stay with you?"

Kate opened her eyes. "Thank you, Mrs Sands, but I need to get home, have a shower and put some clean clothes on."

"Would you like Mr Sands to drive you home?"

"You're very kind, but I'll phone mum, she'll be happy to pick me up. She was coming to fetch me after the skywatch, anyway."

Mrs Sands said to help themselves to anything they fancied in the kitchen, to make themselves sandwiches or a salad, and then left them.

Imogen was hungry now and, so it seemed, was Charlie. He had worked his fingers under the edge of the biscuit tin lid, but his tired fingers were clumsy and the lid popped off and clattered onto the table.

Stuart lifted his head and looked around. "Oh! I thought it was thundering."

"It still is," Imogen said. "That was only the biscuit tin."

"Ah, biscuits," Stuart said sleepily. "I could do with one. Any custard creams?"

Charlie looked in the tin. "Yes. And bourbons, digestives, rich tea. Take your pick."

Charlie picked out a couple of bourbons and slid the tin over to Stuart. Imogen leaned over and grabbed an assortment. Stuart took out some custard creams and then passed the tin to Kate. She shook her head, and said she wasn't hungry.

"I felt my head being stroked," Stuart said. "I hope that wasn't you, Charles."

"Piss off," Charlie said. "It was Imo."

"Thanks, Imo." Stuart looked at Kate. "How are you, my darling?"

"Knackered," Kate said. "I'm going to go home and get some sleep, I think." She stood up, carrying her mug and went to the phone in the hallway.

"I need a coffee or something," Stuart said.

"Have mine," Charlie said. "I'll make myself another."

"Did anything happen while I was asleep?" Stuart asked.

"Nothing," Imogen said. "The phone did ring. I got hopeful for a moment. But it must've been one of Mr Sands' friends."

Charlie sat down again, placed his new mug of coffee on the table. He began to roll a cigarette.

"Do you want one?" he asked Stuart.

"Yeah, please."

The thunder had come closer and the kitchen was gloomy again. The rain rattled against the windows. Kate returned, said her mother was leaving immediately, and would be here in about twenty minutes. She asked if Stuart and Charlie wanted a lift home. Stuart said yes, please, he was knackered and really needed a few hours kip. Charlie also said yes, as his mother had earlier said she would cook him something for six o'clock.

Charlie looked at Imogen. "Do you want me to come back later?"

Imogen wanted them all to stay, but poor Kate and Stuart looked ready to fall down. She would love to have their company later, but she also knew that, if they did go home, she could at last lie down on James's bed and, despite her concerns, readily fall asleep. She'd almost fallen asleep, sitting upright in her chair, while she had played with Stuart's long, auburn hair.

"I'll be okay," she said to Charlie. "Once you've all gone, I'm going upstairs to put my head down. I haven't slept for..." She looked at her watch. "God, nearly thirty-six hours."

They finished their coffee in silence. They heard the doorbell ring, heard Mr Sands greeting Kate's mother. He came to fetch Kate. They all stood, Kate moving to hug Imogen, telling her everything would be all right, that James would be back soon. Then Stuart hugged her and said he'd see her tomorrow. He sounded very tired. Kate took Stuart's hand and led him out of the kitchen.

Charlie took Imogen's hand, lifted it to his lips and kissed it, then clasped it with his other hand and squeezed. "Will you be okay?"

"I'll be fine. I just really need some sleep now."

"I'll pop around tomorrow, before I head off to Devon with Paul."

Imogen followed Charlie to the hallway. Mr Sands held the front door open as Charlie, Stuart and Kate left the house. Imogen watched them climb slowly into Mrs Rix's car, and waved as they drove away. Mr Sands closed the door, looked at Imogen and told her she looked tired, that she should go upstairs and get some shuteye. She said she would, thanked him for letting her stay, and then slowly climbed the stairs. In James's room, she fell onto his bed, where she could smell tobacco, patchouli and Paco Rabanne on the counterpane. She thought back to the conversations earlier in the day and imagined James sleeping on the station platform at Exeter, or sucking on one of his black Sobranie and wondering how the hell he'd arrived at the oddly-named Whimple. Then she fell asleep, despite the thunder that boomed again.

15

When Imogen awoke she felt anxious, although for a moment she'd forgotten why she should feel this way. She soon remembered, though. She was still alone on James's bed. He hadn't, then, quietly returned during the night. The sun shone strongly through the bedroom window. She stood up and pulled back the curtains. Yesterday's thunderstorms had moved away. The sky was as blue as it had been for most of the summer. When she opened the window, a fresh breeze ran across the bare skin of her arms. The heat would build again, she supposed, but at least today would be less humid than yesterday had been. She turned away from the window and caught sight of herself in the full-length mirror. She looked scraggy, she thought. Her long curls were an unruly mop. She still wore the clothes she had put on the day before yesterday. At least, she thought, her face wasn't puffy, and her eyes no longer looked red and tired. She went through James's drawers and found clothes she knew would fit her. One advantage of her being so tall and James so skinny was that she could – with a belt here and a knot there – wear most of his clothes. She found a pair of his Y-fronts and thought they would do for today.

Imogen looked at the clock. It was 10.30 in the morning. She'd slept an unbroken sleep for sixteen hours. *And still no sign of James.* She'd give herself an all-over wash at the sink in the bathroom, she decided, then put on James's clothes, go downstairs and find Mr and Mrs Sands. They were usually up by this time. She met them, ten minutes later, in the kitchen, at the table where she and her friends had spent most of yesterday.

Mrs Sands said good morning to her and said she'd make her a nice cup of coffee. Before Imogen could ask, Mrs Sands said, "James isn't back, dear. Mr Sands has phoned the police. They'll be around soon."

Imogen doubted that Mrs Sands was as calm as she sounded. James's health had always been a worry to her, and if she thought James had been out all night in the rain and wind, memories of his childhood, the aches and shivering she'd witnessed, would have returned to her.

Imogen took the mug of coffee from Mrs Sands just as the doorbell rang. She saw Mr Sands look up at Mrs Sands, who replied only with a nod, a wordless understanding developed across their twenty years of marriage. Mrs Sands wiped her hands on a tea towel and went to the front door. They all supposed it would be the police, rather than James. Mrs Sands returned to the kitchen a few minutes later. She had shown the policemen into the lounge and had come to make tea for them.

"Come on, Imo," Mr Sands said. "They'll want to see us. And you know most about what happened on the hill."

Imogen and Mr Sands walked into the lounge, where they found two uniformed officers. One sat, while the other stood. The one who was sitting had his notebook ready. Mr Sands introduced himself and Imogen. The policemen introduced themselves in turn. Imogen and Mr Sands both sat on the settee. The policeman who was standing asked Imogen about her relationship with James, while the one who was sitting wrote down her reply. Imogen found she'd already forgotten the names of both men and began to think of them as Constables Standing and Sitting. Constable Standing asked why they'd gone to Copsehill, as if he didn't know, and smiled. He had a pleasant, boyish face and his smile helped Imogen to relax. She sipped at her coffee, and then explained that, yes, they *had* gone there to skywatch. Standing asked if anybody else had been on the hill.

"There was only us," Imogen said. "There were no other skywatchers. Nor any walkers."

Sitting wrote quickly. Imogen wondered if he knew shorthand and glanced at his notebook.

Mrs Sands came through the door, with a teapot, cups and saucers on a tray. She placed the tray on the coffee table and poured tea into china cups. She passed cups and saucers to the officers.

Standing thanked her. He asked Imogen for more details of what had happened that night. Imogen told them about the ritual, at which she saw Standing frown. She wondered if he was a Christian, if he'd been to matins before he'd started his shift this morning. She told them James had taken LSD before the skywatch. She'd already decided they had no reason to know that Paul had also been stoned. She wondered if Mr Sands would add that detail, but he didn't. She hadn't wanted to mention James's drug use at all but knew the police might have to ring around hospitals in search of a freak in a coma. She knew he was, anyway, unlikely to suffer anything more than a fine for dropping acid – and he had the money for that, although the car he so wanted to buy might have to wait while he saved his money again.

"Is he a dealer?" Constable Sitting asked.

Imogen shook her head. "Oh no. He's a user, but only very occasionally." She knew this wasn't true of his dope smoking but was of his LSD use.

Constable Sitting looked at his colleague, and then at Mr Sands. "You won't mind if we look around, then?"

Mr Sands looked at Mrs Sands, and then demurred. Constable Standing nodded at Sitting, who asked where James's room was. Mrs Sands led him away. Imogen became concerned, realising they might find more in his room than even she knew about.

"Normally," Standing said as Sitting left the room, "we wouldn't concern ourselves too much over a young lad who'd gone missing. He's old enough to look after himself and he might have his own reasons for vanishing." He paused and looked at Imogen for a moment. "However, Mr Sands told us when he called that James had taken LSD that night, and also mentioned James's previous problems with his health. We're aware that the weather was dreadful later that day. So, we are concerned that James might be in trouble, and we will begin making inquiries."

Standing took his own notepad and pencil from his pocket and asked more questions. "How long have you all known each other?"

"The boys have known each other since secondary school," Imogen said. "Kate and I met them at college."

"Was there any reason to think James was unhappy, that he might have wanted to leave home, or leave the town?"

"Not that I know of."

Standing looked at Mr Sands, who shook his head. "He's always seemed happy enough," Mr Sands said. "We argue rarely and then only about the usual things. Tidying his room up, getting drunk, that kind of thing."

Still looking at Mr Sands, Standing asked if he'd known about James's drug use.

"No, I didn't. although I suspected. I know James is a bit of a hippie, and this is the seventies, after all. But I don't search his room. I trust him to be sensible, even if he is experimenting with... things. We all did, when we were young, didn't we?"

Imogen had always liked James's parents, and was impressed by Mr Sands, who talked cogently and with an unexpected liberality. Of course, he'd been angry when he'd found out yesterday about James taking acid, but that was to be expected.

Constable Sitting reappeared. All he'd found was the hash, still wrapped in its tinfoil. Standing unwrapped the package and sniffed, then rewrapped it and put it in his pocket.

"Are there any other drugs in James's room?" Standing asked.

"James is an occasional dope smoker," Imogen replied. "He's used acid, to my knowledge, twice. He isn't a dealer. The tab he dropped last night was probably the only one in the house."

Standing rambled for a while about the problems of adolescent drug use in today's decadent society, but no longer seemed concerned that James might be one of Dereham's drug barons. Instead, Sitting asked about the ritual. Imogen tried to explain what little she knew about it.

"Do you need any special gear?" Standing asked. "Items. Equipment. Paraphernalia?"

"Not really," Imogen said. "The only thing they *really* seemed to need was the ritual knife, but they don't even-"

"Hold on," said Standing. "Did you say a knife?"

Imogen noticed the sudden interest from Standing. What had obviously been before a rather dull case involving a missing person had taken on a new slant for the policeman. "Yes," Imogen said. "But it's not a *sharp* knife. It's quite blunt. They could just as well use their fingers in place–"

"Does it have a point on it?" Sitting asked. He had a tight little face. His eyebrows were now raised, which had the effect of pinching his face even tighter.

"Yes, it's thin. A bit like a stiletto, I suppose. At least, Paul's is. James has one with a broader blade."

"So it could be used to stab somebody?"

"I used to be in the military," Mr Sands said. "I've seen James's knife. It would be difficult to cut butter with it."

"Ah. They both had knives," Standing noted. "Who had a knife last night, Miss Peek?"

"Oh, they used Paul's last night," Imogen said. "Paul was performing the ritual."

"Did this Paul have any grievance against James?"

The question surprised Imogen. "Oh no! You can't think *that*! James and Paul have been best friends for years. Nothing could happen that would make them fall out with each other."

"Well, they were alone out there, Miss Peek. Who knows what might have happened."

"But they were both completely out of their heads. Paul was unconscious when James left."

"Ah, so your friend Paul also takes drugs?"

Shit, Imogen thought, she had intended keeping Paul out of this. "Yes, but not often, even less than James, which isn't much. He just ate some of that hash." She pointed towards Standing's pocket.

"Why?"

"Oh, because of the associations between ritual and the doors of perception, the cleansing of the way, the widening of perception and–"

Standing stared at her blankly.

"Never mind," she said. "The point is that you don't have to take drugs to do a ritual, but you can experiment with it, as a guide to show you the way."

"I'll take your word for it, Miss. Nonetheless, we do have two stoned lads out there with a knife."

"Yes, but I can assure you there is no way... *no way*... Paul would *ever* have done anything to James."

"What about the rest of you?" Sitting asked.

"What?"

"Well, you had friends with you." Sitting consulted his notes. "Stuart, Kate and Charlie."

"And?"

"Well, we have, according to you, two young men in a field and a knife. Is it possible one of your friends went over to the field and used the knife on James?"

"Why would they want to?"

"Oh, I don't know. Because of a previous smouldering row? Jealousy? A crime of passion? Did any of your friends go off by themselves?"

"Well, yes," Imogen said. "Charlie. But it's ridiculous to suppose one of us would do anything to James."

"This is just speculation," Mr Sands burst out. "We don't even know where James is. He could simply be missing, unconscious somewhere. To suggest that one of his friends might have assaulted him seems to be merely fishing for answers."

"Indeed, Mr Sands. The most likely explanation is that James is in a hospital. Yet what if one of his friends did go for him with this knife? He might have been scared and run away. Perhaps he's hiding somewhere, afraid to come back. Who knows? It's best to consider all the options, don't you think?"

"I suppose it is," Mrs Sands agreed. "But I also know all these boys. They've been friends since they were in their first year together at secondary school."

Standing looked at Mrs Sands and spoke briskly. "Not to worry, ma'am," he said. He then nodded at Imogen, "Miss Peek. In most of these cases, we find that the missing person either returns after a couple of days, or has had an accident and is unconscious in a hospital with little harm done." He was trying to reassure them. "We'll begin our investigations. In the meantime, if he gets in contact with you, or returns home, telephone us immediately."

"Yes, yes, of course we will," Mr Sands said. He stood up, thanked them for their help, and showed them to the door.

Imogen played with the faience bead at her neck. Smouldering rows, she wondered. Crimes of passion? Jealousy?

Charlie?

16

Jane woke Charlie with a kiss. "Wakey, wakey, Charlie," she whispered in his ear. She was so pleased to see him. She still couldn't believe this was happening to her.

Charlie opened his eyes. "That was a nice greeting."

Jane winked at him. Charlie sat up and kissed her, then smiled at her. She thought she would melt. He stretched, stood up, scratched at his beard, and pulled on jeans and a tie-dyed tee shirt. The day was already hot. Jane took Charlie's hand and padded barefoot into the kitchen tugging Charlie behind her. The ceramic tiles felt cool beneath her feet. They began making breakfast.

Jane stared absent-mindedly at the teapot in which the tea brewed. "I wonder if James has come back yet?"

"I should phone Imo or Stu," Charlie said. "I will later. Mind you, I'm sure one of them would phone us if there was any news."

Jane had said nothing to her parents about James. When Paul and Charlie had arrived, late last evening, Paul had told Mr and Mrs Maas only a little of what had happened. He said James had gone missing after taking some LSD, but omitted the ritual and his own hash-induced blackouts. Mrs Maas pointed out the obvious, that Mrs Sands must be really worried, and Mr Maas said James was a stupid boy for causing all this worry and probably wasting police time. After Mr and Mrs Maas had retired to the lounge, Fiona had arrived. Charlie and Paul muddled through an explanation of events at the skywatch, and what had happened afterwards. Their account had been truly confused and jumbled, as Charlie talked animatedly about his UFO sighting and Paul tried to explain where his ritual had gone wrong. Sensible Fiona thought the esoteric explanations – spaceships, Qliphoth and possession – most unlikely and had said so. She thought James was most likely still stoned – possibly hallucinating or having paranoid delusions and lost somewhere – or was in a local hospital, in a coma or suffering amnesia.

After Charlie and Paul had finished their description of events, Jane had suggested that the next day they should go to Blue Tor, and quietly relax in the sun.

Jane carried her mug of tea into the dining room, leaving Charlie to look after the toast. She joined Paul and Fiona at the table. Jane noticed that the *Western Morning News*, delivered every day to her parents, had already been opened and folded to display a short item about James. *Mystery Disappearance at Local UFO Hotspot*. She showed it to the others.

"We've already seen it," Fiona said.

Jane quickly read the article. Charlie came back into to the room with plates and his own mug of tea. "Look at this," she said.

Charlie put down the plates and his mug and took the paper from Jane. He skimmed the article. "That's Patterson," he said. "I recognise the style."

"Patterson?" Jane said.

"The bloke in Dereham who writes about UFOs," Charlie said.

Paul took the newspaper and quickly read the article. "It doesn't mention UFOs."

"Trust me," Charlie said. "It's Patterson. He supplements his income by writing for other papers. He's a... What does he call it...? A *stringer*. There's probably a similar article in the *Western Daily Press*."

When they'd finished their long, lazy breakfast, they stocked up on cold drinks, picked up Paul's portable cassette player and a handful of cassettes, and were just about to leave when the telephone rang. Paul lifted the handset. "Oh, hello Imo," he said. He didn't say much. He said, "Okay," a couple of times, "Oh, that's a shame," once, and nodded a few times. After a few minutes, he said, "I'll try," and then he said goodbye and replaced the handset. He looked at Jane, Charlie and Fiona. "No news. James is still missing."

"How is she?" Fiona asked.

"She sounded tired," Paul said. "She says she hasn't slept much."

"What did she ask you?"

"Just to remember whatever we can."

"I wish there was more we could do to help," Charlie said.

They left the house and began the walk through the narrow lanes to Blue Tor. Jane looked at her watch. It wasn't even eleven yet, but the air was thick and heavy. They walked slowly, dawdling in the heat. When they reached the hill, Fiona found shade beneath the canopy of a tall hedgerow ash and spread out a large blue blanket on the brown grass. They all flopped down onto it, hot after their walk. From their vantage point on the slopes of the hill, Jane could see brown fields, brown hedges and brown trees everywhere. The drought and the ferocious, constant, heat had reduced the world to a brittle brown. Above her, the sky was an intense blue, studded with slow-moving islands of cumulus, as it had continued to be since the thunderstorms.

"I'm sorely tempted to undo that knot," Charlie whispered in Jane's ear.

Her reply was as languid as she felt in the heat. "Knot, Charlie? What knot?"

Charlie touched the loose bow between her breasts. She wore a white tie-front halter-top, with a floral pattern embroidered into it. She knew if Charlie were to tug at one of the strings the knot would unravel and the halter-top would come loose. "Not in front of my brother," she said.

"I don't know what you're whispering about over there." Paul said. "But I don't want to see whatever the consequences may be of such hushed entreaties."

"Pretentious wanker," Charlie said.

Fiona flicked through the cassettes. The plastic lid of the cassette player rattled as it opened and closed. Fiona switched on the tape recorder and Joni Mitchell filled the warm summer air.

"It *is* a most Californian summer," Paul said.

"It's lovely," Fiona said. "And now I'm going to do something *most* Californian." Jane looked over at her. Fiona smiled at Paul, then at Charlie. "Don't be shocked, Charles," she said. She slipped off her shirt, exposing her breasts and torso, and then lay back down on a part of the blanket that was in the sun.

"I see by your tan," Charlie said, "that this is *not* the first time you've done this."

"First time in front of anybody except Paul and Jane," Fiona said. "But I know you're cool, Charlie."

Jane lay back down on the blanket. Charlie probably wanted to be cool, she thought, but she knew he'd seen very few naked breasts, and had seen hers rarely; they had, after all, met only a few times this summer. Jane laughed quietly as she saw him caught between looking at Fiona and looking away. "Just look at mine," she said.

"Are you undoing that knot?" Charlie asked.

"Not with him around." She jerked a thumb towards Paul.

Charlie lay down beside Jane, resting his head on her breasts.

Paul seemed restless. "I wish I could remember more about the other night. James might have said something."

"Like what?" Fiona asked, sleepily.

"Oh, I don't know. Something like, *I'm being chased by a sodding great demon so I'm buggering off to Whimple.*" Paul rolled over and pushed himself up onto his elbows, looking towards the brow of the hill. "Or he might have said, *I am now Orev Zarak and I'm going to London to live a fully human life.*" Paul paused. "Which would have been more worrying."

"You kept blacking out," Fiona pointed out. "I'm surprised you remember anything."

"I'm sure I remember him saying something about the circle being broken." Paul paused again. "I do know, however, that I was very, very stoned."

"You, sir, are an idiot," Fiona sighed.

"So Imo kept telling me."

"I'm not surprised."

Joni filled a moment's silence, singing of California.

"I suppose we could hypnotise you," Fiona said to Paul.

"What?" Paul said.

"Hypnotise you. Some people think you can discover hidden or forgotten information when in a trance."

Jane sat up, Charlie lifting his head away from her as she did so. This intrigued her. Betty and Barney Hill had been hypnotised, and it was only through that hypnosis that they discovered they *had* been abducted.

"Hey, that's a good idea," Paul said. "You could probably hypnotise me easily. All the focusing and relaxation I do before a ritual is like a trance."

"I've got some information on the induction of trance states in my psychology books at home," Fiona said.

"Oh my god, Fi," Charlie lazily drawled. "You're beginning to sound as pretentious as Paul."

Paul turned to Charlie. "Anybody with a modicum of education would sound like a professor of eloquence when contrasted to your natural plebeian rusticity." He thought for a moment. "I do have a couple of books on hypnotism back at the house. In fact, I'm sure I've got a book that's actually called *Hypnotism*. An old Pelican I picked up for fifty pee."

Jane remembered it. "You have. In fact, I looked at it the other day." She flicked through it after reading about the Hill abduction case. "It seemed very... um–"

"Dry? Academic?" Paul suggested.

"I was going to say boring. But yes, that's what I mean."

"Did you notice if there were instructions in there on how to hypnotise somebody?" Fiona asked.

"Yes, I think there were," Jane said.

"Why don't we try it later?" Paul asked.

"Just don't eat any hash beforehand," Charlie said.

They had returned to the house and were lazing around in the back garden. Jane could see the first bright stars flickering in the twilit sky. She and Charlie were now entwined on the same blanket they had taken to the hill with them. Paul and Fiona were on sun-loungers, next to each other, holding hands. Jane reached towards the lemon balm growing in the border beside her, pulled off some leaves, and dropped them into her mug of tea.

"What *are* you doing?" Charlie asked.

"Making my tea taste like Lady Grey," Jane said.

"I don't know what you're on about."

"Lady Grey is a mild, lemon-flavoured tea, suitable for ladies. Like me."

Charlie tutted. "Surely a real lady would say *Such as I*. Anyway, what have those leaves got to do with it? I take it you haven't got a Lady Grey plant over there?"

"It's lemon balm."

Charlie face wrinkled into puzzlement. Jane ripped off another leaf, crushed it between her thumb and forefinger, and held it beneath Charlie's nose. "Haven't you heard of lemon balm?" she asked.

Charlie sniffed. "We only grow cabbage and potatoes at our house. There's no room for exotic flora." Jane dropped the crushed leaf into Charlie's tea. He sipped at it. "Ah, *lemony*," he said. "Cool. Give me some more."

Jane ripped more leaves from a bushy twig, leaned over and dropped them into Charlie's mug.

"When are we doing the hypnotism thing?" Jane asked.

Paul's eyes were closed. "Soon. When we're all relaxed."

"I'm pretty relaxed now," Charlie said. "Anyway, I still think you and James saw a flying saucer."

"You were stoned, too," Paul said. "Perhaps not as stoned as me, but you were. You might have been confused by a twinkling planet."

Charlie was emphatic in his reply. "No way. *No way*. Not after all the nights I've spent on Copsehill. I may not know the names of all the stars, but I can recognise constellations, planets, bright stars, what have you. What I saw, I've never seen before."

Paul shrugged sleepily. "So what if you did see a UFO? It could just be coincidence. It might have nothing to do with what happened to us."

"Seems like a pretty big coincidence," Jane said. "What's that thing you always go on about? Some connecting principle thing."

"Ah yes. An acausal connecting principle," Paul said. Jane recognised the tone his voice had taken on. He was about to lecture her, introduce her to new knowledge and help her make connections. She was used to it. "Acausality," Paul continued, "is the principle behind significant coincidences, or synchronicity as Jung calls it. He theorises that synchronicities tie together separate events to reveal a larger meaning."

"So perhaps it was synchronicity," Jane said. "What if Charlie's UFO connects together everything that happened that night? You and James being stoned, your ritual going wrong, Charlie, the biggest sceptic, being the only one to really see it, James going missing..." She ran out of ideas.

"But what would be the meaning behind all these events?" Paul said. "After all, it should be a *significant* coincidence," he emphasised. "Not just a *mere* coincidence. The convergence of coincidences illuminates some larger problem. But what's the problem? What knowledge could come from all these coincidences?"

Jane wanted to tell them something. She had an idea – a possible explanation for everything. She'd been reading about flying saucers and abductions, about Antonio Vilas Boas and Betty and Barney Hill. Everything seemed to connect somehow – her new interest in UFOs and abductions, and her relationships with Charlie, Paul and Stuart. Perhaps she now knew things they didn't. She was, however, reluctant to say anything. She didn't want to be laughed at or put down by her brother, even though her ideas seemed no more ludicrous than all his strange ideas about the occult and psychology and consciousness. But she couldn't do it, she couldn't say it. She wasn't yet confident enough in herself. She still sometimes felt like a little girl when she was with Paul and Charlie.

Jane stroked Charlie's hair as he sat between her legs on the floor. She and Fiona were sitting on the only two chairs in Paul's bedroom; well, she had a chair, Fiona had a stool. Paul was lying on the bed. Fiona thumbed through the book on hypnosis Paul had found on his shelves, looking for a good description of hypnotic induction. Before sitting down, Charlie had found what he thought would be suitably relaxing music, Tangerine Dream's *Rubycon*. It was a good choice, Jane thought.

"Light a joss-stick," Paul suggested. "Let's involve all my senses."

Jane reached over Charlie's head to the bureau beside her and found an open packet of sandalwood joss-sticks. She took one and held it down towards Charlie, who lit it with his lighter. She placed it in a brass holder. There had been a time, not so long ago, when she had thought the odours and scents drifting from Paul's room rather peculiar – but now she'd grown to love them. When she came to his room, to rummage through his books, she would always catch the faint trace of some exotic perfume.

"Here's something," Fiona finally said. "We'll try this."

She turned to Jane and Charlie and signalled them to silence with a look.

"Are you ready, Paul?"

Paul already had his eyes closed. He nodded. The electronic music burbled quietly from loudspeakers on a bookshelf. The room slowly filled with scented smoke.

"Right," Fiona said. "I'm going to count from one to twenty and, as I do so, you will experience a pleasant feeling in your right hand, which will move from there into your right arm. As I count, you'll begin to feel a twitching in your fingers, a slight, easy movement of the muscles."

Fiona reached over, gently took Paul's hand and moved the fingers lightly. "It will feel just like this. Your arm will feel as if it's lifting. When it does, don't resist. You can resist if you choose but, as you're doing this because you want to, it would be counter-productive to resist, so you might just as well go with it."

The quiet, relaxing voice of Fiona was impressive. She was a natural, Jane thought.

"Finally," Fiona continued, "your arm will fall slowly, gently, across your chest. When this happens, you will be very relaxed, and can go deeper still, and your subconscious mind will be open to our questions."

Fiona paused. Paul's breathing was already light and regular. Jane continued to stroke Charlie's head as Fiona began the induction.

"One," Fiona said. "A tingling sensation moves into the fingertips of your right hand."

Fiona continued with the induction as she had described. Jane was fascinated, and excited, to see everything happening just as expected. Paul's fingers did begin to twitch, his arm did lift until it was at ninety degrees to his body.

"You are now hypnotised," Fiona said quietly to Paul. "There's nothing to worry about. It's natural for your arm to be there. You will go deeper into a trance as your arm floats above you. Your eyelids are too heavy to open now, and you feel relaxed, your whole body feels relaxed."

When her count reached nineteen, Fiona told Paul his arm would begin to fall slowly across his body and come to rest on his chest. Jane watched Paul's arm perform a slow, controlled, but somehow sleepy arc towards him. It came to rest as Fiona counted twenty, and she told Paul he could now go deeper and deeper, that it was natural now to feel relaxed and deep within himself.

Fiona stopped talking, then turned and winked at Jane. "Cool," she whispered.

"Now what are we going to ask?" Jane said quietly.

Fiona shrugged and turned back to Paul. "Paul," she said. "I'm going to ask you some questions, and as I do you feel more relaxed and go deeper as you concentrate on my voice and my questions. Nod if you understand."

Paul nodded.

"I want you to return to Copsehill, three nights ago. You and James have gone to a field to perform your ritual. What do you see?"

"I'm feeling stoned," Paul said quietly.

Fiona looked at Jane and pulled a face. "Oh! Um. Ignore that feeling. Let that float away. Let your subconscious be apart from any sensations caused by the hash."

"Yeah, okay," Paul said.

"Stay relaxed, let your breathing stay even. Tell me what you see."

"We have a bird. It needs to be put out of its misery. James has killed it with the ritual knife. He's letting the blood drip into the circle."

"Good," Fiona said. "What next?"

"I'm starting the ritual. I'm giving cues to James, so he can follow me."

"Do you see anything?"

"Not really, I have my eyes closed, so I can concentrate."

"Huh," said Fiona. "Um. All right. What you can hear? Can you hear anything?"

"Not really. James is quiet. All I can remember is my own voice, giving James instructions."

"Cool. Do the ritual again in your head, keep going until you hear or see something."

Some time passed. Fiona gave Jane a quizzical look.

Paul spoke at last. "James is saying something." He paused. "He says the circle has been broken."

"Ah, yes," Fiona said, "you've told us that before. Is there anything else?"

Paul frowned, and then said, "Yes, James says there's something appearing in the circle."

"How does he sound?"

"He sounds calm... Wait... he says it's heading for him. It's a bright light, very bright, but it has a shape. It's a bird, it's a black shining bird."

"How does he sound now?"

"Like he's panicking, like he's frightened."

"It is a bright light," Charlie said quietly. "But it isn't shaped like a bird, it's round and the lights flash on and off like it's sending a message or something."

"What happened next, Paul?"

"I opened my eyes and could see the bright light James was talking about, but it didn't look like a bird to me, it was dazzling, changing colours."

"Is that because it was spinning?" Jane asked.

"Yes, it was spinning," Charlie said.

Fiona looked at Charlie, then at Jane. She nodded at Charlie. Jane looked down. Charlie's head had fallen forward beneath her hands. She hadn't noticed, so intent had she been on Fiona and Paul.

"Shit, I've hypnotised them both," Fiona whispered to Jane.

Jane was eager to discover what Charlie had seen. "Tell us what *you* saw Charlie."

"I can see a bright light. It seems to be spinning. The lights are flashing on and off... in *patterns*... The patterns seem to have meaning."

"Do you think it was a spaceship, Charlie?" Jane asked.

"I don't know, how can I know? I think it was."

"Shh, Jane," Fiona whispered. "It can't help if you put ideas in their heads."

"Sorry, Fi. I'm just so excited."

"What's worse, now I have two subjects. It all feels a bit... out of control."

"Don't worry, Fiona, you're doing fine."

Fiona turned back to Paul. "Paul, you saw the light too, you heard what Charlie just said. Did you see these lights?"

"Perhaps. The lights might be going on and off. There might be a pattern..." He paused. "Where has James gone?"

"What?" Fiona said.

"James has gone. After looking at the light I was going to ask him if he'd seen it, but when I look over to him, he isn't there. Where is he?"

"Okay, so we know James has gone. What happened next?"

"I'm having blackouts. I'm drifting in and out. There's no sound, there's nobody around. I see the light sometimes, but then it's gone. Now I see nothing." Paul frowned. "I must have lost consciousness."

Fiona looked at Jane and whispered again. "I don't think we can learn anything else, do you?"

Jane shook her head. Fiona looked in the book to find out how to bring Paul and Charlie out of their trances. She counted backwards slowly from ten to one, telling them that on each number they would become more aware of the room, become more alert, that when she counted *one* they would be wide awake. She clapped her hands. Paul opened his eyes. Jane looked down at Charlie. He also blinked sleepily.

"Cool," Paul said. "I remember most of what happened. Did Charlie also go under?"

"Yeah," Charlie said. "I think it was because Jane was stroking my head... I felt really relaxed."

They talked about what had happened and decided there was little difference in what Charlie and Paul had seen. The only differences were those of interpretation – but which interpretation was correct?

"I'm with Charlie," Jane said. "It was a UFO." She looked at Paul. "It was just a coincidence it happened during your ritual."

"I don't know," Paul said. "Whatever it was, something freaked James out."

"But did it?" Jane said. "Perhaps he wasn't freaked out."

"What do you mean?" Paul asked.

She had to say it, she thought. She must tell them that James *had* been abducted. But she couldn't. "Oh, I don't know," she mumbled, instead.

17

Imogen found herself admitting that, yes, Charlie had gone off by himself. She watched as a detective wrote this in his notebook.

She, Stuart and Kate had arrived at Mr and Mrs Sands house to ask if there was any news and had found two CID officers already in the hallway. They, too, had just arrived, and were explaining that they were doing everything they could to find James. Because there was continuing concern that he might be ill or injured, they said, the police had been in contact with and circulated James's details to all local police stations and hospitals. Tomorrow there would be a search of the hills and fields around Copsehill which would involve a substantial number of constables. If James's friends and family wanted to come along and help, they would be welcome.

One of the detectives asked Imogen if there was anything she hadn't yet told them. She shook her head. And then she suddenly remembered that there was one other thing. "Oh! The money! James had two hundred and fifty pounds in his wallet."

The detectives became extremely interested and asked if they could talk to her, Stuart, and Kate. Mrs Sands showed them all to the lounge and then left them. The officers introduced themselves as Detective Constable Prior and Detective Sergeant Wilson. Imogen knew little about police ranks, but these didn't sound particularly senior. It heartened her, in a way. James's case wasn't yet so important that it demanded a Detective Inspector. In fact, Detective Constable Prior looked very young.

Detective Sergeant Wilson spoke first. "Where are your other friends?"

"Charlie and Paul were always going to Devon after the skywatch," Imogen said. "That's where Paul lives, and where Charlie's girlfriend is."

The two detectives turned their backs to them, leaned into each other, talked quietly. Imogen thought she heard Devon and Cornwall Constabulary mentioned.

She knew what the detectives were thinking. James had a large sum of money on him, and that was the motive they'd been waiting for. But she couldn't imagine any of James's friends harming James simply for money. That was absurd.

"Your friend, Charlie," Wilson said. "He wandered away by himself, didn't he?"

Imogen said nothing. She knew Charlie had left them more than once, but she was also sure he had done, and would do, nothing to hurt James.

Stuart spoke. "Just the once, and not for long."

"More than once, actually," the detective said. "Remember, it was he who volunteered to look for James. He was alone there for some time after you returned home, during which he claims to have looked for James."

"Yes, but–" Stuart began, before being cut off.

"And he went for a walk to the copse alone before seeing his... flying saucer, isn't that right?"

Imogen nodded.

"And for how long was he gone?"

Imogen couldn't remember exactly. "Fifteen minutes, twenty minutes?"

"Thank you. And did Charlie know Paul had a knife?"

"Of course. Charlie knows something about the rituals. We all do."

"Was there anything significant about his decision to go for a walk?"

"He just went for a walk," Stuart said, his voice tight. Imogen could hear the frustration in him. "And, anyway, you might as well blame Imo!" he blurted out, to Imogen's surprise. "She also went for a walk alone."

"Really?" Wilson said. "And why hasn't this been mentioned before?"

"That was at the other skywatch, I think," Imogen said.

Stuart looked puzzled. "Was it? Oh, yeah, it was. Sorry."

"Are you sure?" the detective asked.

"Yes, I'm sure it was," Imogen said. "I don't think I was alone, was I?"

"I don't know. I spent a lot of time dozing," Kate said.

"I'm not certain," Stuart said. He sat quite rigid on the sofa, Imogen noticed. He was trying to control himself. She had rarely seen Stuart angry. Only the once, now she thought about it. "The skywatches tend to blur, after a while," Stuart said. "People are always coming and going. They need a pee, or they go for a stroll to the copse, whatever'

"Hmm. Really?" Wilson said. He turned a smile on Prior. "It's quite a little conundrum we've got here, isn't it?" Prior smiled back.

Imogen wondered why. "What do you mean?"

"Well, Miss Peek, in all previous accounts, Mr Woolmer was the only one of you to have wandered off alone for any length of time. Yet we now discover that you might, or might not, have left the others for a while. Miss Rix was dozing, so Mr Garland might have left her for a walk at some point, perhaps while Mr Woolmer was up the copse and you were urinating behind a hedge."

Prior finally spoke. "And, if Mr Garland *had* gone for a walk, Miss Peek was urinating behind a hedge, and Mr Woolmer was up the copse, then Miss Rix would also have been alone."

"Very true, very true," Wilson said. "Well spotted, Prior." He scribbled in his notebook. "So, we've now established that any of you might, in fact, have had the opportunity to be alone with James that night."

Prior changed the subject. "Who had the knife?"

"I suppose Paul had it," Imogen replied. "He would have used it during the ritual."

"Where did James get his money?"

"He's acquisitive," Stuart said. "He saves his pocket money, he works in Bentons and does odd jobs. He even washed my Dad's car once."

Wilson spoke now. "He's not a dealer then?"

"Oh no," Imogen said. "He's just careful with his money."

"And yet generous," Stuart added. "He isn't a miser."

"And the constables who were here the day James went missing found nothing."

Prior spoke, looking at each of them. "Which isn't to say one of his good friends didn't scour the room before any policeman arrived."

"Well, we didn't," Imogen said. "The hash the PC found in his room is the only drug I ever knew about. I didn't even know he had a tab to take."

The detectives finally left them, saying they would see them in the morning, when the search was due to take place.

Stuart bit his nails.

"What are you thinking?" Imogen said.

"About Charlie," Stuart said.

"Surely you can't think he had anything to do with it."

"Oh, I don't know. Sometimes he acts so weird. What if the whole UFO thing was a ruse? He wouldn't do it for the money, but..."

"But what? You're not going to tell me it's to do with me?"

"He was so obsessed with you and your relationship with James and me. He seemed so on edge about it all."

"He wouldn't go that far, though, surely, not to... He's never been violent, has he?"

Stuart fidgeted, and looked away. "Well, yeah, actually. At the skywatch back in April. I asked him about Jane. I just wanted to know if... well, if his intentions were honourable, that he wasn't just on the rebound, from... Well, you." He looked back at Imogen. "Then he started pushing me around, so I... uh, I slapped him."

Imogen remembered now how surly Charlie had seemed that night. "Yes, yes. He was weird when he came down from the copse with you. He seemed angry or pissed off about something. I meant to ask you about it but forgot."

"You never told me this," Kate said.

"Yeah, well, Charlie asked me not to tell anybody and I said I wouldn't. So I didn't. And you and I weren't together then. But things have changed now."

"But it was about Jane, not me?" Imogen asked.

"Yes, it was Jane we were talking about."

Imogen didn't know whether to believe Stuart or not. He would always protect his friends. He was loyal. "I'd better phone Paul," she said. "I'll tell him that we'll be searching for James tomorrow. And that the police might be knocking on his door."

18

Paul ate his muesli and wondered when the police would arrive. He'd told the others little about the call he'd received from Imogen last night. He didn't want to freak out Charlie and Jane. Particularly Jane. He'd told them only that the police would be searching the fields around Copsehill, and that somebody from the local police would visit the house during the day. Imogen had warned him about the kind of questions the police might ask. Paul could see how all their actions, even Imogen's, might appear suspicious. He didn't think Charlie had done anything to James. He knew he also a suspect. Was he the *chief* suspect? He had the knife, after all, and had been alone with James. He supposed he must be.

Charlie and Jane were lying next to each other on the sun-loungers, holding hands, catching the sun before it passed around to the other side of the house. Paul thought it even hotter today than yesterday. Jane still wore her embroidered halter-top, but had replaced her jeans with a pair of shorts. Her legs had become lightly tanned over the last few weeks. Charlie was topless, wearing only his patched and faded blue jeans. His chest was pink. Fiona had left them earlier, promising to return. Charlie had convinced her to hypnotise him this evening. The insistent rhythm of Led Zeppelin's *Kashmir* drifted from the open window of Paul's bedroom. His only concession to the imminent arrival of Devon and Cornwall constabulary was a note pinned to the front door directing any visitors to the back garden. Jane had asked if this was wise, but Paul said he didn't see why he should wait indoors like a naughty schoolboy.

He wondered how the search in Dereham was progressing. Did Charlie feel the nagging guilt he did at not being in Dereham, helping to search for his friend? He didn't know where the police could look that Charlie or Stuart hadn't. Charlie had spent two hours, he'd told Paul, searching the fields around Copsehill, looking in copses, spinneys, sties and barns. And then, later in the day, Stuart had also returned to Copsehill and found nothing. Charlie thought it unlikely the police would find James, or any clues, when he and Stuart had not.

A voice said, "Mr Paul Maas?"

Paul looked toward the corner of the house, where the path at the side gave out into the garden. A smartly dressed man stood there. Paul supposed him to be the policeman.

"That's me," Paul replied.

The policeman looked at Charlie. "And you, sir, you'll be Charlie Woolmer?" Charlie slowly opened his eyes, sat up and nodded.

Jane turned to face the policeman. "Do you need me?"

"You weren't at this... skywatch thing, were you? Wiltshire constabulary only mentioned the two gentlemen."

It seemed odd, Paul noted, to be referred to as 'gentlemen' and 'sir'. He knew how they looked – long-haired and scruffy, like they should be living in a commune, or returning to nature, or something. Charlie stood and pulled on a faded blue tee-shirt.

"What's this about?" Paul asked, although, following Imogen's phone call, he already had some idea.

"As you know, Wiltshire police have been making enquiries into the disappearance of your friend James. They have some loose ends they'd like tidied up."

"And what loose ends could they be?" Charlie asked. "James got stoned and disappeared. End of story, I would've thought."

"Could we talk inside?" the policeman asked.

Paul carried his cereal bowl into the kitchen, put it into the sink, and then took the policeman through to the lounge. The policeman introduced himself as Detective Constable Jacobs. Paul returned to the kitchen to make the detective a cup of tea. He picked up the kettle, but Jane had followed Charlie into the room. "Don't worry," she said. "I'll make the tea."

Charlie kissed her. "Won't be long, gorgeous," he said. He went through to the lounge.

"What else can they ask?" Jane said to Paul. "You told the police in Wiltshire everything you knew, didn't you?"

"I can't imagine what else they need to know," Paul said, although Imogen had given him some idea. He followed Charlie into the lounge.

Paul was surprised by what the detective – and, by inference, Wiltshire police – did want to know. As Imogen had hinted, they were obviously *all* under suspicion. The most urgent questions seemed to be about the knife: where was it that night, who had handled it, had it been out of Paul's sight?

"I can't be sure I had the knife all the time," Paul admitted. "I kept blacking out. I don't know how long I was out for."

"James had a lot of money with him," Jacobs said. "Where had it come from? Why was he carrying so much?"

"He had part-time jobs and generous parents," Charlie said.

"Was James a dealer?"

Charlie snorted derisively.

"How can you be sure he *wasn't* a dealer?" the detective pressed.

Paul looked down at the scratched coaster on the table, which had a Dartmoor scene printed on it. "I can't be sure. None of us knows everything."

"You, Mr Maas, live here in Devon," the detective pointed out. "You can't be certain, at all, can you?"

"I might not live in Dereham anymore," Paul said. "And I know I only see James every couple of months, but we've been friends for years. We write to each other. I'm sure we'd know if James had taken up dealing. We're all close, we're all very open with each other. I can't imagine how James could hide something like that."

Jane brought a cup of tea for the detective and then sat on the arm of the sofa, next to Charlie.

"So, as you're all so close," the detective said, "you'll know Mr Woolmer took at least one unaccompanied stroll that night."

Paul felt the need to lie. "Yes, I did."

"But did you know before Miss Peek phoned you?"

Paul wasn't a good liar, and he wasn't going to carry on with the lie now. "How did you suss that out?"

"Just a copper's intuition. So, did you know?"

"No, I didn't," Paul said. He glanced over at Charlie, who'd also become interested in a coaster on the table.

"You omitted to mention this to my colleagues in Wiltshire, Mr Woolmer. Is it true? It is the recollection of your friends..." he consulted his notebook. "Ah... Misses Peek and Rix, and Mr Garland."

"Well, I was pretty... out of it... myself," Charlie said. "But, yeah, I expect I did wander off by myself. It's one of the things that happen up on the hill. We wouldn't have mentioned it the first time we were interviewed because we wouldn't have thought it a big deal. It's just what happens. The only person who doesn't walk around the hill alone is Stu."

"Why?"

"Because he's a big baby and Copsehill can be pretty freaky."

"Ah, I see," the detective said, nodding and smiling. He consulted his notes again. "Miss Peek also went for a walk alone. And we know Miss Rix spent some time dozing. So Mr Garland, his lack of fortitude notwithstanding, could also have wandered away alone and unseen. And, as Mr Maas has already pointed out, he spent some considerable time unconscious. If that is the case, he cannot always have known the location of the knife. And Mr Sands had a good deal of money on him. There at least is one motive."

"Ridiculous," Paul sputtered. "None of us cares about money. James is our best friend. We wouldn't do something *that* stupid just for money."

"The money, as I say, is one motive. There could be others."

Charlie frowned. "Am I under suspicion for this?"

"Not really, Mr Woolmer. And nor are Mr Maas, Mr Garland, Miss Rix or Miss Peek. Not at this moment, anyway. The police in Wiltshire are keeping an open mind. After all, we haven't found Mr Sands yet, so there is no evidence of foul play."

Despite what Jacobs said, Paul knew that they were all, obviously, under suspicion. The detective had hinted that the money James had carried on him was at least one motive for attacking him. "What other motives could there be for attacking one of our best friends?" Paul said.

"Passion. Jealousy. Envy. Greed. We see them all, Mr Maas. For example, is there any reason any of you might be jealous of Mr Sands? Apart from the money, that is."

Paul could think of nothing. The detective stood, and shook hands with each of them, thanking them for their help.

Paul, Jane and Charlie went back into the garden. Charlie slid onto the same sun-lounger as Jane and put his arms around her.

"You don't care about the money," Jane said. "It's ridiculous."

"Of course we don't," Charlie said quietly. "And all the stuff he said about envy, passion, jealousy. As if we ever felt any of that."

Jane looked at Paul and raised an eyebrow. She knew he'd been obsessed with Imogen, everybody knew that. Was she now wondering, Paul thought, whether Charlie was telling the truth? Because there was one of them who had felt, who had suffered, jealousy, envy and passion.

Charlie.

19

Charlie had originally intended to hitch back to Dereham but had decided to take the train instead. Although the carriage he sat in was hot, if he'd hitched and been left on a road somewhere between Devon and Wiltshire, he would have been hotter still. At least here a welcome breeze squeezed through the open quarterlights. There were few people on the train, despite it being another fine day during this long, hot summer. The train had recently stopped at Taunton and now travelled through the Somerset Levels, across fields of brown, burnt grass. Only small, bright cumulus clouds broke the monotony of the huge blue sky above him. He had been reading one of the books Jane had lent him, but he had instead become obsessed with obsession and put the book down. Charlie was beginning to understand something about himself – he was obsessive. Oh, he'd heard the others say it of him, and he had sometimes wondered at the insistence of his concerns, especially about Imogen. But he'd never really thought he had obsessions, that *obsessive* would describe him, that obsession might, in fact, be a personality trait.

Fiona had hypnotised Charlie last night, but they'd learned nothing new, only that he remained certain he had seen a UFO. He'd been disappointed to find he didn't recall rays of light beaming down from the object and illuminating the field, nor remembered a tractor beam hauling James skyward. Jane had, of course, been excited about what he had remembered. His recollections while in the trance only served to confirm what she believed – that he *had* seen an alien spaceship. Jane's belief in his experience had been welcome; he now knew how his friends must have felt in the face of his past scepticism, when they had been more credulous. He'd faced similar doubts from Paul and Fiona and would undoubtedly face it again when he saw Imo, Stuart and Kate again. He found it difficult to accept. Why wouldn't they believe him? Their scepticism had been easy to understand when the events of that night had first occurred, but time had moved on and

James was still missing. Only he and Jane believed he'd seen something unusual, something that might be connected to James's disappearance. Charlie really needed somebody like Stuart to listen to him.

Charlie was sufficiently self-aware to know that his own long-held scepticism had fallen quickly away when confronted by his own sighting, and this sudden conversion from disbelief to belief in UFOs had certainly confused Paul and Stuart. Of all his friends he thought Stuart the most likely to believe him. It was he and Stuart who had first become interested in UFOs, who had first walked the local hills looking for them. Perhaps, in time, Stuart would listen, could be brought around. Charlie knew it would be difficult for Stuart to understand. What had happened to him and to James was outside their experience. The only things people had ever seen around Dereham were lights in the sky. Patterson had once told him about a young woman who claimed to talk to aliens; but she'd committed suicide back in the early seventies. For a moment, Charlie wondered where his obsessions might take him. He should lend Jane's books to Stuart. Then he'd understand why Charlie felt the way he did.

If there was one good thing about all this, Charlie noted, he was no longer obsessed with Imogen. Instead, he was obsessed with UFOs and Jane. He was particularly obsessed with Jane. They'd at last had love, one star-filled night, lying on the brown grass, the warm earth of Blue Tor beneath them. It had been the first time for them both. At least now he wouldn't be a virgin at nineteen, something he'd been secretly dreading. He and Jane were quite mad about each other. He loved seeing her and being around her. He was sorry to leave her. She'd said she loved him, and he'd said he loved her too. This was the first time in his life he'd said it and, just before he said it, in the split-second when he knew he was going to say it, he'd felt his stomach tighten, not with fear, but with an excited anticipation. And after he'd said it, his whole body had relaxed and, as he wrapped his arms around her and found her mouth with his, he was surprised to find he felt like crying with unexpected joy. *I live in a new world. O! Brave new world that has such people in it. Something like that.*

He rather liked this new world, the world containing Jane and her soft skin, this feeling in his heart, the way he wrapped around her, she so small and delicate, almost as if she'd been crafted by unseen hands to slip so easily into his arms, to lie there so warm against him, curved against each other on that warm night surrounded by the scent of *Havoc* and patchouli.

The scenery outside the train began to change, from flat land to hills. He was, he knew, approaching Frome. He'd been so lost in thoughts of Jane, and of flying saucers, and of obsession, the journey had flown by. In fifteen minutes or so, he would be arriving at Westbury station. He had bought a through ticket to Dereham but hadn't checked the timetable for a connecting train. Whether he would wait for a train, or catch a bus, or hitch, or just walk the five miles across the fields in the brilliant July sun, he didn't yet know. At this moment he felt so free, so happy, that all options were open to him, and all seemed equally good. He was aware, however, that he would arrive in Dereham happy and in love while James was still missing.

Imogen had rung last night and told him about the search. It was late, and the sun was setting after another long, hot day. Imogen was exhausted. The police had stopped searching hours ago, she said. They had returned to their cars and vans and slipped away into the warm, rich, evening light. Many friends and acquaintances had turned out to help search for James, or for clues to his disappearance. James was well-liked, and Mark, Steve, John and Danny from Honeyhouse, Simon, Gaz and Nick, Julie and Sarah, Chrissie and Jake, even Dodgy Len and Geezer and some of their friends from The Swan had been there. They'd walked over the hills, investigated thickets and clumps and examined fields. In the end, they too had all drifted away. Imogen had thanked each one of them, grateful for their help. Then she, Kate and Stuart had walked the search area again. Simon, Danny and Mark had stayed behind and joined them. There had been no sign of James. Nothing had fallen from his pockets, no wallet, no money, no items of clothing. There had been no clues, there had been nothing suspicious at all. Imogen had sounded tired, sad, frustrated. Charlie consoled her as best he could from where he was. He would see her soon he said, and they could talk things over.

He pushed aside for now the feelings within him. For the last few minutes he was to be on this train, he would think only of kissing

Jane. He felt the ghost shape of her, conjured from fragments of sensory impressions – her breasts pressing against him as he hugged her to him, the shape of her hips, the dip at the waist. From behind closed eyes, he saw again the knot of her halter-top, felt the cord beneath his fingers as he was finally, in the still night air, allowed to tug at it and watch the knot unravel.

He felt the train slowing, He opened his eyes. He could see the White Horse, the cement works, and knew he was approaching Westbury. The sight revealed as Jane's halter-top had fallen open and the fabric had slipped, slowly, gently down and crumpled onto the grass between them, faded now. The train slowed, clanking and jerking across points. The red-brick station buildings and grey platforms marked the end, if only for a few weeks, of the dream life he'd been living in Devon and had managed until now to carry with him on the train. Charlie opened his bag to put his books away. He was surprised to find a piece of cord on top of his clothes. He took it out of the bag. Jane must have placed it there when he wasn't looking. She had tied it into a bow. Experimentally, he pulled both ends of the cord. The knot began to slip. Not wishing to unravel it further, he replaced it in his bag. He smiled, then looked out of the window. The train stopped at the station. He stood, sighed, and made his way towards the doors. The train wasn't terminating, but for now the idyll was.

20

Over the years, Imogen had become accustomed to finding articles about Dereham in the Sunday papers. He'd been proselytising the Dereham mystery for years. The frequency at which such articles appeared had, however, diminished over time as what had once been strange and esoteric had become mundane. She was not surprised, therefore, to find an article about Dereham in the paper. This one had obviously been written by Richard Patterson. She read through it. Despite the liberal use of 'perhaps' and 'might', she was unsurprised to find Patterson suggesting that James had been abducted. The article bothered her. She didn't know why it bothered her so much. Perhaps because it made James's disappearance so final. If James ever came back, it was only when "they' – whoever or whatever "they' might be – allowed. But she wanted James back now. She would have a word with Patterson. Or, at least, she hoped Charlie or Stuart would – they knew Patterson better than she did, from their frequent visits to Copsehill and to the UFO Centre. She would suggest it to them.

Mr Sands now firmly believed James had never intended to buy a car. He had taken the money out of the bank for some other reason and slipped quietly away from Dereham, away from his family and friends. He'd used the money to run off to Tibet, or to an ashram, or to a commune. He had deliberately got Paul stoned while only pretending to drop a tab himself. Why James would want to do this, Mr Sands had no idea. He'd asked Imogen whether she and James had argued; Imogen assured him that they had not. Mrs Sands continued to worry that something awful had happened to James, that he was in a hospital somewhere. The police had assured her, however, that no hospital in Wiltshire had admitted anybody fitting James's description, and nor had any hospitals in neighbouring counties.

Imogen liked Mr Sands' theory, because it at least implied James was safe. When the police had kept asking about the knife, and why Charlie had gone for a walk alone, Imogen had begun to think that something terrible might have happened, after all. If Charlie had been here a few days ago, and not in Devon, she might also have started questioning him. But now she too thought that James had simply slipped away, had planned everything just so he could leave without telling his friends, without telling *her*. Yet this idea always bumped up against the one unknown – why would he do such a thing?

She didn't believe any of her friends had attacked James to steal his money, or for any other reason. She did worry, though, that somebody else might have attacked him while he was stoned. He might, she thought, have wandered back into town, or towards Southleigh, and been mugged. The event vividly played itself out again in her imagination. She saw the car pull up beside James as he staggered down a road somewhere. She heard the two men laugh as they took the piss out of him, the way he looked, his hair, his clothes, and then ask for his wallet. James refused, thinking perhaps they were demons that had escaped from the ritual. Then she imagined the confrontation: a struggle, a knife perhaps, and James collapsing, holding his chest. And then the two assailants panicking and bundling the injured James into their car and driving him up onto Salisbury Plain or the Mendips and dumping him there. Anxiety clutched at her stomach again, as it always did when she thought of these scenes.

That hadn't happened, though. She was sure of it. She breathed, tried to relax. James was alive, she thought. Even if he had spent a couple of nights out in the open, unconscious, he would have survived. He was young and fit – well, as fit as an eighteen-year old, brandy-soaked smoker can be. The thunderstorms, which would have soaked him had he been caught in them, had all happened during daylight, and it had been warm ever since. He might anyway have holed up in a barn, copse, or pigsty. James was fine. A little freaked out, perhaps, but basically fine. She knew she was again indulging in the endless and circular speculation which now occupied her waking hours.

If he'd *planned* to go, thought, why not tell her? She'd talked to Stuart and Kate, but really, they got nowhere. Why, after all, would a young man with a comfortable home, a nice girlfriend, money and tolerant parents, run away? The only thing she hadn't know about James had been something Kate and Stuart had told her, after the search, as they walked back to James's house. Trying to find a reason why he might have left, she had asked Stuart if James was upset with her for any reason.

"Not that I know of," Stuart said. "He loves you."

"Do you think he took all that money out of the bank for the car?" Imogen asked.

"Well, if buying a car was a ruse," Stuart said, "it was cleverly executed. He'd been looking for one for weeks. He even asked my Dad what he thought of different makes and models." Stuart shook his head. "He never had a plan to go. Something happened to him on the hill. Whatever that was, it was enough to make him leave."

"Or if you listen to Charlie," Imogen said, "he's been abducted."

Stuart nodded. "Where's that shit suddenly come from?"

"He says he knows what he saw. Now he can't believe it was anything other than a spaceship."

"And Jane's really into UFOs. She's bound to have an influence on him at the moment."

"Was there anything else James was worried about?" Imogen wondered.

"He was worried about what he was going to do next, after college. We all had big plans to go off to university and polytechnic. But he hadn't made any. You know that. I do think he was worried about being left behind. Especially when it was possible he wouldn't see some of us at all for weeks."

"That wouldn't be enough to make him run off, surely?"

"I suppose not. But he was tripping. Who knows what delusions he might have suffered."

Kate had touched Imogen's arm then. "There was one other thing he talked to me about."

"To you?" Imogen had said, surprised.

"Yeah, to me. Because I was your oldest friend. He was worried that when you went to Uni you'd get to know lots of interesting blokes, even freakier than him, brighter than him. And who... drank less than he did. He thought you might be swayed, you know? That you might leave him."

"Stupid lambikins," Imogen sighed. "I wasn't planning to. I love the stupid little freak."

"None of us can know what's going to happen," Stuart said.

"I know. We all know that. How long are you and Katie going to be together? You don't know. None of us do. We're still young. We can be practical and say it won't last forever, this is all puppy love, we'll get over it. But if we accepted that, we'd all just fuck and move on, wouldn't we?"

"Some of us do," Kate said.

Imogen put an arm around Kate and drew her closer. "Yes, some of us do. But at this moment, I would stay with James forever if he would just come back. I hope he didn't leave because of what he said to you. That would be stupid." She paused. "*Stupid*," she repeated for emphasis.

Since then, non of them had come up for with a good reason for James to leave. She had talked to Stuart a lot since then. Out of all James's friends, Stuart was the closest. They shared similar tastes and Stuart was always at his house, listening to music, talking about books, or writing songs with James. Surely he would know if James had been unhappy about something, if he was unhappy with her? He could add nothing, though, to what Kate had already told her. There might have been other reasons for James to leave that she didn't know about. Perhaps he *was* a dealer and had got on the wrong side of some Mr Big. Perhaps he was being abused or bullied by somebody. All her speculations went around and around in circles. The only things she knew for certain, she thought, were what Stuart and Kate had told her that day. And if those were James's fears, they seemed unimportant, silly even. They wouldn't cause James to run away, stoned or not.

Anyway, the plans everybody had made or discussed in spring and early summer were always likely to change. James's best friend now intended to remain in Dereham for another year at least. Although Stuart had planned to go to Plymouth, he still dithered. He simply couldn't decide whether to study something eminently practical like engineering, or something, as he put it, vague and woolly. He had instead decided to take a year out and return to education next year. None of the others were moving far from Dereham. Imogen had only ever intended going to universities in the southwest. Her first choice had been Bath, otherwise Bristol or Exeter. Charlie's first choice was also Bath. Even Paul would be closer if he secured a place at Bristol, his first choice. There had been nothing for James to worry about. And what if she did go to Exeter? It was only a two-hour train ride away. Moreover, James had intended buying a car and learning to drive – he could have visited whenever he liked. They'd already discussed it. And if she got into Bath university – which was likely, as she knew she'd done well in her A-levels – and Charlie and Kate got in as well, then, really, they'd still all be together, just twenty miles up the road from where they were now. James could come and live with them all in Bath, if he wanted. *Or he could live with me, as we discussed.* No, James wouldn't have run off just because the rest of us were moving away, she thought. That would be absurd.

There was a soft knock at her bedroom door. Charlie had phoned yesterday to find out if there was any news on James and said he might be over this evening. He peeped around the door in his characteristic way, before allowing his long body to follow once he was sure, it seemed, that everything was as it should be in her room. He hugged her and kissed her cheek, then he sat on the chair by her desk and began to roll a cigarette.

Charlie looked around the room. "Where's the ashtray?"

"Oh, sorry, yes, the ashtray." Imogen opened a drawer in her desk and removed a glass ashtray which she handed to Charlie. "I haven't needed it often since James disappeared."

The spider plant was wilting, she noticed, another forgotten victim of James's disappearance. Imogen poured water into the pot from a glass she had brought up and placed on the cabinet beside the bed. She turned back to Charlie, who was looking at the photograph on her desk.

"I haven't seen this one before, have I?" Charlie asked.

"Yes, you have. You took it."

Charlie picked up the framed photograph from the desk and

looked at it more closely. "Oh, yes, I remember. You've cropped it, haven't you. That was a good night."

Charlie returned the picture to Imogen. She looked at it and smiled sadly. Charlie had taken the photograph on her camera, after a Honeyhouse gig. Stuart and the boys in Honeyhouse were in the background, their arms around each other. Julie, Simon, Nick and some other friends who'd been standing at the side of the frame had been cropped out. She and James were in front of the band. She was looking at the camera, a smile on her face, while James, barely visible behind his dark, straggly hair, kissed her cheek. She had cropped the photo down to its current size because, although there were other photos of her and James together, none showed them kissing. This was a nice photo, a picture of love and friendship as she and James kissed in front of their friends. They were happy. They were all happy It *had* been a good night, as Charlie said. She carefully placed the photograph back on the desk

Charlie tapped ash from his rollie into the glass ashtray. The glass was clean and sparkling without the ash from James's Sobranie smearing it. She almost felt as if Charlie defiled it, as if she wanted it, needed it, to stay clean until James returned.

"Did you see the newspaper?" Imogen asked. She knew Charlie would know which newspaper she meant. Both her parents and Charlie's parents had the same Sunday paper delivered, although her parents took three Sunday newspapers, whereas Charlie's parents took just the one.

"I saw Patterson's article," Charlie said.

"It pissed me off."

"Why?"

"I don't really know. Because it makes James's disappearance so final. Unsolvable, I suppose. I don't know, it all seems a bit crazy. Why not simply say he ran off somewhere? For his own reasons?"

"Why would he do that?"

"It's what Mr Sands thinks. He thinks James used the money to lose himself somewhere. Whenever I see him, he asks if James and I were getting along okay."

Charlie took another drag of his cigarette. "I'm not buying it. What about the police? What are they saying?"

"Well, I think *we're* in the clear now. Although I can see why they were suspicious. You and I both went off alone that night." Imogen could feel her heart sinking as she talked about this all over again. She wanted to change the subject. "Did you have a good time with Paul and Jane?"

"Well, I had a brilliant time with Jane. I merely tolerated the presence of Paul. Let's face it, he's now turned from a best friend into my girlfriend's big brother."

She was relieved. She had wanted him to enjoy his time with Jane. "What did you get up to while you were there?"

"That's not for your ears, young lady."

"I don't mean sexy stuff. Did you do anything different? Did you go anywhere?"

"It was way too hot. We spent most our time lazing around Paul's garden or going up to Blue Tor. We managed to drag ourselves to Paignton beach once, but it was so crowded, we didn't stay long."

"So, things are good with Jane?"

"They are. I just wished I lived closer. It's okay now, during the holidays, but what am I going to do once we start at Uni?"

"You'll have your grant. You'll be able to get down at weekends. And her parents will probably let her come and see you."

"Yeah, Jane's been bending their ears about it."

"Everything will work out."

"How are you holding up?"

They'd returned to the subject she'd been trying to avoid. "I'm okay, Charlie, but I miss James and I want him back."

"Well, if you're right, he'll probably come back when his money runs out. Back to the bank of Dad."

"Yes. I hadn't thought of that. The bank of Dad." She tried to keep hope from her voice but failed. "He'll run out of money eventually, won't he Charlie?"

"Of course he will," Charlie said.

He was trying to sound hopeful, too. He was doing it for her, she knew. He, after all, believed his daft idea about James being abducted. Any hope James would come back when his money ran out soon faded, though. She knew James too well. he had never been work-shy. If he *had* run away, and wanted to stay away, he'd find a job and keep himself alive.

The bedroom door opened. She looked up to find Stuart smiling at her. He came in and sat down on the bed. He asked Charlie about his trip to Devon. They talked about Charlton and Torbay for a little while.

"And how are you and Jane getting on," Stuart asked.

Charlie took from his pocket the knotted cord he'd taken to carrying with him everywhere. He explained its significance to Stuart and Imogen.

"She's very droll, that girl," Stuart said.

Charlie looked embarrassed for a moment. "I think I love her, Stu."

"Only think?" Imogen said, smiling. "Don't be so reticent. Embrace your emotions." She was genuinely happy for him.

"I do. I know I do."

"I'm not surprised," Stuart said. "She's such a sweetheart."

"Where's Katie?" Charlie asked.

"Oh, I'm on my way to Kate's now. I stop in here to see if Imo's all right. Not that there's anything I can do, but, you know..."

"Yeah, I know. Imo was telling me she thinks he's run off for some reason."

"I don't know what to think. It's certainly the most... *banal...* version of events. Nobody dies, nobody is spirited away."

"What do you think?" Charlie asked.

"I have no idea, Charles, I really don't. I hope he's run off and he's safe. But if he has run away, I don't understand why."

"I don't know why he would either," Imogen said.

"You know what I think," Charlie said.

Imogen grimaced. "And you still believe that?"

"Yeah. I'm even more convinced. The police have turned up nothing. And we know none of us did the deed, guv. And you both have no idea why he would want to leave." Charlie shrugged. "So aliens is all I have."

Stuart stood up, then went over to the teak shelves where Imogen's records leaned against each other. He pulled out Peter Hammill's

Chameleon in the Shadow of Night. Charlie rolled a cigarette while Stuart put the record on the deck and started it playing.

"Want one?" Charlie asked. Stuart nodded. Charlie tossed him the cigarette he'd just rolled and began to roll himself another.

Stuart sat on the bed again. He looked at Imogen. There was a faint smile on his lips. "So, our Charles still believes James is up there," he said, rolling his eyes skyward.

"I do," Charlie said.

"I suppose none of us will know where he's been until he comes back," Imogen said. "If he *is* up there–" she mimicked Stuart's expression. "I hope they're treating him well. And, at least, he'll learn something."

"I wonder if they still have books?" Charlie said.

"I wonder what their sci-fi would be about?" Stuart said.

21

Charlie yawned and stretched. He'd eaten his breakfast. He would see Stuart later, but first he thought he'd have a word with Richard Patterson about the articles in the newspapers. Imogen had told him her concerns. It was a small thing he could do for her. When he arrived at the UFO Centre, he found Patterson fussing around a recently donated electric typewriter.

"Look at this!" Patterson said excitedly. The UFO Centre ran on donations, the meagre fees he charged skywatchers to stay in a room there, and whatever he could scrounge. "You only have to touch a key lightly, and the hammer fairly whacks the paper." Patterson touched a key. A mechanism whirred somewhere in the machine, then there was a smack of metal against paper. "I'll be able to produce the journal so much quicker!"

Charlie sat in a chair on the opposite side of Patterson's desk, amused at his child-like glee. There was an indefinable smell to the room that Charlie always thought of as paper and ink. "Are you going to say anything about James in your journal?" he asked.

"Naturally!" Patterson replied. "It's the biggest thing to have happened around here for a while. I've already written most of the story."

"Do you really think he's been abducted?"

"Why not? Why shouldn't abductions happen in Britain? Especially *here*, in Dereham. We've got more UFOs around here than anywhere else in Europe! James's abduction is big news." Patterson eyed Charlie. "Why? What do you think happened?"

Charlie agreed with Patterson, of course, but didn't want to tell him this. Telling his friends that he believed James had been abducted was one thing; telling Patterson was a step he couldn't yet take. "I'm sure I saw a UFO. But abduction?"

"Oh, thanks for reminding me. I need a full description of your sighting for the story in the journal."

Patterson picked up a notebook and pencil from his desk. "I might get your story in the *Gazette*." He tapped his pencil lightly on his bottom teeth. "Perhaps even in the *Daily Mirror*. What do you reckon, Charlie? Your name in the *Mirror*?"

"Well, you've got to make a living somehow," Charlie said. He described the UFO he had seen and the other events at the skywatch. Patterson stopped him occasionally to ask questions, his eyes bright with excitement as he made notes.

"If James comes back tomorrow, your ideas about aliens are going to look pretty silly," Charlie said, even though he knew he was being hypocritical.

"Even if he does come back tomorrow, he might not remember what happened to him. Look at Betty and Barney Hill, they didn't remember everything until they were hypnotised."

"I've been reading about the Hills," Charlie said. "My girlfriend lent me some books."

"The Hills are famous," Patterson said. "But there have been more recent events. There was Calvin Parker and Charles Hickson in some place called Pascagoula, in America, a couple of years back. And I've heard about one from late last year in America, some guy called Travis Walton." Patterson stood up. He looked though the books and papers stuffed into the shelves ranged about the room. "Here we go," he said. He pulled out some journals and handed them to Charlie. "Have a read through those and tell me what you think."

"Thanks. By the way, Imogen – you know, James's girlfriend? She's a bit upset by what you wrote."

"Really? How on earth could she be upset by what I wrote?"

"Because it makes everything so final, I suppose."

"But if he's been abducted, at least he's not dead, which is what the police were worried about for a while." Patterson chuckled. "At least, that's what they told me."

"They told you?"

"Well, not in so many words. But I've been talking to the police about stories and covering the local courts for years. You learn to read between the lines. Did you know *you* were in the frame, Charlie? Still are, I think. You probably all are. Except for a Miss Rix. Is that Stuart's girlfriend?"

"Yes, that's her." Charlie stared at his coffee. "It was obvious they might suspect me."

Patterson laughed gently again. "Well yes, they would, young man. Until James turns up, you'll all remain under suspicion. What's it all about? Something to do with a wad of money and a knife?"

"I'm not giving you an exclusive, Richard, so stop asking."

"A poor reporter has to try."

"I suppose there's nothing I can say to make you stop writing about James?"

"Who's asking?"

"Imo. I don't care, really."

"Oh well. They can't censor me. Freedom of the press, young man. And so on. Although you can put it more politely to the lovely Imogen."

They stopped talking for a while, the silence interrupted by the clack of Patterson's typewriter. He'd already started typing up the sighting report.

The typing stopped and Patterson looked at Charlie. "I've asked a UFO group in London to give a lecture here. They're really into abductions. Would you come?"

"Yeah, I might do. When is it?"

"In a couple of weeks' time. At the Wool Hall. I'd already arranged it with them, but what with James going missing, we've agreed to bring it forward. It'll cost you a couple of quid to get in."

"You *are* an opportunist."

"As you said, a man's got to make a living."

"True, true," Charlie said. He stood up. "I need to get going," he said. "Thanks for the loan of the articles."

"No problem," Patterson said. "I'm sure I'll see you around town. I'll let you know the date for the lecture."

Charlie hoped Jane's parents would allow her to come up for the lecture. She'd love it. And she could at last visit Copsehill. She'd heard so much about it, had read about it, but had never visited it. When her family had lived in Dereham, she'd been too young to accompany the boys on their late-night jaunts to the hill. And, anyway, they'd only started visiting it a year or so before the family left for Devon. Charlie worked out how old Jane had been then. About thirteen. *She thought we were weirdoes then.* She was now quickly becoming a freak herself. His little weird freako. She'd even surprised him with some music he'd never heard before, some band called The Mighty Ones she'd heard on the radio. She still listened to *Fleetwood Mac*; and now, so did he. He'd rather come to admire its polished professionalism and its well-crafted tunes. And, whatever faults he might otherwise find with it, it was at least better than the Rollers, or Mud, or Wizzard, or some other pop-chart crap she might instead have been listening to.

He arrived at Stuart's house, singing *Rhiannon* to himself. He knocked at the front door but received no answer. He walked down the path to the back garden where he found Stuart lying in the sun, reading a book, listening to the radio.

"Hi, man," Charlie said.

Stuart looked over. "Hey! What's up?"

"Just been down to see Patterson. He lent me these." Charlie waved the journals in his hand. "Abduction reports in American UFO journals."

"Did you tell him Imo was upset?"

"Yeah. He'll just keep writing what he wants though."

"No surprise there. Any other news from the UFO Centre?"

"Patterson is inviting a UFO group down from London to give a lecture on abductions. Do you reckon you'd go along?"

"I might. Do you know when it is?"

"Some time soon, a couple of weeks. Patterson's arranging it for the Wool Hall – he doesn't think the UFO Centre will be able to hold the throng."

"Surely he can fit four people in his front room?"

Charlie laughed. "Make that five. I'm hoping Jane can come up that weekend. I can show her Copsehill and Derebury. We can go for the usual walks. She'll love it."

"She will. Katie and I will come along too, if you don't mind. She doesn't know all our walks yet. And Imo. It would be good for Imo to get out. It would take her mind off things."

"When are you seeing Imo again?"

"Tonight. On my way over to Kate's."

"You're seeing a lot of her."

"Well, it's on my way. I can hitch over to Imo's and then walk the rest of the way."

"What does Katie think?"

"Why should she think anything, man?"

"Well, Imo's a good-looking girl, and you're dropping in there every night. Doesn't Kate ever worry about you?"

"Nobody ever worries about me." Stuart grinned at Charlie. "I'm harmless."

"Yeah, right. What are you doing for the rest of the afternoon?"

"Listening to the cricket and reading."

"Think I'll join you. I'll read these articles." He sat on the grass beside Stuart. "How's the cricket?"

"Willis bowled like a man possessed and got five wickets. England need 204 to win."

"Not much, is it?"

"You'd think not. But, unfortunately, they're already thirty-two for three."

"Shit. Depressing."

The telephone handset was warm in Charlie's hand; he could feel sweat against the plastic. The evening was, as usual, hot and close. He'd already been holding the handset eagerly to his ear for half an hour. Jane said she'd like to read the articles.

"I'll bring them down with me," Charlie said.

"When *is* the lecture?" Jane asked.

"In a couple of weeks or so. Patterson works fast. I'll come down the week before. I can work my charm on your mum and dad. Then you can come back with me and Paul. "

"I'll whine at mum and dad until they let me let me go."

"I've already asked my mum if you can stay here. She says it's fine. You can sleep in my bed and I can sleep on Will's floor."

"I'd rather I slept in your bed and you slept in it with me."

"So would I, darling, so would I. But I don't think mother would appreciate such shenanigans."

"I don't think mum and dad would let me come up if they knew that was the plan," Jane said. "I can't wait to see you, Charlie. You can undo me again."

"Is that our new name for it?" Charlie said.

"I am a woman undone," Jane softly.

"And on that pleasant thought, I'll say goodbye."

"I love you, Charlie."

"I love you too."

Charlie replaced the handset in the cradle, then went to his room, taking with him Jane's books and the journals. He'd read through the journals once at Stuart's house, and now wanted to read them again. Charlie found the stories fascinating. The missing time, the forgotten memories, the physical examinations were all strange enough; but the appeared to be a very strange sexual thing also happening – sperm and egg samples were being taken, and there were naked barking aliens. The abduction scenario seemed simply, at any level, strange. If the UFO phenomenon had previously been odd and exciting, abductions took it to a different level. The contactee cases of earlier decades seemed much less strange than abductions; in fact, they seemed rather mundane. In the end, the contactee stories contained nothing very exciting – that was the problem, Charlie thought. The aliens never provided useful information about anything – no breakthrough technologies, no interesting scientific theories. The aliens seemed only interested in telling contactees how fantastically long-lived they were and how sensible, well-run and organised their societies were. They seemed to have no interest in helping humans become as fantastic as the aliens claimed to be.

The abduction stories were something else entirely. They overturned the flying saucer myth that Charlie had come to know. In the contactee stories there had seemed at least to be a sense that aliens and humans communicated as equals. In the abduction stories, however, the aliens showed a darker side – they took humans without consent, performed strange procedures on them, and then erased the memories of what had happened. Charlie wondered why the aliens hadn't simply asked the contactees – who had, after all, always seemed so excited, so willing, to be part of the alien experience – if they would mind being the subjects of experiments. *I say old chap, would you mind lying on this bed while we stick a needle in you?* The aliens could have explained that the procedures would be harmless and painless, and that, anyway, any bad memories could be removed afterwards if the experience proved too traumatic. Charlie felt there was definitely a break here, a ... he groped for a word... a *rupture*... between one type of UFO story, the one he'd known for the last five or so years, and this new type of story. Before, it had all seemed so unthreatening and, indeed, a little cosy. Now, the UFO seemed more menacing – at any moment, a life could be invaded, and normality shattered.

What would this London UFO group have to say? Very little was known about abductions, so it would surely all be speculation. Would they have an opinion about James? Would they know something Charlie didn't? That if a UFO flashed its lights, it was a sign that an abduction was about to happen? That abductions were inextricably and inexplicably linked to badly executed occult rituals? That aliens liked to pick up hippie-Marxist-capitalist contradictions? When James returned – if he ever returned – would it be with tales of benevolent space gods or sinister space devils?

So many questions. If James *had* been abducted, Charlie thought, at least suspicion of involvement in James's disappearance would no longer fall on him. The police wouldn't accept such a fantastic story, they would think it ludicrous. But it might stop the others – Imogen, Stuart and Kate – wondering if he had done something to James. He knew they had their suspicions, despite what they said. And could he blame them? He was himself still troubled by the blackouts, by the episodes of missing time, and wondered what had happened during those dark moments. What might he have done, what *had* he done, in that time?

Charlie forced himself to think of Jane. Was he as obsessed with Jane as he'd been with Imogen? His feelings for Jane were different. Hopeful rather than hopeless, happy and engaged rather than bitter, twisted and empty. Their relationship felt... nice. A banal word, he knew, but what could be nicer, really, than nice? It was all so easy, so free, so giving and loving and tender and warm and open and...

and... He rested on his bed, floating in a warm sea of tender, relaxing, niceness. The heat pressed on him and he drifted into sleep.

22

Peter Richards and his friends drank cold lager in the fading light of a warm evening.

'If we come clean now,' Phil said, 'Charlie will stop talking about his UFO sighting, and Patterson will have nothing to write about.'

Rob nodded. 'I can't help feeling it's our fault James ran away. Perhaps he saw our lights and because he was tripping thought he was seeing horrible aliens or something.'

'Well, even if I say so myself,' Peter replied, 'the lights were impressive. And they certainly got Charlie going. But, honestly, if James ran away, was it because of the lights, or because of the acid? Charlie hasn't run off, has he? It was just an unlucky coincidence we were there. Anything might have made James run away. James and his mate were doing some kind of ritual thing, we know that from Patterson's stories. Something went wrong. So he might have run away from some demon he thought they'd conjured.'

'Yes, I suppose so,' Phil said.

'And, if we say anything now,' Rob added, 'we won't get to send up the balloon on the Bank Holiday weekend.'

Peter nodded. There was the problem. If they were to reveal that the 'UFO' currently exciting Patterson was really Peter's box of tricks, there would be no more 'experiments'. Ufologists would realise that Peter and his friends had been hoaxing skywatchers in Dereham for some time. And Peter didn't want the world to know that – not now, anyway. He hadn't yet found the proper audience for his new device. Peter had been loath to fly it on the night James had run away. There had been too few people on the hill, and he knew, from previous visits to Dereham that all of his intended – subjects? victims? – were various shades of sceptic. He knew them all by sight, had seen them in the pubs and on the hill, knew they called themselves the Prophets, had even talked to Stuart and Charlie once or twice, which was how he knew them to be more sceptical than typical skywatchers. But Phil and Rob had encouraged him, saying they had driven a long way, and these might be the only skywatchers they would catch. Which had been true – nobody had come to the hill the next night.

Peter was anticipating the August Bank Holiday. A large crowd always gathered at Copsehill on Bank Holidays. Peter couldn't help guiltily thinking that James's disappearance might be a useful occurrence. Patterson's exaggerated and wild stories about James were likely to draw even larger crowds to the hill. And although Phil and Rob also felt bad about James, they too wanted to fly the device on a night when Patterson was on Copsehill, and find out how he and thirty or forty excitable skywatchers would react.

From his few conversations with the Prophets, Peter had supposed Charlie to be the pragmatic, sceptical one, so was surprised to learn that Charlie had been fooled by their hoax, and now seemed convinced UFOs existed.

'Just think,' Peter said. 'If we can convert a sceptic like Charlie, what will we do to a group of people who *want* to believe?'

Peter didn't know if Charlie conversion has been encouraged by Patterson. Charlie's conversion certainly demonstrated *something* – one man changed from easy-going sceptic to believer in alien abductions, simply because of some flashing lights. What a change of attitude! Changes of attitude and conversion, Peter thought, must be a central part of the sociology of ufology. He didn't know anything about these topics. He resolved to find some books in the university library.

"Perhaps we can say something after the Bank Holiday," Peter said.

Phil agreed. "After Patterson has seen his lightshow."

"And written yet more articles," Rob added.

"And we can put Patterson in his place," Peter said. He always wanted to fool Patterson, to catch him hook, line and sinker. His desire was even more acute now, now that he'd seen how Patterson was handling the disappearance of James. Poor James. He had probably freaked out on bad acid at this botched ritual and gone running off into the night and was now holed-up somewhere suffering psychotic delusions while Patterson made money off the back of his troubles. Unless, that is, one of his friends had killed him; there were dark hints in some newspapers that this had indeed happened. The reports implied that the crime – if crime there were – involved knives, money, and beautiful young women who could turn the heads of sensible young men.

"But we can't reveal what we've been doing for some time after the holidays," Peter said. "We need to see how people react. We need to give them time to discuss what they saw and write about it in the newsletters."

They would have to wait at least a couple of months before they received all the magazines produced by the UFO groups, as some were only published quarterly or bi-monthly. Peter wanted to read bare, unvarnished reports about his lights. If people knew the UFO had been a hoax, their memories of what they had seen would be influenced by what they read about it. They would remember what they had seen differently. The knowledge that the sighting had only been a balloon with lights on it would contaminate their reports. It would become obvious to them, retrospectively, that it had all been very mundane. He also wanted the reports to be only about his lights, not about the circumstances surrounding them. Nor did he want to read pontifications on how people could be so easily fooled. No – when the time for pontifications came, he wanted the first to be his. He hoped he could interest a proper journal, a sociology or psychology journal, in his account of the hoaxes. But he knew his article would most likely be published in *Flying Saucer Review* or British UFO Research Association's *Times*.

"We could be discovered at any moment," Rob said.

Peter nodded. "I know, I know. But one good ascent is all we need."

There was always the risk that someone might, one night, catch them setting up their hoaxes. This was even more likely with the current device. They needed to be close to Copsehill, so they could see what the skywatchers were signalling. In fact, the night the Prophets had been on the hill, Stuart and his girlfriend had come too close for comfort while he and Rob had been setting up the balloons. Peter had heard them laughing in the distance, just as Phil had lit a cigarette. The laughing had stopped, and Peter knew that Stuart had seen the flame from the lighter. After a short while, the talking had started again. Peter had recognised Stuart's voice, although he'd been too far away to make out what Stuart was saying. He'd been grateful it was Stuart. Charlie would probably have wandered over to investigate. But Peter knew, from his brief conversations with them, that Stuart, although sceptical, was the most nervous of the group, and was the most likely to shy away from anything unusual on the hill.

Most ufologists walked or drove up Lavington Road to Copsehill. The Prophets, however, were ramblers as well as skywatchers. They knew all the footpaths around the hills and liked to walk them at night. One day, Peter knew, he and his friends would be discovered putting together one of their elaborate devices. "If anybody is ever going to catch us," Peter mused, "it'll be a Prophet."

"It'll probably be Charlie," Phil said.

"Yeah, it'll be Charlie," he said. "And if it is, he'll probably just sit down and roll me a joint."

23

The following evening, Charlie sat with Imogen in her bedroom. She was on her bed, while he was on the chair by her small writing desk. She listened to Radio 3. Classical music played quietly in the background. He didn't understand classical music.

"I saw Patterson," Charlie said. "He's going to keep writing about James. He said, and I quote, *It's a free press, old chap. Nobody can censor me.* And all that shite." He paused. "Only he didn't say, *and all that shite*. I just said it. Just then."

Imogen smiled, and then sighed. "Oh well," she said. "I believe in all that... shite... too."

Charlie studied Imogen. She had bags under her eyes. Her long curly hair was tied back in an elastic band, from which a loose end escaped and fell across her cheek.

"Are you sleeping okay?" he asked.

"It's getting better. I seem to be only one who's worried though. Mr and Mrs Sands are now *convinced* he ran away because of something I did. They think he's perfectly fine somewhere."

"But not Whimple?"

Imogen laughed, despite herself. "No, not Whimple. Stuart believes, more in hope than anything, that he's weirded out and living in a squat somewhere. And you believe he's been abducted."

"It's one solution," Charlie said.

"A pretty far-fetched one, if you ask me."

"What about you?"

"I still worry that he was attacked, like I've said before. Or that he really is in a hospital somewhere, ill and nobody has recognised him yet..." Her voice tailed off. Then she said, plaintively, "He might need me, Charlie."

"Have you seen much of his parents?"

"Since they've come to believe I'm at the root of it all, they've been less welcoming," she said.

"What do they think you could possibly have done?"

"Slept with somebody else."

Charlie was surprised. "What?"

"Those are the dark hints."

"But who? Somebody from college?"

"In a sense."

"What do you mean?"

"Stu."

"Stuart? But he's with Kate."

"Stuart and I have always been close. You know that. There was plenty of opportunity before Kate came along."

"What do you mean, opportunity?"

Imogen blushed and looked down at her lap. "Oh, not like that. But, you know, Stuart and I have known each other for ages, and we were often alone together. It's not as if James had me on a leash or anything. And we aren't always been together, you know that. We split up and then we're back on again. We're very confusing."

Charlie felt suddenly vindicated. At least one of his obsessions had a basis in reality. It wasn't some weird personal grudge or strange fantasy – well, perhaps a fantasy, as nothing had happened between Stuart and Imogen. But his obsessions were not so outlandish that James's parents hadn't also considered the possibilities that Charlie had imagined. Anyway, what was so fantastic about it? Imogen and Stuart hung around together and spent a lot of time alone with each other. They were young and clearly attracted to each other.

Charlie changed the subject, before he fell into the groove again. "Are you coming to the UFO lecture?"

"I wouldn't have gone to one when James was around," Imogen said. "I'm certainly not going to start frequenting them now."

The bedroom door opened, and Stuart entered.

"Hi, kiddies," he said.

"On your way to Kate's?" Charlie asked.

"Not tonight. She's out with her mum at some architectural thing."

"Just her mum?" Imogen said.

"I think so. I've never seen her dad."

"You won't," Imogen said. "There's a lot of bad blood there. It's almost as if he's dead. Kate has hardly seen him since she was eight. Nobody really talks about it."

"Anyway," Stuart said. "They're out. Glugging champagne and eating truffles, or whatever it is posh people do."

"*We* sip champagne and nibble delicately at our crudités," Imogen said.

"Ar, that moight well be true," Stuart said, emphasising his Wiltshire accent, "but give oi "alf a gurt pig and a point o' scrumpy any noight. Us don't need any of your fancy Frenchified cuisine, do us, Charles?"

Imogen laughed.

"Sorry, can't understand your lingo, old chap," Charlie said. "Given any more thought to the lecture?"

"Oh, I'll probably be there," Stuart replied. "I can think of better ways to spend a couple of quid, but somebody's got to keep your feet on the ground."

"I never thought I'd hear you say that about me," Charlie said.

"I never thought I'd hear me say that about you," Stuart said. "I'd always assumed it would be the other way around. If any of us was to go off the deep end, I thought it would be me."

"Do you think I've gone off the deep end?"

Stuart looked at Imogen with a smile. They both nodded emphatically at Charlie. "You've gone bonkers, man," Stuart said.

Charlie wondered if Stuart and Imogen were finally revealing their true feelings about his adoption of strange beliefs. Stuart winked at Imogen. Charlie had noticed a change in her demeanour. Before Stuart had arrived she'd seemed tired, often looking down at her hands and watching them knit and unknit in her lap. Her shoulders were slumped. But from the moment Stuart walked through the door, she'd changed. She seemed brighter, happier. When Stuart had talked nonsense, there had been a twinkle in her eye. *Perhaps James's parents are right.* The idea didn't seem so preposterous. Stuart and Imogen always said they'd done no more than kiss and hold hands, and Charlie had willingly accepted that story right through the worst of his obsessions. And could Stuart have kept something so significant and exciting from him? *Surely Stu would've wanted to talk to somebody about it? He couldn't talk to James about it, obviously. He would've talked to me, surely?* Or would he? Charlie realised that there was for Stuart somebody even better to talk to, somebody distant, somebody removed from the local scene. *Paul.* Might he know something? Stuart had once gone to Paul's alone, Charlie remembered, saying he needed to sort himself out. Yet Paul always told Charlie that his obsession with Imogen and Stuart was absurd. What if Paul was covering for Stuart? It was possible. There must be some secrets in the long-standing friendships between them all that were shared between some and not others. Was this one such secret? The one big secret James had somehow discovered and run away from? Who else did you tell, if not your friends? The only other people who Stuart might have trusted were the guys outside this circle of friends, perhaps Simon, perhaps Mark. Perhaps one of them had finally told James what was going on with Imogen and Stuart.

Imogen pushed loose strands of her unruly hair away from her face with a delicate white hand, revealing her profile. Her nose was small and straight; her lips were full. Charlie's breath caught in his throat. So beautiful, he thought.

For a moment, Charlie was in danger of treading the path of an old obsession, but his new obsession saved him. *I know what I saw.* Something weird had happened that night, and everything seemed connected somehow. James had disappeared on the same night he'd seen the UFO. That couldn't possibly be a coincidence. It just couldn't be. Suddenly, it became clear to Charlie. Abduction was the simplest solution, the sanest solution. If Stuart and Imogen had slept together, everybody's world would turn upside down. It would be more surprising, he thought, more shocking, than James being abducted. Stuart was harmless, everybody said so, even Jane. He was the only one who thought otherwise and, even then, only at the most desperate moments of his confusion. Now he had Jane and despaired no more. He looked across at Stuart, who was now talking to Imogen about something inconsequential, some idle tittle-tattle. Like a girl. *Yeah. Stu is harmless.*

*

The next day, Charlie was back at the UFO Centre, chatting to Patterson. "It looks like Stuart and I will be at your ufological shindig."

"Good, good," Patterson said.

"I might even be able to bring my girlfriend."

Patterson looked at Charlie and raised and eyebrow. "I don't think I've seen you with a girl, Charlie."

"No, it's difficult. She lives in Devon and she's only sixteen. Convincing her parents to let her come up and stay with me is taking some work."

Patterson looked at Charlie mischievously. "Who can blame them? I wouldn't trust my beautiful young daughter with you."

"And you can piss off, Richard," Charlie said with a smile. Patterson often seemed a little staid, remote and otherworldly, off somewhere in the realm of the unknown, but sometimes a more human, humorous person broke through.

"Did you read the articles?" Patterson asked.

"Yes, I did. Fascinating. But if James *has* been abducted, there are some obvious differences with previous abductions."

"Such as?" Patterson asked.

"Well, nobody's been gone as long as James has. Even in the Walton case in America, the guy was back in five days."

"Good point," Patterson said. "But think of it like this. The ones who *have* come back to tell us about what happened haven't been gone for more than a few days because they're the ones who've come back. Obviously. But what about the Kinross case, where a UFO swallowed up a whole jet fighter? A jet fighter! Simply disappeared! Presumably the pilots are still up there somewhere."

"I don't know that case," said Charlie.

"Or Flight 19? You must know that one?"

"Yeah...Those were the planes that disappeared in the Bermuda Triangle just after the war, weren't they?"

"Yes. Who knows where those pilots are? I think they're also up there." A slight lift of Patterson's eyebrows was the only indication Charlie needed to know where Patterson meant. "Perhaps," Patterson continued, "there's one big floating mothership out there somewhere, a kind of space hotel, and that's where all the abductees are taken. Perhaps James is shooting the breeze with the pilots of Flight 19 right now."

"In everything I've read so far," Charlie said, "abductions happen in the Americas, not here. If James has been abducted, wouldn't he be the first British case?"

"Well, no, actually he'd be the second or third." Patterson eagerly rubbed his hands together. "But he'll be the first to be reported in the British press."

Charlie could almost see the pound signs in Patterson's eyes. Charlie didn't think too badly of him, however. Patterson was a reporter – that was how he made his money, after all. Charlie knew that he truly believed in the Dereham mystery and wanted to tell everybody about it. James's abduction was good for Patterson – it was a new topic he could write articles about, it was something exciting that would generate interest in the phenomenon. "How do you know about the others? The articles you lent me didn't mention any British abductions."

"They've all happened within the last couple of years and haven't been written up yet. I did hear of one that occurred back in 1974, but I've yet to find a written report of it. And there's one that happened in February this year, but again, I haven't found a report."

"Shame." Charlie looked at Patterson's bookshelves. "Have you got anything else about abductions I can read?" Charlie asked.

"Probably. What have you read?"

"Just the stuff you lent me and a couple of Jane's books." Charlie told Patterson the titles.

"Ah. Yes, I do have some other books and articles. They'll just repeat what you've already read, but they'll approach the topic from different viewpoints."

"Anything will do," Charlie said. "All this is new to me."

Patterson went to his shelves and pulled out journals and books, passing them to Charlie as he did so. "There's something about abductions in most of these, whether for or against. There are also a couple of books about cases like Kinross, which aren't thought of as abductions in the same sense as the Hills case. But, really, if they've all disappeared into a spaceship, even if by different means and for different lengths of time, it's all the same, isn't it?"

Charlie, who had been flicking through the books, looked up at Patterson. "No. Yes. What was the question?"

Patterson chuckled. "Ah, don't worry. I was talking to myself, really. Anyway, take those and have a read. You'll find out about the missing time in those too. Now that *is* strange. When James gets–"

Charlie stopped him. "Missing time?"

"Really, Charlie, did you even read those books your girlfriend lent you? Abductees nearly always seem to report missing time. Now run along, young man, I have articles to write."

Charlie thanked him and left. Charlie turned toward the town centre. *Missing time?* He'd overlooked something in his recent reading. And what had Patterson said? *All abductees suffer missing time.* Charlie had experienced missing time at the skywatch. Was that significant? Had *he* also been abducted? Was he unable to remember the experience? Charlie had spent the last couple of days talking to Jane on the telephone, and when they weren't talking about each other and their relationship, they were talking about abductions; Jane was fascinated by them. He would once have gently mocked such interests, but now he badly needed to talk to her. *Was I abducted at the same time as James?* The blackouts he had experienced on the hill bothered him. He sometimes wondered if he had, in fact, been involved in James's disappearance. He imagined scenarios in which he stabbed James and then tumbled him into a deep chalk quarry. Then he worried that it *had* happened, that he *could* have done it during a blackout. But surely he couldn't do anything like that, despite his obsession with Imogen. James was one his best friends. And he also knew that, perversely, James being with Imogen never bothered him as much as the intimacy between Stuart and Imogen did. And he'd never wanted to stab Stuart, let alone James – but then he remembered the fight at Copsehill.

It was lunch time. Although today was another hot day in a summer of unceasingly hot days, it was also muggy, and dark clouds broke the endless blue to which he'd become accustomed. There'd been other muggy days during the summer, but the only thunderstorms he remembered had been those that occurred the day after James had disappeared. He felt it should thunder today, yet knew it probably wouldn't. He walked down Five Chains Lane, knowing the lane should be half a furlong, as he'd once learned all the imperial measures, listed on the back of a notebook, when he was fourteen. He'd forgotten most of them now, though. After all, who could possibly want to remember the number of poles in each side of an acre? The lane was no longer five chains, however, as a carpark cut through it. He looked at his watch. Midday. Time for a pint of 6X. As he turned into the High Street, he was surprised to find himself falling into step with Stuart beside him. "Stuart, man. What are you doing here?"

"I'm going to The White Lion," Stuart said. "Is that where you're headed?"

Charlie nodded. "Where else?"

Stuart glanced down at the books and journals Charlie had tucked under his arm. "I see you've found more reading material."

"Yeah. I've just been down to see Patterson. I want to get as many viewpoints as I can."

Charlie so wanted to discuss with Stuart the idea that dogged him. *James has been abducted.* It was so obvious – but also too fantastic. Indeed, Stuart thought it ridiculous. But Charlie needed to talk about it with somebody. He should phone Jane. She'd understand. He didn't care how crazy it sounded. He was sure he was right.

"Are we meeting anybody in the pub?" Charlie asked.

"Imo," Stuart said. "She came into town this morning to do some shopping. She phoned and said she'd meet me there."

As much as Charlie tried to repress it, one thought bubbled to the surface. *She didn't phone me.*

24

Stuart and Kate walked hand in hand in front of Charlie up the long incline towards Copsehill. Everybody was here but for Imogen and, of course, James. Charlie was pleased Jane's parents had finally given in to her demands and allowed her to visit Dereham. Her parents had insisted, though, that Paul came with her. Charlie couldn't understand it. She was sixteen for God's sake! Charlie had been hitching down to Devon and going to the pub at sixteen. Her parents obviously had faith – most likely unwarranted – in Paul's brotherly instincts. Charlie couldn't imagine that Paul would stand in Jane's way should she want to smoke, get pissed or have sex with him. And, anyway, Paul and Fiona were staying at Stuart's house, while Jane was staying at his; Paul could hardly be alert for the sound of squeaking stair treads from a mile and a half away. Fiona had joined Paul in Dereham for this trip – she had told Charlie that it made a nice break before she went to university in October. How close it was now. Soon, everything would change. Kate and Imogen would be at Bath University, Fiona would be at Warwick, Paul at Bristol. Charlie would also be at Bath and had arranged to stay in halls for the first year. Imogen, though, had decided to remain at her parents' house for at least the first term and travel in to Bath. Stuart would still be in Dereham, wondering what he should do. And James? Who knew.

Jane could hardly contain her excitement at finally being at Copsehill. As they approached the white gates, she dashed ahead to see the view. When the others caught up with her, they stood for a while drinking in the view over the sun-bleached, drought-browned Wiltshire countryside, seeing it afresh through Jane's excitement. Skylarks dropped waterfalls of trills from the sky above. Heat bounced back from the grey tarmac. Soon, Jane wanted to head to the copse, the ultimate destination of all journeys to Copsehill – its soul, its heart, the temple of the strange. They followed her up the hill as she skipped and jogged on ahead of them, dust rising from beneath her feet even though she seemed as light as air in her excitement. They entered the copse, which was, as always, dark beneath the arching branches that were heavy with curling leaves. It was quiet, except for their hushed voices, which bounced back at them from the tree trunks, the echoes flattened by the weight of leaf above them. They walked back out into the dazzling sunlight, back into the heat, and walked around the copse. From here, at the top of the hill, the views over the surrounding countryside were extensive.

"Where are we going next?" Jane asked eagerly.

"We could walk over to Derebury," Paul said.

"I've never been there," Fiona said.

Jane shaded her eyes and looked across at the hill. "Has anybody ever seen UFOs on that hill?"

"Yes," Charlie replied. "Some hardy souls who managed to slog the stony footpaths to the hill have seen UFOs there."

"Then we have to go," Jane said. She pointed along the road that seemed to head towards the hill. "Do we go down there?"

"Yes, that's the right road," Charlie said.

"Come on then!" Jane giggled, took Charlie's hand, and began to pull him along the road. She had soon jogged ahead of him, however, eager to get to the next hill. Charlie happily watched her, so bright and full of joy in her new clothes – the tight jeans, the skimpy white tee shirt and the plimsolls so inappropriate to a long hike over the baked fields – her long blonde hair glinting in the endless sun.

"She's looking good," Stuart said to Charlie. This was the first time Stuart had seen her since Easter, over four months ago now.

"She's gorgeous," Charlie said.

"She's certainly changed," Stuart said. "Just as you said. My, how she's changed."

Charlie eyed Stuart suspiciously then, wondering at his interest. But this was Stuart's way. Interested in all the girls, but not necessarily chasing them. And he had Kate now. Fiona had barely laid a hand on him since she'd arrived with Paul.

Fiona also looked different. She had cut her hair short. When she turned around, smiled at Stuart and said he'd better not be looking at her arse, she looked like a pixie. When Charlie had met up with her after she'd arrived in Dereham with Paul and Jane, he'd asked why she had changed her hair. She had shrugged and said she had decided it was time for a change. Paul later explained that Fiona had started listening to the New York Dolls, Iggy Pop and The Ramones. There seemed to be some new cultural movement afoot, he said, and she wanted to be part of it. When Paul had been to her house in Totnes, he'd noticed some blue dye in the bathroom and had asked about it. Fiona had said she was thinking of dying her hair blue. Paul knew little else. The short hair suited her though, Charlie thought. Although, if it was a small signal of something new, hip and happening, it would be another two years before this movement or fashion swept through Dereham, if it swept at all. Totnes had always seemed hip. Dereham was sleepy and backward, somewhere at the nexus of the urban and rural. Charlie idly wondered if it was this summer's heat that was the fire driving this change, or if the weight of the heat was drugging them all, except for Fiona perhaps, maintaining the languid post-hippie idyll in which they all existed.

The UFO lecture that Patterson had organised was taking place tonight. Dereham might be sleepy and backward, but it was certainly at the centre of *something* exciting. Charlie was going with Jane. She was very excited. Paul and Stuart would be joining them; they were less excited.

Fiona had wandered up beside Charlie. "What's all this I hear about abductions? Do you still think James has been abducted by aliens?"

Charlie looked up at the sky. "Who knows? All we know for certain is that James has gone. He's been missing for some time. Nobody has found a body and he's not in any local hospitals."

"But you were always the sceptical one, Charlie."

"And then I saw a UFO."

"Yes. You quite literally saw the light." Fiona laughed.

"Good one."

"Thank you. Stuart thinks you're a bit obsessed with the whole thing."

Charlie looked ahead, where Stuart walked with his arm around Kate. Jane was talking to him. "Stuart keeps an eye on me. He thinks I'm obsessed with many things. Sometimes he's right, sometimes he's wrong. But I know what I saw."

"You turned into a believer overnight," Fiona said.

"Yeah. Well, I saw something, and he didn't. I don't blame him for doubting."

"But that's all it took. Seeing a light."

"You've no idea. If you'd been there, well... You might have changed your mind." He paused for a moment. "I don't think I was ever much of a sceptic, really. I liked acting the part to wind the others up. And I wasn't scared of the dark, or the hill, like Stuart is. But Imo and James are the real sceptics."

"You had me convinced you were a sceptic," Fiona said. "All those late-night conversations at Paul's house about how skywatchers were fooling themselves."

"I still think most of them are."

"I won't argue with that. Except you think you're not."

I'm not," Charlie said. He quickly changed the subject. "What are you doing tonight? I'm surprised you're not coming to the lecture with Paul."

"*Très drôle*. Luckily, there weren't enough tickets. I'm going to the pub with Imo and Kate. We shall probably talk about you while you're gone."

"That's only because I'm so interesting."

"That's one way of putting it."

After the lecture, Charlie talked to Jane enthusiastically about what they had heard. It had been fascinating. Stuart and Paul were less convinced. They'd learned nothing new, Stuart said. The speakers had retold the same old stories they already knew about. Charlie was about to disagree with Stuart when they were interrupted by an odd-looking couple, a man and woman. They weren't strange in the way Charlie knew the Prophets appeared strange to the other residents of Dereham – these people were odd in their own unique way. For a start, they both had crew cuts. This was rare on a woman. Her hair was much shorter than Fiona's pixie cut. Charlie had to admit, it looked good on her. The man was clean-shaven, and the woman wore no make-up. She was tall, only an inch or so shorter than her partner. They both wore identical white shirts with button-down collars, neatly pressed trousers and both wore brogues on their feet.

"Are you the Prophets?" the man said.

At the seriousness with which the man uttered the preposterous nickname they'd given themselves, Charlie almost burst out laughing. Stuart smirked. Paul, who had curbed his instinct to laugh better than Charlie, replied. "Well, technically, I'm not and she-" he nodded at Jane, "is not, but these two freaks are, yes."

"Greetings," said the woman. "I am Mo."

"Greetings," said the man. "I am Jo." He then added, after the beat of a pause. "Without an "e'."

They bowed, in an oriental manner, a slight bob from the hips and a tilt of the head.

"And how can we help?" Stuart said.

Charlie tried to work out what their names might be. Mo could be short for Moira, of course, or perhaps Margaret or Molly or Morgan or–

"Mr Patterson tells us you are the good friends of the one who has gone," Mo said.

"The one called James," Jo added, as if the Prophets might have forgotten their friend's name.

"Yes, we are," Charlie said. Jo could be short for Joe, Joseph, John...

"We would like to talk to you. Are you venturing to Mr Patterson's after the lecture?"

"Well, Jane and I are," Jane wanted to visit the UFO Centre and Charlie had agreed to take her.

"What do you want to know?" Stuart asked.

"We will speak with your friend at Mr Patterson's," Mo said, mysteriously.

They bowed again and left them, moving back beside Richard Patterson.

"They," Paul said, "are weird."

"Yeah, their names are a bit, well, crazy," Stuart said. "You did get it, didn't you?" He looked around the others, who looked back at him blankly.

"Mo and Jo. MoJo."

"Yes?" Paul wondered. "So what?"

"Ah," Charlie said, finally realising. "You obviously haven't got your mojo working, man."

"Oh!" Paul said. "Yes, I see."

"You have to wonder why, don't you?" Jane asked, looking at the odd couple standing next to Patterson.

"You do." Paul said. "And what's with the identical clothes?"

Charlie shook his head and looked at Stuart. He noticed then there was a similarly weird, almost-identical-clothing thing going on with them. Both wore collarless shirts, a waistcoat and patched jeans. The main difference was in their footwear – Stuart wore his stinky baseball boots, while Charlie had favoured his Doc Martens. Other differences were in the details: Charlie's waistcoat was a blue pinstripe, whereas Stuart's was plain brown; Charlie favoured reds in his patches, while Stuart preferred patterns, which were usually from old Laura Ashley dresses Imogen cut up for him. What was striking about Mo and Jo was the very ordinariness of the clothes they'd used to create their uniform.

"Well, it seems like you are about to have an interesting evening," Stuart said.

"You never know. They might have new information, or a new theory," Charlie replied.

"I think I'm going to join the girls in the pub," Paul said. "Are you coming, Stu?"

Stuart nodded and then he smiled at Jane and Charlie. "I hope you find enlightenment."

25

An hour later, Charlie wished Paul and Stuart were still with him, so he could later talk with them about this freaky pair, Mo and Jo. The conversation had wandered all over the place, including the occult, UFOs and astrology. He wondered where it would lead next.

Mo said, "And what of your friend James?"

They had now returned to where the conversation had started. Charlie was baffled. Mo and Jo had cornered him and Jane and had been rambling on for at least an hour about all the well-known abduction cases. They were repeating, essentially, what he and Jane had already heard at the lecture. Their way of talking was, he thought, hypnotic. Mo would speak, then Jo, then Mo, then Jo, one finishing the other's thoughts or sentences, like verbal tennis, but with never a fault or net call. He'd started to think of them as one being – MoJo.

"Yes, what about James?" Charlie asked.

"Do you wonder," Mo said.

"What is happening to him?" Jo finished.

"For if he is gone," Mo started.

"And you believe he was taken by aliens..."

"Then what will become of him in their craft?"

Charlie frowned. "I think they'll do some experiments on him, then let him go."

"Yes, but what kind of experiments?" Jo asked.

"Yes, what kind, for we hear stories, do we not..." Mo said.

"Of syringes being inserted into the stomach, samples taken..."

"But samples of what?"

"We have asked ourselves..."

"Over and over..."

"What it could be the aliens want, what would they want from us?"

"For if they are as advanced as we believe..."

"Not just us, but all gathered here in this room..."

"Then what would they want with mere eggs and sperm and blood?"

"Surely they could recreate them..."

"As we are on verge of doing..."

"With our advances in genetics and biology and medicine."

"DNA," finished Mo, both abruptly and mysteriously.

"You think they want our DNA?" Jane asked, who now appeared to be as confused as Charlie.

"No, young lady," Mo said. "The DNA is, after all, the constituent part of all our bodies, all our cells."

"And if they have the powers," Jo said.

"Of science and technology that we assume them to have..."

"They would reconstruct our DNA from a few skin cells or hairs."

"They could create for themselves the sperm and egg and blood."

"That is what we mean."

Charlie was trying to understand. "So, you think what they're doing has nothing to do with medical procedures or experiments or whatever?"

"We believe what they do to their subjects..." Mo began.

"Your friend James, for example..."

"Is experimental. But also, perhaps, they search for something..."

"Something we have but they do not."

Jane looked at them quizzically. "But what else could they be doing, with these syringes and the blood collection and sperm samples?"

"Do you know about magnetism?" Mo asked.

"Yes, not electrical magnetism, but animal magnetism?" Jo clarified.

Jane giggled and kissed Charlie. "Yes, Charlie has it."

"Very droll, young lady," Mo said, with no hint of a smile.

"Yes, very," Jo added.

Charlie did know, vaguely what they meant. He knew it was a term from mesmerism, that people had once believed all animals contained a special kind of magnetism, a kind of magnetic fluid. "I thought all those old ideas about animal magnetism and mesmerism had given way to hypnotism. Nobody believes that magnetic fluids circulate in humans, do they?"

"But we do believe in such magnetism, such *special* magnetism," Mo said.

"We believe it to be called by many things," Jo said.

"Qi, soul, spirit, élan vital..."

"And yet, even though it *is* called animal magnetism, it serves to distinguish us from other animals."

"Do animals have souls?" Jane wondered.

"An interesting philosophical question," Mo said.

"One which we have obviously spent much time contemplating."

"For would an alien..."

"Obviously another animal..."

"Have a soul?"

Things seemed to have taken a weird religious twist. Charlie wondered if MoJo were about to convert him and Jane to some strange religion.

Jo chuckled. "I see a wary look in Charlie's eye."

Charlie nodded. They had obviously said similar things to many other people and met with the same reaction. But if they weren't trying to convert people, what were they trying to do?

"We have no religion, Charlie," Jo said.

"No religion, do not fear. Yet the problem remains, does it not?" Mo added.

"We realise this would be a profound problem to our religious leaders," Jo said.

"If aliens had souls, that is."

"Yet we know that our pets have spirits..."

"Qi?"

"Élan vital?"

"Vril?"

"So, what is this mysterious... essence?"

"Not DNA, because plants and single-celled organisms share that too..."

"But do we say they have spirit?"

Charlie was unsure whether to say 'yes' or 'no'.

Jane was confused. She spoke out suddenly. "But what does all this have to do with James?"

"We believe they seek the thing we are not yet able to measure..." Mo said.

"Weigh or quantify..." Jo said.

"The thing more developed in humans than in other animals..."

"The eternal spirit, animal magnetism, vril, call it what you will..."

"But we like to call it animal magnetism, because we hold to no religion..."

They stopped for a moment and looked at Charlie and Jane.

"We believe they are taking animal magnetism," Mo said.

"Whatever it is and howsoever you name it." Jo said.

Charlie was momentarily diverted by hearing the word "howsoever' uttered by a real person. "So," he said. "You believe that right now, aliens are sucking out... uh... *something*... from James?"

"Yes," Mo said.

"And there is danger there," Jo added.

"For if they do not know what it is, as we do not know, how do they know how much to take?"

"At what point would your friend become inhuman?"

"Inhuman?" Charlie said. "That's ridiculous."

"Is it?" Mo said.

"Those who return are invariably disoriented, they lose memories, perhaps suffer in other ways..."

"Sometimes, they have marks upon their bodies, they seem uncomprehending..."

"Almost as if they'd lost for a while some vital spark..."

"Some small part of their humanity..."

"Which can only be replenished..."

"When they are back upon the geosphere..."

"The continual, unending source of magnetism..."

"Which fills them with sacred energies again, transformed into animal magnetism..."

"Qi..."

"Vril..."

"Spirit..."

"Élan vital."

MoJo stopped their rapid exchange. Charlie didn't know what to say. Jane stared into the glass from which she was drinking, as if she could scry the meaning of MoJo there.

"But surely," Jane said, "if what you say is true, James would come back as a zombie."

"He would be like unto a zombie," Mo said.

"But that is merely speculation, the worst case we could imagine," Jo said.

"We imagine our alien friends to be benevolent, but that they perhaps lack this miraculous substance and wish to understand what makes us human."

"I thought you said it was in all animals?" Charlie noted.

"Yes, but it takes on a unique, transformed and highly-evolved quintessence within humans," Mo replied.

"And perhaps this highly-evolved quintessence is what the alien lacks," Jo said.

"We do seem to be visited by such a variety of aliens, do we not?" Mo asked.

"The Grey ones, the Nordics, the humanoids, and all the others..."

"They are many and varied..."

"Almost as if there is something special here, something we possess and for which many alien races search..."

"And what we have in abundance is soul, animal magnetism..."

Charlie expected them to start listing synonyms again, but MoJo just looked from him to Jane and back again, smiling at them.

"We only wish to warn you," Mo said.

"That when your friend James returns," Jo continued.

"You may notice differences in him..."

"Differences caused by the depletion of animal magnetism..."

"And we hope he still has soul enough to live among other humans..."

"And he is not so empty that the geosphere cannot replenish him, that he can regain his human quintessence."

Charlie wanted to say something but wasn't sure what it was. The whole thing sounded preposterous, somewhere between science, religion and voodoo. Hoodoo voodoo, Charlie couldn't help thinking. Then, suddenly, MoJo performed their strange little bow.

"We will leave you now," Jo said.

"To think a little about what we've said," Mo added.

They did leave, then. Charlie watched this odd couple return to Patterson, talk to him for a few moments, then bow and walk out through the door.

"Wow!" Jane said. "Could they talk!"

"They certainly could," Charlie concurred.

"I didn't understand half of it," Jane said, combing some of her long hair away from her face with her fingers, resting the loose strands behind her ear. Charlie loved the way she did that, the smooth movement of her soft hands, the sudden revelation of her face; it seemed so familiar, yet so new.

"I kind of understand where they're coming from," Charlie said. He'd read enough books on the occult to have some idea of what they were talking about. But this was the first time he'd met anybody who so explicitly linked occult notions to flying saucers. "Perhaps we should talk to Paul about it."

"Perhaps, first, you should kiss me," Jane whispered.

Charlie woke with a start. He'd been dreaming, but of what he couldn't immediately recall. He also thought he'd woken at some point during the dream. Or had that been before the dream? He remembered a tightness in his chest, or a tension, a pressure, a weight bearing down on him. It was all rather hazy. He was thirsty but was afraid of waking Will. He remained, instead, dozing in his sleeping bag on the floor, trying to clutch at the tantalising wisps that remained of the dream that had become vague now. He was sure he'd been afraid at some point. Was it because of the tightness in his chest? Had he thought he was having a heart attack? That might have been it. But it had felt like a weight rather than a tightness. He was close to drifting back to sleep again, but suddenly remembered seeing something, or somebody, in the room. He returned to dozy wakefulness. What was it he'd seen? It had moved about the room, he was sure, and it had seemed vaguely human in shape. He thought it had picked up objects in the room and examined them. What was it looking for?

Perhaps, he thought, it had been Will. Charlie sat up to look for Will, to ask him if he'd got out of bed during the night, but he wasn't there. So, Will *had* got out of bed. Odd. Charlie slipped out of his sleeping bag, pulled on some clothes and went downstairs. He put the kettle on the hob quietly, as it appeared to be early. Even his parents were still in bed. He wondered what the time was, but his watch was upstairs. He went to look at the clock in the front room. Will was sprawled on the sofa. He had obviously come downstairs to sleep. Charlie wondered why. The clock on the mantelpiece told him it was only half past seven in the morning. He went back to the kitchen, ready to catch the kettle before its whistle woke the house. Perhaps, then, the figure he'd imagined in his room had only been Will. He wondered what time Will had come downstairs. Yet, something didn't seem right. For if it had been Will, he would only have needed to step across Charlie in the sleeping bag, and then leave quietly through the door. Why would he wander around the room, picking up objects before leaving, and risk waking Charlie?

The kettle began a low warbling, a portent of its whistle, so Charlie lifted it off the hob. He dropped a teabag into his mug and poured the just-boiling water over it. He leaned on the worktop with his elbows, his chin in his hands over the mug, sleepily watching the bag steeping in the water. He wondered if Jane was still asleep. The night had been hot again. Jane might, he thought, be naked, right now, in his bed. He considered sneaking up and sliding in next to her. Yet what a scene there would be were he discovered! He took the milk from the fridge and dribbled some into his tea. He fished the teabag out of his mug and threw it in the bin, dripping tea over the kitchen floor as he did so. He didn't really notice. He was thinking about his dream again.

With a shock, he realised the figure he'd seen might have been one of *them*. Perhaps they *knew* he'd seen their spaceship at Copsehill. But then – perhaps he'd been in their spaceship that night. Had they come to take him away? Again? To do experiments on him? To suck out his soul, if MoJo were to be believed? If the aliens had taken him, he wouldn't have seen Jane today. She would have been upset. He felt a momentary sense of loss, then had a moment of empathy with Imogen. *So this is what she feels like, every day?* If this was how she felt, perhaps it was just as well Stuart dropped in on her. *If I'd been taken, at least Paul would be there for Jane.*

He hadn't been taken, however. He was still here, after all. He sipped his tea, slowly. Yet... perhaps he had been taken. Perhaps he'd been taken and then returned. Perhaps his memories had been erased. Hadn't he read that abductees had distorted memories of events, that they couldn't remember everything? If he *had* been taken, would he remember? For a moment, he felt disoriented. The pit of his stomach fell away and panic rose in him. How would he know? How would he know if he'd been abducted? How would he know if he still in possession of a soul?

Hypnosis, he thought. That was how memories had been recovered in other cases. Fiona was in town and she'd successfully hypnotised Paul. *And me, accidentally!* She seemed to have a natural flair for it. Should he ask her to hypnotise him? It seemed the obvious thing to do. Although when he thought about asking her, he felt anxiety within him. Because what if he *had* been abducted that night? Who knew how long twenty minutes might last on an alien spaceship. Would he find himself admitting to strange sexual encounters in front of the others? And though he thought MoJo were a little crazy, what if they were right? What if his soul had been taken? Would he know if he were soulless? *I'm sure Jane would tell me if I'd become a weirdo.*

Jane appeared in the doorway then, rubbing her eyes, pushing her long, blonde, night-tangled hair away from her face, and wearing a long white tee-shirt that reached to her knees. One of his, he noticed. She walked over, smiling a sleepy smile and put her arms around him. She smelt of sandalwood, soap, and shampoo. She picked up his mug and took a sip from it. Then she kissed him. Her tongue, warmed by the tea, slipped into his mouth. He ran his hands over her, felt the soft cotton of her underwear, then moved his hands under her tee-shirt, up her sides and felt the smoothness of her skin, the curve of her breasts. At that moment, he didn't feel soulless.

26

Paul agreed with Charlie; the dream had been most odd. But then, weren't all dreams strange? Charlie had asked William why he'd been sleeping on the sofa, and William had said that Charlie had been tossing and turning and talking in his sleep. That wasn't strange either, Paul supposed. After all, when he and Fiona managed to sleep together, he would sometimes hear her mumbling as she talked to the people in her dreams. Charlie had also asked Will if he'd looked at the objects in the room before leaving. Why would he do that in his own room, Will had asked. This had made Charlie even more determined that Fiona should hypnotise him. Paul knew that all the mystery, intrigue and excitement surrounding the dream had to be weighed against certain facts – Charlie had been drinking after the lecture, he had been listening to MoJo for most of the evening, and he was, because of Jane, and because of what had happened on the hill, currently obsessed with abductions.

Charlie's parents had gone out for the evening, for which Paul was grateful. He couldn't imagine what Charlie's parents would think of the dream and of what Fiona was about to do. They'd probably tell Charlie to stop being so silly, it was only a dream brought on by all the weird conversations and the drink the night before. Charlie's parents now thought the same as all the other parents. James had run off somewhere, there'd been a row with Imogen, or he'd upset somebody, or something. Good old, solid, sensible parents, Paul thought. They lived in a grown-up world, where odd things happened for mundane reasons. He was determined never to become so pragmatic. Yet Imogen had also begun to share the same belief as all the parents, even though she, who should know best, had no idea why James would run away.

There would only be the four of them at Charlie's this evening. Stuart would, of course, be heading over to Burnt Norton to see Kate. And he would, of course, also drop in on Imogen on the way, just as he did most evenings. Paul wished Stuart were here. Somebody had to keep their feet on the ground. He seemed to be increasingly sceptical of any occult explanation for James's disappearance. That was Imogen's influence, no doubt. Fiona had always been sceptical. She was happy to indulge Paul's interest in the occult, although she didn't for a minute believe that anything other than the psychological happened during a ritual. Fiona was interested in his practices and rituals because, as she had once said, they mixed up art, performance, Jungian psychology and symbolism in a fascinating way. She baulked, though, at UFOs, aliens, contactees and abduction.

Fiona would be sceptical enough, Paul supposed. Yet she would also be taking the lead in what could turn into a psychodrama. *Stuart should be here. We need him.* Still, human psychology fascinated Fiona – Paul had known as soon as Charlie asked that she would hypnotise him. Fiona thought everything that was happening bit silly, she'd said so earlier. But she did want to experiment with hypnotism again. She was still intrigued by what had happened when she'd hypnotised Paul, even if, as she said – and it was true – they hadn't really discovered anything new. Perhaps, though, Charlie *did* have hidden memories that only she could recover through hypnosis. Paul wondered what she might discover.

Charlie was now lying on his bed. Fiona began to talk to Charlie, relaxing him, and then, recalling all the steps she'd previously used with Paul, slowly put him into a trance. Paul noticed that Charlie had gone under long before Fiona suggested it, as if he'd somehow been ready. Paul wasn't surprised. When he prepared for a ritual, the mere act of opening his bureau to create the altar had the effect of changing his consciousness.

"Are you feeling okay, Charlie?" Fiona asked.

"I'm feeling great," Charlie replied quietly.

"What do you remember about your dream?"

Charlie repeated his dream to them again. The details remained the same as he'd told them before.

"Do you remember anybody in your dream?"

"There's somebody in my room... No, not my room, Will's room."

"And it isn't Will?" Paul asked.

"No. It's ... somebody different.... Something different."

"Do you remember any details?" Fiona said.

"No. Wait. Yes. It's looking down at me..."

"Where are you?"

"In my sleeping bag. It's looking down at me... it's got really big eyes."

"Is it human?"

"It looks human. A bit like a baby, you know... small features... Big head. And big eyes. But they're dark, almost black."

"Anything else?"

"Yes. Something weird..."

"What do you mean?" Jane asked.

"Like... oh, you know, what's it called. The pupil. It's not round. It's weird, man. Like, it's a slit. Not round. Like a cat."

Fiona glanced at Paul. He raised an eyebrow but remained silent. This was... odd, he thought.

"I'm not in my bag anymore," Charlie said, with a note of anxiety.

"What bag?"

"The sleeping bag. I'm not in it. I'm somewhere else. It's like... when it looked into my eyes... I went somewhere."

"Can you describe where you are?" Fiona asked.

"It's a room, all white. Not much in it. Some kind of... trolley? I'm on a bed. Something like a bed. Lying down. I can't move. I'm paralysed. I'm... I'm..."

"Yes?" Jane said.

Paul looked at Jane. She stared at Charlie, her eyes wide, chewing at the tip of her finger.

With a sense of wonder, Charlie said, "I'm next to James!"

"James?" Paul asked.

"He's on the bed thing next to me. He's got something in his arm. He's asleep. Unconscious. Hypnotised? Hypnotised... or something. He doesn't see me."

Well, thought Paul, that was unexpected.

"What's happening now?" Jane asked.

"They're attaching something to my arm. It's like they're taking blood or something. Samples of something, anyway."

"I hope it's not your soul, Charlie," Jane said, anxiously.

Fiona snapped at Jane. "Don't put MoJo's crap into Charlie's head, please Jane."

Jane looked peevishly at Fiona. "It was just an idea."

Fiona had spoken sharply, but Paul thought she'd probably been right to do so. *We don't really know what we're doing. We don't know how what we say will affect Charlie's thinking. Not while he's in this state.*

Charlie spoke, still calm in his trance. "Don't worry, darling. It does just feel like they're taking a blood sample."

"What about James, though?" Paul said. Then he wondered if he should have mentioned James. By doing so, wasn't he merely confirming Charlie's fantasy?

"I feel like he was here before me and he's had this thing attached to him for some time... Somebody's checking something by his arm."

"What is it?" Jane asked.

"I don't know. It looks medical, I suppose. Shiny, stainless steel. James has something around his arm. Like at the doctor, when they take your blood pressure. There's a tube leading out of it to a... shiny thing... like a steel bottle."

"What's the alien doing?" Jane asked.

Fiona didn't snap at Jane this time, but Paul noticed the implication she had missed. *How do we know it's an alien?* Jane seemed so certain. This situation was so difficult to control.

"It's like... like it's checking something. Or... looking at a dial, or something. I don't know. It seems very interested, though. I can't turn my head far enough to see, I–"

Charlie paused.

"What's happening?" Fiona said.

"I don't know. Suddenly I went dizzy and I'm back in the sleeping bag, on the floor in Will's room. My chest hurts."

Charlie was again silent for a few moments. "I think that's when I fell asleep again," he finally said.

Fiona sighed, glad it was over; Paul saw the characteristic relaxation in her posture, as if she had finished a particularly difficult area of one of her paintings. "Okay, Charlie," she said. "I'm going to bring you back to the room now." She counted down from ten and when she reached one, clapped her hands. Charlie opened his eyes.

"Do you remember what just happened?" Fiona said.

"Yes, I remember it," Charlie said. He looked around at them. "Now do you believe James has been abducted?"

"I've always believed it," Jane said.

"No," Fiona said. "This makes no difference. All you've been reading about for the last two weeks is abductions. And you were at Patterson's last night, talking to MoJo."

Paul was uncertain. There was something odd, unsettling, about what Charlie had told them. "I don't know," he said. "Charlie couldn't remember any of this until you hypnotised him. If it *was* a dream caused by what he's been reading or talking about, surely he'd have remembered fragments of it, like you do when you wake up from dreams."

"But he did remember fragments," Fiona said. "Somebody moving around the room, the weight on his chest."

"But he didn't remember the really odd and important things until you hypnotised him," Paul said. "Like seeing James, which would be a big deal. If he woke out of a dream, you'd expect him to remember something so meaningful."

"Or he could be creating it for us, now," Fiona said.

Charlie looked at Fiona in surprise. "Why on earth would I make up something like that?"

"Don't get me wrong, Charlie," Fiona replied. "I don't think you're deliberately making it up to fool us or anything. I mean, it's like... the pressure to perform, to find a coherent story for what you felt last night. Something that makes sense to you and to the rest of us, especially in the current circumstances, with James missing and your UFO sighting."

Paul shook his head. "I don't know, I just don't know."

Fiona looked at Paul disdainfully. "Surely, *you're* not going to start believing in aliens now?" she said, with a certain exasperation. "Do you really believe that James has been abducted, that Charlie wasn't dreaming? It's a *story*, a *performance*, a way of making sense of recent events. He's taken fragments of his dream, fragments of what's happened, fragments of what he's heard and read and fused them all together."

Charlie's voice was firm, measured. "I don't think that's right, Fiona. I think the dream is a memory of something that really happened. It's what I saw."

Jane went over to the bed and gave Charlie a hug. "I believe it too. But I don't think they got your soul."

Fiona's shoulders hunched. She was frustrated by what was happening. Paul himself was wavering. He knew he wanted to believe Charlie, that he too wanted this crazy story to be true.

When Fiona next spoke, her voice was heavy with sarcasm. "I'm going to make some tea," she said. "Who believes they want one?"

27

A day had passed since he'd been hypnotised, and Charlie still couldn't understand why Fiona doubted him. He sweated as he walked over to Burnt Norton in the warm, late-evening sunshine. He wondered if the summer would ever end. The low sun threw the long shadows of hedgerows and trees across brown fields. A red tractor belched black fumes into the evening air as it bumped across the hard earth, raising behind it a cloud of dust cast orange by the setting sun.

Jane had gone with Fiona and Paul to see Fiona's brother Dominic at Southampton University. They intended to stay the night at Dom's place. Jane had suggested Charlie come with them, but he said he'd take the opportunity to see Imogen and Stuart. He'd seen little of Imogen during Jane's visit and felt he was, in some way, neglecting a friend in need. He knew if he saw Imogen, he'd likely see Stuart. He might be lucky, though – he might miss Stuart and catch Imogen by herself for a change. Since James's disappearance, he'd rarely seen Imogen alone. Yet Kate didn't seem to mind that Stuart saw Imogen so often – which was weird, really, as Stuart was supposed to be going out with *her*. But then, Charlie supposed, she did live only a mile or so along the road from Imogen – perhaps it wasn't so odd that Stuart should pop into to see Imogen first. Charlie would like to have her to himself for a while and tell her about his dream and about how Fiona had hypnotised him, and what he'd remembered. Should he also tell her what MoJo had said? Perhaps not – it would be too freaky. He did so hope Stuart had already gone on to Kate's. Imogen's scepticism would be bad enough, without Stuart there to reinforce it.

When he arrived at the house, Imogen's well-spoken father, the lawyer, let him in, asked how he was and asked about his new girlfriend. Charlie made small talk for a few minutes, turned down the offer of coffee, and was ready to head for Imogen's room, when Mr Peek asked him a question.

"Where do you think James has gone?" Mr Peek said.

Charlie was surprised. He hadn't been asked this question by a parent for a couple of weeks. A lot had happened in that time.

"I don't know," Charlie said. He wanted to say more, about his dream, about MoJo, about the books he'd been reading, but decided that lawyerly Mr Peek would be the most sceptical of them all and might subject him to all kinds of questions. As he took the stairs two at a time to Imogen's room, he wondered why all the parents simply assumed James had run away. None of them had a provided a plausible reason why he would do so – nothing beyond speculation, at least. Abduction was as likely an explanation as any other. Given his own experiences, he felt it now the *most* likely.

He knocked at Imogen's door and, as he opened it, stuck his head through the gap. He was disappointed to see that Kate and Stuart were already there. They greeted him warmly as he entered the room. He sat on the floor, his back against Imogen's stripped pine wardrobe. Imogen was on the bed, Kate was on the chair next to the desk, and Stuart also sat on the floor, between Kate's legs.

"What's new, Charlie?" Imogen asked.

Charlie didn't know whether now was the right time to launch into what had happened over the last two nights. He tried to make light of it. "Same old weird stuff," he said.

Imogen asked if he wanted a drink.

"No thanks. I was just talking to your dad. He asked me if I knew where James was."

"Father thinks one of us knows where James is and why he left," Imogen said. "He was probably trying to catch you off-guard."

"Although you *do* know where James is," Kate said to Charlie. Her smile was mischievous.

"It's a possibility," Charlie said. Was Kate trying to bait him?

"I heard you had fun at Patterson's," Stuart said.

Charlie described Mo and Jo in detail for Imogen and Kate. He made them out to be even more eccentric than they had been.

"I heard they'd been bending your ear," Stuart said.

"Really?" Charlie said.

"Jane told Paul," Stuart said. "Did you believe them?"

"I don't know. It all sounded plausible. Mad but plausible."

There was a brief silence during which Charlie began rolling a cigarette.

Echoing her father, Imogen said, "*Have* you heard from James?"

Charlie looked up. "Me? Why would I have heard from James?"

"He might have got in touch with you. He might have been in touch with any of you boys and you might be keeping it secret because he asked you to. And he'd be more likely to get in touch with you than Stu."

Charlie shook his head and wondered why James would contact him rather than Stuart. Just as he was closer than the others were to Paul, James was closest to Stuart. Surely, if James wanted to talk to anybody, it would be Stuart. Unless there was something he didn't know. *What aren't they telling me?"* If he'd contacted me," Charlie said, "you'd be the first to know."

"You better be telling the truth, Charlie," Kate said. "I'd hate to have to make you squeal," she added, doing a passable Humphrey Bogart impersonation.

Charlie laughed. "I bet you like to make Stu squeal."

"Oh no, he makes *me* squeal," she said, playing with Stuart's auburn hair.

Stuart winked exaggeratedly at Charlie.

"So, you didn't save yourself for me," Charlie said, with mock despair. "Despite all those promises we made when we ran together in the spring sunshine!"

"No," Stuart said. "So you'd better return that locket I gave you."

"Hah!" Charlie exclaimed. "A gentleman never asks for the return of a gift. Besides, despite your indifference, I shall treasure your gift for ever."

The mood was light. This would be an appropriate time, Charlie thought, to talk about his dream, even though he was talking to three sceptics. "I had a weird dream the other night," he said. "After talking to those MoJo people at Patterson's."

"I know," Stuart said. "Paul told me about your adventures in hypnotism."

"What dream? What hypnotism?" Imogen said.

"Stuart hasn't told you anything?" Charlie said.

"I thought it best that you tell the story," Stuart said.

"We are agog, Charlie," Kate said.

He described all that happened over the last two nights. When he'd finished, he was unsurprised to find himself looking at three doubtful faces.

"So, let me get this straight, Charles," Imogen said. "You really think you were taken by aliens? And you saw James while on their..." she hesitated. "Spaceship?"

"It seems to fit," Charlie said meekly.

"You've been reading too much weird stuff," Stuart said.

"What's happened to you?" Charlie asked. "You used to believe in the weird stuff more than the rest of us. Now *you're* the sceptic."

"Oh, I don't know," Stuart said uncertainly. "It's just that... well... In the last few weeks, since..." he hesitated. "Well, you know... since James disappeared, I've watched you construct this weird world in which you take it for granted that people are abducted by *aliens*. And why? Because *you* saw a flying saucer. And because *you* saw it, suddenly they're real, even though you'd always been so sceptical. And also, in those few weeks, you've fallen in love with quite the loveliest little flying saucer nut. You spend all your time reading books and articles about abductions and talking about flying saucers with her. Is it any wonder you've convinced yourself that James has been abducted."

"Do you think I'm making this up? Or do you think I'm deluded?"

"No. *Making it up* sounds so... what's the word..."

"Pejorative?" Imogen offered.

"Yes, pejorative," Stuart continued. "If I say you're making it up, it makes what you're doing sound bad. How can I put it...?" He looked around the room, in search of inspiration. His eyes alighted on the spines of the books in one of Imogen's bookcases.

"It's like a story. We've all made up stories to account for James's disappearance. At first we thought he'd run off, stoned, and got lost in Whimple. And then Imogen thought he'd been stabbed, and his body dumped somewhere on the Plain. Now, all the parents think he's run off. My parents are now wondering if he had another woman."

"I'll cut his nuts off he has," Imogen said.

Stuart laughed and then continued. "You know, it's a big thing. James is our best friend, Imo's boyfriend. Suddenly there's this *hole* where he used to be. Look at us now. Before James disappeared, we were always at his house, drinking his booze, smoking his fags, listening to his records. Now we're here at Imo's. Our world is... *disrupted*. It's not a *really* big thing, you know, like a parent dying, or finding out one of *us* is going to die. But still, what *has* happened is big enough. So, we construct stories to explain it. Like Imo's story, or James's parents' story. It's a mystery. It needs a solution. Every story we've made up is an attempt to solve the mystery, to provide a... framework. Your story, this abduction, is just one of the stories. And the more I think about it, the more I believe the whole UFO phenomenon is a story created to explain the unexplainable."

Has he been talking to Fi? Charlie wondered. "But what about the abductions?"

"Same thing," Stuart replied, simply.

"But why would anybody create such crazy stories to explain... What? Dreams? Trances?"

"Because these dreams *are* crazy? Because they make no sense? Because the elements of the dream are so weird, no normal explanation will do? I don't know, Charlie. I'm no expert on all this. I've only been thinking about it so much because of your sudden change of attitude." Stuart paused. "It's like I now need a story to explain *you*."

"So it's all stories?" Charlie said.

"Not everything. Imo's on the bed, Kate's stroking my hair, Imo's spider plant is dying, it's bloody hot, and one of the books I can see on the shelf is *Animal Farm*. That's all really... real."

"You only think I'm stroking your hair," Kate said.

"No, I don't only think it. Charlie and Imo can see it. And unless you're willing to deny your own reality, you also know you're stroking my hair."

Kate cuffed Stuart lightly around the side of his head. "You have an answer for everything,"

"I only think I have an answer for everything."

They all laughed.

"I only know what's happened," Charlie said. "I saw a UFO. James disappeared. I seem to have been abducted. And I saw James."

"I wish you had," Imogen sighed. "I really do. I want to know where James is."

"It seemed real to me," Charlie insisted. "I really do think I was abducted. And James has been abducted too."

"Oh, for Christ's sake," Imogen said, despairingly.

"But that's what I believe. And all those other witnesses I've read about can't just be making up stories. Something real is happening. And it's happened to me and James as well. If Kate stroking Stu's head is real, why the hell can't my experiences be real?"

"Because... because... it's crazy talk," Imogen blurted. She stood up. "Does anybody want coffee?"

They all said they did. Imogen walked towards the bedroom door. Stuart said he'd help her. He stood and followed Imogen, giving Kate a kiss on the cheek before he left.

"Ah, my kiss of reassurance," Kate said, absent-mindedly.

Charlie looked at Kate. "Why won't anybody believe me?"

"We've talked about it a lot, Charles. You must realise, to us, your ideas sound a little... wild. Look at it from Imo's point of view. If you *were* on board some alien spaceship, then why were *you* allowed to come back and James wasn't?"

"I don't know," Charlie admitted.

"If we believe what you say, you got away and he didn't. Therefore he might never come back."

But Kate's earlier comment had returned to Charlie and now nagged at him. "What did you mean by what you said just now? What was it? *Kiss of reassurance?*"

Kate's cheeks reddened slightly. "Nothing, nothing," she said, vaguely.

"Come on, Katie, you're usually pretty straight."

Kate sighed. "Well, he *has* been spending a lot of time with Imo lately, so he does little things to reassure me."

"You're not worried, are you?"

"I wouldn't worry about Stu and Imo."

"So why say it?"

Kate chewed her lip and then looked down at the floor. "I shouldn't have said anything."

"They do spend a lot of time together, don't they."

"Yes, a lot. But I accept that. I've always known how close they are."

Charlie persisted. "He does spend a lot of time here. How can you *not* be worried?"

"Because Imo is my best friend," Kate said. "She wouldn't do anything to hurt me."

"Why would she do anything to hurt you, anyway? She loves James, doesn't she?"

"Yes, she most certainly does."

Charlie wasn't sure why these feelings had returned to him this evening – perhaps because Jane was away, perhaps because he felt disturbed by his friends' doubts – but the beat of his old obsession again drummed inside. "So, what is there to worry about?" Charlie continued, uncertain that there was anything to worry about at all, and yet afraid of something.

"Nothing," Kate said. She looked away from him, out of the window towards the sky that was now nearly black.

There *was* something, Charlie thought. *She's hiding something.*

Kate ran her fingers through her hair and turned back to him. She smiled reassuringly. "Nothing, Charlie. Nothing."

"Come on, Kate. What are you hiding?"

She bit her bottom lip again, seemed to be considering what she should say next.

"Charlie–" she began, but then tailed off. She took a breath before continuing. "I don't know why nobody has told you. Well, I do know, but I'm not going to bend to your obsessions any longer. And anyway, you've got Jane now, so what does it matter?"

Charlie felt a knot in his stomach.

"What? What haven't I been told? Is it Imo and Stu? Is it something to do with them?"

"Oh, Charlie, Charlie." Kate shook her head and frowned. "Of course it is. Why are they so close? Why does Imo always go to Stu when she's upset?"

"Because they're good friends, I thought. Because Stu used to fancy Imo."

"Don't be a thicko, Charlie."

"What? What do you mean?"

"It wasn't only Stu who fancied Imo, you know. Imo *really* liked Stuart back then."

The muscles in Charlie's chest tightened. He hadn't known! He could hardly breathe. During all those months he and Stuart had fancied Imogen, he'd believed neither of them had a chance. Yes, he knew that there had been that night when Imogen and Stuart had kissed, but at least she hadn't gone out with Stuart. But she *had* really liked him. Which made Charlie feel... *inferior*, second best. He'd felt inferior before, but he'd handled that feeling well, he thought, when she had preferred James to him. When she had started going out with James, a chapter had closed. She had rejected him *and* Stuart.

"But she went for James in the end, didn't she?" Charlie said. "Stu's as pathetic as me."

"Yeah." Kate said. "Yeah. Almost."

The last word hung in the air between them.

"Almost? What do you mean?"

Kate looked him in the eye, steadily. "Come on, Charles. Catch up."

Charlie shook his head, baffled.

There was exasperation on Kate's face. "Oh crap, Charlie! Don't you get it?"

"What?"

"They slept together!"

The room turned around and flipped over. Charlie had never fainted before and he wondered if this was how you felt just before you did. The pit of his stomach felt heavy and his blood pulsed and boomed with a dark energy. He stood up. He twitched with the adrenaline now running through him. He needed to do something. He wanted to leave, he needed to be alone, needed to think. He wanted to run all the way back to Dereham, to the quiet of his room. He heard the footsteps of Imogen and Stuart on the stairs. They came through the door, smiling, each carrying two mugs of coffee. Imogen handed one to Kate and put her own, on the bedside cabinet. Stuart put his on the desk and turned to hand a mug to Charlie. And as he turned, he looked at Imogen warmly, reached out with his free hand

and stroked her back. Charlie had seen him do that so many times, but now understood that action in a different way, imagined that Stuart, in that touch, must remember the feel of her naked flesh against his palm as he gently ran his hand down her spine, must know the texture of the soft skin beneath her tee-shirt, must remember how she looked, naked beneath him.

Charlie recalled now how Stuart had slapped him that night on Copsehill, to calm him down, all righteous and smug. Anger had now replaced shock. Stuart still held out the mug to him. Charlie smacked the hand that held it, cuffing it from below so the hot coffee exploded into Stuart's face. He blinked the coffee away. Charlie punched him, a right hook to the cheek that sent him sprawling across Imogen's bed and tumbling onto the floor, knocking over books and mugs and records and plants as he went.

"You lying little bastards!" he shouted, looking at Imogen.

They'd all known, even Kate, the newest member of the gang, and they'd all kept it from him. Why? He pulled the bedroom door open and ran down the stairs. Mr Peek was in the hallway, asking what the hell was going on.

"Better ask your slut of a daughter," Charlie said, leaving by the front door, slamming it behind him.

Charlie jogged down the road, the night dark but still warm. He needed to burn off this anger. He'd regretted calling Imogen a slut almost as soon as he'd said it. But he was angry. Angry and jealous. Jealous because Stuart had held something he'd so badly wanted to hold. Angry because everybody, except him, had known about it. Why hadn't they told him? Jogging felt good; he could feel it burning up the remaining adrenaline. He was sweating now, which also felt good. He didn't regret punching Stuart, who was a fucking hypocrite who had slapped him when, it now turned out, he'd been speaking the truth. Perhaps all the parents were right. Perhaps Stuart and Imogen had been sleeping together again, behind James's back, and he'd found out and run away.

An owl hooted in the trees. Charlie's jog had slowed to a fast walk as the urgency of his feelings faded. The smell of warm earth came to him. He caught the sweet fragrance of some plant whose name he didn't know.

Why hadn't they told him? The question returned, time and again, accompanied by images of Imogen's naked body in bed with Stuart. Part of him wanted to believe they'd kept this knowledge from him so they could mock him behind his back. But he knew that wasn't true. The real answer also kept coming to him. The others hadn't told him because they'd feared his reaction. And weren't they right? *Didn't I react exactly as they expected?* Even now, when he was supposed to be in love with Jane, what he had learned from Kate had broken him, had made him violent. What if he'd been told earlier, before Jane, during the height of his obsession? He knew now what they'd all known for so long. He had been obsessed with Imogen, even if he hadn't seen it that way at the time. The constant visits to her house, the flowers he had sent, the pubs he only visited because he knew she also visited them, the many phone calls – all of it had, at the time, seemed so normal. He could see now, as the others must have seen, that his behaviour around Imogen had been unusual.

He peered into the darkness ahead of him. There was no moon tonight, and he could see very little, but he knew the roads between here and Dereham well, he had walked and cycled along them often enough. In an hour and a half, perhaps less at the pace he was walking, he'd be home. The house would be empty. Once his parents had been certain that Jane would be away for the night – and they could thus safely leave the house without unwittingly breaking their unspoken covenant with Mr and Mrs Maas to protect Jane from Charlie's ravages – they'd driven with Will down to his aunt's in Bournemouth. They would be back tomorrow evening. Charlie was glad he would be alone. He needed to get his head straight before Jane returned, also tomorrow evening. He was sure he could, in time, square things with Imogen and Stuart. They must realise what a shock it had been, Kate blurting out the truth like that. They were probably berating her now for telling him something they'd so obviously wanted to keep secret.

Charlie had just put the kettle on and was upstairs, changing out of his sweat soaked shirt, when he heard a knock at the door. He looked at his watch. The time was just past eleven. It was an unusual time for somebody to come calling. He must have left Imogen's at about half past nine, he calculated, given that he'd run part of it. The door was knocked again. He remembered that there were no parents to answer it, and there was no Will either. He would find Stuart at the door. Charlie put on a clean shirt and then walked slowly down the stairs. If Stuart had left Imogen's as soon as he'd picked himself up off the floor and straightened himself out – even if Imogen and Kate had tried to hold him back, had tried to reason with him, had told him to forget about it – he would arrive here just about now.

Better prepare for a smack in the gob.

He straightened his shoulders as he stood before the door, then reached up and turned the brass knob of the Yale lock. He was greeted not by the angry face of Stuart, but by a smiling face, happy to see him.

28

Charlie stared with something bordering on wonder. Were his eyes as wide as they felt?

"Are you going to invite me in?" James asked.

"Well, yes. Come in. Do you want a coffee?"

"I should say so. I've been on trains without buffets for hours."

Charlie led James through to the kitchen. James had cut his hair and shaved off his beard. Charlie wondered if there were other differences in James he was, as yet, unable to see.

"What are you doing here?" Charlie said.

"Well, I didn't phone anybody before I left. My decision to return was rather... uh... precipitate. I guessed Stu would be at Kate's, if they were still together. Imogen would most likely be asleep and my parents almost certainly are." He shrugged. "I thought you were the most likely to be in and still awake. And you are!"

Charlie thought it most likely that Imogen remained wide awake and was talking to Stuart and Kate about what had recently happened. Charlie didn't want to get into that now, though – he had a more urgent question. "How did you get off the spaceship? Did they let you off?"

"Spaceship?" James said. "What are you on about, Charlie?"

James appeared to be genuinely baffled, which surprised Charlie. "You were abducted, weren't you?"

"I've been in Leeds!"

"But I saw you!" Charlie exclaimed.

"Where?"

"On the spaceship!"

The kettle began to whistle.

"Charlie, have you been smoking tonight?"

Charlie found himself holding the handle of the kettle tightly as he lifted it from the hob, as if gripping it would stop the spinning sensation. "No, I haven't been smoking. I've been... I've been... You were on the spaceship, don't you remember?"

"I haven't the foggiest idea what you're on about, Charles." James nodded toward the kettle in Charlie's hand. It was suspended above a mug, tilted but not pouring. "If the wind changes direction, you'll stay like that," he said.

"What?"

"Pour the water, Charlie. You need to tip the kettle a little more."

Charlie looked at the kettle, then at James, who gave him a smile of encouragement. He poured water into the mugs and stirred.

"Charlie, you had a bagful of marbles when I left. Have you lost some? Has everybody gone loony while I've been away? Is Imo even now gibbering in her room? Are Stuart and Kate in padded cells?"

Charlie poured milk into the coffee, trying to understand everything. "I still have all my marbles. But you *were* on a spaceship. I saw you."

"How could you have seen me?"

"I was abducted too."

"What do you mean, you were abducted too? The tenor of the conversation leads me to assume you harbour a belief that I was also abducted; that is, in addition to you."

"Yes, you were."

"But I have, as I already mentioned, been in Leeds. Do you have any biscuits? I'm ravenous."

Charlie took a tin from a cupboard and clattered it down onto the worktop in front of James.

James gave Charlie a puzzled look. "Hey, man, calm down."

"Sorry. It's been a bit of a freaky evening all round."

"Really?"

What did it matter if he said something? Everybody knew. "I found out about Stu and Imo. Kate told me tonight."

James looked at Charlie. It was a studied look. Finally, James said, "Ah. Well... You can understand why nobody wanted to tell you before. You were a little... obsessive."

"Alright, yes, yes. I can accept that. But whenever I said anything about Imo and Stu, you all denied it and treated me like I was mad. Which pisses me off."

"You were mad. Mad with love. We were bored with hearing about it. If we'd told you, you would have become even more boring."

Doesn't it bother you?"

"Well, now I'm in love with Imo, if I trouble myself to think of the two of them shagging, why, yes, I do believe I *am* capable of jealousy. But it was a while ago. And she loves me. And Stu is cool. So, I don't think about it."

"But they still touch and hug and kiss all the time. Doesn't *that* piss you off?"

"Stu's like that with everybody though, isn't he? Fiona, Kate, Julie, Jane. In addition, Imo likes to hug as well. I'm not bothered. What happened, happened."

Charlie wondered how James could simply ignore the kind of thoughts that had so tormented him during the journey back from Imogen's – Imogen and Stuart naked together, Imo and Stuart in bed, curled in each other's arms.

"Let's sit down, Charlie," James said. They walked into the front room and sat next to each other on the sofa. "Do you want a fag?"

"I'll roll my own," Charlie said.

"No wacky baccie, though. You're weird enough as it is."

James took a Players Number 6 from a packet. "Hey man," Charlie said. "Why are you smoking those shitty little sticks?"

"I'm short of money, Charles."

"Now, there's a first. You didn't come back just to tap up your dad, did you?"

"No. It was just time to come back. I'd got my head straight again and I missed Imo and the rest of you guys. I missed Dereham. I missed Copsehill."

"Why didn't you tell anybody you were coming back?" Charlie asked.

James frowned. "You may find this difficult to believe, but I was scared."

"Scared? Of what?"

"I just ran away, man! Went! I was out of it, Charlie, I really was. For a couple of weeks, my head was all over the place. I was scared. I was scared of what would people say when I came back. How would Imo react, my friends, my parents. I knew I couldn't *plan* to return. If I *planned*, I'd want to see Imo. But I needed to catch you or Stu first."

"Where were you?"

"Keep up, Charles! Leeds!"

That's what you say, Charlie thought. "So... why Leeds?"

"Leeds was the one town I could remember the name of that wasn't Dereham. I didn't want to be in Dereham. I really, really wanted to be somewhere else. And Leeds was the only place I knew that seemed... homely, somehow."

"How did you get to Leeds?"

"It was weird. It's like I was split in two. I could do ordinary things. I could walk. I could ask for train tickets. I could take money out of my wallet. But it was... automatic. I just... went. I kept performing automatically, trying all the time to put distance between myself and here. I walked from Copsehill to Westbury station. I thought I heard voices in the trees near Derebury, which freaked me out. So, I started running. The ticket booth at Westbury station wasn't open, so I caught the first train that arrived. I paid for a ticket on the train. I was asking for a ticket to Leeds and the inspector kept trying to tell me the train was heading to Torquay. Eventually, I understood and paid for a ticket to Exeter. I slept on the station there."

"Hah! We talked about that. The day after you went. We were sitting around the table at your mum and dad's house. I said you could be anywhere, depending on what train came through Westbury. Exeter was one of our suppositions. Oh, and Whimple."

"Whimple?"

"Yeah, it's a station on the Salisbury to Exeter line. It became a kind of running joke. We thought you might have fallen asleep there and then woken up wondering how you'd got to Whimple and where the hell it was, anyway."

"Well, I did fall asleep in Exeter and then woke up and saw... it... and... well, jumped on the first train I could find that was pulling out. And that train was on its way to Birmingham."

"Saw it? Saw what?"

"The Raven."

Charlie remembered what Paul had said all those days ago in the hot kitchen. How close they'd all seemed then, drinking coffee, wreathed in cigarette smoke, worrying about James. "The Raven of Dispersion?"

"That's the guy," James said. "What do you know?"

"Only what Paul said. He's a false guardian... a... what do you call them?"

"Qliphoth?"

"Yeah, that's it."

"I only worked it out when I got to Leeds, when I was straight again. I remembered reading about it when I was preparing for the ritual."

"Paul said he heard you say something about the circle being broken. Although I'm surprised he remembers anything. He was stoned out of his bonce."

"He only ate some of my hash, didn't he?"

"Seems you bought some good shit. Or bad shit, depending on how you look at it. He kept blacking out, couldn't keep the ritual together. He can vaguely remember what you said, even thinks he can remember hearing your feet in the grass as you ran away. And then he blacked out completely for a while. When he came to, you'd gone."

James nodded, his eyes distant for a moment, recalling that night. "What happened then?"

"Well, at first we thought you'd gone for a walk to clear your head. But you didn't come back. The sun came up, Paul was puking, so the others went home. I started looking for you. I assumed you'd also gone home, but we knew you were tripping, so it seemed sensible to have a look around the fields and make sure you weren't flaked out in one of them."

"I probably had a good hour on you. I expect I was at Westbury station by then. I was walking pretty fast. When I wasn't running."

"Running? Why were you running?"

James looked down at his coffee, frowning. "I was scared. I thought I was being chased by an eight-foot tall something-or-other with the head of a raven."

"Shit! What was he going to do to you?"

"Ha! Well, that's the thing. I didn't know, which was scary in itself. I thought I might be taken to the Plane Eternal."

"The Plane Eternal?"

"Who knows, Charles. I just had this image of my soul being sucked out, and my empty hulk of a body endlessly wandering the Plane Eternal. The phrase just kept going around in my head. The Plane Eternal." James frowned. "I'm not keen on the sound of it, even now."

Charlie's attention had settled on something else. James had said something about his soul being taken away. *Sucked out*. Wasn't that exactly what MoJo had talked about? Perhaps James *had* been abducted, after all. Was he hiding the memory of it behind a different memory, a story that made more sense to him?

"More coffee?" Charlie asked.

James nodded. Charlie went to the kitchen, alone with his thoughts. James's story sounded plausible. It agreed with what Paul had said about Orev Zarak. That James would want to go to Leeds was also credible. Yet why would he think this Orev Zarak wanted to *suck out* his soul? Moreover, Charlie couldn't deny what had happened to him. He'd seen James on a spaceship. If James's story was true, then his own story wasn't. And Stuart – *lying bastard Stuart* – thought Charlie had created his story to answer the question of why James was gone. Now James had returned, he was discovering the *real* story. But was this the real story? James could be denying reality by making up another story, something frightening that would prevent the *really* frightening memories returning. Perhaps the aliens had found images of Leeds and railway journeys and Orev Zarak floating inside James's brain through some mind-reading technique, then created *this* story and implanted it, so he wouldn't remember what had really happened.

Charlie returned with the mugs just as James lit another Number 6.

"That stubby little thing looks pitiful, man," Charlie said.

James dragged on his cigarette, blew smoke into the room and then looked thoughtfully at the glowing end of it. "What happened later? When did you realise I'd gone?"

"It might be obvious to say, but when you didn't come back. I mean, we didn't worry too much on the first day... Well, Imo and your mum worried a lot, we were merely concerned. We thought you'd got strung out and gone to sleep it off somewhere. We all expected you to come back at some point during the day, or the next, when you'd got your shit together. Your mum wanted to phone the fuzz, but we didn't think it was a good idea, with you being stoned. Your mum was so freaked out Imo had to tell the kiddies you'd dropped a tab. Sorry, man."

"I thought somebody might tell them. Which is why I wanted to check with one of you guys before I saw them."

"So why didn't you phone Imo before coming back?"

"Stupid, really. I thought she might be mad at me. Another thing I wanted to check."

"She's been worried about you. I expect she'll kiss you, slap you, then kiss you some more."

That's if she wasn't kissing Stu, Charlie thought – but he also knew it was a stupid thought and wished he could stop thinking like this.

"I think she's been lonely," Charlie continued. "But Stu's been looking after her."

"I knew he would. I knew she'd have somebody to turn to."

"She could have turned to Kate."

"Yeah, but Kate doesn't really know the rest of us, does she? Stu is one of us. A Prophet. She'd turn to one of the gang for comfort, to one of my friends, to somebody who knows me."

"Doesn't it bother you?"

"What?"

"How much comfort Stu might have given her."

"Not really," James said. "Unlike you, I trust them both. And anyway, if something more than hugging happened, I can't say I'd blame either of them. I was the one who ran off, after all. Who was to know why I ran away? I bet some people thought I'd gone because of relationship hassles."

"You're right there. Most of the parents thought you'd either run off with another woman, or you and Imo had argued about something."

"Because they thought Imo had slept with somebody else?"

"Well, yeah. Why do you say that?"

"Simple really. She's gorgeous and I'm a hairy..." he rubbed his cheeks. "Or rather, I *was*, a hairy hippie. We boys look rough while the girls look exotic."

"What did happen to your gorgeous flowing locks?"

"I cut them off. I was advised to cut them off at the hostel."

"Hostel?"

"Well, to continue my adventure." James tapped his cigarette in an ashtray. "Having reached Birmingham, I got my shit together, kind of. I worked out the platform for the Leeds train. The Raven was nowhere to be seen, which was good. I fell asleep on a bench on the platform and dreamed about the light I saw at Copsehill, and the Raven, and the walk, and train journeys. Some kind soul woke me when the Leeds train arrived came in. I got on the train and left the station–"

"Hold on. You sound like you were more rational by then. Didn't you know what was going on?"

"On some levels, yes. As I said, it was like having a split personality. There was sensible James, but he was below the surface somewhere, waving, trying to get attention. And there was slightly mad James, who could only think of Leeds, how everything would be better in Leeds, a town I could hardly remember. And then there was scared James, who was just completely freaked out. I felt like I was full of adrenaline all day, pumped with it. My legs were aching and my head, man. God! It thumped so much. Then, somewhere near, uh, Tamworth, I think, I saw him."

"The Raven?"

"Yes. He was in the next carriage. He was just sitting there, looking at me. Like he knew where I was going. I felt I couldn't get away and now he'd been unleashed he would never go away until ... Well, I thought I'd have to do another ritual, to put him back in the circle. But the idea of doing another ritual was also frightening. I moved to the carriage behind me. I thought then I wouldn't be able to see him. He just moved to the carriage I'd been sitting in and continued to stare at me. There was nobody sitting opposite me, so I swapped to that seat, so I had my back to him. Then he moved to the carriage I could see from that seat, along the corridor and through the door. He was a demon, after all. He could be anywhere he wanted."

"Why didn't he come into your carriage?"

"Because he didn't *want* me then. He was mocking me. I knew it. He was going to follow me all the way to Leeds and get me at a time of his choosing."

"What do you mean, *get you?*"

"I wish I knew, Charlie. All the time, don't forget, this idea of the Plane Eternal is going through my head. It's like a mantra following the clattering of train wheels. Plane Eternal, Plane Eternal. And I have this image in my head of my soul being sucked out."

There it was again. James had thought his soul would be taken from him. *It can't be a coincidence, can it?* The idea was so close to what MoJo had suggested. James wasn't lying when he said he hadn't been abducted. James had constructed a story – or the aliens had constructed a story for him – to hide the truth. *But then, that's what Stuart said about my story.* Charlie was becoming lost in stories. Did Orev Zarak exist? Did UFOs exist? Did aliens exist? Had he been on a spaceship, or had he imagined it? Had James been on a spaceship and imagined he'd been in Leeds? Charlie felt panic rising in him as stories clashed and collided, each one making sense in its own way, each one equally true. And always, at the back of his mind, beneath the flow of narrative and counter-narrative, there recurred technicolour images of Stuart and Imogen locked in sex, or Imogen rising naked from the bed, a Pre-Raphaelite beauty with long red, curly hair falling over her shoulders and breasts, looking down at Stuart in the bed, her full breasts ruddy in the morning sunlight through a bedroom window, the tangled triangle of pubic hair between her long legs, Stuart reaching out a hand to run down her slim thigh, she asking if he wanted tea, as if it were any other day, not the day it now was, the day that would live in Charlie's imagination for ever, replayed in a hundred different ways as he constructed and reconstructed the story of Stuart and Imogen, never able to know the real story, never knowing where they'd made love, how many times, never knowing what it really felt like to be with Imo, to be inside her, which Stuart now did, Stuart the lying bastard, Imogen the lying shit.

Charlie had drifted away. James was still speaking. "...and so I had the money in my pocket, but I knew it wouldn't last long."

"Where did you stay?" Charlie asked, knowing that he asked to make it seem as though he'd been listening.

"I burned a lot of money in the first week. I stayed in one of the best hotels in Leeds. I didn't know it was the best hotel until I handed over some money. Given what I looked like, they didn't want to give me a room. They changed their minds when I took out the wallet and they saw the 200 quid."

"Where was Orev?"

"Somewhere behind me. I ended up staying at the hotel for five days. I got through about half the money. It was good to be clean though. And the food was good. I didn't go out much, because he was out there. I could see him through the glass doors. Sometimes, when I thought about going out, I'd find him waiting in the lobby, so I'd return to my room."

"What did you do?"

"In the end I had to leave, I knew my money couldn't last much longer. I got cheap digs for a while but left them after two weeks. I wandered the streets, slept rough for two nights, but knew I couldn't do that for much longer, either. Orev was on the streets, too. In the end, I thought I would either have a breakdown, or recover, and I was the only person who could change things. Even if Orev *was* real. So I went to a psychiatrist."

"What? You went to a shrink?"

"Yeah. I saw a doctor in Leeds, and I was sent to a shrink. And, uh, do you know what? She helped. She was understanding," James mused. "She was... very good. She didn't doubt the existence of Orev at first. Just played along with me. She did just one thing to break through it all, to begin clearing my mind."

"What was that?"

"Prescribed Librium for me. Four tabs a day. Oh, and she found me somewhere to stay. A hostel. Where they advised me to shave my flowing locks. Lice, you know. I helped out at the hostel. I wasn't as far gone as some of the alcoholics and down-and-outs who were there. And the food was free. I felt I should give something back. Especially as staying there was saving me money."

"Did Orev follow you there?"

"For the first couple of days, yeah. But I began to sleep, which was a relief. Thoughts of Orev had been keeping me awake. You know, where would I see him next, what he would do with me when he'd finished toying with me, that sort of thing. When the Librium kicked in, though, on the second or third day, I slept like a log and then eventually slept soundly every night. Or nearly every night. I'd wake up and the Qliphoth wouldn't be there, in my head. Imo, or you guys, or Copsehill might be. Orev became... dim. And when I went out into the streets, I didn't feel like he was behind me all the time."

"So, he was gone?"

"Not quite. Things came to a head, I suppose, about a week into the Librium, when I woke up one night and thought Orev was in the room with me. I thought he was trying to cut into my arm, trying to take something from me, blood or something."

Not blood. Your soul. How often we return to that.

"I started screaming and some of the hostel staff came. They asked what I was shouting about. I told them Orev was in the room. They pointed out, as calmly as they could in the face of a screaming loon, that I was the only person there, there was nobody else. One of the guys moved a curtain, I don't know why, he just did, rearranged it, smoothed it down. And I suddenly became conscious that there had never been anybody else – *anything* else – in the room. Orev had disappeared. There never had been a giant bird-man following me around, there never had been an Orev Zarak. Probably against doctor's orders, I dropped another Librium and went back to sleep. I woke the next morning and Orev was gone. I knew it."

"How long ago was all this?"

"A couple of weeks ago. As I said, I was kind of scared to come back. And I wanted to help out there for a bit longer, as they'd been good to me. But this afternoon, I just wanted to see you all again. I've missed you all. Even you, Charles."

"Hah! Shut up, you'll have me in tears in a minute."

James looked at his mug. It was empty. He lifted it and shook it in front of Charlie.

"More coffee, vicar?" Charlie said.

"That's the gist."

Charlie went to the kitchen again. His mind was racing. It all sounded so very plausible. Orev Zarak had merely been a delusion, a demon conjured up by the acid. The Librium had calmed James and broken the spell. No demons, no aliens, no spaceship, nothing weird, just a poor stoner lost in Leeds. *But it doesn't tally with what happened to me.* He knew he'd seen a spaceship; he knew he'd been abducted. And there was this odd correspondence between what James said and what MoJo had said. James kept talking about his soul and something being taken from him. What did it mean? Charlie wondered how he'd know if James had no soul. James *seemed* all right. The James that Charlie had always known seemed to be sitting in the front room. A James with a wacky story, true enough. But he looked no different and behaved no differently. He seemed liked the same James – apart from the hair and beard. They had gone, and it was slightly odd to see the James he remembered from the fifth-year in school, rather than the slightly sozzled freak he'd become used to seeing.

The kettle whistled. Charlie took it from the hob and poured it into the two mugs.

James came into the kitchen. "Where are the kiddies?"

"They've gone down to Bournemouth," Charlie said.

James looked at his watch. It was gone midnight. "Can I crash here tonight?"

"Of course."

"And can we go upstairs and listen to some music? I haven't heard anything for weeks."

Charlie handed a mug to James, then picked up his own mug and the biscuit tin and followed James up the stairs.

James sat on the bed. Charlie asked what he wanted to hear. He said he didn't care. Something long, loud and raucous. Charlie found Van Der Graaf Generator's *Godbluff*, put it on the record deck and flopped at the other end of the bed. The sound of a pensive flute drifted from speaker to speaker. James took out a Number 6 and put in his mouth. He went to light it, but the lighter refused to work. Charlie reached for his lighter and then remembered that he'd left it downstairs.

"I'll get it for you," James said.

"No need. There's a box of matches in the drawer." Charlie pointed to the cabinet beside the bed.

James slid the drawer open and found the matches. He then reached further into the drawer and pulled out Charlie's ritual knife. "Hah! I'd forgotten you had one of these."

"I've never used it for anything," Charlie replied. "In fact, I rarely think about it."

"Brings back bad memories for me," James mused.

"Chuck it over here," Charlie said.

James smiled. "How hard?"

"Pass it, then."

James passed the knife to Charlie.

Charlie looked at it. "Why did I bother buying it?"

"Caught up in the excitement, I suppose. Didn't we all buy one that day?"

"Yeah, you, me and Paul. From the shop in Glastonbury."

"Yes, I remember."

Charlie fingered the blade. "Pointless, really."

"The knife, or your life?" James said.

Charlie tested the point of the blade with his finger. "Ouch! Must be my life then." He chuckled. He spun it through the air, so that it landed handle first in his palm. "I've never used this. Not for anything at all."

"Juggling?" James suggested.

"Not even juggling. It just sits in the drawer month after month. Occasionally I go in there for a match or a pen or something and then I remember I have it."

Charlie wondered if James could be this genial and laid-back if he'd lost his soul. What would it be like to lose your soul? Jane had said she would know if Charlie lost his. Would he be able to tell if James had lost his? Charlie didn't know. He couldn't imagine what it would be like. Would you lose empathy and sympathy? Would you be unable to understand humour and kindness and sadness and love and affection?

"How are things with Jane?" James asked.

"Cool," Charlie replied. "We've started going out together. In fact, she's here this weekend."

"Where?" James looked around the room. "Has she learned the secret of... invisibility?"

Charlie laughed. "No, she went to Southampton with Paul and Fi. Fi's brother is at the Uni. She'll be back tomorrow. You'll see her then."

"Dominic? That's his name, isn't it?"

"Yes, that's the one."

"Nice to know I haven't lost my memory," James said.

But have you lost your soul? How can I tell? How will I know?

"Still, at least you aren't obsessed with Imo anymore, right?"

"Hah," Charlie spluttered.

"What?"

"I ... uh... punched Stu tonight."

"You did what?"

"I punched him. In Imo's bedroom. I was so angry when Kate told me."

"Why, man? It's all in the past. And if you've got Jane now, why does it matter?"

"Because you all kept it secret, I suppose. And because I had a fight with Stuart about... Well, about Jane and Imo."

"You had a fight? When did that happen?"

"When we were up Copsehill a couple of months back. At the skywatch. The one before you disappeared."

"I didn't know."

"Are you saying Stu didn't tell you? Or Imo?"

"No. He might have told Kate, I suppose. But he didn't tell us."

"Hah," Charlie said again.

"Why the surprise?"

"I couldn't imagine Stu keeping his mouth shut about something like that. Stupid Charlie goes mad over Imo again. I thought he'd tell everybody."

"Man, Stu is many things. Arrogant, flirty, a show-off. But he's also loyal. And discreet. He never said a word about any fight."

"It wasn't much of a fight anyway," Charlie grumbled. "I pushed him around a bit, then he slapped me."

"You idiot," James said. "You've got Jane! Let Imo go!"

"Oh, I know, I know. It started off with me thinking Stu would flirt with Jane and ruin my chances with her. Then it got back onto Imo again... I was pissed. We had drunk quite a lot of your Martell. And smoked a lot of weed."

"That's no excuse, Charles," James said.

"You know I found it hard to get over Imo. And the amount of trust you have in Stu! Especially after what I heard tonight. How do you do it?"

"I just don't think it's important."

"But it must be."

"It isn't. What's important is knowing Imo loves me and that I have good mates. Even if you are a little weird tonight."

Charlie persisted. "But Imo, man! You love her, right? So how can you just forgive Stu? I'd worry about him all the time."

"I don't," James said.

"Why not?"

"I just don't. Look–" James stopped.

"What?"

"Doesn't matter."

"What doesn't?"

"Ah, fuck," James said. "Kate told you about Imo and Stu, right? About them sleeping together before Imo and I started seeing each other? That's what she told you, yeah?"

"That's right. That's what she told me."

"But there's one other thing nobody knows, not Kate, not Paul. Only Imo, Stu and me."

Charlie could feel the anxiety building within him, just as it had earlier in the evening at Imo's. The tension in his muscles, the feeling in his gut. He felt as if he were awaiting another slap.

"Stu and Imo slept together again, after I'd started going out with her. "

The pain swept over Charlie like a wave. He groaned.

"Imo and I had a big fight about my drinking and the dope," James explained. "She left and said she wasn't coming back. We were apart for a while, a few weeks, and then we were on and off after that."

"I had no idea," Charlie managed to say through a dry mouth.

"Well, remember Imo and I didn't see each other so much in the early days. She lives in Burnt Norton and she couldn't stay over at my house like she does now – or did. So, if we didn't see each other for a while, you wouldn't have noticed. We didn't make a big deal out of it, we were still friends." James paused, and looked at Charlie. "There was a party, at which Imo got very drunk. Stu was there. Imo said we'd broken up, and there was no way she was getting back together with me. One thing led to another, and..."

"But how can you not care?" Charlie wondered.

"I did care. But what can I say? I was way too much of a pisshead in those days. You remember what I was like. I'd only just turned eighteen and was on a bottle of Martell a day. What she said was right. What she did might have been wrong. But it was a real shock to me. A bucket of cold water."

"But what about Stu? You must have hated him!"

"Why? I knew he'd always loved Imo. And she made it plain to him that as far as she was concerned it was over. Stu took her word for it. He thought that what was happening might be the beginning of something beautiful."

"But how could he do that? To you? To her?"

"Because he wanted her, too. And she said what she said. We're young, Charlie. I'd only been with her a couple of months. It wasn't like we were married or anything. It was just a colossal fuck-up. And here's the thing. I promised to cut down on the drink and the weed. And I did. So, after a couple of weeks, a month, Imo came back to me. And in doing so, she dropped Stu. Can you imagine how he must have felt?"

Charlie was calculating. "Hold on. Was that the time he went down to see Paul by himself? First time he went without me? He said he wanted to get something straightened out, but I didn't know what."

James nodded. "Yeah. And he told nobody what happened, not even Paul."

Charlie found himself conflicted. He was impressed by James's ability to forgive. He hated Stuart even more than he had earlier, yet felt empathy with him because Charlie knew what rejection felt like. But he was mainly amazed that all of this had happened without him knowing about it.

Charlie looked at James, who smoked another Number 6 and seemed lost in contemplation. Still, Charlie wondered, how could James not care that his girlfriend had slept with his best friend? It seemed soulless somehow.

Soulless! Everything fell into place.

James had no soul. That's why he didn't care, that's why he could just sit there, smoking his cigarette as if nothing mattered. It was obvious. He *had* been on the spaceship, there was no Orev Zarak – not because the Librium had banished it, but because there had never been a demon. James had never been chased by anything, had probably not even been to Leeds. He'd been returned here just this evening, dropped back in Dereham with a host of memories implanted by *them*.

There was only one story: his story He hadn't dreamed about James's abduction, it had *not* been a fantasy on his part. He *had* been inside the flying saucer with James. *Everything* he'd thought and believed was true. Imogen and Stuart were as close as he'd always imagined, they *had* slept together, he *had* been abducted, he *had* seen James next to him with a contraption wired to his arm. *My senses wouldn't lie.* It was as MoJo had said. The aliens were trying to get at the essence of what it meant to be human, but they didn't know what they were trying to capture; they didn't know how to measure it, they didn't know when to stop. James had been drained of soul, of emotion, had been left empty, and then finally dumped back in front of Charlie's door.

"You *were* abducted," Charlie said, with a note of wonder. "It's all true."

James looked up. "What?"

"I saw you. I know I saw you. You were on a spaceship with me, with a tube going into your arm. I know! I was there! You just don't remember, they've messed with your head, man. They've sucked something out of you. You've got no soul. If you had a soul, you'd hate Stu, you'd hate Imogen for what she did! You probably did before the aliens took you, you just can't remember hating them, can't remember what they did."

"I don't, didn't, hate them," James said, confusion in his voice.

"How would you know! You were still drinking Martell, you were still smoking dope, or don't you remember–"

"Not like–"

"Crap!" Charlie shouted. "It's all shit! No wonder you drank so much. You were trying to blot it all out. Now *they've* done it for you."

"Who?" James asked, puzzlement in his voice.

"The aliens, man," Charlie shouted excitedly. "They've wiped your memory, sucked your soul away, you are dead to Imo. I can see it! I can! You're dead! Emotionally dead! How can you not care about Imo? I'd kill Stu if he did the same to me. She's a goddess! If I was with Imogen, she'd be on the highest fucking pedestal I could find!"

Charlie wondered why James ignored him and stared instead at the doorway to the bedroom.

29

"Charlie!" The voice was Jane's.

Charlie turned towards the door. Jane was there. Charlie knew she was crying, even though she looked at the floor. "Jane? Jane, what are you doing here?"

She didn't look up. "Paul and I caught a late train," she sobbed. "We hitched the rest of the way. We walked the last four miles from Hayton. All because I wanted to get back tonight. I knew your parents were out, and I wanted to be with you." She turned to go. "I wish I hadn't bothered."

Charlie was dumbstruck.

It was James who spoke. "Hang on, Jane. Don't go. Charlie's had a surprise, that's all. He's a just bit *confused*. I'm sure he wants you."

Jane stopped in the door with her back to the room, her head still down. "How can you be so sure, James? What do you know? You've been missing for weeks. How do you know how much he loves me? I heard what he said. Imo, Imo, Imo.... He'd put her on a... a ... *fucking pedestal*, would he?"

She turned and walked back into the room, over to Charlie and slapped his face. "You told me you didn't care about Imogen anymore." Her young voice was angry. "You loved me, you said, you wanted to move on with me, and leave Imogen and all your feelings about her in the past. That's what you said. Well, is that moving on? Is it? Putting her on a bloody pedestal?"

"I didn't mean it like that." Charlie suddenly, to his surprise, began to cry. He was so confused, so angry, so frustrated. "I didn't mean it. I meant if I was James, if I was in James's place, if..." He squeezed his palms into his eyes. "If..."

"If *what*, Charlie? I heard what you said! I heard it! It sounded like what *you* would do, what *you* would like to do *even now*."

James stood up, spoke quietly. "I'd better go."

"No! You can't go, you soulless zombie," Charlie said.

"I'm going," James said. "You need to sort things out with Jane."

"I don't want to sort anything out," Jane said. "I want to go to Stuart's."

"Stuart. Bloody Stuart," Charlie said. "He's at the centre of everything, isn't he!"

"Stay here," James said, gently, to Jane. "He needs somebody to talk to. Listen to what he has to say."

"You're not going anywhere, zombie," Charlie said to James. "If you had a soul, we wouldn't be doing this. Everything would be okay. You should have punched Stuart months ago and shown that slut Imogen the door–"

"Don't call Imo that," James said.

Charlie hurried on. "But you blotted it all out with drink and dope. And now you're back here, you just don't care. Because you have no soul."

"I don't understand," Jane whimpered. "What's going on?"

"You do understand Jane! Remember what MoJo said!"

Jane rubbed her cheeks and face with her hands. "What? I'm confused! What about MoJo?"

"They said the aliens were taking away souls. They've taken James's soul, Jane! I know it. He should *care*. But he doesn't, he doesn't."

James looked from Charlie to Jane and back again. "Who, or what, the bloody hell is MoJo?"

Charlie shouted. "It doesn't matter! The point is, they were right! I was right! I was right about everything. About you being abducted, and Stuart and Imogen, and nobody bloody believed me. Nobody!" He stood and moved towards Jane, his arms open. He still held the ritual knife. It glittered in his right hand. "Nobody but you Jane! You believed me, didn't you! You believed me."

She moved away as he came closer, shrugged off his attempts to hold her. "What? What did I believe? I believed you'd got over Imo, that you'd left those feelings behind you, that's what I believed. But that's not true, is it?"

Despite what he was saying, Charlie now found it difficult to sort fact from fiction, truth from lies. Did he love Imogen? Did he love Jane? Where had James been?

He remembered one true thing, and he would cling on to that one memory, that one *real* memory. "I *was* abducted," Charlie said. "James was on the ship. You believed me, didn't you? You believed I'd been taken away."

"I don't know, Charlie! What does James say?" Jane turned to James. "Where have you been?" she asked desperately.

"Leeds," James said.

"Leeds? You weren't abducted?"

"No."

Charlie screamed. "*That is not true!* Why are you lying? I saw you. *I fucking saw you!* You had something attached to your arm. They've wiped away your memories, James, believe me. They've sucked out your soul, they've sucked the real you away. You're empty, a husk, a shell, not human!"

Charlie could feel the weight of the ritual knife in his hand. It felt right, sitting there. A ritual knife. Just the thing he needed to kill this zombie. It wasn't James he was looking at – it was something else, something other. He wouldn't be killing James. He'd be killing nothing except a bag of water. The real James was... what? A vapour in a bottle? Weighed, measured and now frozen as he was transported back to some distant planet? What did it matter if the flesh should die? Wouldn't he be doing James a favour? This couldn't be the real James, here, this James who didn't care about Imogen, didn't care what she'd done, what she'd done to them all. She'd broken them all, broken all their hearts. He even again found himself momentarily sorry for Stuart, to whom she'd offered so much only to snatch it away. But Imo couldn't return to James this time. Because James wasn't here. There was only this empty thing.

Charlie knew he had to do it, he had to remove this offensive, empty zombie flesh before him, had to erase from his world this travesty, this walking void, this robot, this... He raised his hand, knew how easy it would be to end it now, before the others were fooled by this non-James, before they came to love this sac, welcomed his soulless shell back into their world. The sharp point of the knife was arcing towards James's heart, almost without volition. James's eyes were wide. Then Charlie heard a sharp "No!" beside him and was surprised by a weight crashing into him. The point of the knife entered James's left shoulder, dug in deep and ripped flesh as Jane's weight carried Charlie across to the bed. James fell backwards onto the bedside cabinet, his mug crashing to the floor, the brass alarm clock clattering off the wall, then he sank to the floor, holding the handle of the knife.

Jane sat on top of Charlie. He was surprised to hear himself screaming. "Kill the zombie Jane, kill the zombie, do it now, do it now!"

Jane slapped Charlie's face. "Charlie! Come back to me!"

"Get off me, bitch!" Charlie snapped. "Are you one of them? Did they abduct you too? Is that where you've been tonight? Is that why you're back early? To protect James?"

Charlie struggled to get free, but Jane was strong now, and had the advantage. She slapped Charlie again, harder this time.

"Charlie, stop it! Stop it!"

Charlie was suddenly overwhelmed with fatigue. It had been a long day. A lot had happened. He stopped moving. He began to cry again.

Jane looked over at James. Charlie followed her gaze. Through the tears, he could see James holding the handle of the knife. Blood oozed from his shoulder, staining his velvet jacket. James looked at the knife, his face pale. He chewed his lip.

"Don't," Jane said. "Leave it where it is. If you pull it out, you might bleed to death." Her voice caught as she spoke. She was crying too. She wiped tears from her eyes with her sleeve. "Can you move?" she said to James. "Do you think you can get downstairs okay?"

"I think so," James said through gritted teeth.

"Then do it. Do it now. Phone for an ambulance."

"What about the police, Jane?"

"I don't know, James. What should we do?"

"If we phone the police, he'll go down for assault, possibly attempted murder. Do you want that?"

Murder? Charlie thought. A mercy killing, surely? He turned back to Jane, who was looking down at him sadly. Her face was soft, but her eyes were still full of tears.

"Of course I don't want that," Jane said. "But he did try to kill you,

James. I saw him. I saw what he was trying to do. I saw where he was aiming the knife. I saw the look in his eye."

"So did I."

"That's not the Charlie I love. He needs help'

They were both silent for a while. Charlie wondered what would happen, how long he would be trapped here beneath Jane. If only he could get up, he could finish what he'd started. He could feel James's eyes on him.

"I know what to do," James finally said.

Jane was softly crying again. "What?"

"Leave it to me."

He slowly stood, forcing himself upright. He walked unsteadily towards the door. Jane heard the stairs creak at each slow step he took.

Charlie's thoughts were still incoherent. Had *they* planned to take James all along? It couldn't all be coincidence, surely? They wouldn't take just anybody they found on any old hillside. They had to take somebody *special*, somebody they particularly wanted, for whatever reason. They had to be always watching, always waiting, for the right moment. Perhaps all his friends, even Jane, had been part of *their* plan all along. Was he the only one who was, for some reason, unaffected? Were they all soul-less zombies? Had Jane herself always been a zombie? Had she been sent to prepare the way? No girl had ever been ready to love him, not Imogen, only Jane. She'd changed so much for him. There had been no need for her to do that. She'd been happy with her friends, listening to crappy music and going to shitty Torquay nightclubs. Charlie forced himself to open his eyes. *Now look at her.* Her long blonde hair fell like a golden waterfall. Her oval face and big blue eyes were so beautiful, he wanted to reach out and touch her. Her soft lips needed to be kissed. She was a *siren*. She had attracted him so she could watch over him, be ready to control him if he ever learned the truth. Who else would learn the truth? If Stuart had ever seen anything, he would have run away, and when Paul and James did see the light that night they had called it a ghost, an elemental, a spirit, a delusion. No, he was the only one who would recognise a UFO when it appeared, so he was the only one who would know what was happening, he was the one who had to be watched,

"You're one of them," Charlie said to Jane. "You're one of the zombies, controlled by *them*. You don't really love me. You've been sent to watch over me."

"Charlie," Jane cried. "Don't be ridiculous Charlie! I love you. I've loved you since I was fourteen, I think."

"They play a long game."

"Look at me, Charlie. Do I seem soulless to you? Did I lack soul that night on Blue Tor? When we made love, did I seem like I was sent here to watch over you? Didn't I show you love? Didn't we share *something*? Didn't our *souls* meet?"

"They programmed you well," Charlie said. He struggled against Jane's weight again. "I've got to get away from you. From all of you. If you're not zombies, then you're all sluts like Imogen."

"Forget about Imo," Jane said.

"I can't," Charlie said. "It all fits together. She was obviously sent first. To mess with my head, to confuse me. I can't think straight because of her. I can't... think straight. If I could think straight, I'd have known what was happening."

"What *is* happening?"

"I don't know, do I? How can I know? I can't think straight because *they* send beautiful women to mess me up. I'm confused because *they* want me to be. *Need* me to be."

Charlie wriggled on the bed, trying to break free from Jane's grip. Then he stopped struggling as a new realisation dawned. "Perhaps it's Stuart?"

"What?"

"I don't know how it all fits together. Only *you* know. But he's always at the centre of everything, isn't he. He's always around, all you girls love him. He obviously controls you all. Perhaps *he* isn't a zombie. Perhaps *they* let him keep his soul, so he can entrance people like you. And when you fall under his spell you do what he wants. I bet you love Stuart really, don't you? I bet you sleep with him when I'm not around. I bet you never even went to Southampton tonight. I bet you were with Stuart until you got the message about James."

Jane spoke quietly. "Listen, Charlie. None of this make sense. None of it fits together. None of it."

She sounded so reasonable. *But then, she would, wouldn't she.*

James came back through the door and slid down the wall onto the floor again. The silver handle of the knife jutted from his shoulder still. He grimaced and shifted painfully. "It's not aliens, Jane, you know that, right?"

"Yes, I know. It's Imo. He always loved her."

"He's learned too much tonight, had too many surprises. His belief in these... *aliens*... is a distraction, a comfort even."

James had no idea what he was talking about, Charlie thought. *Or perhaps he does, and it's more lies.*

"Poor Charlie," Jane said softly. Charlie felt her hand on his cheek.

Charlie found himself sobbing, he couldn't help it. His breathing was ragged. He found it hard to look at Jane, and stared past her instead, up at the ceiling. He, too, reached a hand up, and touched Jane's cheek. "I did love you, Jane."

There was a knock at the front door. A few seconds passed and then there was another knock. A few moments later, there were footsteps on the stairs.

A suited figure, carrying a brown bag, appeared around the bedroom door.

"Hello, Dr Ambrose," James said.

"James?" The doctor asked.

James nodded.

"Where *has* all your hair gone?"

"A long story."

The doctor squatted down and looked at the knife. "You need an ambulance, not a GP. If I remove this, I might not be able to stop the bleeding."

"I thought you might say that. I need you here for another reason."

The doctor looked at him, puzzled.

James winced. "Although... first... a pain killer would be good."

"Are you taking any drugs?" Ambrose asked.

"Yeah, Librium,"

Charlie turned to look at the liar James. "Hah! Don't believe that shit."

James reached painfully into his pocket and took out a dark plastic bottle and rattled it. The doctor took the bottle from him and read the label. "Yes, 25 mg, three times a day."

"It's shit," Charlie said. "They planted them on him, planted them, don't you see? They wanted everything to look normal. Normal! You understand. Normal!"

Ambrose gave James an injection. "You might start to feel a bit dopey. I'd better get an ambulance here soon." He looked over at Charlie. "What wrong with him?"

"There's nothing wrong with me!" Charlie shouted, twisting beneath Jane again. "It's them. They're all soulless zombies. You'll understand. Look at them. Look into their eyes! You must be able to see it, you're a doctor, you save souls."

Ambrose shook his head. "That's what priests do. I try to save lives."

"Then phone for a *priest*," Charlie shouted. "Let's get this sorted out! I know they're all in this together. Jane and James, Imogen and Fiona, Paul and Stuart. I just..." Charlie paused. "I just can't see how, yet..." He carried on quietly. "They were sent to confuse me."

Ambrose spoke. "Is he the reason I'm here?"

James sighed. "Yes. I want you to section him. Section two, I believe."

"That's a big decision, James."

"He tried to kill me."

"Police?"

"I don't want to press charges. I just want him to get better."

"You'd better tell me what happened."

Charlie listened as James explained everything to the doctor. His story was preposterous. When Jane added what she knew, it was as if his all his friends had turned against him.

Jane is the great deceiver. Stuart is the organiser. Or the manipulator. Are they all in this together? I can't work it out. Perhaps Imo is the only innocent one left. But she isn't innocent, she fucked Stuart too, I don't know, there's no reason to believe, but why should she want to, what's so I mean it's not as if I'm... And Jane is so beautiful you are beautiful Jane but you are and James is and Stu is... And what is it and what do they want with me where will they take me why send James back I don't understand because it makes no sense none of it and you doctor you must be one of them why are you here where did you come from so quickly I don't recognise you you're not from around here and Jane I wanted to love you so much Jane, everybody could be them and they could all be watching me all the time, always have done, sent Jane to me to watch me, stop me knowing finding out Jane finding out. Imogen and Stu they didn't want me to know why didn't they want me know it's just Imo and Stu fucking what does it matter unless it's something bigger much bigger than them something they're part of do they know they're part of it do they know do they Jane who knows who knows Jane what it all is why these girls why Stuart why Imogen Imo ImoImo...

Epilogue

Charlie heard the chair beside the bed scrape backwards. When he opened his eyes, he found Stuart sitting there.

"Ah, the great deceiver," Charlie said.

Stuart grabbed Charlie's hand and held it. "I'm sorry, man."

"What for?"

"For everything."

Charlie said nothing for a while, only stared at the white ceiling. Then he spoke again. "What are you doing here?"

"I came to apologise."

"How did you get here?"

"Dad brought me over. He's waiting outside in the car."

"How can he bring you here, Stu? Only *they* can bring you here."

"Who are *they*?"

"The guys in the white coats and uniforms."

"You're allowed visitors, Charlie. Any of us can come at any time."

Charlie laughed mirthlessly. "Don't be ridiculous."

"It's true. I'm sure Jane will come and see you soon. And James and Imo, when James is better."

Charlie was silent again. "You're another one of them, aren't you?" he finally whispered. "I know what you're doing. I know what's happening here."

"What's happening, Charlie?"

"Your soul's been removed. If you were the real Stuart, you wouldn't be here, you'd run away, run as far as you can. But you have no soul, so you're under their control. You've been sent here to try and keep me calm while they do whatever they like with me." He shouted at Stuart then. "Well, you can piss right off! Tell them I see through their game! Tell them that I won't give in, that I'll hold out for as long as I can! Tell them to stop sending zombies in to see me. Just tell them they can all go! All of them!"

Charlie thrashed around in his restraints, hoping that, just this once, he would be strong enough to break free. Stuart stood and backed away. A doctor came into the room and inserted a syringe into Charlie's arm.

Charlie began to relax. He didn't want to feel like this. "Have they told you what they're doing to me, Stu? You think they're injecting something into me, don't you. But they're not. They're taking something from me. They're sucking my soul away. Drop by drop by drop."

Charlie's eyelids fluttered, but he forced his eyes to stay open and stared at Stuart. "If only you weren't one of them. Then you'd help me. You'd undo these straps and set me free."

However, Stuart had turned to go. "Bye, Charlie."

Charlie didn't reply. He looked around the room. The walls were a monotonous faded white, unrelieved by pictures or any other features, except for a pair of pipes, also painted white, that fed a radiator. The bed was plain, simple, grey metal. Charlie's pyjamas were white, as were his sheets. The blankets were grey, like the bed. Everything was very clean, very functional. Too functional.

He stared up at the white ceiling of the spaceship, wondering when they would next come to suck away his precious soul.

Drop by drop by drop.

www.ingramcontent.com/pod-product-compliance
Lightning Source LLC
Chambersburg PA
CBHW061940170626
46813CB00006B/2475